Praise for *The Passion of Tasha Darsky*

"With this first novel, Yael Goldstein offers us an exploration of the intense passions and pains of creativity . . . The writing is smooth and supple, enticing you into the story and easily persuading you to read every word. There are moments of great clarity here, descriptions that flash out to illuminate small, intimate human truths."

—*San Francisco Chronicle*

"Passionate, moving . . . a literary treat."

—*Tucson Citizen*

"Until *The Passion of Tasha Darsky* I never would have believed an author could successfully use words to convey something that can only be heard. But Goldstein does it. It wasn't that Goldstein's writing made me hear that sensual, angry violin. It was that she made me ache to."

—*Berkshire Eagle*

"An impressive debut . . . Goldstein paints a vivid picture of the world of the arts from behind the scenes: the studying, composing, selling, and performing and the people who are driven by the need to create."

—*Library Journal* (starred review)

"A splashy literary debut . . . a highly refined tale of love among musical geniuses."

—*Kirkus Reviews*

"Offers a vividly distinctive voice."

—*Washington Times*

"Goldstein utilizes language in such a way as to make even tone-deaf readers hear strings in their minds."

—*Jerusalem Report*

"*The Passion of Tasha Darsky* is a sweeping tale of love, fame, and power in the world of classical music. It's a wonderful debut from a promising author."

—*Jewish Woman* magazine

"Chick lit for the literary set."

—*USA Today*

"Sophisticated yet accessible, intellectual but also sensual."

—*Time Off*

"A marvelous first novel—sophisticated, nuanced, and sexy. A precociously gifted woman trades romantic love for artistic passion, then must learn to balance motherhood with her art. This narrative is as tense and vibrant as an extended note from a solo violin. Goldstein writes about musical composition in a way that approaches music itself."

—Emily Raboteau, author of *The Professor's Daughter*

"An intoxicating symphony about love, a moving love story about music, *The Passion of Tasha Darsky* is a truly marvelous debut novel. Encore!"

—Katharine Weber, author of *Triangle*, *The Little Women*, *The Music Lesson*, and *Objects in Mirror Are Closer Than They Appear*

"Yael Goldstein has given us a delightful, passionate book about the life of the mind, the life of the body, and the life of the heart. *The Passion of Tasha Darsky* is a mesmerizing and wise novel, simultaneously unsparing and tender, and compelling from the first page to the last. This is a big book in the best possible way."

—Rachel Kadish, author of *From a Sealed Room* and *Tolstoy Lied: A Love Story*

"Yael Goldstein's passionate, precocious novel of creativity and love understands with great wisdom the way all of us—parents and children, artists and appreciators—must fight to find our own voice so that we can be free without resentment to love the world that made us."

—Jonathan Rosen, author of *Eve's Apple*

The Passion of Tasha Darsky

The Passion of Tasha Darsky

YAEL GOLDSTEIN LOVE

Formerly titled *Overture*

BROADWAY BOOKS

NEW YORK

This book is a work of fiction. Names, characters, businesses, organizations, places, events, and incidents either are the product of the author's imagination or are used fictitiously. Any resemblance to actual persons, living or dead, events, or locales is entirely coincidental.

Published in the United States by Broadway Books, an imprint of The Doubleday Publishing Group, a division of Random House, Inc., New York.

www.broadwaybooks.com

A hardcover edition of this book was originally published in 2007 by Doubleday under the title *Overture: A Novel.*

BROADWAY BOOKS and its logo, a letter B bisected on the diagonal, are trademarks of Random House, Inc.

Library of Congress Cataloging-in-Publication Data
Goldstein, Yael.
[Overture]
The passion of Tasha Darsky : a novel / Yael Goldstein Love. —
1st pbk. ed.
p. cm.
Originally published in 2007 by Doubleday under title: Overture.
1. Women violinists—Fiction. 2. Genius—Fiction. 3. Music—Fiction.
4. Mothers and daughters—Fiction. I. Title.
PS3607.O4859O94 2008
813'.6—dc22
2007047000

ISBN 978-0-7679-2979-0

PRINTED IN THE UNITED STATES OF AMERICA

1 3 5 7 9 10 8 6 4 2

First Paperback Edition

TO MY MOTHER,

FOR A LEVEL OF GENEROSITY IN ART AND IN LOVE

THAT I CAN ONLY HOPE ONE DAY TO MATCH

ACKNOWLEDGMENTS

For insight into the life of a professional violinist, many thanks are due to Sonya Chung. For answering questions about the contemporary composing scene, my gratitude to Dmitri Tymoczko. (Any mistakes I made in applying his answers to this book, are, of course, mine alone.) For reading and commenting on early drafts of the novel, I am indebted to Mimi Cheng, Samantha Goldstein, Ilana Kurshan, Tom Kelly, and Nicholas Weiss. For reading and commenting on far too many drafts, I am even more indebted to Alexis Offen and, especially, Rachel Elkin Lebwohl.

I could not have written this book without the emotional and financial support of Tom Kelly, nor the brilliant insights and suggestions of my agent Sarah Burnes. Sarah's assistant Chris Lamb knows everything about everything, and while that occasionally makes me nervous, I still can't believe my good luck in having him available to me as a resource. The warmth and understanding with which Deb Futter embraced this book eases my worries about sending it into the world, and the cheery emails from her assistant Dianne Choie ease all sorts of other worries.

Finally, in terms of love and encouragement, I have been incredibly fortunate to have in my life such extraordinary people as my sister, Danielle Goldstein, my father, Sheldon Goldstein, Steven Pinker, Gabriel Love, and, of course, my mother, Rebecca Goldstein, who continues to inspire me by accomplishing the seemingly impossible every day: being a better mother because of her art, and a better artist because of her consummate mothering.

I

I AM SITTING IN MY LIVING ROOM, AND THE REPORTER is eyeing me nervously, tapping his foot out of sync with the salsa beat drifting down the stairs. He looks as though he's raced here straight from the offices of a high school newspaper, Adam's apple jumping in his delicate neck, large blue eyes set wide with earnest curiosity in a smooth, egg-white oval of a face, though I understand (he's brought me a collection of clippings as proof) that he's more established than he looks: recent arts editor of the *Yale Daily News*, minor freelancing assignments everywhere from the *Village Voice* to *People* since he graduated from college last June. His specialty is arts profiles, as he let me know the moment I opened the front door, pushing into my hands the two quarter-page jobs he's done for *Entertainment Weekly*. I'd pretended to recognize the names; we share some tenuous connection, this boy and I, and I'm anxious to put him at ease. He is the son of the cousin of the brother of God knows who, a line that eventually traces back to my college mentor, Robert Masterson. But, more than that, I like him. I like his youth and eagerness, his undisguised excitement. I like him for not noticing—at least not visibly—what a dull and tired woman Tasha Darsky has turned out to be.

And so I've been trying for nearly an hour to show a hint of the dazzle he's come here expecting. Sometimes I can catch it from the mere anticipation, scoop up some of the phosphorescent run-off from a reporter or a fan's unrealistic idea of me. But today it isn't working.

"And that was 1998?" he asks. He's good at this—incisive, thorough—and I can't help thinking he deserves a better subject for an interview that marks—he's told me this twice—"the most awesome day of his career."

I nod, noticing a ring of something sticky on the coffee table.

It's then that he shifts a certain way in his seat, a funny, aborted wiggle like a child impatient with a heavy diaper, and I realize that he's got a question he's been holding back, his clincher, his killer. It's possible this question is going to be dopey—the supposedly trenchant ones often are—but I find that I have faith in this boy. I find, moreover, that sometime in the past fifty minutes I've decided that we're in this together, poised at the start of a brilliant career. It's a nice place to be, and I don't want to blow it. God knows I'll never be here on my own again. And now, finally, I start to feel that slow prickle of warmth under my skin, that trickling creep of sparkle that once came out of me as something singularly—puzzlingly—crowd-pleasing.

And so I'm a little disappointed when, after a long pause, he says in an overly loud voice: "Would you say there's been any single aspect to your life"—he's biting his pencil between words—"an aspect, or an event, or a . . . well, the aspect that's the pivotal one? The one that, you know, made you what you are, the most famous violinist since Paganini?"

"I'd hardly compare myself to Nicolò Paganini," I say, because it's true but also because the tone of his voice has set off a vague sort of alarm. I hear a burrowing, wheedling edge there, and it makes me think, just for a moment, that I've been reading this man all wrong.

"Oh, but haven't people been making that comparison for decades? Since Vienna, in fact?" he stammers, pushing the blunt-cut bangs off his forehead. When he returns his hand to his lap, I can see beads of sweat have appeared on his wrists, of all places. The sight makes me think, quite suddenly, of a penguin with a shock of spiked hair we saw in a Budapest zoo fifteen years ago; Alex, all of two years old, had insisted that she knew its name to be Mr. Levin for reasons that never became clear to me. The memory makes me briefly giddy.

"No, not since Vienna. Certainly not that early," I relent, feeling a new protective swell along with my burst of silly, hopeful joy.

"So what was, you know, what would you say it is, the pivotal thing, if there is one? Would you say there is one?"

I look at the beads of sweat, the leg tapping now on the downbeats, the floppy bangs fallen back into eyes fixed onto mine, and I want to throw him something he can use, something good.

"Maybe the people I've loved," I say.

"Love." He repeats the word like it's revelatory, but not in a good way; as though I've said that cars run on happy thoughts. His eyes have gravitated away from mine, and I can't catch his gaze. I'd tried to throw him a line and now he's floundering, and so am I.

But we're saved by a voice booming down the staircase, mingling with the salsa music. "That's a weird thing to say," the voice—like a bell trying hard to sound grumpy—calls. "It's so weird that if I didn't know better I'd say you were actually being honest. That'd be wild."

"Is that Alexandra?" the reporter asks, swinging his head around.

Just then she slouches to the bottom of the stairs.

"I didn't know she was here," the reporter exclaims, looking back and forth between us. "Could we possibly? Would it be possible to speak to her as well? I'm such a big fan. Of both of you."

Usually I'd leap at the chance to pull Alex into an interview—reminisce about our performance of the Van Rheede duet in Brussels back when she was twelve, or the London concerts when she was fifteen, set loose some nostalgia in the air between us and see if it catches—but because Alex is looking at me with narrowed eyes I'm quick to say, "I don't think so. We don't have much time. I have a lunch date, as I mentioned earlier?"

"Just a few more questions to you, then." His voice is petulant, aggressive, but I notice this the way you'd notice a slightly stale smell in the bathroom of a four-star restaurant, a skimming, shallow jolt. All my real attention is turned to Alex, to the very unpromising look she is giving me.

"I wanted to ask about Jean Paul Boumedienne," I hear the reporter say, as I mentally tick through the ways I might have pissed Alex off since breakfast. I stop ticking at the sound of the name, surprised but not yet stunned. The words "Jean Paul Boumedienne," spoken in the reporter's high-pitched voice, echo in the room with us, but I'm certain he didn't really say them. *One too many sleepless nights*, I think, a little amused, even, at what a messy mind will throw at you. It's true I've barely slept in the weeks since Alex showed up at my doorstep, unexplained and furious. Out of habit, I turn to look at her again; it's when I see her eyes have gone hot and white and ghastly that I know.

"Your relationship with him," the reporter is pressing, and his face, staring intently at Alex, not at me, no longer strikes me as young. "Do you think, perhaps, that *that* could be the singular thing that made you who you are?"

I want to say, "Where'd you learn to link that name to me?"

I want to say, "What makes you think you have the right to know?"

Most of all, I want to shout, "Alex, why're you looking at me like that?" but the reporter is already answering the less urgent of these questions, saying, "It was Robert Masterson who suggested I ask. He told me that Boumedienne was how it all began."

I watch him long enough to see his thin lips form the words, then whip my head back around just in time to catch sight of Alex's left foot as it follows the rest of her swiftly out the door.

ASK HIM IF HE WANTS COFFEE, I THINK. *ASK HIM IF HE wants water.* Hold him at bay and hold him in the dark.

The reporter is sitting ramrod-straight several feet from me, and I can tell, without looking at him, that he's dissecting the scene in his memory: did something just take place or didn't it? I'd like to think I'm not sure myself, but I am. Something has taken place. I just don't know what. This, in itself, is no surprise; it's been a long string of I-don't-know-whats with Alex.

I try to form the words I should say next, that perfect something to deflate the last two minutes, to get him out of my home. I breathe deeply and close my eyes, but what I see is Jean Paul's face: heavy-lidded blue-black eyes, pale lips curled subtly in unexpected places. So darkly beautiful. So unwelcome. *Open your eyes,* I demand, but I don't want to. I don't want to see the reporter's boyish face aged with anticipation, or the bland and beige room around us, a room so tasteful it's clearly not the product of any real person's taste. I don't want to swing my feet off the plush white carpeting and tuck them beneath me in a feint of intimacy, to hide that the answer I'm about to offer answers nothing. I have the strange thought that what I *really* want is to fling my eyes open onto my parents' West Village brownstone circa nineteen sixty-something. I want to see the narrow staircase crammed with books, the dozens of paintings jostling for space on the walls; when I look toward the dining room, I want to see reds and blues and golds rain down onto my hands from the stained-glass windows above.

I should see all that, because that's where I am. The reporter is feet away from me, rigid and waiting on the Eames chair upholstered in blandest cream, but I am decades away, under a shower of color, tracing lines across paper. It's a shame the reporter can't be here with me, because this is probably the closest I can come to answering his question; this is how it all began: sitting at a dining-room table rescued from the original *Queen Mary,* my five-year-old fingers alive with vibrant shades, but not with talent. What's really alive is the living room below, shaking beneath my seat, the wood groaning and the glass tinkling its displeasure at one of my father's foot-stomping tirades. Light swells of jazz mingle beneath this, and supporting it all is my father's ecstatically violent voice. My mother is hovering around me, her flower-scented arms close, her ghostly pale hand reaching down every now and then, but too lightly, almost afraid to touch the paper I'm carefully filling with lines and curves, though there are canvases of hers littered throughout the house. I hear a door slam, and a small man scurries past the bottom of the stairs, in and out of my peripheral vision in an instant. My father is in the dining room seconds later. He stares for a moment as if trying to place us, and then he says, with marked relish, "I don't think we're representing Milton anymore," before gliding away on his elegant rage. I am trying to capture all of this in my drawing, but I am finding it infuriating, because I have no idea *how* one captures anything in a drawing, I am not good at drawing, and what I really want is to make something that sounds like everything I've just heard. I turn to my mother and ask how to work sound into a picture. The next week, they start me on violin lessons.

This memory is before me and gone in the time it takes to breathe, once, deeply, in and out. *Open your eyes,* I think again, but I allow myself one more beat of close-lidded silence, because the one memory has unleashed another, and now I am six years old, and up way past my bedtime, afloat in a murky world of cigarette smoke and clinking glasses that has materialized in our living room. Large, well-dressed bodies cram the space, and either push past me or, worse, stop to ask me questions and then laugh at my perfectly reasonable answers. I long to be away and also dread the moment when I'll be banished to bed, and so I stick close to my father, who I know has only the vaguest sense of my presence. I watch from behind his left leg as he gleefully holds forth about "simplicity on canvas," "honest art," and "finally, finally bringing the sublime into this shit hole of a world" to a group of people who worship him for making them rich. My father has an enormous talent for damning people and movements, and even I know that the fad he's calling "sublime" tonight, he'll be calling "criminally naïve" by next month. He is, after all, that famous Abe Darsky who was declaring Abstract Expressionism dead just months after he'd established a gallery to serve as its epicenter. He is that Abe Darsky who spent his childhood dreaming of becoming an artist, yet never felt the need to try his hand at drawing or painting until he entered an art class as a college freshman at Columbia. After two frustrated days of slow and clumsy sketching, he declared himself unworthy to proceed, and turned himself toward the task of revealing who *was* worthy. He opened his gallery on his twenty-first birthday—funded by the fortune his own father had made with a revolutionary new flushing mechanism and the sheer suction force of his charm—and was a resounding smash not so much because of the work he included in his first show, as because of the much-touted works he rejected by declaring they'd be much improved if hung with their faces to the wall.

These stories are legend to me; my father himself is still legend to me as I cling to his leg and listen to him rant to his guests. I am the only person who takes him seriously when he declares, as he so often does, "Funny to think, isn't it, that if my old man hadn't thought up a great new way to flush, American art would still be in the international toilet." That my father (and my mother, whom my father calls his "business brain") is responsible for all good art in the country is the easiest thing to believe—all one has to do is listen to the brutal thrum in his voice, so mesmerizing and so frightening. So frightening that, standing right beneath it, feeling the force of its tremor shoot through his body into the left leg I'm clutching, I have a sharp need to know where my mother is standing. My eyes wander the room for the sight of her glittering in the background, filling glasses, flashing smiles, being an incandescent work of art herself, the perfect hostess, but also wondering behind that docile face whether her husband has to go on to *quite* this extent, because surely he couldn't really think that Michelangelo and da Vinci were pale harbingers of de Kooning. (This I know because she says it later, while tucking me in that night, in that light, delicious way she has of saying impossibly unknowable things as if I know them.)

My eyes are well trained to spot any inch of her from any distance, and so it's just an instant before I know she's not here. I make my way through a mess of legs toward the hallway, and up the stairs, climbing toward the slant-roofed fifth-floor room that will soon be my bedroom but right now is still her studio. That I know to go there is strange, because I cannot remember the last time she used that space. But I know and I go, and I find her staring at an empty canvas with her hands limp at her sides, five long, bejeweled fingers clutching a paintbrush dipped deep crimson. "It's the lighting, I think," she says without turning around. I see her in profile. "The lighting in this room is impossible." The clamor from downstairs is rattling the tubes of paint on the ground, and after a moment she says, "Or maybe the noise." She turns around then, and her face takes on the look that precedes a command, so I brace for her to shoo me to bed, but instead she says, "Go practice the violin, will you?" I think this is the funniest thing I've heard in a long while, a brilliant joke, though I don't quite get it, and we share a strangely wild laugh together before we descend back into the party, to find my father frantically searching for her because someone is asking about last quarter's profits.

I push forward in my mind, weeks, months, I'm not exactly sure, and now I see a ratty brown couch covered with a plastic sheath that sticks to the underside of my legs in the heat; there's a strong smell of cabbage in the air, and pictures of smiling faces everywhere I look, so many that even my new violin teacher, Mrs. Blau—who has replaced Mrs. Peacocke, my kind but not terribly talented first teacher—doesn't know who they all are, though she's assured me now several times that, whoever they are, she loves them. Surrounding us is the most remarkable sound I've ever heard, being pumped at us from Mrs. Blau's phonograph. "Too crazy you never hear the Fifth," she had laughed, her breath giving off the scent of the sticky Hungarian pastry we were sharing between us. And then there'd come this music, which is nothing like the music my parents play, those meandering lines of sound that move like life, without a theme, without an obvious pattern. Moments ago, I was ashamed that I had never heard of this very important fifth piece of music by an apparently very famous man, but now there's no room for shame. I feel as though I'm in one of those dreams where I discover a fantastic new wing to my house or an amusement park in my backyard. I know that I want to be in this part of myself forever, but I'm afraid because I realize that I might never be able to get back here on my own—that this fantastic wing, the best in the house, where music like this exists, might not be in me at all, but only dreamed, beautifully, through that dreamlike name suggesting an odd aquatic being, Bay-toe-fin.

That night, in my tiny new pink-and-gold bedroom on the fifth floor, I thrash around in my sheets, trying to remember every note of that music, to not let any of it out, because without it I'm lost. Beneath me my father's flinging around his elegant contempt again, shouting about "idiots" and "boors," linking all the world's ills to the lack of artistic sensitivity in the population, and I'm inspired with the kind of terror that Calvinists probably feel when contemplating the likelihood that they're among the damned. Hearing my parents talk incessantly about the immortality of this one, and the godliness of that one, I have constructed a metaphysics that calls out for a score by Wagner. I've taken my parents' pagan beauty-worship and confused it just enough with the Jewish heritage that my grandparents try to sneak into my bedtime stories to arrive at a picture of the world in which God's Chosen People are a group consisting of all great painters, certain avant-garde composers, and a handful of writers. These people are temporally unbound, spatially unlimited, and imbued with certain superhuman powers, like the ability to bring "the sublime into this shit hole of a world." They are also, of course, immortal. Naturally, I want more than anything to be one of God's Chosen, so that my mother can adore me in the special way she adores her clients, and my father will never be forced to hurl contempt my way, but also because I have come to believe, even more deeply than those two fanatics, in the special worth of this group. Music like Beethoven's proves it to me, and keeps me up now inspired with terror. How and when will I know whether I matter in the world, I wonder. What can I do to ensure that I do? What will happen to me if I don't?

That was how it all began.

WITH THE REPORTER GONE THERE'S AN ANXIOUS STILL in the apartment. I begin to pace and repeat what in recent years has become a mantra of sorts: do not go after her. The wisdom of this mantra has been thoroughly substantiated, and to make sure I don't go and substantiate it all over again, I force myself back down onto the couch, where, since I have nothing better to do, I slip back into recalling.

Memories swim up and swim away, less distinct now, merging and melding and ambiguous as music. I see a girl with a thick smattering of freckles who may or may not belong to the name "Becky Hobbs," which floats up at me along with the face; I see classrooms, lunchrooms, playgrounds, but mostly long afternoons in Mrs. Blau's apartment, the only place aside from home I truly like to be. Those afternoons I remember distinctly: the remarkable giddiness of letting the world's purest beauty course through my arms and fingers, and burst out through my violin.

Music spilled out of me in a way that drawing never had—naturally, satisfyingly. It was almost too pleasurable, too much fun, to even seem worthwhile. But my parents were convinced that it was very worthwhile, especially when I began to win a slew of competitions for young violinists, even placing first in the New Jersey Symphony Orchestra Young Artist Search at age ten, beating out dozens of musicians nearly twice my age. My father was so impressed by this particular victory that he decided to yank me out of school after the third grade. "It's a crime to waste whole days on geography and arithmetic when you've got a gift like that," he told me, while I whined about how lonely I'd be. "Loneliness is an emotion you would do well to know better," he said. "Anyone unfamiliar with the contours of loneliness has no contours herself." My mother said: "One day you'll be grateful for this decision." (I only later learned that the end of my formal schooling happened to coincide with a bitter argument between my father and the school's headmaster—the headmaster had been uncouth enough to declare himself a fan of Andy Warhol—and, perhaps more relevantly, a marked downturn in our family's finances.)

So, starting when I was eleven, Monday, Wednesday, and Friday mornings were spent with my mother, reading history, literature, French, and Latin. On Tuesdays and Thursdays, Dan Bryson, a graduate student studying physics at Columbia, would come by and teach me math and science. But afternoons were devoted to music.

Because of those afternoons of music, in particular my Tuesdays at Juilliard, I never did have to become intimate with the inspiring contours of loneliness. I found a whole new batch of friends who liked to do strange and fun things like ride the subways for hours just to watch the people, and sing along with the musicians in Washington Square Park. Among this group one was far and away my favorite, a skinny, pimply-faced boy named Julius Rassner, with whom I was timidly in love between the ages of twelve and fifteen. Julius's skill on the piano was matched only by his skill at making up silly titles for himself (my favorite was "the Terrifying Puny"), and one day, while we all rode the subway to nowhere, just a few months after I first started at Juilliard, I slipped my sweaty palm against his. We kept our hands entwined for hours, pressed between us so that no one else would see. We never spoke about our romantic encounter, and it never happened again, but after that there was a special bond between us, and I felt comfortable confiding certain things in him.

Or, more precisely, I felt the *need* to confide certain things in him periodically, in the hope that one confession would lead to others. (Our mutual love, for starters. Oh, wasn't it mutual, didn't he remember fondly the feel of my sticky hand?) That was why it was Julius I ultimately went to with the guilty secret of my young life, which was that playing the violin had never quieted the fear that I was not worthy.

Over the course of seven years, Mrs. Blau had taught me to make music with my whole being. She was constantly interrupting me in the middle of a piece to ask me questions like "Vat are you feeling as you play that movement?" At first, if it was a happy piece of music, I'd say that I was feeling joy; if it was sad, I'd say I was feeling heaviness; and she would just shake her head and say, "You, you, nut the violeen." For months, maybe even years, I had no idea what she was talking about with this "You, you, nut the violeen" talk. But at some point I began to pay more attention to what was going on inside of me as I played, beneath the fixation on technique and the flimsy feelings that the piece evoked on its most obvious level. I realized, much to my surprise, that when I played the violin that place inside my mind that I'd first discovered while listening to Beethoven's Fifth was filled with rich images. It wasn't long before I figured out that when I attended to these images my music changed. After one particularly layered rendition of a Dvořák concerto, Mrs. Blau nodded her head in approval and said, "Now the violeen is begeenning to feel what you feel." I went home that night feeling that I could turn every bit of sound in the world into music.

For years now I'd believed in this invigorating delusion, and yet something still urgently pounded away inside me. The same something that couldn't be expelled through paintbrushes or pencils hadn't been expelled through my violin. I confided this to Julius one day while we were fetching sodas from his family's sugar-filled marvel of a refrigerator. I'd volunteered us for the job while the rest of our friends sunned themselves on Julius's Upper East Side rooftop; I was constantly trying to get him alone. He shifted some cans from the crook of one elbow to the crook of the other, then, furrowing his hairy brow, said, "Why don't you write your own music?" and I felt the world tilt itself to a fantastic new angle.

It had never occurred to me until then that normal people

could write music. Sure, some people—Julius, for instance—took composition classes, but did a person just set out to write a concerto or a sonata or a rondo the same way she might set out to memorize state capitals or tackle some long division? Was this something I could aim for?

By the following summer—the summer I turned fourteen, which I spent mastering Mendelssohn's Violin Concerto and mooning over Julius—I had managed through sheer willpower to write several pieces that my new composition teacher at Juilliard called "eminently promising," including a twelve-tone piece that he'd shown to his own teacher, Milton Babbitt, the undisputed father of dodecaphony in this country, in order to prove that the aging idea remained vibrant among rising young talents. As fun as playing was, though, composing was not. I could rarely get a firm grip on the fuzzy swirls of sound that seemed so promising from a distance, at least not firm enough to yank them out into the world as something with definite shape and weight. Groping around in my mind for the notes was like groping for a dream in the first blush of wakefulness. Still, the thrum in my mind was quieted as long as I kept at it, and so I did.

The summer I turned fifteen, I earned a spot at Tanglewood, ostensibly to study the violin. But in my mind the violin was just a means to an end, a way to stay close to music until I figured out how to *be* music. I spent the whole summer ducking violin practice to trail after the composer Gunther Schuller. My hope was that he'd notice me lurking and ask, unbidden, if, by any chance, I had some scores I wanted to show him. Of course, he never did notice me, and instead all I managed to accomplish that summer was to mutate, shooting up and out in all directions as though I were just one more piece of lush Berkshire foliage. This was a development I could have done without. I hated my new body, with all its messy, un-Twiggy-like contours. I hated that the boys stared and the girls asked me unanswerable questions. (How did that happen so fast? Could they do anything to encourage such a metamorphosis? As if I knew.) I hated that I went from being the girl who played first violin to the girl with the big boobs over the course of one month. I hated that if this had to happen, and so fast, it also had to happen miles from home, when I was surrounded by other kids. But, then again, walking past mirrors, windows, lakes, I couldn't help tossing my head in the direction of my reflection and marveling that that form was mine: a form that demanded to be seen, that boldly seized space from the world. It looked like a body that was not afraid of anything. It looked like a body that wanted things I did not yet know how to name, things far more dangerous than holding hands with Julius Rassner a second time, which until then had been my highest erotic aspiration.

My father was the first to catch sight of me as I stepped off the bus toting a small suitcase, my violin, and the body of a 1950s pinup, and I could actually see the usual insouciance melt from his face. It was the one time I saw my father at a loss for words. "Oh my, don't you look nice," is what I think he managed to offer, smiling weakly. My mother had also taken me in by then, and covered me up in her pale arms, which no longer felt ample enough to keep out the world.

I noticed as we embraced that I was now taller than my mother—only by an inch or two, but the new balance to the ratio seemed wrong. I was fairly convinced that, to my parents, *I* seemed wrong. They had every right to expect that I'd grow into a body like my mother's, with long, clean lines, or perhaps that I'd never grow up at all. I'd given them no reason to fear that one day I'd sprout this thoroughly unmodern form. They probably considered it bad art.

In the changing room at Bonwit Teller the next day, my mother allowed me my privacy, something she had never done before. Though I was relieved to be left alone with my monstrosity, I also experienced a pang of abandonment, as if I'd been thrust out of childhood cold-turkey. While I was inspecting the bulge of my hips in a skirt I would have loved to have fit me more flatteringly, I sensed her smiling her glittering smile at me, blood-red lips still managing to curl around a cigarette, eyes alive with some bit of comfort to wrap me in. I looked at her expectantly, waiting for her to tell me how to view this in the most soothing light.

"I know you're seething," she began, putting her hand on my arm. "And that you hate how you've changed. But, sweetheart, one day you're going to love that body . . ." She paused, laughed, tossed her glossy hair, and blew a ring of smoke. "Until then be careful. A body like that is very . . . volatile."

A quick jerk of my arm, and she was off. I had not been seething, but now I was. It can't be true that I'd never been angry at her before, but that's how I remember it. It was as if a new emotion were being born in me: a constricting, dirty, ticklish, overwarm mix of anger and shame and resentment. How did she know I would come to love this body? Why hadn't she prepared me for its coming? And why was she laughing? It was a conspiracy against me: my flesh and my mom together. I wanted to strike out and hit her.

Later that afternoon, as the cab crawled through bottlenecked streets, I thought through what she'd said more calmly, turning the word over in my head. "Volatile." What did it mean? It didn't sound like a good thing, though it didn't sound bad, either. Exciting, unsafe. Even bohemian, free-spirited, maybe, like my parents and their friends. But to whom did my body pose a danger? To me? To my parents?

Certainly to my long-standing tutor, Dan Bryson.

Dan Bryson on a Tuesday morning in September: physics, calculus, and biology books in hand, goofy smile on face, inevitably a few stories about his summer vacation (long hours on the dissertation: "Grad school isn't the blast it's cracked up to be, heh-heh") tucked neatly into his brain, waiting to ease over our always awkward reunion. He was just as unprepared for my transformation as I'd been. "It's been quite a summer for you," he somehow found it fitting to say, before a coughing fit seized him, his face awash in red—and not from the stained-glass windows. As he lunged for the table, the hefty physics book slipped from his sweaty fingers and landed on his toe. My mother, who'd been pretending until then not to notice from the other room, caught my eye and winked. *Volatile.*

I liked the way Dan Bryson treated me that day and every day after. No longer like a child, but like an equal. No, almost like a superior. Because of a body, a talentless lump of matter? It just might be. I thought about asking my mother, but every time I geared myself up to broach the topic, that warm, ticklish feeling came over me, and I needed to think strongly about something else in order to recover.

I also thought about asking her why, on Julius Rassner, my body seemed to have the opposite effect. During our tremulous reunion (tremulous on my part, probably not on his), he barely looked at me, and he was strangely patronizing, painstakingly explaining the most elementary concepts to me while talking about his summer internship at Carnegie Hall, as if I didn't know just as much about music as he did. The next day, he called to say that I had changed over the summer, become a different person, or that perhaps he was the one who had changed, but either way we couldn't be friends anymore. By the time the semester started up at Juilliard, he'd found a new group with whom to shift aimlessly through the tunnels of New York.

It was a few days after this call, pulling the plug on three years of feeble desire, that I attended the opening of an important show at my parents' gallery. I was feeling betrayed and guilty, alluring and disgusting, and all of these conflicting emotions had coalesced that morning as I lay in bed thinking about Julius into one overarching desire to will the rest of me up to my body's level by becoming an adult in every way. An adult was the sort of person who didn't care whether she was rebuffed by the man of her dreams; an adult simply glittered on in the face of heartbreak because she valued what my mother called "independence," and perhaps even relished loneliness along with my father. So that night I acted like an adult by smearing myself with makeup from my mother's vanity and flitting around the brightly lit halls with an unlit cigarette in one hand, an unsipped martini in the other, making small talk about the work on display, and trying to act as blasé as possible about my months at Tanglewood, while still managing to work my summer activities into every conversation; I tossed my hair, and pouted my lips, and I was so mesmerized by my ability to blend in as just one of the fashionable crowd that it didn't even strike me as odd that one of the more prominent painters my parents represented, a man who was considered one of the best artists of his period, which, granted, had long passed, spent two hours soliciting my opinion on Pop Art. I didn't find it suspicious when he smoothly guided us away from the crowd, into one of the back rooms of the gallery that my parents used for storage. Being the naïve and eager-to-impress dolt that I was, I thought it made sense that he'd want to be able to focus on my patter more single-mindedly; it wasn't every day, I reasoned proudly, that a member of the youth culture came along who was able to articulate the views of her generation so eloquently. I imagined that I was giving him invaluable insight into the audience of tomorrow.

It wasn't until he'd moved his agingly handsome face so close to mine that I could see the wrinkles that grooved the skin around his mouth and eyes, and his copious white hair was tickling the top of my forehead, that it first dawned on me that he hadn't been attracted by my analysis of Claes Oldenburg. I should have been disgusted—here was a man well into his sixties, a respected member of the art community, as well as an outspoken opponent of amorality in the public sector, putting the moves on a fifteen-year-old girl—but I wasn't. I wasn't exactly excited, or even happy, but I wanted him to proceed. As I backed against a stack of large canvases that were waiting to be shipped out to a client in California, all I could think was "I am about to be kissed by the man who painted *Bird with Lines*." He didn't kiss me, though. Instead, he pulled away and left the room abruptly. I left the party minutes later, after catching sight of him with his arm draped over a woman closer to his own age.

Late the following afternoon, I came home from Mrs. Blau's to find a message waiting for me on the kitchen table. Our housekeeper, the seventh in an unending string of Croatian relatives attached to one of my parents' discoveries, had scrawled, "Art lesson continues," followed by an address. As I read this strange note, I found myself thinking, as though it were the most natural thing in the world, "So today will be the day I kiss the man who painted *Bird with Lines.*" An hour later, I was on the subway, headed uptown, decked out in a pair of old jeans that I could still squeeze into, a beaded peasant top we'd bought a few days earlier to accommodate my relentless form, and just a touch of my mother's signature deep-red lipstick. As I examined my unfamiliar reflection in the train's darkened, dirty windows, I wondered if he knew how old I was, and, if so, if that didn't make him kind of a creep. But it was hard to consider these questions seriously when my mind was busy trying to imagine the same hands that had painted those huge, darkly luminescent canvases reaching for me.

The address turned out to be his studio, a cavernous, window-filled loft, littered with art supplies and partially painted canvases. When I knocked at the door, he called out that I should let myself in. The second I caught sight of him, I lost whatever semblance of poise I'd been successfully feigning. He was standing in the middle of the room, staring at a canvas, naked except for a dark-blue towel that hung around his waist. His body was surprisingly muscular. The transition from the Terrifying Puny to this could not have been more stark.

It took him several seconds to turn away from his canvas and toward me, standing, uncertainly, several feet from the door, and when he did look at me it was with the same menacing intensity of concentration he'd given his artwork. I was just beginning to think that I'd gotten his message horribly wrong, that he hadn't wanted me to come here, though I couldn't imagine what it was he *had* wanted, when he broke into a bashful smile and held his arms out toward me in a gesture of defeat.

"You make me take humility in my work, Tasha," he said. "Do you know why?"

I shook my head.

"Because I could never paint anything as beautiful as you look standing there, even if I tried my whole life to do it. Which, by the way, I have been. For me it's a daily torment to create the sublime. For you it's a matter of existing."

Part of me was thinking what an unexpected mess of cliché this was, coming from someone whose paintings showed such glorious originality and restraint, but the rest of me was celebrating the discovery that someone—this someone—thought I was beautiful.

"How old are you, Tasha?" he asked next, unaware of the revolution taking place inside of me.

"Sixteen," I responded, though I was months away from my sixteenth birthday.

"And why are you here?"

"Because I thought you invited me." Again I felt a surge of panic. Had I misunderstood his message, reading in what I'd wanted to believe?

He laughed, a dry, raspy laugh that reminded me of the sound of hot caked sand crunching underneath shoes.

"Yes, I know I invited you, but why did you come? Aren't you frightened by a lecherous old man like me?"

"I'm not that easily frightened." I managed to bring off the line with the sultry offhandedness of a Marlene Dietrich character.

"No, you're certainly not."

"And I don't think of you as old," I remembered to add.

"But I am," he insisted, his eyebrows raised as if daring me to challenge.

He had started coming toward me, the towel swaying threateningly, though mercifully keeping its grip on his lower body. I thought of running, but found myself firmly rooted to the floor.

His silver hair was wet—this detail was a relief; it suggested the towel wasn't just some kinky setup—and smoothed away from his generous forehead, exposing his weathered features in all their severity. I noticed that his mouth and nose looked cruel but his eyes looked kind, and that it was the effect of these mismatched signals together on the same face that made him so sexy. I was on the verge of mentioning this, then thought better of it.

"Come on in, Tasha." He said it as if I'd just that second walked through the door. "I want to show you what I was painting today."

He led me to where he'd been standing when I first came in, in front of a painting that was much smaller than the canvases of his I'd seen before, with lines that weren't as clean, and colors that were much more strident.

"I love it," I said honestly. "It's different from what you usually do, but I love it."

"That's good, because you inspired it."

I must have looked startled, because he laughed again, his warm, raspy laugh that made me think now of two sun-baked bodies rubbing gently against each other, an image that brought a rush of heat to my cheeks.

"I started it when I came home last night. I wanted to paint something like you—tentative and brash at the same time."

Without knowing how else to respond, my mind retreated to its old standby of precocious girl, and I considered asking whether a painting that was meant to be like me didn't go against the ideals he himself had outlined in an article decades earlier—art as its own self-definition, not meant to represent anything outside of itself. I wasn't sure whether he'd be pleased with my erudition, or disappointed by my inability to recognize the fluidity of the laws of creativity. I wisely decided to remain silent on the issue.

"I'd like to paint you sometime," he murmured. The words sounded more like something he was saying to himself than to me.

"I didn't know you did anything realist anymore." I'd added the "anymore" hoping he'd be impressed with my grip on his history, but he didn't seem to be, and I was beginning to feel the frustrating conviction that I was saying all the wrong things and not saying any of the right ones. Without knowing quite what I was doing, I reached out and gave his towel a tug. The swatch of blue terry cloth came off in my hand, leaving him bare, erect, and startled. I was startled, too, both at my boldness and at what it had uncovered. I'd never seen a live naked male form before, and expected something more like the pale marble version I knew so well from trips to the Met, but I think I did an excellent job hiding my revulsion at just how colorful and alive the main attraction was. It took him several seconds to recover his calm, and then his wry smile returned, this time tinged with a hint of what almost looked like reverence.

"Who are you, Natasha Darsky, age sixteen? And how is it that you exist and are in my studio?"

Before I could respond (I wasn't sure I was supposed to), he had disappeared to a far corner of the room. He came back wearing pants.

"Hungry?" he asked, taking a shirt from a basket near the wall lined by tall, arched windows. "Because I was just about to go get some Chinese food when you showed up."

By the time I said "sure" he was halfway out the door.

I wandered around the wide space for a while, inspecting every piece in progress, trying to think of staggeringly insightful comments to throw out when he returned. There must have been at least thirty paintings that he was working on simultaneously. After I'd looked at every canvas twice, stopping for longest to stare at the one inspired by me, a vibrant, angry swell of blue and green and black that looked neither tentative nor brash to me, I sat down on the floor, leaned my head against one of the wall-length windows, and watched the traffic crawl by on Columbus Avenue. Though he was gone for over an hour, I never once suspected that he wasn't coming back. When he returned, though, he seemed not to have had the same confidence in me: "You are still here," he said when he saw me, emphasizing the "are." But when he sat down beside me on the floor, and started unloading white cartons between us, he seemed happy enough to have me there. I stayed until almost 10 p.m. We sat on the floor beside the windows, eating mediocre Chinese food and talking about art, music, and politics. He acted interested in what I had to say, even deferential to my musical opinions, and so when I said "goodbye" I only felt slightly unhappy that the one time he'd touched me was by accident, when handing off a packet of duck sauce.

Outside, the night was small, cozy, and unthreatening. *This is what it's like to be an adult,* I thought, putting my mother's sashay into my walk. Was it my imagination, or did I glitter in the dirty subway windows?

On the stoop of my parents' brownstone, though, I turned back into a panicky child. I could hear my mother crying, and my father screaming without any savage pleasure in his voice. *What's happened?* I wondered for a desperate beat or two, before I realized that I was the cause of this pandemonium. My parents allowed me a lot of freedom; after my music lessons, my days belonged to me to do with as I pleased. But I had never stayed out this late before. My mother never worried about anything until given a legitimate reason, but once given such a reason she instantly assumed the worst.

I skulked through the door, softly calling out that I was home. Both of my parents were before me instantly. "I told you she was fine," my father said, and disappeared back up the narrow staircase. "I was going to call the police," my mother whispered breathily (she got breathy when she was angry), her face rigid and tear-stained, her arms awkwardly held out in front of her, wanting to embrace me but also not. "I was sure something had happened to you." For a moment I felt guilty almost beyond endurance, and then, without warning, the guilt disappeared, leaving me resentful and aggrieved. "I'm not a child," I insisted, trying to recapture the poise I'd discovered earlier that day. "Yes, you are," she countered sharply, looking angrier than I'd ever seen her. Angry at me, which she never was. I stormed up four flights of stairs to my bedroom, but after lying on my bed for a while, I couldn't conjure up the anger anymore, and I reverted to guilt. I crept downstairs, where I found my mother sitting on the couch staring out the window. I curled up in her perfumed arms, and she rested her chin on my head. Sitting like that, I forgot what had appealed to me about a paint-splattered loft and a strangely small and unthreatening night.

But I woke up the next morning remembering the appeal with gut-gripping force. Again I set off uptown and, though this time he looked startled to see me, again I stayed for hours. I went again a week later, and again and again. I was never invited, exactly, but I was never greeted with anything other than eager hospitality, either. And, anyway, I at least made myself useful. I learned how to clean brushes properly and how to stretch a canvas, and I took to tidying up the cartons still filled with Chinese food that would otherwise linger for weeks. Sometimes he would let me sit and talk to him while he painted, but other times he wanted silence, and so, if there were no minor tasks for me to do, I would sit on the floor against the windows with some staff paper and try to compose. I worked well there; being around him made me so frenetically happy that even my music jumped when he was near; I could reach into my mind and pull out notes almost as easily as I could launch them from my violin.

Every now and then, he'd ask me to hum what I'd written; he couldn't read music, which struck me as incredible. One time he let me hum an entire rondo while he touched up the small canvas that was supposed to be inspired by me. The moment struck me as intensely sexual, but this might only have been projected fantasy; his continued failure to touch me was a source of constant irritation.

I had somehow gotten it into my head that what we were having was an affair—a very chaste affair. Julius Rassner was a puny memory of a puny emotion compared with what I was feeling now. I was dying to tell my mother; I thought she might be bohemian enough not to care that her daughter was head over heels for a senior citizen. But whenever I seriously considered confiding, I decided it was too much of a risk. What if she forbade me to see him? Just as I was blithely certain I was in the midst of a torrid but virginal liaison, I was also convinced my mother had no idea I was sneaking around behind her back.

Naturally, my mother had an idea. She saw the change in my walk, in my talk, the look in my eyes. A few days after my sixteenth birthday (which I celebrated rinsing brushes and clearing cartons), she finally confronted me. What she thought she knew was almost the truth; it was the truth in everything but one small detail: she pinned the rap on poor Dan Bryson. Sweet, goofy, awkward, and fired. For some reason he took his dismissal gracefully, not even standing up for his innocence. So I heard; my father was the only one present. But I could imagine not wanting to press my luck with that sort of anger facing me down; better just to bolt. Anyway, it was lucky for me. I decided that this misunderstanding had to stand, though I hoped that Dan would get some blessing in recompense. A finished dissertation and a job with an Ivy is what I tried to negotiate for him as divine recompense. If my mother disapproved this heartily of my consorting with a twenty-something, I reasoned, who knew what irreparable damage would be done if she knew I'd been hanging around with a sixty-something? If she knew . . . then what? Would she hate me? Would she deem me unworthy of her constant care? One thing was for certain: if she knew, she would never let me see him again.

With the Dan Bryson fiasco I lost my stomach for deception, but I only fell further into my infatuation. I knew I was filthy, shameful, and mean: I had hurt Dan, I could have hurt my great artist, but worst of all I had hurt my mother. I knew that a good person would not keep sneaking around. A good person would be open and honest, and start spending afternoons helping out at the gallery, practicing the violin, and writing music in the innocence of her own bedroom. So this is what I forced myself to do. Hardly a day went by when I didn't imagine racing to that manic, paint-filled studio. (How surprised he'd be to see me again, after such a long, unexplained absence!) For over a year, I lulled myself to sleep with clippings of his work I'd snipped from catalogues and stuffed in a shoebox I kept under my bed. I'd convinced myself that he was pining for me, too, and we were sharing these same thoughts at the same moments each night. That he'd never made any attempt to find out why I'd dropped from his life was just proof of our psychic connection; not once did it occur to me that he might have been indifferent to my visits to begin with.

Since the best tangible connection left to me from my days in his studio was the many pieces of music I had started there, my composing, at least, continued to go well. I would compose at night, thinking of him, the way other teenage girls might lie awake in the wee hours writing teary love poems, though if anyone had made that comparison then I'd have been mortified. I didn't think of my music as being *about* him, or even about my feelings for him. It was simply that being inside of that music was a way of remaining in his studio, and so my music was a place I wanted to be—no longer a threat but a comfort. The whole world was comfortable, just one large waiting room to my bliss, because I had formulated a foolproof plan: on my eighteenth birthday, I would show up at his studio, and we'd make our implicit love affair explicit.

As far as I could see, there was only one large obstacle keeping me from this happy eventuality: my father's sudden insistence, soon after my seventeenth birthday, that I begin applying to colleges. Was it out of retribution for my bad behavior that my father decided to banish me? Was it because I had made too much of a nuisance of myself? Whatever the reason, I wouldn't have wanted to go even if I weren't in love. Neither of my parents had a college degree, and they'd turned out perfectly well. And, anyway, I belonged at Juilliard. I'd always figured that once I reached college age I'd move from the after-school program to the conservatory. But this was my father I was up against, and so I lost: soon we were filling out applications, going on interviews, and then packing my bags.

I was three weeks shy of leaving home the day my father asked me to drive with him to New Jersey to drop off a painting at a client's house. My mother couldn't come along, for the usual reason: a famous astrologer had cornered her at a party years earlier and told her, with no provocation, that she would die on an interstate. She hadn't crossed state lines by car since. My father hated to drive alone, so along I came, as I so often did.

For the umpteenth time in my life, I drove to New Jersey with my father. I'm sure we spoke about the virtues of photorealism or the implications of Richard Estes's insipidness. I'm sure he was silent and brooding for part of the trip—he had been periodically strange around me since I'd upped and sprouted breasts, and seemed to downright hate my presence for weeks after the Dan Bryson fiasco. (We were almost a year past the hating stage now, but it resurfaced at odd times, even if only for a few seconds of discomfort.)

On the way home, there was no traffic. That was the shocking thing—it was a high-traffic time of day, but there was no traffic—and so we got home an hour earlier than we'd expected, and stumbled on a scene that I was just three weeks shy of never stumbling on: a man standing on the red-and-orange Oriental rug in the front parlor holding a half-filled tumbler; my mother paused halfway between him and the door, caught mid-stride; guilt cast thickly over both their faces; an unsurprised anger on my father's.

The first emotion I had upon taking in the scene, amazingly, was joy: a reflex at seeing the man I loved for the first time in nearly two years. There he was, standing on the red-and-orange Oriental rug in the front parlor, holding a half-filled tumbler. There he was, in the flesh, in my house, outside my mind. My great artist.

And then came the terrifying thoughts, in quick succession: First, that we had been discovered, that Dan Bryson had sleuthed up the truth in a mission to clear his name, or that guilt had overtaken the husband of my heart and he'd confessed all. Second, that we were not the ones who'd been discovered.

My father shot up the stairs, his fluidly elegant back stiff. My mother sashayed up behind him, her steps as light and buoyant as ever.

I stood dumbfounded beneath a wall-sized painting by Barnett Newman. Then my great artist caught my eye, and in an instant he was there with me in the high-ceilinged vestibule. He was there, just as he was there every night in my mind: his body close, his breath smelling of scotch. My heart was beating furiously, my eyes were stinging from the tears I was blinking back, and my parents' raised voices were drifting, muffled, through the ceiling. But other than that it was just like in my fantasies. He pulled me into our first true embrace, pressing gently against me, but it was more of a father's hug than a lover's. His face was close to my ear, and when he breathed in, I could feel the hairs on the side of my head shivering toward his open mouth. And then he was gone. The tumbler was sitting on the floor where he had just been; I hadn't noticed him putting it down, and this upset me.

I stood listening to the muffled sounds of my parents' raised voices, then found myself running, heat pressing up against me, hair sticking to my forehead and whipping in my eyes. He had a quick, jaunty walk, but it was no match for my youthful legs in flight, and soon I was right behind him. He had been about to hail a taxi.

"Wait," I called out, huffing and puffing, sweating and wheezing.

He turned around and took me in with that detached look, which I now saw was not appraising lust but simple distraction. He took me in, and I don't know what he saw.

"You and my mom?" This was all I could manage to produce.

He looked dumbfounded, though not overly concerned—I could see his hand sorting through his pants pocket, perhaps for his cab fare. Then recognition spread over his face, and he let loose his wry laugh. "Oh yeah, we're sneaking around behind your father's back, all right. But not in the fun way."

"Not in the . . ." I repeated the words, trying to form them into something I understood.

"He doesn't want to sell my stuff anymore. You must know the drill by now." He shook his head with irritation. "He's cut me slack longer than most, but you know as well as anyone I'm out of sync with the principles he's calling holy today, and will scrap tomorrow. Fucking dictator could rip the creativity right out of you if you gave him the chance. Christ, look at your mother."

I must have started at this, because something horribly like pity flickered through his eyes and he said, "So I hear you're going to Harvard."

"Yeah."

"Not bad. Send me a letter if you remember. Why'd you stop coming by, anyway?"

I'd had the perfectly crafted answer ready for this question for years now, but this was not the way the question was supposed to be posed—not by a long shot—and so, instead of telling him how our love had to be kept secret until my eighteenth birthday, which, incidentally, I had let pass the month before without acting on my increasingly detailed fantasies of unstayed passion, I just shrugged, trying, though I'm sure failing, to seem as indifferent as he did.

"Well, write me if you remember," he repeated. His arm was up again, flagging the taxi hurtling toward us, which swerved abruptly toward the curb. With his other hand, he reached out and touched me lightly on the shoulder, saying, "Take care of yourself, little girl," before stepping into the waiting car.

I let the sting of the "little girl" travel through me several times. When I began to walk home, I felt several feet shorter.

Back at the brownstone, I was on my way up the stairs, ascending into my parents' muffled voices, when I caught sight of the small canvas hanging outside our dining room in a tiny alcove partially hidden from view. It was by my mother, who'd forgotten since then how to paint, and it was not at all like the other art in our home. I wondered for the first time why my father had agreed to let it hang at all, even in a partially hidden alcove; it was the stark opposite of the works he championed in his rants. It was dark and subtle; nearly monochromatic, any emotion a barely audible whisper. It showed a dockyard at dusk. The colors were delicate but visceral as well: there was the deep gray of the ocean, the dirty-white foam tips of the nearly vertical waves—angry waves, water with an attitude—the decaying brown of the dock. Men scurried with an understated urgency in between the hulking, rusting ships, which were draped in algae and dirt, loading and unloading, doing God knows what, really, but looking important and carefree at the same time. And off to the side, there was a girl. All the lines of the painting, once you noticed her, pointed you straight to that child.

I wanted to tear the painting down. It was clearly the best thing my mother had ever done, and I felt while staring at it that I was hearing all at once the specter behind nightly terrors, the sadness behind my mother's glittering smile, the smirk behind my father's rage, and my longing for a lecherous old man who, in the end, just thought of me as a child.

I was face to face with failure, and I swore, standing there, that I would never know it.

I LEFT NEW YORK ON A BRILLIANT URBAN MORNING, and arrived by late afternoon in someplace gray and indifferently unfamiliar. My new home looked like an old English asylum I'd once seen in a photo, the scene dominated by austere red brick buildings set in a gloomy, grainy sky.

"A sanitarium for privileged loonies," I said out loud, but my father was busy looking for parking and ignored me.

He'd been ignoring me since we left New York, lost in some recent aesthetic indignation I refused to digest, and I was glad for his distraction. I was glad that my mother was at home, afraid to tempt the fates of the interstate (I pictured her still standing at the curb, rubbing mascara out of her eyes), that my home was a memory, that my great artist didn't love me, though he also didn't love my mother, not in that way, which I had to admit was something of a relief. As we drove, I kept reminding myself how grateful I was for all this, for both the small reprieve and the outsized outrages, and I even half believed it. Probably I was just reeling from my heartbreak, but I imagined myself as reeling from my history: from every family crisis, every rant of my father's, every abandoned painting of my mother's, every night I was kept up by the specter of my cosmic unworthiness. I was determined to shake off all vestiges of my life until that point. I was glad to have this chance to remake my life.

At least I told myself I was glad. Really, I was desolate, a feeling that was getting worse with every minute, as the realization that I was *actually* going to be living in a new place gained force. It was a revolutionary notion, almost beyond comprehension, that my life would take place here from now on: not beneath the reds and blues and golds of the stained-glass windows in the dining room, not on the narrow staircase crammed with books and canvases, not in my pink-and-gold bedroom thick with fantasies of music and affairs with iconic, aging geniuses, but beneath this gloomy, grainy sky, amid these austere red brick buildings, far from my parents, my great artist, and everything else that anchored me to reality, allowing me to live in my strange, insular, obsessed world without noticing that that was where I was.

Climbing up the staircase of my dorm with the battery of suitcases packed by my mother, beside the huffing, puffing, linen-suited figure of my father, I heard students effortlessly starting up friendships in the hallways, rock music drifting up from the quad below, parents being impatiently shooed back home, and I knew that I'd entered a world where I would no longer be afforded the luxury of obliviously and blissfully *not* belonging. I deeply regretted asking for a single room, which seemed now like the only quiet space on campus. I was ashamed of the quiet of my room.

When my father hauled in the last bag and said he was going to head back, I cried. He escaped from my embrace, patted me on the head, winked, and left with a quick "Good luck," even his elegance not sufficient to dissemble his scurrying out.

In a daze, I made my way down to the orientation address, a pompous, self-glorifying speech riddled with the phrase "Harvard community," of which the speaker (some doddering dean or other) wanted us all to be a vibrant part. Being told that I now had the privilege of becoming a part of this world, whether I wanted to be or not, only made me lonelier, but I reminded myself that this was the prelude to great things, my remaking. I was finding this refrain harder and harder to believe amid the throngs of students who all seemed to know one another already, or at least to know much more than I did about getting on with strangers. I spent the rest of the day holed up in my room, pretending I was eager to unpack, when really I was just eager not to be the one strange girl standing off to the side in Harvard Yard.

It was with a joy bordering on mania, therefore, that I entered the freshman dining hall the next morning and caught sight of someone I knew. Tiny, blonde, and lovely, Amy Wyatt was moving through the cereal line with the same studied grace I'd admired through three summers at Tanglewood. Amy had been the star flutist of our age group, as well as the star tennis player, and, just generally, the star. She was one of those people no one seemed to like but everyone wanted to be around, possibly because she emanated a sense of entitlement as large as her family's estate out in Westchester horse country, or possibly because she had embraced so many causes—feminism, Marxism, a strangely militant vegetarianism (at Harvard she later founded a movement called "Vegitas")—that it was difficult to speak freely without offending her in some way, and yet equally difficult not to admire someone who cared so deeply about so much. Watching her spoon cornflakes distastefully into her bowl, I remembered none of this about her. That I recognized this girl and that she would recognize me was too momentous a fact to allow any others to crowd my mind.

I positioned myself near the archway between the food lines and the tables, and, pretending to inspect a counter full of fruit as meticulously as the Amy Wyatts of the world would, waited for her to mince by.

"Tasha Darsky!" she called out as she neared me. "Is that you?"

I turned around and gave her my most winning smile. "Wow, Amy Wyatt. Hi."

"I had no idea you were going to be here," she cooed, her most winning smile putting mine to shame. "Where were you this summer? We missed you out in the woods."

I shrugged, trying not to indulge the memory of hot days spent dreaming of an old man putting paint to canvas. Instead, I told her about my composing breakthrough, the way the music had loosened inside me two years earlier. It hardly seemed worth taking out time for the violin when there was music to be written, I explained.

She seemed taken aback by this pronouncement, but also impressed, and, as if in direct response, asked if I was eating with anyone. "Well, come join us," she said when I told her I wasn't. She began to move away, and gestured with a wave that I should follow. I gratefully took off after her, clutching a banana and realizing with empty-bellied dismay that it was the only food I'd picked up in my excitement. Afraid to lose her, I stuck close as she wended her way through the maze of tables, once again admiring her graceful glide, more wafting than walking. With a satisfied "humph," she set her tray down across from a boringly handsome boy who looked like he could be the brother of half the other males milling around the place. He was talking to two other people, the first an artfully unkempt Israeli boy, the other a girl, the first heavy person I'd seen on campus.

"Tasha Darsky, meet Graham Rockwell, Ari Ben Haar, and Adrian Brown," Amy said, gesturing toward them with her adorably pointy chin.

Graham had already given me his cursory glance and was now letting his eyes wander around the dining room in search of something more interesting, but the other two were smiling warmly.

"Graham and I grew up next door to each other. We're practically related."

I slid self-consciously into the seat next to Amy's, and placed my paltry banana as unobtrusively as possible on the table in front of me.

"Graham is a novelist," Amy added. "He's brilliant beyond belief."

Graham let his gaze wander back onto me, and told me, without a trace of self-mockery, that he was currently "percolating" his first book.

"Ari is Graham's roommate," she continued her introductions while she spread butter delicately on toast. "He's a sculptor. And Adrian is my roommate. A poet. And Tasha here," she declared earnestly, ignoring the look of embarrassed but not displeased amusement the three of us lesser lights were sharing now, "is a brilliant violinist, who has recently become a composer as well."

I smiled at each of them in turn, feeling both cowed and important to be described as such a definite something when I was a nothing. I wondered whether the others were feeling the same. I wondered whether they liked me. I wondered whether I'd ever see them again. Naturally, it didn't occur to me that in this small group I might have found the new home in which I'd been only half believing for weeks.

My new home, it turned out, wasn't a place, but a time, the time at the end of the day when we'd all trickle lethargically into one or another's rooms, too tired to study or read or lie on our beds wondering what our life was all about. Within minutes of gathering, our lethargy would fade, and we'd be shouting maniacally about the futility of a new ethic in postmodern art, or the death of atonal music, or the artistic responsibility to work toward "the good"; none of us had discovered irony yet, not in the deep, despairing sense.

Of course, it wasn't only the inspiration of one another's enthusiasm that awakened our study-dulled senses, but a good deal of narcotics, most of it obtained for us by the one nonartist in our group, a boy named Gregory Mandell who had mysterious and well-supplied contacts down the road at MIT. (Because I almost never joined in the mind-altering aspects of my friends' fun—I wanted more control over my faculties, not less—for a while I got stuck with the unclever nickname "the Anti-Gregory.")

Gregory joined our group late in the first week of school. He was a recent Russian immigrant and math whiz, whom Amy *needed* to befriend because of his tendency to act out the plots of Russian novels when he was high. The next day, Amy found Michael O'Shea in her expository-writing class. He was the ninth of ten children from an Irish Catholic family in South Boston, who also played the violin and had what seemed at the time irrational plans to become the conductor of the New York Philharmonic by the time he was thirty. That was the same day our late-night gatherings began in earnest.

Despite the hours we logged together that first semester, I continued to be secretly terrified of both Amy and Graham. There was no topic, no matter how obscure (even if you'd just invented it that minute), on which Amy did not already have a firm opinion. And Graham had that typical boarding-school sense of recklessness about him, I guess stemming from the knowledge that, no matter what he did wrong, his father's money and influence would save him. He was heavily addicted to cocaine, slept around as though out of a sense of duty, and consistently spoke as if he were parodying someone very, very pompous. That Amy and Graham liked me remained a bit of a happy mystery, one I believed was best left unprodded. What was clear was that they *did* like me; Graham even confided to me once during midterms that I was the only person other than Amy to whom he'd ever felt close, which led me to feel sorry for him for several days before I realized he'd probably just said it because he was high. Gregory, too, was almost always hopped up on drugs, and, anyway, never seemed terribly interested in any of us except Graham, who tolerated the constant hovering because it meant getting all his coke at a discount. I never felt I knew Gregory well.

Around the other three, though, I felt an ease I'd never felt before with people my own age. Unlike my Juilliard crowd, Michael, Adrian, and Ari weren't aggressively quirky; they were strange, certainly, but not on purpose. I never felt I had to impress them, and yet they consistently impressed me. When Ari would talk about the way he learned to see sculpture rise out of natural formations during his two years as a weapons officer in the Israeli army, or Adrian would genuinely laugh at her tragic childhood (her drunken father had smashed his car against a tree when she was eight, leaving her mother and her barely to scrape by financially), I wouldn't think, *God, my life is pretty lame compared with theirs*, like I would when Graham or Amy spoke about their many accomplishments, but just, *Wow, these are far more substantial people than I am*. They made me want to be more substantial myself, though I was pretty certain that explicitly contriving to become more substantial trapped me firmly in the trivial range.

Sometimes in the middle of one of our gatherings—when Gregory was carefully miming, and Michael was furiously conducting an invisible orchestra, and the rest of the room was shouting emphatically about the virtues and vices of Stockhausen's serialism, or Ligeti's experiments with texture and density, over the blare of Boulez on the stereo—I'd crawl into a corner of the room and watch the scene from there, convinced that life could not possibly get any better. I'd feel then as if I'd been born, age eighteen, at the eastern edge of Harvard Yard.

At the same time that my new friends were expanding my

conception of what a social life could be, I'd also acquired a new violin teacher who was expanding my repertoire. Mrs. Blau had called in an old favor with the legendary teacher Annabelle Scherr, and arranged for me to meet with her once a week at her ill-lit home in East Cambridge. I hadn't been too keen on the idea at first, concerned that further violin study would distract me from composing, but even I didn't have the gall to turn down Annabelle Scherr.

My first few lessons with the four-foot-seven, eighty-nine-pound powerhouse were miserable. There was an unpleasant stench of goulash permeating the cramped gilt-and-velvet-infested rooms, and her Hungarian sternness was a startling contrast to the Hungarian grandmotherliness of Mrs. Blau. But under her unforgiving eye, my fingering began to improve exponentially, and my tone was enriched. Walking briskly through the cold Cambridge nights after my lessons, I would often be seized by my childhood delusion that I could turn every bit of sound in the world into music.

Back in my room, though, I would remember that *I* was having trouble turning out any music, glorious or otherwise; it was only other people's music that came flying vibrantly out of me. I could still hear music in my head almost constantly, but when I came at it with a pencil and staff paper it tended to evaporate. I was back to my old state, unable to translate my mental music to notes in the real world. The frustration of this regression, and the clear implication that my two fruitful years had relied on something as simpering as a crush, upset me so much that I often ended a writing session in tears and surrounded by shredded sheets of staff paper.

One night, after starting and shredding three efforts in the space of two hours, I collapsed on my bed in exhaustion and picked up an old copy of the *Crimson,* the student daily, which must have been lying there for weeks. Surrounded by the shameful carpeting of paper bits, recently removed from the indulgence of a tantrum, still reeling from my failed efforts, I read a name and all my thoughts turned instantly toward it. Robert Masterson.

The article was a profile of the twenty most eccentric professors currently teaching at Harvard: the ones to stay away from and the ones to seek out. Robert Masterson was number two, and the suggestion was to seek him out and cling to him at all costs if you had any musical ambition. His advanced-composition seminar was brutal, the profile warned, but there was the potential for achieving alchemy if you had the right chemicals to start with. Competition for a spot was fierce; out of the thirty or so who applied every year, Masterson chose five. I knew right then, sitting on a snow bed of failure, that I needed him to choose me.

At that time it was unheard of for a freshman to apply, much less to win a seat, but I was convinced that getting into that seminar was the only way to save myself from artistic doom. I never told my friends why I was so hell-bent on getting in; they thought I was just displaying the sort of noble arrogance we all pretended to share, and cheered me on heartily. Amy even began referring to "our grand seminar crusade."

I agonized for two weeks over which score to submit for judgment, and settled on the rondo I was writing as a final project for my intermediate-composition class. Although I was furiously unhappy with it, my professor had called it "wonderfully lyrical and densely interesting," and I prayed that Masterson would agree with the assessment. Luckily, it seemed that he did—or he at least saw within it some sort of promise—because when the names were posted on a bulletin board in the music building mine was among the chosen.

My friends took me out for a celebratory dinner that night to our favorite hole-in-the-wall Italian place. We drank too much cheap red wine and became giddy with optimism about our collective future; I'm pretty sure that's the night that we conceived the idea of the Illuminati School, which would revolutionize all the arts, with each of us leading the movement in his or her respective medium. We would talk about this school a lot over the years, and though we never came up with even the germ of an ideology, we did manage to write the first three words of our manifesto: *We the artists* . . . (Only Amy took this seriously.) After dinner, everyone was tired from the wine and wanted to turn in early, except Adrian and, of course, me, still animated by my triumph. The two of us walked and talked along the spectral banks of the Charles River until early morning, sharing all sorts of things that neither one of us ever shared with other people, and feeling free because of it. I think that night might have been the lightest I've ever felt, high on the prospects of the future, and also on Adrian's hypnotic conversation.

I believed that this was the beginning of everything, that my new life had begun in full force, and that I wouldn't abandon it for all the world. But, of course, I didn't anticipate Jean Paul. Nor, for that matter, did I really anticipate Masterson.

IT'S EASY TO IMAGINE HOW ONE OF ROBERT MASTERSON's ancestors might have earned that particular surname for future generations. If the original Masterson was anything like his descendant, he was an imposing man in every way—appearance, voice, demeanor, and accomplishments, just to name a few—and he positively radiated a sense of mastery the way other people radiate fear or arrogance. The Masterson I knew was a strikingly large man, nearly six and a half feet tall, and exceptionally broad. His face would have been handsome, but it seemed unfinished; there was a lack of contour that always made the impression on me of a sculpture that hadn't been fully carved. But the unfinished face somehow only added to his general aura of unwavering and all-encompassing ability, in a way a truly handsome face would not have.

Like so many of the unflappably confident men I've known, Robert Masterson began life with the odds stacked firmly against him. He was born into a family of six, and was encouraged, like his brothers and sisters, to drop out of high school and help his parents run their grocery store. He stubbornly remained in school, won a football scholarship to the University of Illinois at Urbana-Champaign, and embarked on his career as a pre-eminent musicologist. He went on to do graduate work in musicology at Columbia, much to his parents' bafflement, then passed through several stints as a junior faculty member at impressive places, before landing a chaired professorship at Harvard at the age of thirty-five. By the time I met him, ten years later, he was widely considered to be the best man working in the field, and had every accolade to prove it. All four of the books he'd written were instant additions to the scholarly canon, and any movement he smiled on was taken seriously by the music community. He'd also composed several original works, and all had received positive attention. One of them had even been conducted by Pierre Boulez at a small concert in Greenwich Village that I'd gone to with my first love, Julius Rassner. (I'd had no idea at the time who Masterson was, but the early confluence in our lives now made me proud, and I made sure to mention it to everyone else in the seminar.)

Naturally, all of Masterson's students revered him, but the self-assurance that had come along with his effortless success made him a terrifying teacher. When he was sitting at the head of the large seminar table, critiquing our work as if we weren't there, I'm certain I wasn't the only one who wished Masterson had had just one significant failure in his life, some public error of judgment that would make him more sympathetic to our fragile egos. He wasn't a sadistic man, but he had no qualms about saying that something was awful when he thought it was, and unfortunately all of the work his students produced was awful when compared with Mahler, who was his standard of all that was worthwhile.

Within a week, I was wishing I'd never made it into his seminar, and wondering how I could get out. We started each class by dissecting a student's work, beginning with the scores that had earned us all the right to sit there and be humiliated, and though Masterson must have originally heard something praiseworthy in the pieces, he didn't give much evidence of that during class. He never came right out and said a piece was garbage, but when you weighed the good comments against the bad, the natural conclusion to draw was that this piece should never have been written. I was scheduled to present my work last, which meant during the third week of classes. I spent those three weeks busily working myself into a hysterical frenzy.

The piece that had landed me in this misery of a class was a rondo in the neoclassical style, spare and, to my ear, empty. I could think of a million unkind things to say about the work without Masterson's help, but that didn't make the prospect of hearing Masterson say them any less terrifying. Even though this piece was only one effort among many, and the purported idea behind the critiques was that they would help us to improve enormously over the course of the semester, hearing Masterson bash my work came to amount in my mind to hearing God declare that I was absolutely not on his master list of the worthy.

I came into class the day of my presentation looking like a victim of a random act of violence. I hadn't slept in two nights, hadn't bothered to shower, and was finding it difficult to stand up straight since my knees had lost the ability to lock in place. I don't remember walking into the class, but I do remember finding myself seated in my usual spot, staring numbly at Masterson's work-in-progress of a face.

I could barely hear myself mumble through the synopsis of the work I'd prepared the night before, and the comments the other students made were lost on me. We always made encouraging comments to one another; a sort of camaraderie had developed among us, like it does within platoons. We were bound by the fear of attack by a common powerful enemy. But as soon as Masterson's voice started booming around my ears, I could hear every word distinctly.

His complaints came fast and furious, with the words "trite" and "turgid" making appearances. It was no worse than what he'd said about anyone else's work, and to hear it said about my own music was not as harrowing as I'd expected. The negative adjectives stung, but I found myself agreeing with most of what he said, and not being devastated by that fact; after all, I probably hated this piece as much as anyone could. I would have left that day happy, feeling mature for having dealt well with severe criticism, and relieved that he hadn't called me an impostor or an outright disgrace to the musical tradition, even if he hadn't shocked the whole class by ending on an uncharacteristically positive note.

"Despite my reservations about this work—especially as regards the convoluted third and fourth contrasting themes (I will remind you all again, I hope for the last time this semester, that ugly does not equal interesting), I am gratified to tell you that we have just critiqued what is in my view the first salvageable work of the semester. The main theme is nothing less than enchanting, and some of the harmonizing borders on the very good. With a lot of work, we could have a delightful rondo on our hands."

And then, without a smile or any further word of congratulation, he moved on to discuss the assigned reading. As he rambled on about counterpoint, I wasn't the only one not listening to a word he was saying; everyone was looking around trying to read everyone else's face: should they be jealous, happy, bitter, gracious? I tried to avoid their eyes, because I couldn't hide my swooning.

Later that week, in the afterglow of my triumph, I resolved to visit Masterson during office hours. My purported intention was to discuss the new piece I was working on for his class, an aria set to one of Medea's monologues in Euripides' eponymous play. The assignment had been to write any form of music using counterpoint, and the particular passage had always sounded to me as though it were written for counterpoint to begin with: "O Zeus, and Justice, child of Zeus, and Sun-god's light, now will triumph o'er my foes . . . On victory's road have I set forth; good hope have I of wreaking vengeance on those I hate . . ." But it was fairly obvious to me that I was visiting Masterson's office largely in the hope that he would dole out more praise. Ever since he'd called my rondo "salvageable," I'd been working better than I had in months.

I'd expected to wait in a long line for an audience, given his iconic status in the department, and so I was surprised to find the hallway deserted. I later learned that everyone else was too intimidated to show up uninvited, which probably explains why he seemed genuinely surprised to see an undergraduate standing in his doorway. I'd interrupted an intense perusal of what looked like a score, which he shoved off to one side of his desk. While he cleared a stack of books off the only other chair in the tiny, cluttered room, I looked on, petrifying, wondering how I'd gotten the notion that coming to see Masterson was wise.

"Well, Ms. Darsky, what can I do for you?" he asked when we were both seated, I with the stiff and awkward air of anxiety, Masterson looking oddly loosened. I wondered whether he was using that tone—so full of patience it was encroaching on sweet—to mask how irritated he was at being bothered.

In Masterson's presence, we all quite consciously assumed his slow, deliberate speech, which we, in our ignorance, considered the essence of confidence, but which was just the rural Illinois accent of his childhood. And so it was in his voice, but coming out too loudly, that I told him about my idea for the next assignment. He looked distractedly out the window as I spoke, nodding from time to time, though not at intervals that made any sense in relation to the words dripping out in my unmastered Masterson. Once I'd said all I could think of to say, we sat in silence for several seconds, listening (at least I was) to the faint, chalky tapping echoing down the hall. He turned to me with an expressionless look, and, in six words, directly pinpointed the weakness of my conception.

"Those two melodies sound terrible together."

I nodded solemnly, trying to formulate a mature and professional response, and all the while nodding and gathering myself together for what I knew would likely have to be a wordless exit. He indicated with a quick motion of his hand, though, that I should remain seated.

"It's convenient that you came by today." He was looking out the window again, speaking as if I were taking dictation.

I froze mid-rise, hovering half an inch above the unforgiving wooden seat. A few of the papers I'd hurriedly gathered for my escape slid off my disappearing lap. I stooped, thought better of picking them up, and sat back down instead.

"I'm an old friend of Annabelle Scherr's. I'm not sure if you knew that."

I let out a shallow breath, every expectation I'd conjured instantly ruled out.

"I didn't know," I said. It didn't surprise me, though. I was sure all great musical personalities knew one another well, the way my parents seemed to know everyone in the art world.

He handed me the papers he'd been looking at when I entered, and I glanced down at them uncertainly. "I was wondering if you might do me a favor on her behalf."

My first thought was that he was asking me to bring them to

her, a possibility which annoyed me, to the extent that I could be annoyed by anything related to Masterson, because I wasn't scheduled to go back to her house for another week, and didn't want to make the long trip an extra time.

"It's a score I've been working on," he explained.

"Do you want me to bring it to her?"

"No, she's already seen it. I'm having it debuted at my house in three weeks. At a birthday celebration."

"Neat." It was a word I had never before used, and it hung in the air like a blaring signal of my inanity.

"Yes, I think it's going to be, provided I find my away around one sizable problem."

I waited expectantly, a fatuous smile twitching its own counterpoint to my helplessly nodding head. Ingratiating smiles and nods, and a Master-ful voice declaring the word "neat," too loudly, combined in my mind to paint a self-image of unparalleled lameness.

"The piece is a violin concerto, you might have noticed, and I had Annabelle in mind as the soloist. While I know she doesn't perform anymore, I did think that for such a private thing, and for me . . . But she said no."

"Do you want me to talk to her?" The idea seemed absurd to me.

Apparently it seemed absurd to him, too, because he laughed. It was the first time I'd ever seen him laugh; he managed to pull it off without smiling.

"No, no. Thank you, but no. I was hoping you might fill in for her."

"I don't think I . . . Isn't there someone you'd rather have?" In my surprise I dropped the drawl, my words coming out at their usual thoughtless speed.

"If there's one thing I trust Annabelle about, it's her judgment of a violinist, and she says you're the woman for this concerto. I'd pay you, of course."

I glanced through the pages, primarily to break contact with those freakishly pale blue irises. The part, I decided as I turned the pages, didn't look terribly complicated; three weeks would give me enough time to learn it and still get my work done. The only thing I thought might suffer was my fledgling ode to revenge.

"My aria, is the only thing. I was hoping to devote most of my time to that."

"I'd be willing to give you an extension, since this would be a favor to me." While he said this, he reached behind his head and, without turning to look, pulled a book down from a low shelf. It was one of his own books, *Sound and Sensation in the Classical Era,* and I thought he was going to give it to me. Instead, after glancing briefly at the spine, he merely put it down on his desk, preparing to resume his more important duties as a scholar.

I thought about the proposition for several seconds more, aware that he wanted to be rid of me, and realizing that there was no way I could refuse a request from Robert Masterson.

"Sure, why not?" I bent to retrieve the papers still littering the floor between us.

"Very good." Without standing, he grasped my hand in a vigorous shake. "It's a deal, then."

"Good," I repeated, feeling important for having a mutually favorable deal worked out with Robert Masterson. I knew I should leave then, and there was nothing I wanted more than to be away, but instead I stood there, paralyzed by the notion that there was something tangible now linking me to the greatest musical mind I personally knew, and that by exiting I would weaken that connection. I only got my legs to carry me out the door when he started leafing through the book in his hand, acting as though I'd already gone. I bolted then, and ran all the way home, holding the score tightly against my chest.

LATER THAT NIGHT, when I put his score on the stand and began to play, I saw that Annabelle had suggested me with good reason. It wasn't just because she wanted to foist the task onto her one remaining student. Or maybe it was, but, regardless, it was clear that I was well suited to Masterson's music. I tended to play my notes slowly and deliberately, always afraid to let a tone go by without exploring its full implications. The style didn't fit well with certain pieces; in what was probably a pretty unusual turn for a teacher of young violinists, Annabelle was often yelling at me to stop paying so much attention to every sound. But it was exactly right for Masterson's mournful, meditative concerto.

Though I'd only agreed to help because I couldn't say no to my demigod of a professor, I ended loving that music. I loved the way the overtly Romantic style hid something distinctively modern beneath its warm chords. I loved the periodic slips into atonality, the disenchantment these conveyed. I loved how, the deeper I sank into the piece, the clearer it became that it wasn't so much a piece written in the Romantic style as it was a piece trying to hide itself beneath that style, that the slips into atonality were the audience's chance to see through the trumped-up Romantic delusion to the real music underneath. I had the strange sense of wanting to protect this score, and I came to think of it as belonging to me as much as to Masterson.

Sometimes it seemed to belong to me even more than to him. Sometimes I forgot he'd written it. It was hard to reconcile the vulnerability of the music with the impenetrably confident man who led my seminar and occasionally asked me how the piece was coming, only to ignore my response. Reconciling this disconnect became a minor obsession. I tried to pry information out of Annabelle, but she batted away my questions as fast as I could throw them at her.

"Is he married?"

"Yes."

"Are they happy?"

"How do I know such things?"

"Well, do they seem happy?"

"They seem married."

A few days before the performance, the entire ensemble gathered at the Masterson home in order to rehearse. I was on the lookout for telltale signs of a marriage gone to pot, but his wife wasn't around, and the large, well-appointed house revealed nothing but considerable sums of money. *From her?* I wondered. *Has he sold himself into a loveless marriage?*

The members of the ensemble were all adults, and they all seemed to know one another; I think they were all friends of

Masterson's. There were a few famous faces in the group, and I stood off to the side eavesdropping once I'd already made my way around the room to inspect every photograph (all of Masterson with various musicians rather than with family members, much to my disappointment). Putting together the scraps of musical chatter floating in the room distracted me from the worry that had been gaining momentum all day: How would I feel if Masterson tried to correct my phrasing, my pitch, or any of the other crucial variables that I knew in my bones to be right? Would I even be able to slip comfortably into the music, knowing that he'd be listening and considering it his to alter?

The answer turned out to be "yes." With the full ensemble behind me, I felt more firmly rooted to the piece than ever. Each time I escaped into one of the enchanted, fevered reveries, I experienced it as a personal triumph against the musicians seated behind me. When it came time for my last cadenza, I was so filled up with the need to keep on clinging to my fight that, instead of playing the short, technically challenging line Masterson had written in for me, I improvised an impassioned, desperate snatch of slides and cadences. When the rest of the ensemble came back in, it had never been more obvious or heartbreaking to me how badly the violin had lost the struggle.

Under Masterson's direction, we played through the score several times, focusing primarily on the opening, where the phrasing in the percussion wasn't striking him as right. When we broke for dinner, it occurred to me that he'd never said a word about my playing—not any corrections or suggestions, but not any praise, either. The other musicians had surrounded me by this time, and were exclaiming on my preternatural maturity, my sensitivity, my interpretive power. Old men were clapping me on the back, and women were calling me "dear" and shaking their heads in admiration. I knew I ought to be pleased, but instead I felt wounded. I was fixated on Masterson, hovering toward the back of the room, talking to the withered bass player. I couldn't shake the feeling that I'd just *been* him, and yet, despite that intimacy, he was hardly aware of me.

I still had schoolwork left to do that night, and decided not to stay for the buffet dinner Masterson's housekeeper had set out, though several of the musicians tried to get me to change my mind. As I was walking out the door, Masterson came over to see me off.

"Impressive improvisation," he said, stiffly.

"Thank you," I returned in my best faux-Masterson. As he closed the door, I wondered why he'd chosen that particular aspect of my performance to comment upon; I forced myself to dismiss the idea that he'd meant to remind me just whose music it was.

I didn't practice at all the next two nights. Each time I started to play, I pictured Masterson cold and ungrateful in the doorway, and I put down the violin. On the day of the performance, I considered calling in sick. But, in the end, I forced myself back there. This was no time to act like a spoiled child. Anyway, I wanted to play that music again the way I had two days earlier, lost in the struggle, fighting for every note.

When I arrived, the housekeeper tried to usher me into the party, but I asked her to bring me to a quiet spot instead. With the sounds of the party trickling in, I sat in the grand living room with the abandoned musicians' seats arrayed behind me, and ran through the more difficult parts of the score several times. "This music *is* mine for tonight," I told myself as I threw myself into the notes, and by the time the other musicians and guests began streaming in, I believed it, at least enough to enjoy my performance. This time I improvised two out of the three cadenzas, the last one for nearly a minute and a half. The audience exploded when we reached the final bar, and Masterson rushed toward the front of the room to collect his laurels, beaming like a little boy.

While the crowd trickled out, I packed up my violin, still lost in the music. I was surprised when I looked up to see that I was alone in the room. I was trying to remember what I'd done with my coat when Masterson wandered back in. He nodded in my direction, and I nodded back, feeling my body tense into the petrified mode of unfinished movements, dopey smiles, and unceasing nods. And then the process reversed. I had the tangible sense of caution dissipating, and impetuousness taking hold—the overwhelming desire not to nod and smile and speak to him too loudly in his own voice, but to do exactly the opposite. Masterson was moving toward the sherry cart in the corner, ignoring me.

"Happy Birthday." I thrilled to the sound of my incautious voice.

He didn't look up as he gave a dip of the head, continuing to pour his drink. This only deepened my perverse resolve.

"You could say 'thank you.' "

"For the birthday wishes or for the performance?" He turned in my direction, and fixed me with the pale-blue irises. His tone was pleasant. This disappointed me.

"Both, I guess."

"Well, thank you, then, for both." He moved toward me, holding a glass filled with blood-thick liquor. It looked as though he would pass me and return to the party, but instead he stopped inches from where I stood, blocking me from the door.

With my exit route cut off, the reckless impulse started to fade, and, mumbling a deferential "You're welcome," I tried to escape. I had gingerly stepped around his looming figure when he said again, this time more firmly, and in a tone more like a rebuke than an expression of gratitude, "Thank you."

I wanted to smile, but couldn't, and so instead just nodded.

"Do you want some sherry?" he asked.

Without bothering to wait for my response, he handed me his glass, then crossed the room and poured another thick stream of liquid from the glittering decanter. I looked nervously toward the door, not sure if I wanted another guest to disturb us or desperately hoped no one would. He was clutching his glass in both hands, so that it disappeared inside his mammoth fingers, and I wrapped my left hand around my right, to hold my glass the same way.

"Sit," he commanded.

I sat automatically, not even bothering to check whether there'd be a chair waiting to catch me. Luckily, there was. He sat down beside me and took a long sip from his glass; I imitated the gesture. The sweetness caught in my throat. For a while, we drank in silence. I kept a watch on him out of the corner of my eye, noticing that he never once looked in my direction. I tried to think of a conciliatory parting remark to put me back in my place so he didn't have to, but the alcohol was starting to have an effect on me as the wordless minutes passed. My mania returned. I began to think about the man who wrote tragic music, hidden somewhere within the mountainous figure seated next to me. The hidden artist had never seemed so close to emerging as he did right now. This might well be my last chance to find him.

Moments after I'd tipped the last droplets of sherry onto my tongue, I steeled myself, closed my eyes, and let the words fly out. "Why would you want to debut this piece at your party?"

I flung my lids open, expecting I-don't-know-what, but finding Masterson's usual indifferent stare.

I looked at him squarely in the eyes, in an attempt to convince myself that I was as brave, or stupid, as I appeared, and pushed onward. "I mean, in particular with your wife here and all. I never heard a piece of music so down on love."

It struck me then that I hadn't gotten a look at his wife, and that I wished I had. Had she actually been there? She must have been. Not that it mattered. I simply wanted a reaction to my words. I wanted him to draw himself up threateningly so that he seemed about ten feet tall, a solid wall of rock. I pictured him opening his mouth, and small gray boulders flying out in my direction, pummeling me back into submission. I eagerly braced myself, but he slumped in his seat, and shook his head.

"I don't know. Why are you acting so impertinent to a man who clearly terrifies you?"

I met his pale-blue irises with eyes just as intent.

"Because I'm a twerp?"

"Same here." He made an expression vaguely like a smile, with his lips pulling outward but not upward. It was a fairly expressionless expression, but it struck me as promising and somehow flattering.

"I don't know if I understand," I admitted.

"Well, neither do I, naturally."

He laughed, and the smile became lovely, happiness leaking out the upturned corners, miraculously pulling together the unfinished features of his face, finishing them, so that he was, briefly, handsome. But the smile fled, and several seconds later I hardly believed I'd seen it. "To be honest," he said, in a most Master-ful drawl, so slow and deliberate that it almost sounded childish, "I didn't think that anyone would hear that I felt, um, down on love, as you say, from listening to that music."

"Are you surprised I did?" I was proud to have exceeded his expectations, ever the precocious child.

"I'll admit, I was taken aback when I first heard you play it. I could tell you were on to me."

"Is that why you acted like such a jerk?" A strange sense of intimacy had infected the conversation through his upturned lips.

"I'd hardly say I acted like a jerk."

"But is that why?"

"It's possible."

I considered his admission carefully.

"You shouldn't have put it in there if you didn't want anyone to know."

"I guess not, but what did Schoenberg say? 'The wonderful thing about music is that one can say everything in it . . . and yet one hasn't given away one's secrets.' "

"Guess he was wrong."

"I guess he wasn't counting on Natasha Darsky."

I could feel the sherry creeping into my cheeks, and I turned away, breaking eye contact for the first time since we'd begun this exhilarating exchange. Before I could look back, he'd stood and, in what seemed like one smooth motion, escaped the room.

"I'm sorry," I called out, but he was already gone.

The next day, in class, there was no indication that anything out of the ordinary had passed between us. He neither avoided nor sought out my eyes, agreed with my comments when they were good, disagreed when they were bad. I volleyed between relief and severe disappointment, and in both states found it impossible to concentrate. But when class ended, Masterson asked me to remain behind.

As the other students filed out, casting an array of sympathetic and envious looks in my direction, I shifted uncomfortably in my seat, arranging and rearranging my books and papers into stacks. With the last student gone, Masterson marched purposefully toward the door, which he then shut and, as if as a further precaution, leaned his massive weight against.

"Did you find today's class boring?" he asked.

"No, definitely not. No." I bit at the inside of my lip and kept my eyes trained on the table, strangely terrified of having our gazes meet, as if he might destroy something crucial and precious in me.

"You seemed bored." Without looking up, I could tell from his tone that he was smiling, slightly but expressively, and I raised my eyes.

"I'm sorry." It struck me that this was the last thing that I'd said to him the night before, and I blushed at the insertion of yesterday into today.

"That's fine." He was looking out the window behind me and seemed to have forgotten I was there.

"Did you want to talk about the extension?" I eventually asked.

"What?" He wrapped his powerful hands around the back of a chair.

"You're going to give it to me, right?" It had occurred to me he might take back the offer because of my bad behaviour. He didn't seem above that sort of thing.

"Yes, of course. I said I would." I cringed at the irritation in his voice. He let go of the chair and pulled himself up straight, all six and a half feet of him staring down at me.

"It seems to me, Ms. Darsky, that I'm guilty of being ungracious."

I tried to object, but he held up his hand, silencing me.

"Last night," he continued. "You were right. What you did for my concerto . . ." He waved his hand impatiently, as if we both understood what he meant, though I had only the vaguest idea, and certainly wanted a sharper one if a compliment was lurking there.

"It's fine." It took all my effort to keep the quiver out of my voice.

"No, it's not. You played with extraordinary care and sensitivity. I'm inclined to say you played it better than I'd bargained for." At this he raised his eyebrow, almost conspiratorially. "But thank you for forgiving me. I'd like to take you to lunch. As an extra act of gratitude."

Another class was clamoring outside the door. I made a move to get up.

"Are you late for another class?" he asked, looking at his watch.

"No. I'm done for the day."

"Then this couldn't be a better time for lunch."

We were seated several minutes later in the formal main dining room of the Faculty Club. I'd wondered on the way over whether it would be like the night before—with the intimacy that had crept in with his expressive smile—but it wasn't. We spent the meal, naturally enough, speaking about music—safe, third-party music. Charles Wuorinen's, to be precise. It could have been pleasant—he was taking everything I said so seriously!—but instead it felt like an exam: an exam I was passing with flying colors, but an exam nonetheless. I nibbled at my plate of fruit. He returned to the buffet four times.

I had to fight with myself not to be disappointed after the next class meeting, when nothing out of the ordinary passed between us. I had to fight with myself after the following meeting as well. I don't know what I'd expected, but there were hushed rumors in the music department about the chosen among the chosen, the Masterson protégés who came along every decade or so, and I suppose I'd hoped I'd be officially inducted. But by the third meeting, I forgot about wanting anything special, and went back to being grateful I'd won a spot in this seminar at all: my Medea aria was coming together, and even in these early stages, I could tell it was my best work. Plus, there was the hint of a new man in my life, a junior named Peter who I'd met through Amy. We'd gone to coffee twice, and I'd even, waveringly, imagined taking him to bed.

It was right before I was supposed to meet Peter for our third date—dinner and a movie, followed by, I was pretty sure, a long makeout session at the very least—that I finished my aria. I was surprisingly satisfied with it. It wasn't great music, but it was real music, music in the thick sense, and I couldn't wait to show it to Masterson. Though it was late on a Friday afternoon, I decided to take a trip over to the music building and slip it under his door: maybe he'd stop by over the weekend and find it. The building seemed deserted, and so I was practically running through the halls, humming my music, when I collided with a tremendous figure that turned out, when I stepped back, to be Masterson.

He barely acknowledged me when I stammered an apology, but when I showed him the papers I was holding, he was gracious enough about inviting me into his office. I sat down in the extra chair, while he leaned heavily against his desk and, without a word, started to read through the score. I tried to distract myself by staring out the window, but it looked out onto an empty interior courtyard. Stealing glances at Masterson, I couldn't help noticing that his spirits were not improving as he flipped through the pages. I tried to turn my thoughts to what I'd wear out that night.

I was deciding between jeans and a skirt, and panicking about the possibility that whatever I chose might be removed by someone other than me, when I heard Masterson say, "Better."

"Better than 'salvageable'?"

"Let's just say 'better.' " He smiled. "Good, even."

And then, just briefly, he looked at me in a peculiar way. Probably there was nothing to that look—a glare from the setting sun, a memory that passed through his mind—but it reminded me of the way my great artist had looked at me when he'd said he wanted to paint me and sent my whole body shivering with an anticipation I had yet to fully shake. When I rose to my feet, my knees weren't quite as solid as I would have liked. Though I wished Masterson would say more about my piece, I could tell I'd have to wait for the written comments. Anyway, it was getting late; I was supposed to meet Peter in less than an hour. On the way out, I offered Masterson my hand in a shake, which made sense to me until I saw it waiting there between us. He looked surprised, but gave me a firm pump, which I returned. I knew I ought to let go after that, but I didn't want to. Perhaps my reluctance had to do with that peculiar look, though it could just as easily have been my usual fear of severing any connection, however flimsy, I'd forged to this great man. I kept my grip. It had just occurred to me that there was no elegant way for me to end this moment, when he pulled me toward him. I felt his lips on mine. It was quick, and as soon as we separated I was terrified, all the possible ramifications of what had just happened assaulting me simultaneously. I was so nervous that when I felt his huge hands snake behind my head, and guide me toward his face again, I thought he might be teaching me a lesson—that at the last moment he'd bolt back and laugh, and tell me what an unappealing fool I was.

It was his tongue that convinced me that he wasn't mocking me; it lightly traced the line of my lips before plunging in and filling my mouth. Then his hands were on my hips, pulling me firmly toward him.

It felt like a long while later when we pulled apart. My lips tingled. I was sure there was something I ought to say, but he had walked over to the window and was staring out, and all I could think of was to ask when he'd have the written comments ready.

He didn't respond, and so I left.

MASTERSON DIDN'T SHOW UP FOR CLASS THAT MONDAY. A departmental secretary came in to tell us, basically, that it was none of our business why. But rumors were already flying around the music building: he had a daughter sick with leukemia, and she had taken a turn for the worse. That this explained his foul mood on Friday afternoon—that it might even explain the bizarre thing he'd done—was not lost on me, but I was in such a confused state that I was not thinking much about Friday's events. All weekend I had kept my mind narrowly focused on schoolwork and avoiding Peter, whom I'd stood up, like a coward. Now I dragged that willful numbness into another week.

By the following Monday, I had nearly convinced myself that the kiss had never happened. Masterson's stolid presence at the head of the seminar table made it easy to believe. There was no way this guy had pulled me toward him, held me firmly, leaned against a desk beneath me with one of his legs caught between both of mine. There was no way. And if he had, well . . . If he had, my God. Had this man *kissed* me? Me? Tasha Darsky? This absurd little girl? I spent most of the class looking around at the other students and imagining what each of their reactions would be if they knew.

After class, I rushed from the room, but he managed to catch up to me in the hall. It didn't surprise me that we were alone, the corridor more deserted than I'd ever seen it on a weekday afternoon. I think I half believed he could control that sort of thing.

"I imagine . . ." he began.

"Of course," I said.

"Of course what?"

"I wouldn't tell."

"No, I didn't think . . ."

"Never."

"No, of course."

We continued to walk in silence. We'd emerged from the music building, and were nearing the edge of campus, where Harvard Yard met tony residential Cambridge. I wanted to break off and head back to my dorm, but I wasn't sure how. The crowds of students thinned, then disappeared. We turned down several tree-lined streets. We continued to say nothing, but stopped in front of a large Tudor-style house that it took me several seconds to place as his.

"Will you sit with me for a while?" he asked. His voice was weak and pleading. He sounded like the father of a sick child; perhaps that was all true. I followed him inside, wondering why I would.

He took me to his study, wood-paneled and richly leathered. I sat down in a deep chair, and picked up the book lying on the arm. It was another one of his early works. I thought it was strange that he seemed to be constantly reading his own books.

"Nothing fazes you, does it?" he asked, breaking into my idle thoughts.

He was standing by the window, looking out. It seemed to be a favorite position of his. There was something challenging in the tone, so I decided not to respond.

"I'm sorry about your daughter," I said instead.

He shot me a look of disgust before turning back to the window. Then he wheeled around and came toward me. I stood, thinking I should leave, but he pulled me against him, this time much less tentatively. Though I was afraid, it didn't occur to me I could stop the embrace, and, anyway, there was a fluttery voice in my head saying, "*He* wants *you*." Perhaps I was just gratified to find out that at least one old genius liked me, but it felt more exciting than that: it felt as though, scared as I was, my body wasn't. My mother had been right: this lump of matter attached to me was volatile. Upstairs, behind the thick velvet curtains his wife had chosen in order to keep out the prying eyes of neighbors, my body shed its clothes easily. I was surprised by how easily, and perhaps he was, too. He seemed to think I knew what I was doing, and so I didn't disabuse him. I was glad he didn't notice my grimace of pain.

Afterward, both of us lying above the sheets, several inches apart, he said, "God, you're something."

I tried and failed to guess what this something was over the course of the next week, during which time I didn't hear from him. I thought of telling my friends what had happened, but in the end I didn't. It could have been a one-time thing, a mistake he'd made, and I'd only end up embarrassing myself. But when he caught up to me after our next seminar and walked me back to his house again, I thought instead that perhaps we were becoming real lovers, the kind who cling to each other, wrong as it may be, and who eventually lose each other in a rain-soaked scene of regret.

"You know," he said to me as we were getting dressed, "I was going to say you bring out a man in me I didn't know was there, but, honestly, I don't think he *is* there when you're not around. I think you put something into me that's all your own, just like you did with my concerto. You alter me."

I laughed, thinking it was the nicest compliment I'd ever heard, and in response he called our lovemaking "inspired intercourse."

The next time I visited Masterson after class I asked a terrible question.

"Let's say there were no Jennifer." We were lying on our backs in bed, our sides just grazing each other. I had just been marveling, as I'd done several times before, that a warmth rose off his body like it would anyone else's. This seemed far too vulnerably mortal to be right. "Would you still feel like you owed something to Marilyn?"

I'd meant to ask whether he would have felt any obligation to his wife if they'd never had a child together—that is, if he believed in the unbreakability of the bonds of holy matrimony. But he thought I was asking what he'd do in the likely event that his child should die. He flew into such a rage I thought he was going to throw me from the house, naked, but I managed to explain myself above his tirade. As I was heading out the door—unaccompanied; he was still lying undressed on the bed—he said, "Does anything frighten you?" in such a mean-spirited voice that it seemed possible frightening me had been his purpose all along.

The next time I visited him, the sex was violent and painful, and I left seconds after he rolled off of me.

That night, I called Adrian and asked her to come over.

"Don't ever sleep with him again," she said when I told her what had been going on. But I knew that I couldn't do that. Not even if he hated me.

"It'll break my heart," I told her.

"Well, of course it's heartbreaking," Adrian had sympathized like a true poet. "Anything legitimately romantic is. But you should still turn him over to the administration and get his ass canned ASAP."

That what we were doing was against the rules hadn't even occurred to me, but now I took it as evidence that he did care for me after all. Why would he risk his career if he didn't? I determined to be more understanding of my complex and troubled lover. But I never got the chance. The next Monday, I waited for him after class for fifteen minutes, and when he didn't materialize I walked to his house alone. He opened the door with the written comments on my aria in hand.

"Sorry this critique's taken me so long," he said. "My daughter's been sick, you know."

He led me to his study, and we sat for a short while, discussing my ode to revenge. He liked it very much, he said in his old expressionless way. He thought it had promise, he thought *I* had *great* promise. When he walked me back out, he said, "Let's meet in my office next week to talk about your final project," and shut the door before I could reply.

Without any warning, I had been demoted (or was it promoted?) from Masterson's mistress to his newest protégé. The transformation was so quick, so seamless, it was hard to believe that for three weeks we'd been anything other than teacher and student. On my slow way back down the tree-lined streets toward campus, I almost convinced myself that we hadn't been; perhaps that was just what students and teachers did, the way of the world, meaningless. When I collapsed minutes later onto Adrian's bed and let loose this hypothesis, she stared at me wide-eyed for a while before musing, "One day I'm going to figure out once and for all if you're pathologically naïve or just preternaturally debased. My guess is a little of both."

Whatever I was, I was no longer worth hiding behind thick velvet curtains. Soon Masterson and I were meeting two or three times a week, in his office, in coffee shops, for walks around campus—it didn't matter where, since all we did was talk about music, mainly mine. I was becoming known around the department as that very thing I'd most wanted to be just a month before: Masterson's latest find, the chosen among the chosen. I should have been happy about this, and part of me was. Certainly, cautious artistic praise was more helpful to me than sweet nothings, and my work was steadily improving. But it was impossible to ignore the rejection that accompanied my being chosen. It felt like my great artist all over again, and so, rather than happily accept this arrangement that, deep down, I preferred, I found myself trying subtly to seduce him whenever we met, placing my hand on his, letting my hair fall against his arm when we looked over a score together, keeping track of where every glance he gave me fell. (They never fell anywhere good.) One time I joked that we weren't following the guidelines for complicated affairs, that in our situation couples tended to lose control every now and then and jump into the sack for a nostalgic romp. He looked at me with genuine puzzlement and said, "You think that was an affair?"

On the last night of classes, my friends and I went back to the same Italian restaurant where we'd celebrated my hard-won entry into Masterson's seminar. I spent the night tragically shoving linguine into my mouth and wondering whether Masterson had ever cared for me at all. On the way home, Adrian pulled me aside.

"Get it through your head, Tasha," she told me in her gently firm tone, while the others walked on without us. "You need to use this guy like he used you. He can make you, Tasha. And he will, too, at this rate."

That night, instead of studying for my first exam, I started reworking my Medea aria. Adrian was right: instead of sabotaging this opportunity, I needed to milk it for all it was worth. Though I ended up sacrificing each of my final exams to the effort (I managed to bring my GPA down from a pre-exam 3.9 to a post-exam 2.8), by the time I arrived back at the brownstone, I was certain Masterson would award my Medea aria with an adjective more flattering than "salvageable." That label had certainly proved less gratifying with each successive use.

I spent most of the next three months lying on the beach at our new summer house in the Hamptons, reading Agatha Christie novels and polishing the other two works I'd composed for Masterson's seminar. For a week at the end of August, all six of my friends came to visit, and though they irritated me by finding my parents too fascinating, they made up for it by filling my head with nothing more taxing than what we'd cook for dinner, what beach we'd lie on, and who among our classmates was sleeping with whom. By the time I returned to school in the fall, I'd almost recovered, though my equanimity was tried by the only piece of mail waiting for me in my dormitory mailbox: an invitation to a garden party at the Mastersons'. Adrian, who, along with Amy Wyatt, was now my roommate in Adams House, thought that I definitely should not go. I agreed. The second I saw Robert Masterson surrounded by his wife and admiring guests, I'd undo all the progress I'd made.

On the day of the party, though, something compelled me to attend. I've never been able to give up the belief that the mysterious force that guided me to the Mastersons' home that afternoon was somehow in league with that most ardent proponent of inexplicable forces and cosmic connections, that devotee of the inevitable and the inescapable.

That party was where I first heard Jean Paul's name.

II

p a tempo
p a tempo

I HAVE BEEN PACING BACK AND FORTH BETWEEN THE couch and the door for hours now, waiting for the phone to ring, and knowing it won't. I'm surprised to see, when I stop my feet from moving, that the windows are blackened and the room is dim. I head outside, where the streets are crowded with commuters, exhaling into their gloved fists as they elbow past each other in an effort to get someplace—anyplace—warm. I manage to hail a cab easily—I would be shocked at this luck, given the day I'm having, except that I'm too distracted to fully form the thought—and direct the driver uptown to Morningside Heights.

Adrian, looking the same as she has through all the years I've known her, burly and unaging, is surprised to see me, and so I know instantly that Alex isn't here, and that I've made a mistake.

"Come on in," she says, gesturing into the small, cluttered apartment that has always depressed me, and now depresses me even more, since it threatens to keep me trapped at a time when my daughter might be returning home any minute. I step gingerly around the boxes, which have been waiting to be unpacked now for close to fifteen years, past the dead plants, across the brown linoleum floor marked with stains that look like blood but are most likely coffee, and lay my coat—it's sweltering in here—on a chair beneath the high, grated windows that let in such a surprisingly dismal amount of sun to the home of a poet famous for her descriptions of the physics and metaphysics of light.

"Alex came home a few weeks ago," I say, sitting down.

"You're kidding." I can tell she's hurt no one bothered to inform her. "That's wonderful. It's been so long since she visited."

This is a nice way to put it, though I wouldn't expect anything less of Adrian. Until Alex showed up three weeks ago, it had been almost a year since I last saw my daughter. For much of that time, I didn't even have a way to reach her; she claimed not to have a phone, which was the sort of thing you could believe of Alex. I would imagine her out there in the bland flatness of Indiana, in some dingy, heatless room (wouldn't a room without a phone also lack heat?), huddled against the cold in sweaters and scarves, but unaware of the chill, engulfed in her swells of melody. She'd call once a week—I always wondered, but never asked, where from—but these were short and evasive conversations which mostly consisted of her telling me she was working on something "wonderfully new" but refusing to divulge any more details.

Adrian leans down to clear off the couch, and as she lifts a thick stack of manuscript paper says, "Graham's latest. 'Look How Clever I Am, Part IV.' " They both work in Columbia's M.F.A. program, and if they weren't such old friends they would be the bitterest of enemies. Under normal circumstances, I would make a joke about our college chum's gleefully incomprehensible writing, but instead I say,

"So you haven't seen her."

I don't really suspect it, of course, but this was once a haven for Alex, a place she would run in those stormy years of her early adolescence, when she was feeling the first hints of finding me unbearable. "I don't know where she is. I thought maybe she was here."

Adrian shakes her head, and is clearly imagining one of the hot and quick flash-fights that used to be so common and—to her, at least—not a cause for much concern, because her next question is "So what brought her back, anyway?"

I think of the night three weeks ago when I lifted the receiver to hear her voice, choked with a muffled sob, saying, "I'm coming home," how I said, "I'll come get you," feeling I could fly through the wires with the sheer force of my desire to be near her, and how she'd replied, "No. I'm here, I'm on my way up." Minutes later, she glided in the door, looking thinner, paler, tired, her long blond hair filthy beneath a moth-eaten stocking cap. She shot me a tragic look as magnificent and overwhelming as anything she'd ever displayed onstage, and I could see every age of her in that look, and wanted to take all those Alexes and stuff them somewhere secret, where I could try to raise them all over again.

"Do you want to tell me what's wrong?" I'd asked, and she'd replied, "Not really," already escaping up the stairs with her small suitcase, the bedroom door slamming heavily behind her.

"I don't know," I tell Adrian, honestly. "Something upset her."

"It's the age, isn't it?" she offers.

"Is it?" I'm wondering whether I get cell-phone reception here, and whether Alex might be trying to call.

"Seventeen? Sure. It's a bad one. You're away at college, feeling independent. Then, suddenly, boom, you're back at home for Christmas and your mother still thinks you're nine."

"I don't think she's nine." I fiddle with the phone in my pocket, checking to make sure it's on vibrate in case I don't hear it ring.

"Well, I know that. You were never like that, obviously. I'm just saying what the age is like. For some people. Don't you remember?"

Adrian gets up to make us tea—she does this without asking, every time I come over, because I have never had the heart to tell her I don't like tea—and as she putters around in the kitchen, I think about the long nights I have spent since Alex came home, lying in bed, awake, wondering what sent her back to me. I consider what Adrian might say if I told her that on those nights what I did to occupy my mind was try to reconstruct the last piece of music Alex had let me hear, at a student concert last March. Adrian would laugh, I'm sure, tell me that not everything in life is buried in a score, though she'd be wrong in this particular case.

From the first time I'd heard that music of Alex's, it had unsettled me. In fact, the notes had struck me as sickeningly exposed, like eggs on the underbelly of a sea creature. I'd wanted to grab them out of the concert hall and stuff them in my handbag, which of course seemed a ridiculous overreaction at the time. It has only been in the last few weeks, with Alex locked in her bedroom, home with no explanation, more furious at the world and at me than when she had stormed off to college, that I've started taking my initial reaction seriously. Perhaps there *had* been something sickening in that music. Perhaps that something was responsible for chasing her home.

Adrian comes back with two steaming mugs, stepping with the mincing lightness that used to strike me as a strange contrast to her sturdy body, before I understood how well it fit. She places one of the mugs on the coffee table, directly on top of Graham's manuscript, and two large splashes escape the rim and soak through the pages. The other mug she holds out to me, as she asks, "Sorry, what was it again that you said made her run off today?"

"I didn't say."

I realize I'm being ungenerous with my information, but, as much as I don't want to tell Adrian about trying to unearth some barely remembered music, I want even less to tell her that I am now certain I was right to suspect it held my daughter's secrets. That hunch, I think, was confirmed last night. Alex and I had just finished a tense, silent, typical dinner when it happened. I was lying on the couch, marking up a score, and she was seated at the piano. She'd sat there many times since she'd come home, but she'd never touched the keys, so I thought nothing of it. I was only aware that she sat, as usual, with a silence that emanated straight from those narrowed eyes, daring me to pry. So I sat silently, too, wanting to gather her in my arms and remake the world for her, knowing that there was nothing she wanted less than for me to involve myself in her new life, which was inviolably hers and hers alone.

I was pretending to be engrossed in the score in front of me, and so I didn't see her position her hands above the keys or close her eyes to see the notes she keeps tucked away in her mind. Even when the music started, I didn't look up at first. I hid behind the score, and only subtly let it drop, over the course of several bars. But soon I forgot myself, rose, and stood behind her so I could watch her long fingers fly across the keys. I was taking such pleasure in the surety in those hands, sure since they spanned barely a quarter of an octave each and in the sound they were bringing forth, the "something wonderfully new" she must have been working on all these months. In fact, what she was doing was not so new—was disturbingly familiar—but she brought it off with such masterful subtlety that she was halfway through before I heard just how familiar it was.

What she had been struggling toward in that earlier piece, but had not achieved, she had accomplished with stunning effect here: over the course of twenty minutes of music, she had squeezed melody out of dissonant chords, spiraled them exquisitely into control, from atonal chaos toward a sublimely melodic climax. She had managed to pull off what only one person before her had thought to attempt, and I heard him in this masterpiece as clearly as if he were in the room. Jean Paul was speaking directly to us through the tricks and techniques she had borrowed. It was the sound of him that had been taunting me from my daughter's music all along, and I had known it, really, known it with the musical part of me, known it the way I know how to play a Bach fugue. But though the musical part of me may have heard it months ago in the echoes of his ideas, the mothering part of me, even last night, could not believe that man had found his way into my daughter's life. There had to be some explanation for how she'd stumbled on his tricks and techniques on her own. It was a tiny world, the world of avant-garde composition, and the conservatory at Bloomington was one of its few hubs, so, naturally, she would brush up against his music there—there would be teachers who'd been taught by him, there would be people who knew him well, and knew his music better. Yes, this was so possible as to be inevitable, whereas the alternative was not. That man, with his notions of beauty in music so rigid they could be called a madness, and a madness so musical it could almost be called beauty, had not infected my daughter. There were so many ways I could imagine him making a musical child miserable that I was not able to let the possibility of him into her life, not able to let the smallness of the elite musical universe tighten to quite that extent. As she laid her hands across the keys, I let my thoughts dissolve into a gush of praise. She indulged me for a minute or two, then escaped back upstairs, and shut her door with a softer bang than usual.

Left alone, I broke down and wondered: *did* she know him, and, if so, did she know that I'd once known him, too? I knew I couldn't ask her these questions, not yet, and so I pushed the thoughts aside, and might have pushed them off indefinitely if a bumbling, prying reporter had not spoken the one name he should not have spoken this afternoon.

"Tasha?" Adrian prompts, and I realize I have not even taken the mug from her outstretched hand. "It was a bad fight?"

"Fight? No, it wasn't a fight."

I try to consider what to tell her as I take the mug and balance it on my knee, but all I can think is *Jean Paul*, and I cannot bring myself to say his name until I figure out what connection it bears to Alex.

"Oh, so it was . . ." Adrian trails off, confused but unwilling to inquire. For some reason the patience underlying Adrian's words impresses on me that I cannot sit here any longer.

"I should go." I place the untouched tea next to hers on Graham's well-stained manuscript. "She may have come home by now."

She pats my arm warmly at the door, and says, "Send her my love."

I'm about to slip out when it occurs to me that there is one piece of information I can give to Adrian—another person I can blame for my missing daughter. It was Robert Masterson, after all, who thought it appropriate to sic a reporter onto raw bits of my past. Feeling relieved to let Adrian in on this, at least, I say, "Would you believe we're in this mess because of something Masterson said?"

"Completely." This she delivers like the final line in one of her love-weary poems, before letting the door fall shut.

I have just emerged onto the street when my cell phone rings. The voice on the other end is indistinct, and it takes me a moment to recognize my mother's whispering. "I've been trying to call forever. Where have you been? Alex is here." Her voice is raspy and strained. "She says she's going back to Indiana tomorrow. What's happened?"

Again, I hail a cab easily, but the traffic is infuriatingly dense, and as we inch our way toward the West Village, I lose the battle with myself and fall back into remembering.

THE DAY OF THE MASTERSONS' GARDEN PARTY, I AWOKE to the sound of an assault on the slanted eaves of my new dorm room. My eyes searched out the skylight that let in my only glimpse of the outside world, and identified the offending noise as rain. Watching the patterns splash and disperse, I thought, *Good, another reason not to go,* and rolled over. But, lying there, I felt restless. When I heard Adrian and Amy head out of our suite together, arguing about whether the dining hall was still serving breakfast, I shot out of bed, pulled on some clothes, and made my way out the door in record time. I began the long trek toward Masterson's house with an umbrella held unsteadily in one hand, and the three scores I'd worked on over the summer tucked under the other arm.

I arrived to a houseful of soaked and sulky professors cracking unhappy jokes about the charm of an indoor garden party, and headed straight for the bar, where I asked for a bourbon, which was what my mother always ordered at such events. I wandered through the rooms with my toxic drink for a while, afraid to break into any conversations, and then returned to the bar to exchange my bourbon for something drinkable. It was while I was waiting for my new drink—a martini, which also turned out to be too strong for me—that I finally ran into Masterson. He acted happy to find me there, and, using the word "student" at least ten times, introduced me to his wife, an attractive, vintage Cliffie type who didn't look anything like she appeared in the photos on their dresser, but looked a lot like I'd pictured her before I'd seen any of those—younger than her forty-four years, though in such a way that if she were as young as she looked she wouldn't be aging well. Her neat black hair was heavily sprinkled with gray, fine wrinkles lined her large green eyes, and the trim frame lost its sharp edges around the waist. It was apparent, mainly from the way she held herself, that she had once been extremely attractive, and I had to work hard to stifle the concern that he'd unfavorably compared me with her younger self. Though she was affable, even gracious, I detected a cold interior. I didn't like her, and liked even less that Robert was so unconflicted about introducing us, and so, when the pair of them excused themselves to greet another guest, I decided I'd stayed long enough.

I was heading to the closet for my raincoat when I ran into the one other guest willing to talk to me. She was one of the musicians from Masterson's birthday performance, a woman who'd played the flute with the Boston Symphony Orchestra for thirty years. The first time we met, we'd shared a substantial conversation about her eleven-year-old grandson's unfortunate preference for rock music over "real" music. She'd been under the misimpression that my youth gave me insight into kids.

"Are you leaving already?" she asked, laying her hand, which smelled not unpleasantly of stale roses, against my arm.

"I think maybe I am."

"But you can't, of course, dear." She held on to the crook of my elbow, as if aware that I planned to grab my coat the minute she turned away. "You'll miss the performance."

"There's going to be a performance?" There hadn't been anything about a performance on the invitation, and I felt my stomach clench at the knowledge that I hadn't been asked to participate.

"Oh, you know," she told me, leaning in conspiratorially. "That young composer who's come here to study with Robert."

"To study with Robert?" I repeated. It was the second time in a row I'd parroted her phrase, and I wished I could take back not just those words but the whole conversation. Now I was stuck here. I couldn't very well leave knowing some upstart was trying to steal Masterson from me. Not when I'd finally managed to get those three pieces right. I'd have to stay and do reconnaissance.

Terrified of being afloat in the room again, I clung to my friend as long as I could, trying to re-engage her on the topic of her grandson, but eventually she was stolen away by one of my professors. I sidled up to the outskirts of a few conversations, but I could never break all the way in, so after a short while I gave up and wandered into the library, where the four musicians were setting up their instruments. I found a seat in the front row and tried to arrange my face into an expression that suggested I quite enjoyed sitting here alone.

Other guests began trickling in before long. Robert and his wife were among the first. He sat down next to me.

"Tasha, you stayed. I'm glad. You're going to love this," he said, before turning to the man directly behind him and striking up a conversation about Stockhausen's *Sirius.*

When the music started a few minutes later, I didn't love it at all. I didn't know what to think of it. The sounds were strange and hard to understand, a dense polyphony that played around the edges of listenability. Perhaps I would have just tuned out, dismissing the music as yet another overintellectualized attempt to create originality without musicality, if it weren't for my conviction that these unusual sounds were just off the mark, that there was something big just narrowly eluding their grasp. Under ordinary circumstances, I might have found this exciting; the possibility for a wholly different sound was a new obsession of mine, fostered by my forward-looking friends, and a sound that was still being groped toward was even newer than new. But, given the blatantly unhushed comments flying around me, it was clear that, according to the rest of the audience, Masterson most of all, the Something Really Big was firmly within this young composer's grasp. And so, instead of excited, I was outraged.

I focused my envious scorn on the oboist, because he was small and feral, the sort of person who just looked like he'd be overrated in his own time and forgotten by posterity. I had decided, on this basis, that he was the composer, but after the recital, when I went up to congratulate him, partly hoping he'd immediately reveal himself as a musical impostor, he corrected my mistake. He hadn't written this music, he told me in low nasal tones which only deepened my desire for things to be otherwise. Jean Paul Boumedienne—hadn't I heard of him?—was the composer. And where was this Jean Paul? Though the party was apparently in his honor—*It was?*—he had failed to put in an appearance.

I huffed my way back to the bar. I planned to track down my handbag, which I'd noticed during the recital was missing, and then to make a hasty retreat. I felt simultaneously beaten and triumphant: triumphant because I was the only one who could peg this impostor for what he was, beaten for the same reason. Masterson, for God's sake, had thrown this party in his honor. In his honor! A man I had never heard of until today. I swore that I would make no effort to seek out this Jean Paul—that I would outright ignore him—if he ever deigned to show up in person at an event.

But Masterson had noticed me talking to the oboist and assumed that I'd become an instant fan just like everyone else. I heard him walk up behind me while I was peevishly combing the area for my purse.

"Did you like it?" he asked.

"Yeah, it was a great party." I kept my head down, scouring the Oriental rug for a swatch of Indian silk.

"I meant the music."

He smiled one of his expressive smiles. It had been many, many months since I'd seen one of those smiles. It did nothing for me, and I acknowledged this fact with a surprised twinge of loss.

"Would you like to meet him?" I was still forming my response to his first question, trying to strike a balance between meanness and dishonesty, but this second question took me by surprise. I could tell Robert thought he was being kind, and so I said "sure" when I was really thinking "no."

"I'll call you later this week." As he walked from the room, he gestured toward a low table in the corner, where my purse lay amid a pile of discarded cocktail napkins. "We can all have lunch. Just me and my two favorite students."

I grabbed my purse, and was already out the door when I realized I was still carrying the scores I'd been slaving over all summer. I thought of going back in to give them to Masterson, but the idea of entering the house again was too unappealing. Instead, I tucked my head against the rain, and ran all the way home.

OVER THE NEXT FEW DAYS, I picked out classes, I worked on my new music, and I tried to go at least one day without hearing the name that had started to sound like nails on a chalkboard. Jean Paul Boumedienne. You couldn't set foot in the music building without hearing it. What had apparently started as a buzz that summer had become a veritable din in the wake of the Mastersons' garden party. Just from walking the halls, I already knew he had graduated from the excellent but somewhat renegade music department at Yale two years earlier. (This I took as an excuse to further denigrate what I remembered of his music; Yale was the sort of place where they were already agog over Glass and Reich, Nancarrow and Partch, composers we at Harvard were still calling gimmicky anti-intellectuals.) I knew that since leaving Yale he'd been studying in his native France at the Paris Conservatoire; that he was here to study with Robert, the august composer of Polyphony in C, which had made a monumental impression on Jean Paul. I would have thought that at a place like Harvard it would take more than a promising graduate student to get the faculty's imagination running wild, but the department was in raptures. All the hubbub confirmed Jean Paul in my mind as a self-promoter extraordinaire, someone I definitely would not like. I had a distinct picture of my rival for Masterson's regard: soaring ambitions, minimal talent, maximal networking skills. I was sure I could smell him out of a lineup.

When Masterson invited me to lunch with Jean Paul in a small French restaurant in downtown Boston, I was shocked to find that he was nothing like I'd imagined. Soft-spoken, easily embarrassed, self-effacing: these were unusual qualities to find in a shameless self-promoter. Perhaps even more disconcerting was his complete lack of resemblance to the undersized oboist whose image I'd been stubbornly clinging to as Jean Paul's. His face was a perfect mixture of dark and light, harsh and delicate, his mother's soft French features blending with his father's dusky Algerian ones. I was struck by his eyes in particular, a blue so deep they almost looked black, standing out in sleepy defiance underneath heavy lids. And his lips, too, which were blanched and thin at the edges, but curved subtly to fullness in their centers. And maybe also by his strong jaw, prominent, bold nose, and thick, dark hair. What struck me most, though, was his unmistakably tragic air—not so much of someone in despair as of someone waiting for despair to grip him, who knew that eventually misery would engulf his life and was only biding his time until that happened. Though I'd tagged along with Robert hoping to expose Jean Paul as a fraud, I was struck dumb by that solemn air, felt an almost sacred respect for it. I hardly said a word, content to stare.

AFTER OUR FIRST MEETING, I DIDN'T SEE JEAN PAUL FOR two weeks. Sometimes I'd look for him when I was in the music building or walking across campus, but he was never around. Robert arranged our second get-together as well. Jean Paul had written another piece, and it was going to be performed in front of the department and select guests. They were assembling an orchestra and needed a violinist to play first chair. Robert naturally suggested me.

I was surprised all over again by just how attractive Jean Paul was when I walked into Robert's office to find him sitting in the one extra chair. (He stood and offered it to me.) I'd begun to degrade his appearance in my mind. But during this second meeting, it was Robert who had my full attention. He was acting in a way that in other people I might have called "fulsome," and it made me embarrassed for him. At least, that's what I told myself it made me feel. He was throwing around words I'd rarely heard him use to describe a living person's work: words like "inspired," "revolutionary," and "masterpiece." I wished the word "salvageable" would work its way in there just once. I couldn't understand why he thought he had to sell me on the piece; he must have known I never would have refused anything he asked of me. I had a strong and dangerous urge to tell him to put a sock in it.

Of course I said I'd love to be involved, and where was the score, and when was our first rehearsal? Then I raced back to my room, slammed the door shut, and ripped open Jean Paul's folder. The new piece was similar to the one I'd heard at the garden party, only this time it was arranged for a full orchestra. Once again, he was playing around with polyphony and counterpoint in strange ways, creating something like an auditory illusion, so that while it sounded on the surface like atonal music it was straining, slowly and not wholly convincingly, toward a tonal resolution. Analyzing the score for myself, I again felt the conviction that he was on the trail of something big.

Later that week, after I'd started learning my part, I decided to get on the trail myself—that is, to try composing a piece using his method. If I could bring Jean Paul's style to its logical conclusion, Masterson would have to be impressed. I started the project assuming I'd probably drop it before too long, but, as it turned out, it only took one afternoon for me to become entrenched in the rigorous logic of the work. Soon I was spending most evenings trying and failing to force atonal lines to turn tonal.

Realizing just how hard this was to do well, I was quickly gaining respect for Jean Paul's ambition. Our regular contact at rehearsals was also forcing me to acknowledge that the man I was devilishly trying to depose was a saint; not that this shamed me into giving up my quest. An almost freakishly patient conductor, he never raised his voice, and spoke only to praise, even with the wind section, which everyone else agreed was lousy. In fact, the only way we knew our beneficent leader's opinion of our playing was by looking at his eyes, which shone brighter the better we played, so that on those few occasions when we nailed it he looked truly unhealthy.

He was also far from stingy with his praise, particularly his praise of me. "Extraordinary, Natasha. Extraordinary," he would say whenever I walked past him out the door. One time, as I was playing a solo, he knelt in front of me so close that I was in danger of taking his eye out with my bow. "Breathtaking," he said, when the rest of the orchestra came back in. "You play it better than I wrote it." It was both the creepiest and the sexiest thing I could imagine a man doing—though, as I rehashed the moment in bed that night, it took on a romantic glow.

Most of us in the ensemble were undergraduates (there were two graduate students as well), and of these all but me were members of the official Harvard-Radcliffe Orchestra. I had refused to join the orchestra, despite Amy's campaigning, on the grounds that I was not a violinist but a composer. Because I was the only undergrad in Jean Paul's ensemble not also in the HRO, I felt like a bit of an outsider and usually skipped out right after rehearsal rather than join the others for a bite to eat. I'd race home and slave away at my Boumedienne-inspired composition. But one evening, Amy, who was in the sorry wind section, persuaded me to come along. It had been a rainy, depressing day, and now it was a clear, chilly night, and the prospect of strolling outside among a pack of exuberant young musicians was far more appealing than the prospect of locking myself in a dim room with a pencil and some staff paper.

Naturally, Jean Paul was the topic of conversation during our meal of burgers and fries, and as we sat around the pushed-together Formica tables trading dubious but hard-won bits of gossip about our maestro ("Did you know his father was some sort of secret agent?" "Did you hear he has a pitch so perfect there's a special name for it?"), it eventually became clear that the vast majority of females, and quite a few of the males, were deeply infatuated. Apparently this was common knowledge among the group, but no one had bothered to tell me. Not that I was surprised; I probably would have been more surprised to find out that no one had become infatuated yet. But I did feel another sort of reaction come over me. When Amy—the only girl other than me to declare no such crush—delightedly scoffed that there was absolutely no way Jean Paul would be interested in an undergrad, much less one of the undergrads sitting around our table, I found myself feeling pretty offended.

"Is it impossible to imagine he could ever be interested in one of us?" I asked as casually as I could, later that evening, as Amy and I walked down Massachusetts Avenue toward our dorm.

"That who could?" she asked after a confused moment, a hint of irritation in her voice.

"Jean Paul."

"When did I ever say he couldn't?" The hint had blossomed

into full-blown peevishness, but peevishness came as naturally to Amy as breathing.

"Tonight. Like, an hour ago."

"I thought he was an 'overrated impostor,' according to you."

"I might have been wrong about that."

"Well, Jesus Christ, someone alert the dogs, Tasha's going in for the hunt," she spat, rolling her eyes. "Lord Almighty, you can really be conceited sometimes."

The day of the performance came and went without much fanfare. We played on a Friday afternoon, in a lecture hall, to forty enthusiastic professors and spouses. It wasn't until I was gazing at Jean Paul from across the post-performance wine-and-cheese reception that it occurred to me that the end of rehearsals meant the end of our regular contact.

I stayed up all that night finishing my composition, and called Jean Paul's apartment as soon as it seemed reasonably light enough outside, left a message with a woman—*a girlfriend?*—that he should call me back at his convenience, and fell gratefully into bed. I woke up in the late afternoon, gripped by a sense of acute loss, and wandered into Adrian's room, hoping that she wasn't there and that I could squirrel her Joni Mitchell albums away without anyone's being the wiser. But she was sitting on her bed with Amy. I tried to act as though I'd come in looking for them and not for music to sulk to.

"Good morning, queen of dreams," Adrian said brightly. This was something she called me often, usually referring to my ever-swelling hopes, but sometimes, like today, to my tendency to sleep until well past noon.

"Good morning."

"A late night," she observed without any hint of curiosity. Adrian never asked, and she expected the same courtesy.

Amy, however, always asked.

"Might this have anything to do with a sexy young Frenchman?" She flashed a nasty smile.

"I was finishing that piece I've been working on." I forced myself to look nonplussed.

"Jean Paul called this morning," Adrian said.

"Oh? What about?"

"He just said to call him back."

Amy had turned away and was rustling through a stack of sheets on Adrian's desk. There had been a strain in our relationship since the evening she accused me of being conceited. The idea that she might think I was trying to woo Jean Paul just to prove I was capable of such a feat put a damper on my high, but only until I heard his voice on the other end of the receiver.

"Is this Jean Paul?" I asked, even though I knew it was. It would have been hard to mistake his strange accent, a mixture of Exeter and southern France, coming at a whispery depth.

"It is."

"Hi, this is Tasha Darsky. Returning your call," I added for the sake of my roommates, listening from the other room.

"Natasha, yes, hi. It's nice to hear from you."

"You, too. Um, I wanted to tell you. I wrote something I thought you might like. I thought maybe you could take a look at it sometime." I lowered my voice to say this, hoping to maintain the illusion among my roommates that Jean Paul had contacted me first. My voice came out like a less husky, colorless version of his. It made me think of my un-Master-ful drawl.

"Really? I didn't know you wrote music, too." I tried not to let this upset me, but I did like to imagine that when Jean Paul and Robert were alone together my music occasionally came up; it seemed only fair, since whenever Robert and I were alone together Jean Paul's music came up every few minutes.

"Sometimes," I replied meekly, when the bold and slightly arrogant witticism I was longing to toss off failed to present itself.

"Well, that's wonderful. I'd love to take a look at whatever you've written. You're not free early this evening, are you? I'm going to be on campus anyway."

I was free as of right then, but I didn't want to give him the impression that I was the sort of girl who had no Saturday-night plans as of late Saturday afternoon.

"I'm busy," I lied. "What about tomorrow afternoon?"

"Tomorrow afternoon I'm taking my mother to the airport. Tomorrow night?"

His mother! The woman on the phone!

We agreed to meet the following evening in a subterranean, smoky coffee shop that Robert and I often frequented. Jean Paul was the one who suggested the spot, and I felt betrayed that he knew of its existence.

When I got there, he was already waiting at my favorite table, the one all the way in the back right corner.

"This is my favorite table," I said as I slid in across from him.

"Mine, too." He smiled. My God, that smile. I forgot to be annoyed by the obvious fact that it was both of *our* favorite table because it was Robert's.

"So where is this music of yours?" he asked, and I realized I'd been smiling at him longer than I should have.

I took out a folder. It was the same one in which he'd given me his score. I'd transferred it there as a symbolic act, though I was not at all decided on what it ought to symbolize.

He looked over the pages thoughtfully and then began reading through, first skimming the piece in its entirety, then flipping more slowly through the sheets. I noticed his fingers moving inadvertently on the table, pushing imaginary keys, the way mine always fingered imaginary strings when I read music I took seriously.

"This is good," he said.

"Really?"

"Yes, very good. I guess I should say I'm honored, right? You're my first student."

I blushed.

"You seem to understand my ideas."

I nodded, even though I didn't understand them as well as I wanted to, and I didn't think he quite understood them, either. Though I'd written a piece in his style, it had also come out missing the mark, just like his. I hadn't been able to break through to whatever it was we were now both hovering around.

"I mean, I guess I should say 'our ideas.' Once you use a musical idea, I think you own it as much as anyone."

That seemed noble to me—like he was extending the spirit of scientific endeavor to the aesthetic realm.

"I'd like to be your student, though. I'd like you to teach me." I'd meant it wholeheartedly when I started saying it—I wanted him to lead me wherever he was heading, I wanted us to become a co-operative whose aim was to produce great art—but by the time I'd finished the declaration I hated myself for it, and hated him more for looking flattered. There was the old jealousy again, the part of me that wanted to be, at the least, something better than the less promising Masterson protégé.

I was grateful that he didn't respond directly, instead launching into a monologue on his Idea. He called his method Sublimated Tonality, he told me, saying the words as though they were nuclear-war plans. As I had suspected, he was trying—not successfully yet, he himself was quick to point out—to turn atonal music into something organically tonal, to spin chaos into control, raw sounds into resolution. The crucial aspect, he claimed, was the imperceptibility of this transformation: he was going to use it to force a state of uncertainty on his listeners, to make them rethink their approach to music.

"Most people don't pay attention to the music when they listen," he told me, his eyes shining their unnatural bright. "They let their minds wander. They let the music carry them away to extramusical places, places that have nothing to do with the music itself. They start thinking about what the music evokes in them—emotions, scenes, stories, episodes from their lives. But as Stravinsky wrote, 'If music appears to express something, this is an illusion and not a reality.' Incredible, isn't it? What most people pay attention to when they listen to music is an illusion!"

His jaw was set defiantly, as if he were challenging me to defend this state of affairs. I nodded in sympathy, trying to look as outraged as he did. In fact, I was outraged. Even though I'd always disagreed with that famous Stravinsky quote—even though I'd always thought that what made music so extraordinary was its ability to transfer one person's inner life into another person's mind just by plucking the right notes—I found myself distraught that the ignorant majority was flagrantly ignoring music for the extramusical, and looked eagerly toward Jean Paul to right this wrong. I had been conditioned all my life, I guess, to respond to artistically minded rants, Jean Paul's words so far just being a variation on my father's old theme of "Most of humanity are irredeemable bores."

"I want to force people to listen to my music. Make them pay attention to the sounds themselves and not what those sounds evoke in their subconscious. I want them to be wondering where are we with this music, are we anywhere at all, are we still where we were five seconds ago, am I hearing what I'm supposed to be hearing, or am I confused? They won't be able to take the sounds for granted."

I asked him if he thought serial music was on the right track, since it was devoid of a dramatic expressive element. The mixture of pity and disappointment that flashed across his face made me vow to seriously reconsider asking any more questions. Where was the soft-spoken conductor who'd never raised his voice? I wanted to know. But I didn't miss him; this Jean Paul was scarier, but far more tantalizing.

"Dodecaphony just replaced the cult of expression with the cult of mathematics," he explained. "It's true that mathematics underlies music; it's in there, yes, and so, in a way, the cult of mathematics is not as misguided as the cult of expression. But in another way it's much worse. Composing music based on mathematical principles is like setting out to write a novel and, instead of worrying about what story you're telling or whether you're telling any story at all, you just concern yourself with how many letters are in a word, on a line, on a page. In any book there'll be this element—there'll be a certain number of letters, words, pages, yes—but to explicitly take those into account when you're writing, in any but the most special cases, is absurd. The point of the book is its story. The point of music is its sound. All that matters is how it sounds to the human ear. Each sound and the relation between them, that's what's important, that's what music is. Yes, I admit you could give a mathematical description to the sounds and the relations between them, but who cares? You could describe the story mathematically, too, but if you did you'd miss the point of storytelling. Same with music. If instead you are thinking about numbers, you are not even listening to music. Do you see what I mean?"

I nodded my head enthusiastically, though I was tempted to show my approval in a much more dramatic way—shouting "Yes!" at the top of my lungs while genuflecting before him, was the instinct that sprang to mind. In the short time I'd been sitting across from him, I'd somehow caught his fervor; my heart was pounding, my face felt flushed, my eyes were burning because of the heat I seemed to be generating in unnatural amounts. If someone else had handed me this theory of music, I probably would have either laughed or scowled, depending on my mood, but because it came from Jean Paul, and came the way it did—with a shining, optimistic rage—I found myself silently screaming "Yes!" to everything he said.

I unambiguously wanted to be his student now; I wanted to tell him that I believed every word he was saying, that I hadn't understood his idea initially but I did now, and it was wonderful, and right, and he would be music's salvation, and I would help him in any way I was able. But I couldn't bring myself to interrupt the fluid rise and fall of his words. Instead, I let him go on—two hours' worth of on—about the cult of expression, and the cult of mathematics, and the solution that Sublimated Tonality offered. His energy was unbounded, his enthusiasm inexhaustible. I got the impression he could have gone on indefinitely if he hadn't caught sight of the clock on the wall, and realized he was twenty minutes late for a dinner date.

He walked me out still talking about his Idea, our Idea, and didn't even bother to say "goodbye" when we parted ways. He finished his sentence, gave a satisfied "Well" as if he'd just taken the last bite of a good meal, and set off in the other direction.

I WOKE UP the next morning already plotting out a few coy turns of phrase to use in our next conversation, well-hidden guideposts to steer things toward more personal topics ("So what is it, exactly, that fails to get expressed in your music, Jean Paul?"). When he unexpectedly, wonderfully called that night, though, I hardly had the chance to get a word in, much less to redirect the flow of the conversation. He started in immediately with his religious zeal—the point of music, the meaning of sound, the world his Idea was opening up. "Now, here is something you might find interesting," he began that night. "There are few instances in history of a composer openly stating that his work, and, of course, I refer here only to purely orchestral works, means this or that." These words launched a conversation that continued for weeks, always picking up around 11 p.m., always ending an hour or two later, always remaining tightly tied to the topic of music, of Sublimated Tonality, in particular. Not that he was domineering in these conversations; not that he couldn't listen. Far from it. He had gotten it into his head that what I thought about his work was terribly important. I was even becoming part of the fluid rise and fall of the words, saying things lit with his ecstatic hopefulness, and I was beginning to believe that we were on the trail of a history-making sound. We. Together. A collective whose aim was to produce great art. So why would I force us to talk about movies and childhood and favorite books?

Amy and Adrian were sure that Jean Paul and I were on the verge of moving our discussions onto rumpled sheets, and I didn't try to set them straight. Sometimes I told myself that I didn't care if anything overtly romantic developed between us, that I was content to be his sounding board, his partner. If nothing else, our contact was having wonderful effects on my own work. Though I wasn't yet making another attempt at composing according to his stringent rules, I was working on a number of other pieces—mostly for a one-on-one tutorial I was doing with Masterson—and each of them was flowing with the giddy, inspired ease I hadn't experienced since the days when I was pining after my great artist. Though I worried about the implications this had for my artistic depth, there was no denying that I wrote best when I wrote for an audience of one. And, unlike my great artist, Jean Paul was an invested muse, or would have been if I'd only let him hear anything. He kept asking what I was working on, but I was afraid to show him unpolished efforts.

Jean Paul told me he'd never worked better, either. My opinions, he said, had a revelatory rightness to them; he could tell they were right as soon as I said them, and as he pondered them, folds of profundity continued to fall open. (Jean Paul spoke that way; it didn't sound absurd in his voice.) Being treated as a musical oracle was more fun than composing, though it's also true that believing myself to have oracular properties took a lot of the self-flagellating sting out of writing music. I began to live my days toward his phone calls in the weeks following our date in the coffeehouse. I always made sure to be back in my room in time to answer the phone, even on weekends. Often I'd go out again after we hung up—my friends and I were still meeting nightly to argue zealously about everything from art and politics to the best place to get a late-night pizza in Harvard Square—but by then I was usually too distracted to pay any attention to what was going on around me. I'd remain lost in his words—and my words, too—and the only time I'd take active part in an immediate conversation was when I could steer it onto Sublimated Tonality. Luckily, my friends had a high tolerance for this particular topic; they were attracted to any revolutionizing movement, especially those with claims to purism. Soon we were something of a focus group for Jean Paul's theories, generating our own ideas about, and justifications for, them.

"It's got ties to the formalism movement in visual art," Ari Ben Haar, our sculptor, pointed out the first night I'd brought it up. "Drawing attention to the materials so you focus on the art as art."

I'd had that thought as well, but I'd been too afraid to point it out to Jean Paul; I wasn't sure he'd want to see parallels between his work and anyone else's.

Jean Paul loved to hear about the ideas we'd come up with in our frenetic discussions. He would say things like "Yes, keep thinking about this, Tasha. Your thoughts always amaze me."

It was because of these remarks that I felt justified in considering myself his partner. Thinking that I was his partner made it more tolerable that I hadn't seen him since that day in the coffeehouse, over a month earlier, and that he didn't seem to care whether he ever saw me in person again. I cared very much about when I'd get to see him next, and whenever I left my room my eyes were constantly searching him out. But he was never around. Occasionally, I'd suggest reasons why we should get together—saying things like "Oh, I'd like to see that," or "Could you play that for me sometime so I could get a better sense?"—but he always found a way to grant my requests over the phone, holding the receiver up to the piano, describing vividly what I thought I'd needed to lay eyes on, and so on.

Based on his reluctance to get together and my complete failure ever to bump into him, I started to get the idea that, besides the occasional trip to Masterson's office, he never left home—which I pictured as a tiny apartment, so cluttered with books and sheet music that you couldn't sit or stand without trampling on something of intellectual or artistic value. I liked the image of him as a genius-recluse, and even told my friends about it as if it were established fact. Amy had definite ideas about the artist's responsibility to society, and being a recluse didn't fit well with those, but everyone else agreed that his self-imposed isolation nicely embellished his romanticism.

I might have gone on forever believing that Jean Paul was a monk cloistered in his shrine to pure sound if I hadn't managed to bump into him one unseasonably warm Wednesday night in early November, in the tiny Italian restaurant my friends and I frequented. I was there having dinner with Micheal O'Shea, the south Boston boy who dreamed of heading the New York Philharmonic someday in the not-too-distant future. He was telling me about the latest girl he was trying to get in the sack—number eighteen, he made sure to mention several times. Seduction was his new art form, and he was even more gifted in this realm than he was in music.

I was so wrapped up in the tension of Michael's story—the "casual" run-ins, the ambiguous trip to the movies, the accidental brush of fingers on knee which turned into a brush of fingers on thigh—that I didn't notice Jean Paul come in, and only became aware of his presence when a whispery deep voice drifted my way. He was seated at the next table, but there was a column between us, blocking him from view, which is why I hadn't yet noticed him. I had no idea if he'd seen me, and normally I would have gone over to make sure that he did; I'd been waiting for just this coincidence for over a month, and it had come when I was wearing my most flattering pair of jeans. Except that he happened to be seated across from a woman who, unfortunately for Michael and his story, was not at all obscured by the column.

She looked about Jean Paul's age, tall, blonde, and she had an infuriatingly sweet Southern drawl that was getting a surprising amount of airtime. They were both speaking softly—were they whispering lovingly?—and I could only make out detached fragments of sentences. Jean Paul was not raging about the state of music; that I would have been able to hear. They were surely talking about just those personal topics I'd been trying to steer us toward to no avail; I heard the word "Paris" once, and later on I distinctly heard him say "remarkable film." I could tell he was relaxed and charming—the Jean Paul who had conducted his orchestra with kindness and panache, not the rabid, single-minded Jean Paul I'd come to know. There was a lot of hushed laughter coming from the other side of the column.

If Michael noticed I'd stopped speaking, he didn't let on. When he finished his story, we ate in silence until he thought of another. I didn't even try to follow. Urgent questions pounded at me: How long had things been going on with this woman? Were there others? Had there been women in his apartment, in his bed, while he lectured to me over the phone? ("You'll have to excuse me a second, Holly, I need to call a student." She rolls over and pulls a sheet around her shimmering body.) I tried at first to work myself into a fury over Jean Paul's betrayal—how he'd taken me for a ride, making me think he was a fanatic loner when he was really a Lothario—but I found it hard to get around the truth: that he'd never tried to make me think anything at all. We'd never discussed a topic outside of music. I'd taken it upon myself to invent a world for him, and I'd concocted his life with arrogance as my main guide, concluding that he was a hermit from the flimsy fact that he didn't want to see me.

My self-esteem was plummeting about as quickly as my wine was disappearing, and it wasn't long before both were nothing but a bit of sediment. I hit my low point when she got up to "powder her nose" (I was amazed that someone *actually* used that expression, but I had to admit it sounded charming in her voice) and I saw that she was narrow and delicate, with the clean lines I'd never stopped thinking of as more "right" than my exaggerated curves. I felt tremendous and obscenely shapely, with a grating, lumbering voice and uninspiring talent. How could I have ever hoped Jean Paul would love me, with women like that in the world? I almost kissed Michael when he took it upon himself to order another bottle of the house red.

We were polishing off the second bottle, Michael still chattering on with increasingly less coherence, when Jean Paul and his date got up to leave. I buried my face in my oversized wine goblet, but he didn't even glance in our direction.

That night, he called as usual at eleven. I'd been hoping he wouldn't, both because I thought it would prove that the night's events had been an aberration for him, and also because I was drunk and belligerent. I also knew, though, that if he didn't call I would be beside myself with grief.

His voice on the other end of the line sounded normal, and he didn't notice the hard edge in mine. He launched right in with that day's soliloquy on sound. I let him go on for about ten minutes, for the first time letting his words fly past me without paying them notice.

I think he was telling me what Webern once said about Brahms when I ordered him to "Just shut up already."

"Excuse me?" He sounded not so much insulted as confused.

"Why do you always talk to me about music?"

"What is this?"

"A question. Directed at you. Not about music."

"Are you angry at me?"

"Why would I be angry?"

"I have no idea. Do you feel we didn't talk enough about your piece? I've been waiting to talk to you about it. I have it by my bed and plan to go back to it soon. I was waiting until I had my mind clear of my own work."

"That should be any day now, then."

"What is going on here? You sound drunk. Are you drunk?" Now the horror and insult were creeping into his tone.

"Maybe."

"I'll call back tomorrow, then."

"Wait!"

"Why?"

"Because. I asked you something important."

"You asked why I always talk about music."

"I asked why you always talk about music to *me.*"

"To you, right. I am not going to talk to you about anything when you are drunk." He sounded angry, sad even, but that only made me more eager to keep him on the phone.

"I'm not drunk," I lied.

"I think I should call back tomorrow night."

"No!"

"Yes."

"I saw you tonight!" I screamed it just in case he'd already taken the receiver away from his ear. I heard him breathing on the other end of the phone.

"Jean Paul?" I thought maybe I'd deafened him.

"I'm here."

"Sorry for shouting."

"I saw you, too. I didn't know you saw me."

"Why didn't you come say 'hi'?"

"I could ask the same."

I didn't respond.

"I'm unsure what's going on here." He paused. "And I'm a little afraid."

"Afraid? Afraid of what?"

He ignored my question.

"Tell me honestly, are you drunk?"

"A little, maybe."

"Then I do not think we should have this conversation now."

"What conversation?"

"The conversation . . . the conversation I think we are about to have."

"Are we about to have a conversation?" My heart was racing. It was possible, just possible, that this was a very good thing.

"I don't know. We should hang up. We can talk tomorrow night."

"And then we'll have the conversation, or then we'll only talk about music?"

"That I don't know."

"I can't just talk to you about music anymore." I hadn't

known I was going to say it until it came out, but, once it had, I knew it was true. I couldn't stand it anymore, just being his sounding board. It was more or it was nothing.

"Why are you doing this?" He sounded pained.

"Doing what? What am I doing that's so terrible?"

A long pause followed, with heavier breathing this time. I was afraid I'd blown it; maybe he'd had no idea what I'd been getting at, and now he did. It sounded like he was getting ready to hang up on me.

"Come over," he said. "I have to see you."

I TOOK A CAB TO THE ADDRESS HE'D GIVEN ME, TRYING not to think about the conversation we'd just had or what would happen once I got there. I had the definite feeling that things were going well, but I was wary of getting my hopes crushed.

His apartment was half of a grand old Victorian that had been cut down the middle, not at all the typical graduate-student digs I'd expected. It looked from the outside as though it would be spacious and charming, with wood paneling and fireplaces in every room. He was waiting at the door.

When I stepped inside, he made a move like he was going to touch me, then backed away. His apartment was an exact cross between the promise of the façade and the image of it I'd had in my mind until then: old New England elegance, cluttered everywhere with books and papers, with a stunning Steinway in the center, rising up like a cliff from the sea. I went instinctively toward the piano, ran my hands lightly across the keys.

"It was my mother's when she was a child," he said. He was standing several feet behind me. I was glad I'd changed back into the open-back shirt I'd worn to dinner.

"It's magnificent. Is this where you write?" I turned to face him, my fingers still resting on the piano. I felt safer for the contact.

"Yes."

He took a few steps toward me.

"What?" I asked. He'd looked like he was about to say something.

"Nothing. It's just strange to see you here."

"Did you want to see me here?" I could tell I was blushing as I asked it, and I was glad. I didn't want to seem too forward, after my performance on the phone.

"I did." He took another step toward me, then stopped again.

"So why didn't you ever ask me? I would have come."

I moved toward him. He backed away.

"Tasha," he said, holding one hand up in front of him protectively, "What are we doing now exactly?"

"I thought . . . You're the one who asked me here. Why did you tell me to come?" A second ago, I'd felt like the most irresistible seductress; now I felt I was being fended off like a drunk frat boy.

"Because you told me that you cared for me. Isn't that what you were telling me?"

"Was that bad?" My voice came out pitiful and pleading.

"No, it was . . . It just makes it difficult to lust from afar."

"Lust from afar? Why would you want to lust from afar?"

"Is that not what one does here, lust after you?" He was smiling now, but he didn't look particularly happy.

"I don't get it."

"We can't be together," he said matter-of-factly, looking past me toward the piano. "It wouldn't be fair."

"To whom?" I demanded. I was still feeling the wine, and my mind moved sluggishly through the possibilities. I came up with one; it was the right one.

"Robert, of course."

I lowered my eyes, feeling a flush of shame spill over me. I wasn't sure what I was ashamed of. If anything, Robert was the one who should have been ashamed.

"You understand?" he asked.

I shook my head "no," but still couldn't bring myself to look up.

I felt him over me, felt him reach out and tuck a renegade strand of hair behind my ear. I caught his hand and held it for a second before letting go.

"He's the one who ended things with me," I said. I was peeking up through my hair now, and noticed an expression of surprise cross his face. It occurred to me that I'd revealed too much.

"It doesn't matter. I've heard the way he talks about you."

"No, you're wrong." I wanted to reach out and take his hand again, but I didn't have the nerve. "I'm his student. A boring, regular student. Not like you and me. I have nothing with him like our music."

"So you still like our music, then?" He smiled, and I smiled back, unsure whether anything had just been resolved. We stood there for a while, looking at each other uncertainly, and then he asked me if I wanted some hot chocolate. His kitchen was cozy and neat, and we nestled at the end of his narrow wooden table, close enough so that we could feel the heat from each other's mugs. We stayed there for the rest of the night, talking about movies, books, paintings, Paris, New York, my friends—everything except music.

When I left the next morning, we were both awkward, fumbling with goodbyes; it was hard to believe we'd spent the night just chatting and drinking cocoa. I agonized through my classes that morning, itching to be back in the cluttered warmth of his townhouse, wondering whether I would frighten him if I showed up unannounced that afternoon. But by the time my last class ended, I was past caring about frightening him off; I needed to see him. I ran all the way to his house, and as soon as he opened the door I could tell from the bashful smile that greeted me that he'd been thinking about me just as intensely. And yet, again, he wouldn't even let me touch him, backing away as I tried to brush against him while passing through the door. We headed straight for the piano and stayed there for hours, fooling around with some of the ideas we'd talked about in the past month. He played the beginning of his latest piece, and then he listened, as attentively as I could have dared hope, as I played the piece I was currently working on. He offered a few suggestions that I knew, instantly, were right. Afterward we ordered a pizza and sat on the floor beside the piano, eating and talking about our childhoods.

Disbelieving both that I could be pouring something so personal into Jean Paul's ears, and yet also that he didn't already know, I told him about the brownstone bursting with art and outsized ambitions; about my father and his elegant outrage, his rigid yet ever-shifting tastes, the fortune his own father had built on a revolutionary new flushing mechanism; I told him about my glittering mother, her gift for making a sale, and how she'd forgotten to paint, despite her dozens of canvases lining our walls and the one masterpiece hanging, in defiant contrast to every fashion my father has ever deemed worthy, in a tiny alcove partially hidden from view; I even told him about my great artist. Telling all this, I thought my life sounded interesting, but it seemed embarrassingly bland the moment he started in on his history. His past was as remarkable as everything else about him.

His father, Anton Boumedienne, had been an Algerian nationalist and communist, and his mother, Françoise de Rochert, was the scion of an old French family famous for their vineyards and cognac distillery. They'd met at the Sorbonne, fallen in love at first sight, and married three months later. It wasn't until after the ceremony that Françoise brought her revolutionary husband home to meet her parents. The old aristocrats couldn't understand why their gentle, well-bred pianist of a daughter would choose to spend the rest of her days with an armed *pied noir,* and they weren't too keen on spending the rest of their days with him. Jean Paul wasn't clear if this was by direct order or just his mother's sense of delicacy, but that visit was the last time the Rocherts saw Anton Boumedienne.

When Anton was forced into exile during the early 1950s, at a time when many Algerian nationalists either fled or hid, the Rocherts were only too happy to set up the young family—mother, father, and Jean Paul's older sister, Clarisse—far from them, in the United States. Françoise was happy in their new home in Connecticut, where she offered piano lessons to local children, but Anton was eager to return to the battleground. When the National Liberation Front declared war on France in November 1954, with a spectacular series of simultaneous attacks on government buildings, military installations, police stations, and community facilities, Françoise begged her husband to stay in the United States and be a father to their daughter, but Anton couldn't resist the revolution. Françoise and Clarisse returned to France with Anton, but they parted ways in Paris, he staying there to join the NLF, the two females continuing on to the banks of the Charente and the splendid quiet of the family vineyards. Though Anton and Françoise now lived apart, they continued to see each other sporadically, in brief, furtive trips to intermediate locations, and it was during one of these meetings that Jean Paul was conceived.

During his early years, Jean Paul was raised primarily by his mother and grandparents, but he also saw his father on a semiregular basis, spending exhilarating weekends with him in Paris, before Anton was killed in 1962 in an accident involving a pipe bomb, three months before Algeria won independence. In Cognac, and then later in Paris, Françoise taught piano at the conservatory level, and devoted herself to her children's education. Everything was pleasant and comfortable for them in Paris, but Françoise was anxious about her children's futures. She was afraid that they would be stigmatized because of their father's reputation: he was well known as a mastermind behind numerous terrorist attacks, although Jean Paul now swore, implausibly, that his father had nothing directly to do with terrorism. Though she herself couldn't bear to uproot again, she didn't see her children's futures in France. When they reached high-school age, she shipped one and then the other off to boarding school in the States, which is how Jean Paul ended up at Exeter and then Yale.

"When I think of my mother, I think of music," Jean Paul told me that day. She'd taught both her children to play the piano at the same time she taught them to speak. "But when I think of my father, I think of passion. I think of the drive to make things perfect in the world, instead of settling for working within the constraints of its faults. I see my mother every few months, but I see my father every day."

With this operatic history tacked on to the brooding genius before me, my infatuation reached its zenith. Jean Paul transformed from a great musician with revolutionary ideas, to a great revolutionary with musical ideas. I didn't see him in terms of a Mahler or a Schoenberg anymore, but in terms of a Gandhi or a King—someone who would usher in a new world order.

We decided to go for a walk then, to undo the dazing effects of the pizza, the darkened room, the dreamy cadence of voices reaching back in memory. We'd just grabbed our coats when we simultaneously lunged for each other.

The taste of him when our mouths met was so familiar I thought perhaps I'd guessed it from the smell on his breath while we were sitting so close beside the piano, but the feel of his hands cupped behind my head, sliding down my back onto my waist, creeping toward my breasts, also seemed to have belonged there always. Even when he pulled off my shirt and began unbuttoning my jeans I didn't feel that anything new was taking place. And though an unrobed Jean Paul was something to behold—his dark skin luminous against the hardwood floors, his muscles tensing gracefully, his features deformed, and yet made more alluring, by intensity—it didn't occur to me to think how an unrobed me might strike a man like this. We ended up making love right there on the floor, several feet from the front door. Afterward we lay in the pile of our clothes, talking about our Idea and the revolution we would single-handedly bring about. And then we made love all over again.

I WOKE UP THE NEXT MORNING ALONE ON HIS FLOOR, wrapped in a wool overcoat. I was pulling on my clothes when he came bounding toward me, a look of alarm across his face.

"Are you leaving? Are you late?" he spluttered, not at all the purple-prosed Casanova from the night before. "I made pancakes."

"Pancakes?" I repeated, as though I'd never heard the term before.

"Yes." His voice was solemn. I had to laugh, and he joined in, and we laughed like that for a while, holding our sides from the utter hilarity of the word "pancakes" followed by the word "yes."

We decided over breakfast that I should tell Robert that Jean Paul and I were together now. It was the mature thing to do, and, anyway, what right did he have to object? I headed over to his office later that afternoon. He reacted, just as I knew he would, with complete indifference.

"Do you want my blessing or something?" he asked, staring at me stonily after I'd made my stiff speech.

"No. Well, I don't know. We thought maybe you'd want to know."

"Well, swell, I guess." Like the first time I was in there, he was taking books off the shelf and inspecting them while we spoke.

His reaction struck me as yet another sign of his transcendence, his status as a purely objective ear who had faltered three times by pretending to be a whole human.

"You're so naïve," Jean Paul sighed when I reported my interpretation over dinner that night. "I could feel him hating me today. Palpably."

When I ran into Robert the next morning, he did seem stonier than usual. A month earlier, the idea that Robert could be jealous over me would have been thrilling, but now I didn't care. I didn't even feel the twinge of self-doubt that should have come along—didn't ponder the question "Is *this* why he spent all that time on my music?"—because my yelping ego was quieted. *Jean Paul* had chosen me, after all. Chosen me so intensely that before long he was speaking as though the indestructibility of our bond was an unquestionable tenet, like the immorality of genocide or the desirability of happiness—too fundamental to discuss. Questions such as when Jean Paul would return to Paris, where I would spend my winter break, and even what courses I should take in the spring semester, or what I would do on any particular night, always began from the Axiom of Us—that the only thing above sacrifice was our togetherness. Because I couldn't imagine a better man with whom to link my fate, this axiom seemed wonderful to me.

Even more wonderful was the way Jean Paul turned increasingly toward me for musical guidance. Though we both still met with Masterson regularly, Jean Paul was adamant that our maestro disliked us, and that we would have to be each other's mentors now. We'd discuss over dinner, we'd analyze while we cleaned the dishes, we'd dissect while we lay in bed at night, and we'd play always, running our fingers along the piano, the table, the couch, each other, trying to force the other to hear what we could not yet put into notes. Although Jean Paul was always one step ahead, in both developing and implementing ideas, I never thought of us as leader and follower, or master and pupil. I thought of us as a partnership, because that's what Jean Paul said we were. He called his music "our music," his ideas, "our ideas," and his talent "our talent." It didn't escape my notice that he never called my music "our music," but I assumed this was just because I wasn't yet working within the rules we'd so carefully outlined together. There was no denying that he gave my scores a great deal of serious attention, and under his care the music continued to flow out of me with relative ease. Masterson had even called one piece "good."

A few months into our relationship, soon after winter exams had passed, Jean Paul casually suggested that I move in with him. It was midmorning, right before I was supposed to leave for class, and I was in the middle of pulling on a pair of jeans. I stopped to stare at him with one leg on and one leg off.

"Why not?" he asked, when I continued to stare, not sure what to make of the offer; it didn't fit with my vision of the college experience. "You're over here all the time anyway. Why waste valuable hours apart, when we could be working together on our music?"

"But I like the dorm," I bleated, unsure, in fact, why his offer didn't exhilarate me.

"It could be fun." He shrugged. "You'd still see your friends, if that's what you're worrying about."

WHEN I DID MOVE in a few weeks later, though, I stopped going to my friends' late-night gatherings. The trek back and forth took too long, and their odd hours left me out of sync with Jean Paul's schedule. Jean Paul tried to encourage me to go now and then, but I think he was secretly pleased that I never did. He'd never done a good job of hiding just how laughable he thought my friends were, taking themselves and their artistic destinies so seriously. I didn't share his dim view of them (in fact, I didn't think they took themselves any more seriously than, say, Jean Paul), but I also didn't want him to think I liked them *too* much; I was afraid that might make me seem laughable, too.

Soon I saw hardly anyone other than Jean Paul, except in classes. I still went to study the violin at Annabelle's once a week, but I moved through our lessons deafly, focused only on routing out the expressive side of any score. "Vat are you doing to this music?" she'd shriek at me, but I'd hardly hear her as I ran out the door, toward home. I was never sure why she kept seeing me. I hoped every week that that lesson might be our last, but it never was; the old bat was as stubborn about keeping me on as she was about everything else.

Though I still made the occasional lunch or dinner date with my friends, these became markedly less frequent as the months of the spring semester progressed. I didn't want to linger on campus any longer than I had to; it was too tempting to return to our townhouse. I loved how, even from the upstairs closet we'd converted into my study, where I locked myself every afternoon to do schoolwork and perfect my own compositions, I could feel the floors shaking from the force of Jean Paul's hitting the piano. Sometimes I would sneak down and watch him compose for long stretches, and though his eyes were open he never noticed me. When I did interrupt him, no matter how well he'd been working, he was always happy to see me, eager to share his progress, to hear my opinion.

Not that our life was all about music. Funded by his family's fortune, we dined out extravagantly, went to parties and plays and, of course, concerts. He taught me to cook, and we created rich French feasts together several nights a week. And we made love, constantly, frantically, as though it were our natural state and all times apart were amputations.

We were so happy together those months between January, when I first moved in, and May, when we took off for the summer, that I can pinpoint the two times I felt at all dissatisfied. The first took place the weekend I brought Jean Paul home to meet my parents. We'd only been together three months when my parents asked me to come to New York for a particularly important opening, but I decided to bring Jean Paul along. I felt it was time that both sides got acquainted. I wasn't concerned about the big event, because I knew that my parents would love Jean Paul, and that he would love them back. But everyone ended up loving each other more than I'd anticipated. The minute we stepped in the door, it was clear that the match would be perfect. "Oh, Barnett Newman. Do you represent him?" Jean Paul had casually asked by way of greeting, taking in the wall-sized painting.

My mother, looking far more like an emaciated version of a 1940s glamour puss than I remembered her, took me aside while we were still in the foyer. "He's incredible," she whispered. "Why didn't you tell me? What a question—why don't you ever tell me anything! But, Tasha, he's a god. You'd think he was a movie star.

You, by the way"—she let her eyes trail my new figure up and down—"we'll discuss that later. But him! And a fan of Barnett Newman's! Handsome and smart."

I pointed out that he'd never said he liked the artist.

"Give me a break," she said, laughing, but I could see her considering my comment. Over dinner, she tried to pry out his artistic tastes. They happened, by chance, to be right, but it wouldn't have mattered if they weren't. My parents, like me, fell deeply into love by way of Jean Paul's rage.

"What an acute sense of the sublime you have!" my father declared that evening after Jean Paul had delivered his sermon, with no less fire and brimstone for the folks. Jean Paul didn't wince. Instead, he smiled broadly. I wasn't sure if I should be relieved or concerned.

"Your parents are fascinating," he told me later that night. "They're so much like you. You never told me your father set out to be a painter."

"Well, he never painted a thing." We were lying uncomfortably on my narrow bed, where my parents, proud bohemians that they were, had insisted we both spend the night. "He was at Columbia three days before he discovered he preferred looking at art to making it."

"That's precisely what I find so fascinating about their minds," Jean Paul insisted, rolling onto his side to face me. "They have this unique gift for seeing and understanding art."

Three days went on like this, a mutual love-fest, with accolades whispered in my ear every time I was alone with one camp or another. ("Your mother has an impressive ear." "He's so passionate, what's he like . . . No, don't tell me.") I reveled in it, naturally; the three people most important to me loved each other, almost as much as I loved each of them. But something about the weekend set me on edge as well. The more they built up a wall of myth around one another, the more I saw of their faults. In my mother, I was assaulted by traces of the secretary she had been when Grandpa Darsky spotted her graceful good looks, perfectly accessorized by a Jewish name, among his legion of employees and brought her home to meet his son. I heard the lapses into a once-heavy herring-tinged accent. I chafed at the volume of her whispers, the histrionics her hands played out when she spoke, the firm belief in astrology she didn't see fit to hide in front of guests. In my father, I saw the pomposity, the grandiosity, the streak of cruelty, and the deep well of contempt, not entirely hidden by impeccable manners. I prayed that Jean Paul would not also begin to notice these things. And Jean Paul? What did I notice in him?

Right before we left for the airport on Sunday morning, my mother pulled me aside.

"Tasha, I never thought you'd do it. I never thought you'd find someone worthy of you. But you have. It's like you were made for each other."

The whole way home I thought about that. *Made for each other.* Both Jean Paul and my parents seemed to think so. I did, too, of course, but there was an inchoate disenchantment gnawing at the edge of my consciousness. When I looked at us through their eyes, something didn't fit. I couldn't, or didn't want to, understand precisely what it was.

The second instance of dissatisfaction I can recall came just a few days after this trip. I returned home from class that afternoon to the sound of Jean Paul wailing, "They'll crucify me, Tasha. They'll crucify me!" while playing through the first movement of the garden-party piece. He was trying to choose two works to be performed by the Cleveland Symphony Orchestra for their new Emerging Composer Series. At first he'd taken childish delight in the task; he'd been bounding around the apartment for days, bursting with the honor of being one of three artists selected, the only one under thirty. But this morning he'd woken up in a foul mood, and declared while we were still lying in bed that everything he'd ever written was worthless junk. Since then, he'd been going though a routine to which I'd grown accustomed: his hands caressing music out of the keys, while his mouth railed against it.

"They'll love it," I promised.

"Then they're imbeciles!" He delicately tapped out a brief, angry snippet of a melody.

"Well, then, I'm an imbecile, too," I shouted back, not because I was angry—how could I be?—but because the melody was now pounding chaos.

He stopped playing for several beats, gave me a severe look, then returned to a variation on his first theme.

"You're just in love with me." Though he seemed to take a perverse pleasure in insulting himself, he could never tolerate an aspersion cast at me, particularly if I'd cast it. He'd get annoyed when I so much as said that a certain dress didn't flatter me. He flew off the handle whenever I mentioned that I needed to lose the weight I'd gained from all our rich cooking. He told me my mother was trying to make me into a skeleton, just like her, and when I told him the scale didn't lie, he looked so exasperated I wondered if he thought he had a hold on a truth deeper than objective fact. "You're the furthest thing from an imbecile."

He was playing in silence now, and his face had regained the appearance of drunken reverie, which meant that he was enjoying his music again. I felt myself fill with that joyous look, the extraordinary sounds flying around us, the honeyed tones of the spring afternoon, and experienced something that I can only describe as a sense of completeness. And yet this very sense of completeness made me think of what my mother had said—that we were perfect for each other—and form the question, just briefly, whether our being perfect complements belied the claim that we were equals.

That was the last time I had such a thought. A month after the school year ended, Jean Paul and I packed up the townhouse for the summer and spent a month and a half with my parents in the Hamptons, followed by a month and a half in his family's vineyards. Both visits were unqualified successes. In the Hamptons, Jean Paul and my father spent most of their days antiquing and golfing, while my mother and I sunbathed. At night, Jean Paul and I would sit on the beach and alternate between writing and making love as fluidly as if they were two parts of the same exercise. We were melodramatically dispirited when we drove away, talking about all the things we would miss—the seafood; the sand; my father's rages, which seemed ludicrous now that I had someone with whom to laugh about them; my mother's eccentric warmth, which seemed so much nobler now that someone else had confirmed its therapeutic strength—but the contentment came with us to Cognac.

The de Rochert estate on the banks of the Charente was like something out of a movie, with grand staircases, formal dining, servants, horses, and a refined family looking over it all like gentle deities. Jean Paul's grandparents were so old they seemed hardly alive, and I amused myself during the stuffy formal dinners by wondering whether there was some servant whose job it was to place them around the house like statues; you never caught sight of them in transit. Jean Paul's mother, on the other hand, I only ever saw on the move: svelte and elegant with her short black hair, compact body, and designer suits, she was constantly rushing into Paris to attend events or organize charities. When she was home she was either preparing for the courses she still taught at the Conservatoire, or running around rearranging imperceptible aspects of a room while constantly chattering about every lofty topic imaginable—usually in French, though occasionally she switched to English for my benefit; she refused to believe that my vocabulary was as good as my accent, which I found infuriating, even if wholly justified. The only times I saw Jean Paul silenced were in her presence. Though she was never warm to me, she was never cool, either, and we did share some chats about Jean Paul and about music that I thought laid the bedrock for eventual closeness. As on Long Island, Jean Paul and I spent most of our time making music and making love, though this time we made our music at the grand piano in what I could never get myself to call "the salon," and saved our physical collaboration until we were behind the thick walls of his bedroom. For the last three days of our stay, Jean Paul's older sister, Clarisse, and her three young daughters drove over from Orléans, and under their athletic, ebullient influence, I learned to ride a horse, stomp grapes, and test the clarity of cognac.

The final few weeks of the summer we spent back in the townhouse, repainting all the rooms in bright colors because I had read somewhere that bright colors stimulate creativity. I had grown so used to our life of leisure that I was legitimately surprised when Jean Paul reminded me one night that classes were starting in a few days, and that I ought to start looking at the course catalogue. It struck me as unfair that this season had to end, but the summer transmuted effortlessly into autumn, as we continued to bask in our music, our life, and our destiny, and I went on believing blithely in our genius.

It probably would have been our music, our life, and our destiny forever, just as Jean Paul so adamantly insisted, if I hadn't suffered a moment of weakness in the early-morning hours of a stormy November day that also happened to be our one-year anniversary. A few notes had popped into my head just before dawn, waking me from a troubled sleep, and I'd wrenched myself out from under the pile of blankets in order to jot them down before they faded away. Because my closet-study was typically cold and leaky, and in bad weather uninhabitable, I set myself up in the dry comfort of the kitchen. I was feeling achy and possibly feverish (probably this, and not the notes, was what had woken me in the first place), but for nearly an hour I fought through exhaustion and a bone-deep chill, wandering between the table and the piano in the next room, watching the patterns forming and dissolving on our windows, trying to force out the pattern I hoped was in me. It had been months since I'd written something I liked, and these notes had seemed promising. But eventually I had to conclude that tonight was not going to be the night I broke through my block. With some relief, I decided to make myself a cup of hot chocolate, then head back to bed. It was while I was sipping my cocoa, savoring the burn it traced through my shivering body, that I noticed Jean Paul's handwriting peeking out from under my reams of blank music paper.

I like to think that normally I would have quashed my curiosity out of respect for his privacy, but I don't know whether that's true. At that moment, my exhaustion and my desire for distraction were enough to convince me that if he didn't want me to see what he'd written he wouldn't have left his letter lying around.

I pulled the light-blue stationery (pilfered from my desk) out from under the pile and saw that it was addressed to his mother. For no good reason, I took this as further justification to read on. I stumbled over the French here and there, but I mostly understood, especially since I was already familiar with his news—about the music he was currently writing, the commission that looked as though it was going to come through from the Boston Symphony Orchestra, the anniversary that we'd be celebrating that evening. It was right after I found out where he was planning to take me for dinner that night (it wasn't the place I'd been expecting, and I was disappointed) that the letter segued dangerously onto the topic of me. I put the letter down and washed my mug. But as I walked past the table again on my way toward the door, I couldn't help myself. I was still standing, pretending that I wasn't going to go through with it, but I read on.

> *I'm so glad that you enjoyed your phone conversation with Tasha, and I can assure you that she enjoyed it just as much as, if not more than, you did. She wanted me to ask you how Nicole's recital went, and whether she managed to take first prize. You're right, by the way, to point out that Tasha is a very empathetic person; I think that is the quality in her that I admire the most, and that makes us so perfectly paired. It's what makes her such an extraordinary violinist and what makes her so invaluable to my own progress. Sometimes I think that she is able to understand what I write better than I understand it, and that helps me to write even better the next time. Sometimes this even makes me sad for her.*

He began to talk then about a favorite horse that was going to have to be put down. I returned to the paragraph about me and reread the last sentence several times, trying to find a flaw with my translation. Sad for me? Why would he be sad for me? It couldn't be, could it, that it was because he thought my talent was *only* for understanding? That he called his music "our music" not because we were equal partners in its creation but because he regretted that I couldn't produce any worthwhile works of my own? It couldn't be, I was sure of it, but the more times I read the paragraph, the more inescapable this conclusion seemed.

The following morning, I woke up to find that my feverish feeling from the previous night was indeed a high fever. Jean Paul wanted to stay home and take care of me, but I convinced him to spend the whole day at school so I could sleep, and even—though this took persistence—to take a friend from the music department to dinner and to the concert for which we'd bought tickets months in advance. I didn't want to have to face his solicitude when all I could hear in my head was his voice saying, "Sometimes this even makes me sad for her." I left my anniversary present for him—a bound volume of his works to date—on the kitchen table, and let him believe I was asleep when he came in to thank me. I stashed the present he gave me under a pile of papers in my study. It was also a bound volume of his works to date; we never mentioned the coincidence.

For the forty-eight hours that it lasted, I was actually grateful for my flu. I slept for most of that time—dreamless sleeps—but whenever I was awake, I pored over the letter in my memory, stretching it every which way, first to make it as innocuous as possible, then as painful, and back and forth. The efforts at a benign interpretation were not so easy, and so I also began to plot my escape and vindication: I'd run off as soon as I got better, clearing every last trace of myself out while he was in a seminar; I'd steal away when he thought I was sleeping by his side; I'd pretend I was going home for a while and never come back; and, in every one of these fantasies, I would eventually write the most moving piece of music anyone had ever heard, and dedicate it to him. But soon my anger and vengeance were spent and I was simply sad; after all, could he help discerning when discernment was part of his prodigious gift? And could I blame him for keeping his unflattering opinions to himself? The discernment and the kindness were essential parts of him, and what made me love him far too much to run off. And, after all, hadn't I known? I knew I was no Jean Paul. I knew it, and that was why it was so easy for me to understand what he'd meant in that letter, ambiguous as his words may have been to someone else.

By the time my temperature returned to normal, I was prepared to pretend I had never seen the letter. Outwardly, I returned to acting loving and happy. I *was* loving and happy, mostly, though not a day went by when I didn't think, *He's sad for me, because I don't have it.* I had completely given up doubting that perhaps I'd misinterpreted his words. The more I thought about it, the more obvious it seemed not only that he had said it, but that he was right. What had I ever produced on my own? Nothing worth speaking of. Without Us, I was no composer, and so I decided to stop torturing myself by chasing after strings of notes that led nowhere. I took an incomplete in my composition workshop, knowing full well that I would be forced to take a failing grade, putting me in danger of repeating my junior year. Repeating a year seemed better than pretending to be something I wasn't.

In order to drown out the sound of my musical ideas clamoring to be explored, I began to practice the violin constantly. At night I'd lie in bed playing a work in my head over and over until I fell asleep. But it was the expression of the music, not the pure abstract sound of it, that I found so comforting, and I couldn't convince myself any longer that that wasn't a central component of why I chose the music that I chose. Because of this, Jean Paul's dogmatism began to annoy me, though I tried to tell myself it didn't. When he'd rant, I found myself silently arguing against him. *What makes you so certain that there's one and only one thing that music is and should be? Music just so happens to evoke emotions in everyone, so who are you to say that it shouldn't?* I never voiced any of these objections, but maybe my face expressed them, or maybe he could hear in my playing that I no longer accepted them. Either way, the diatribes soon stopped flowing freely through our home.

In addition to the reinsertion of expression into my notes, something else began to change in my music. I began to confront Jean Paul with my violin. To tell him what I'd seen was too much for me. The idea of voicing those words, to *see* him pitying me—it was far better just to pretend it had never happened. But to have it out with him in my music was easy—and not only easy, but thrilling. Every composer was Jean Paul, and every piece was a fight. *These notes are mine as well,* I'd insist from inside the score; *I own them, too, and I am creating.* Soon I couldn't play without having this struggle take over, so even at Annabelle's it had to come out. The first time this happened, the struggle had become such second nature to me that I wasn't even aware of what I'd done until I finished the small piece of the Mendelssohn concerto I'd prepared for the lesson. The look on her face made me think of a jilted lover whose darling had come crawling back.

"I knew there was something remarkable waiting to come out of you," she murmured. "I knew it was only a matter of time. Please, play it again."

Soon, at Annabelle's request, I was going there three times a week instead of once, and I was relishing our lessons rather than dreading them.

Jean Paul never mentioned that I'd taken up the violin seriously again, not even to complain about my unrelenting playing, which made it difficult for him to work at home. Without a word of protest, he simply began composing at school. His quiet accommodation was almost as painful for me as finding the letter had been. I took it as an indication that he was pleased I was focusing on what he thought of as my real talent—pleased that I'd relegated myself to lesser ambitions I could actually fulfill, ambitions he wouldn't embarrass me by naming. One afternoon, I remembered something he'd said about my father: "Fascinating, like you. A unique talent for seeing and understanding art." Yes, he was surely relieved that I, like my father before me, had realized what I was and was not suited for. I spent the rest of the day moping in my closet; I couldn't even touch the violin.

It was around this time that Annabelle mentioned entering an international competition. I dismissed the idea initially, but it sounded increasingly reasonable each time she repeated it. As a child I'd taken part in a number of minor competitions, and had fared surprisingly well. But I'd been planning to leave all that behind me with college. Competitions were for virtuosos, and I had no interest in becoming one of those. Yet now all I did was play the violin, and so it made sense to direct all this effort toward a goal.

The day I found out I'd passed the screening stage of the Vienna competition, I stayed out late walking around town, figuring out the best way to tell Jean Paul that I wouldn't be spending our winter break holed up in the townhouse, drinking his delicious hot chocolate and critiquing his glorious compositions, but rather in Europe, showing off my skills, such as they were, before of a panel of distinguished judges. I knew he'd want to help me practice and come with me to Austria to act as my accompanist. I also knew that I didn't want him involved.

"When do we go?" was his predictably enthusiastic response, when I came home to find him waiting for me with a ruined soufflé.

It was difficult to force out the words "Not we."

"But won't I be your accompanist?" Standing in the middle of the living room, his encouragement still hanging limply on his face, he looked even more hurt than I'd anticipated, and I almost faltered in my resolve. "Can't you bring your own accompanist?"

"I'd rather do this on my own." I laid my hand on his arm. "Do you understand what I mean?"

He shrugged. "Sure. Of course. You need to do it on your own."

But he couldn't have understood that I wanted him to stay away because I was mortified—he couldn't possibly have known that I hated that he was proud of me, because his pride in my playing reminded me of my limits. If my choice continued to bother him, he didn't let on, though if he had let on I'm not sure I would have noticed. I had turned single-mindedly toward my preparation.

The next two months were a welcome blur of practice—for me, the equivalent of eight solid weeks in an opium den. I had a large number of pieces to prepare, many of them on a more technically advanced level than I was used to. For the preliminary round especially, the focus was on virtuosic gymnastics, with lots of super-fast bowing, my weakest point. Annabelle and I spent hours just trying to choose the Paganini caprice and Bach solo fugue that would present the fewest difficulties for me. I settled on Bach's C-major Fugue, and the difficult Caprice No. 4 against Annabelle's advice, because I found those two to be the most interesting and figured I'd be more inclined to practice them incessantly, which I did. The last part of the preliminary round was the commissioned work, a six-minute frenetic thing by a Dutch composer named Ebels.

Through Annabelle's expert pedagogy, I managed to get all three of these pieces under my belt, gaining precision and speed steadily if not exactly exponentially. That left me the rest of the time to focus on the pieces I thought could win the thing for me, should I happen to be among the lucky twelve who made it past the preliminaries. For the semifinals I prepared Beethoven's Sonata No. 3 and the Paganini-Kreisler *I Palpiti,* both of which I'd been playing for a long time, including at a few competitions in the past. It was the pieces for the final round—the concerto segment—about which I was most confident. I chose Mozart's Concerto No. 3, and Mendelssohn's Violin Concerto, two of my favorite works, for the Mozart and Romantic portions of the competition. Both Annabelle and I agreed that if I made it to the finals I had a solid chance of placing, even if based solely on my Mozart. Few young violinists had the patience to give Mozart concertos the subtlety of inflection they required, but patience was exactly what I had.

I rarely saw Jean Paul during those couple of months. Half the time I spent at Annabelle's, and the other half I was in my closet fiddling away, or making halfhearted attempts not to flunk out of school. Jean Paul tried at first to arrange his days according to my erratic new schedule, so we could at least eat dinner and go to bed together, but soon I started eating while I played, and sleeping in brief snatches. I don't know if I was using my immersion in the violin as an excuse to avoid Jean Paul, or if I honestly was too busy to lead a normal life. I think I was probably happy I didn't need to decide which of these descriptions was more accurate. Once again, Jean Paul didn't complain, and whenever we crossed paths he asked me how my preparation was going in a way that I knew meant that, as far as he could hear, it was going phenomenally well and he was proud.

There was one exception to our general estrangement during this period, and that was the week before the first read-through of the piece he'd had commissioned by the Boston Symphony Orchestra. He'd shot this one out in record time even for him—twenty-eight minutes of music in under a month—and I thought it was his best. He thought so, too, which was why he was so anxious about its reception. He padded around the apartment like a man haunted, his face twisted into a permanent silent howl, his proud back slumped with defeat. It was enough to cut through the layers of distancing emotion that had grown up around me—the guilt, the inferiority, the residual shadows of resentment—and I felt our interests were fused again. That week I returned to a more human schedule, making time to sit with him at the piano and reassure him, to cook dinner with him, to make love to him as many times as it took to exhaust him into sleep. The read-through, when it came, went even better than we'd hoped. Everyone agreed that this was his most monumental work to date, and that the première might well put him on the international map. I stuck around long enough to celebrate with a bottle of champagne, then disappeared into my closet for another three weeks.

I went back to focusing on the caprice and the fugue, the pieces I was sure would be my downfall if any would. My fancy fingerings had improved, but I doubted they could compare to the skill of someone who'd spent the past few years studying in a conservatory. When I decided to enter the competition, it had been primarily to attach a goal to my playing, but now I didn't want to lose. I didn't necessarily need to win, but I wanted to make it to the final round. I wanted people to hear my Mozart concerto. I saw the Paganini and Bach as the hurdles I had to cross, and I treated them as such, attacking them viciously and taking no joy in mastering them. But I did master them, and I mastered the other pieces, too. I felt them becoming a part of me, sinking into my fingers, where they could be released at will. I felt so full of music that I didn't even think about the gap left in my life, where my own compositions had once been. Where once there had been Jean Paul to bolster a drooping confidence, now there was Bach and Mozart and Mendelssohn and Paganini.

One day, on my way home from a lesson at Annabelle's, so lost in the Paganini-Kreisler *I Palpiti* that I didn't notice where I was going, I ran headlong into Robert Masterson. I hadn't seen him in months. He acted happy to have found me.

"Where's your music?" he asked, when we'd been through the usual niceties. "I keep waiting for more. That last piece showed remarkable progress. I thought you were on the brink of a breakthrough."

"I'm more into playing the violin these days," I said, wondering if maybe Jean Paul had been wrong to damn me so quickly, before I remembered that Masterson's judgment of me was clouded by nonmusical considerations.

"That's a shame," he replied. "Come see me one of these days, and let's change that."

But of course I didn't.

A week before I left for Vienna, Jean Paul put up a mild fight for the right to come along. He'd already bought his plane tickets, and I almost gave in.

"You only said I couldn't be your accompanist, not that I couldn't come," he protested, as we walked back home from a seminar together. I was already in a foul mood, as I always was after that particular seminar, following two hours of being all but ignored in favor not only of the incomparable Jean Paul, but also of some real nitwits around whom I knew I could talk circles if only the professor didn't cut me off after every third word. He was a famous misogynist, known for declaring that Harvard's doom was sealed the moment they allowed cross-registration by Radcliffe students.

"I don't know," I said, trying to think back to that first conversation. I was sure I'd told him he couldn't come with me to Vienna altogether, but maybe he'd misunderstood. "I feel funny about it."

"Please? I have these tickets already. They're nonrefundable."

The thought of him sitting there in the audience, proud of his fiddler playing other people's music for want of another option, was too unnerving. I remained adamant, and he backed down.

Despite this final insulting blow, the night before I left for Austria, he took me out for an elegant dinner. While we ate, he massaged the sore fingers of my hands and tried, not very effectively, to keep my mind off the competition by talking to me about our summer plans. He even indulged my taste for illicit public affection, running his long fingers up the inside of my thigh during dessert. I let him act like we were uncomplicatedly happy, even enjoyed pretending that we were, but I was planning to put an abrupt end to the evening when we got home. I wanted to lock myself in my closet and practice one last time on familiar turf, and I wanted him out of my mind when I arrived in Vienna. Back at the apartment, though, he told me to wait in the living room while he ran upstairs.

He returned with two gift-wrapped boxes, one small and one large. I opened the large one first. It was a violin case, old and magnificent, in soft, fine leather. It couldn't have cost less than a few hundred dollars, and I shook my head in disbelief. I tried to kiss him, but he backed away.

"Open the other one," he said.

I opened it slowly, afraid that it might contain something I didn't want, something white and sparkling that would ruin my chances in Vienna completely. When I pried the small box open, I was so startled by the sheer glitter of the thing that I wasn't even sure what I was looking at.

"It was my great-great-great-grandmother's," he told me, reaching for the box himself, and lifting out a delicate strand of diamonds and rubies. "It passes through all the women in my family."

"What about Clarisse?" I asked. I felt I couldn't possibly accept a gift this extravagant. I didn't want to.

He shrugged. "My mother sent it. She wants you to have it. Clarisse doesn't wear jewelry anyway."

"Where *would* you wear something like this?" I asked.

"I was hoping you'd wear it at the competition." I knew family history meant a great deal to Jean Paul, and for him to give me something like this necklace was no flashy and empty gesture.

I tried to thank him, but I couldn't speak. I felt happy and miserable, and guilty and grateful, and angry, and in love, and nostalgic and optimistic all at once, and all I could do was fling myself at him, and hope that he took it to mean what he wanted it to.

I SPENT THE FIRST FEW HOURS OF THE WORLD'S MOST glamorous music competition lying on the itchy bedspread in my hotel room.

I was determined not to think of Jean Paul and what he might be doing at that moment, entertaining myself instead with the program booklet I'd been handed in the lobby. I was halfheartedly sizing up the competition, trying to project the winners based solely on the intensity of their expressions, but I was distracted by the realization that I was way out of my league among the forty hopefuls, many of whom had other major wins to their names, and all of whom had attended conservatory beyond the high-school level. That I was an impostor (even my picture was wrong—I was the only one staring straight at the camera, rather than down into the left-hand corner of the frame, violin tucked purposefully under chin) was clear, and this inevitably brought me back to Jean Paul, which brought me to confusion, which ended when I picked up the booklet and began leafing listlessly through again until it was time to head over to the opening ceremonies. It dawned on me then that I had no idea how to get to the Musikverein, home to the Vienna Philharmonic. I ventured down to the hotel lobby, hoping that there'd be a group forming to head over, but in the five minutes I waited, no such group materialized. Luckily, a legacy of my early travels with easily distracted parents was an impeccable intuition for foreign streets, and I managed to find my way there myself.

It was evening by then, and since I hadn't eaten a thing since morning, my first impression of the legendary building was that it looked uncannily like a festive cake, smothered in a deep-raspberry icing, with moldings in a buttery cream. There was a large crowd gathered outside, fellow hopefuls mingling with a music-loving Viennese public. While we waited to enter the halls of this classical confection, I tried to drum up some anxiety: I wasn't simply in a wonderful new city, I was in the city where classical music had been born, and I wasn't here just to see the sights and observe the other competitors, but to test my own worth as a violinist. Johannes Brahms had conducted the Philharmonic in this building, and I would play inside it if I lasted until the final round. I ought to have been nervous. But I wasn't. All I could think about was Jean Paul, writing away, missing me.

In the famed Golden Hall, with its swarming gods and goddesses overhead, I slid into a seat and admitted to myself that my utter lack of nervous energy was making me feel alien and alone. I wanted to *be* here. I wanted to partake in the thrum of disquiet pulsing through the rows of plush seats.

As I was lamenting my cool, the woman sitting next to me turned, pointed at the ceiling, and said in a thick Spanish accent, "Apollo and his muses." I glanced up at the swarming gods and goddesses, and murmured, "Isn't it weird how muses went from being the active force of creation to passive catalysts?" She looked at me warily for a moment—I couldn't blame her—and then laughed.

"I'm Maria." She held out a well-manicured hand, bearing the largest diamond I'd ever seen. "And you are fascinating."

She was twenty-six, she told me as the orchestra tuned up their instruments, and had been giving recitals for years without much recognition. Just a few months earlier, she'd come in third at the Queen Elisabeth competition in Belgium. In the wake of that win, she'd been invited to perform with several moderately important orchestras, mainly in Latin America, and these concerts had gotten some positive press attention. Her manager felt strongly that a win here would catapult her into a solid touring schedule, whereas a loss could be devastating to her momentum, particularly since she had a husband with political ambitions, to whom a working wife could only be justified by heavy doses of fame and fortune.

She pulled out a press kit and showed me some photographs, some clippings, a glossy press release.

"Do you have a press kit?" she asked.

I shook my head. "I'm just getting started."

"You need to get one as soon as possible," she warned ominously. And then, under her breath, "It's tough. For people like us, pictures can help."

I felt a momentary pang of excitement at being a part of something so glamorous and cutthroat, but then I thought, *What true artist relies on a press kit?*, and went back to my detachment.

I hardly enjoyed the concert at all, feeling too unmoored to take in the sounds. Back at the hotel room afterward, I thought of calling Jean Paul, but fell asleep before I had the chance.

I woke up late the following afternoon to the sound of street musicians playing a Slavic song beneath my window, and after a hearty breakfast in the hotel dining room, wandered over to the Konzerthaus to hear my new friend, Maria, perform in the preliminary round. She was good, but it was clear from the first bars that she lacked the distinctive musicality that would push her on to the next level. The picture of her defeated return to her dictatorial husband—I pictured him stocky and with a handlebar mustache—was vivid for me. I wanted to sneak out before she found me. But I'd heard that morning that the boy who was performing right after her, an exceedingly tall and thin twenty-year-old from the U.S.S.R., shaped more like a parabola than a line, was extraordinary, and so I ended up staying in my seat. Vladimir Stobetsky was the violinist whom all the competitors were here to beat; he'd already won two minor international competitions, and rumor was that this was his last concert before he launched on a solo career. To hear him play was to be invited into a peculiarly intimate moment, to be asked to confront the music along with him, and to love it exactly as he did. He reminded me a lot of the legendary Yehudi Menuhin, whom I'd once heard perform live at Carnegie Hall, but there was also something unique about this young man's playing, something raw yet exquisitely controlled. Maria must have slid in next to me in the middle of the performance, but I failed to notice her until Vladimir was bowing his concave body in flopping sweeps to the roar of the modest audience.

"That was unbelievable," I said, turning toward her.

"I know." I noticed there were tears in her eyes, though I couldn't be sure if she was mourning her own performance or simply moved by his. Either way, it had been insensitive of me to praise him without saying a thing about her.

"You were wonderful, too," I pointed out. "Great chops."

"The Paganini kills me." She shook her head. "I spend so much time trying to master the fingering, I forget to make it music. My husband will be happy, right?"

"That's far too pessimistic," I said, but I knew as well as she that there was no hope of making it past the preliminaries with a Paganini like that.

We watched a few more performers, most of them better than she had been, none anywhere near Vladimir's level, and then set out in search of dinner.

We ended up in a café a few blocks from the Konzerthaus, where the virtuoso from the U.S.S.R. was already cradling a coffee cup in his unnaturally long fingers.

"Mind if we join you, Vlad?" Maria asked. She was a longtime veteran of competitions, and knew a lot of the violinists crawling over Vienna, so it didn't surprise me that she knew Vladimir Stobetsky.

Vladimir pushed aside a pile of newspapers, French, German, English, and Austrian. I later learned that until the Iron Curtain lifted Vladimir spent at least 90 percent of his time abroad reading anything he could get his hands on. As far as he was concerned, the special travel visa granted him as a world-class musician was nothing more than a glorified library card.

"Please." He motioned to the empty seats.

"I hope you don't mind my saying, but you're incredible." I took the seat across from him. "I once heard Yehudi Menuhin play in Carnegie Hall, and you remind me of him."

"But my name is Vlad," he responded with a disconcerting smile.

"Tasha." I stuck my hand out tentatively, awed by a cockiness so lofty it would refuse a comparison to Menuhin. Instead of gripping my proffered fingers, he kissed them.

"Natasha Darsky."

"Yes. How did you know?"

"I remember your picture. In the book." He shooed away further discussion with his spaghetti fingers.

"We need to talk about sausages." He solemnly looked down at the menu. "Maria, I am having the hardest time deciding what to eat. Why does everything in Vienna involve pig? I don't like to eat pigs. They're too smart. Natasha Darsky, do you care for pig?"

"Not really."

"No, because you are Russian, and Russians don't care to eat their equals."

"I'm only half Russian," I corrected, not sure why I was bothering. "And I'm not even that. That is, I'm Jewish."

"Another people that respects the pig. We will not eat any pig at this table. Which means, of course, that we will have to eat lots of sugar, because that is the only other item I see on the menu."

Vladimir continued on in this way, dictating the conversation's direction with his heavy hand—or the heavy tongue in his cheek, more accurately—until Maria excused herself, claiming that she had to start practicing again early the next morning. Without Maria there, he calmed down, became almost placid.

"So." He leaned back in his chair, a cigarette dangling precariously from his mouth. "Now that we are without that big mouth Maria, tell me why it is you want to win the Vienna competition."

"I don't really," I replied. "I mean, I couldn't. But I wanted to come. I wanted to play."

"Ah, to come and play. Yes, it's fine to come and play, isn't it? It's first-rate."

"Why do you want to win?" I asked, hating that he was making fun of me, and wanting to turn the conversation in another direction.

"Why do I want to win? Now, that is really a different question altogether. I want to win because that's what I have to do. But don't worry, I'll win."

He picked up one of his newspapers and started to read again, but after a few seconds he peeked out over the top to make sure I was still watching him.

"Don't you want to know why I need to win? You'll be impressed that I'm so calm."

"I have a vague idea."

"Well, it's a half-vague reason. If I win, a distinct life of freedom and luxury. If I lose, a vague life. Probably in some Siberian orchestra, or, if I'm lucky, a provincial concert circuit."

"From just one competition?"

"Sure, why not? Efficiency. I like it." He picked up the newspaper again, perhaps secure now that I appreciated his insouciance in the face of overwhelming pressure, which I did.

"I should get going." I pushed back my chair, though I was reluctant to leave.

"You won't sit with me longer in this starlit Vienna night? I was hoping we could read the paper together. Out loud. You know, like love poems."

"I should get to bed. Shouldn't you?"

"Later," he said. "I'll see you tomorrow."

I sat back down, lulled by the soft light of the street lamp falling through the windows onto our wrought-iron table, the laughing voices swirling around us, and the promise of being read the *Herald Tribune* like a Shakespearean sonnet.

"OK, read to me," I said, but he passed the paper across the table.

"You read to me. It's nicer from a woman's voice."

THE NEXT MORNING, I woke up early, hoping to fit in some sightseeing before I had to go onstage. Annabelle had always warned me never to practice on the day of a concert, and it was advice I didn't have much trouble following. I hadn't seen much of Vienna the day before; my travels had taken me the length of the Ringstrasse and back. I felt that a musical tour might inspire me.

I bought a map, shrewdly targeted at music lovers, in the hotel lobby and set out to conquer the major sights by early afternoon. I breezed through the Johann Strauss Memorial Rooms, where the "King of the Waltz" wrote the "Blue Danube," then lingered in the pleasantly furnished Haydn Wohnhaus, where the great composer wrote his later oratorios and gave lessons to Beethoven. I took a break in a café to wolf down some pastry, ordering everything *mit Schlag,* then sped on to the Beethovenhaus, which had held the actual man only one year but now housed the best collection of his memorabilia.

In the Figarohaus, the respectable middle-class dwelling where Mozart had spent the few happy years of his life, I hit a stroke of good luck. I bumped into an American tour group with a knowledgeable guide. They didn't seem to mind my tagging along with them from room to room, so when they left I followed them to the squalid building where Mozart had died at the age of thirty-five, while working on his Requiem.

The room where Mozart took his last, labored breath was cramped and dismal, but to me it seemed cast over with something darkly luminous, like one of my great artist's paintings, the spirit of that haunting, vaunting music that had come spilling out of him in his final hours and was now playing mournfully, if triumphantly, through me. I closed my eyes and tried to picture the scene: the dying man scribbling furiously into the night—or had he dictated it to his wife, Constanze? I seemed to remember reading that somewhere—giving the world an expression of the mortal condition more articulate than any life had been.

All morning I'd been falling into theatrical reveries, but here I fell harder than ever. I was caught up in clichéd but sincere raptures—wondering how it could be that music that sounded like God's blueprint for sound had come from one man's mind, and shuddering at the thought of what a poorer world it would be had he never been born—when the piercing voice of one of my fellow countrywomen broke through my thoughts.

"Isn't it tragic? A genius like Mozart, and this is how he dies?"

She was a type I knew well, a staple customer of my parents' gallery: Brooklyn loudmouth cum Manhattan socialite, costumed in a tasteless armor of expensive jewels, and probably the proud owner of a tremendous monochromatic canvas she secretly thought was just a bunch of paint, but waxed ecstatic over whenever someone "artsy" came for dinner. My parents had likely sold it to her. I'd been discreetly avoiding this woman since the Figarohaus, when she casually and confidently asserted right into my ear that in her opinion Mozart's greatest work was the *Brandenburg* Concerto, but she'd managed to gravitate next to me without my noticing.

"Isn't it tragic?" she wailed, again to no one in particular—maybe the portly husband, who also tried to keep his distance.

Tragic? I wanted to shout. *Mozart is tragic?* The idea that this woman, dumpy lump of inglorious flesh—squat and solid, with every particle gravitating toward the dirt—could pity the greatest musical mind that had ever lived—eternal and ethereal, with every neuron straining toward the heavens—set something off in me. That Mozart could be pitied! That Mozart could be patronizingly sighed over as tragic! What I wouldn't do to die squalid and tortured and writing the Requiem.

I was short of breath, staring hatefully into the heavily mascaraed eyes of my confused adversary. The misty, romantic stupor that had been steadily building over the course of the morning had dispersed without a trace.

"Callicles skulks at Socrates' side," I shouted inexplicably at her before running out into the street, leaving behind a crowd of questioning looks.

It was a line from one of Adrian's poems, a dialogue between the life-embracing hedonist Callicles, and the life-sacrificing philosopher Socrates, but my friends and I had adopted it as a mantra of sorts; we thought it perfectly summarized the correct ordering of priorities: misery and genius over earthly pleasure and, well, nongenius. Secretly, I'd always considered the notion stark and melodramatic, but saying it now, posing the relevant choice of lives right outside Mozart's home, minutes from the homes of Beethoven, Brahms, Haydn, Schubert, Schoenberg, et al.—in the promised land of the Tribe of Greatness, so to speak—and acknowledging that the choice was not mine to make, that it had been made for me, when God or chance or whoever decided I would just be another plodding plebeian mind, not even capable of composing a few worthwhile scores, I was transported to a state I can only call complete breakdown.

I sat on the low, dirty stoop of a house that may at one time have belonged to an inconsequential neighbor of Wolfgang Amadeus Mozart, and I cried. I don't cry often, and, in particular, I hadn't cried since I'd stumbled on Jean Paul's letter months before—I'd moped, I'd sulked, I'd teared, but I'd never cried. Now I was sobbing, I was wailing: for not being who my parents had so wanted me to be, for not mattering in the only world I cared about, but, most of all, for not being the sort of woman who could love Jean Paul despite.

The group of American tourists I'd recently shocked with my antics tried to stay as far to the other side of the street as possible when they came filing out of Mozart's home. I didn't care that I was making a spectacle of myself. The extremity of the moment was simplifying and invigorating; and when the sobs began to peter out into sighs, I discovered that I felt wonderful. I felt that I wanted to win this competition. It was a delicious feeling, inspiring and electrifying, and though I wasn't in any danger of being late, I began to run toward the hotel to pick up my violin, and then on to the Konzerthaus, where I was scheduled to play Paganini's Caprice No. 4 in an hour. I arrived early, of course, and sat backstage, relishing the churning in my gut, the fluttering in my fingers. When I climbed onto the stage, I said to myself, *You'll play this better than you ever have.* As it turned out, it was far from an interpretively brilliant rendition; my fingers behaved like disconnected machine parts, automatically playing the notes they'd memorized like one of those ghostly player pianos that are always showing up in Bugs Bunny cartoons—but it was technically flawless.

On my way out, I ran into Vlad.

"You have a marvelous tone," he told me, holding open the door. I was tempted to stick around and hear what else he had to say about my playing, but I was more eager to begin practicing again. While I muted my instrument, I tried to call Jean Paul, more out of a sense of duty than from a desire to talk to him. He wasn't home. It was unusual for him to be out at this hour of the day, and it occurred to me that he might be staying away because the apartment felt empty in my absence. The idea that he was missing me made me perversely angry at him, and then at myself for being so illogical and unfair. I ordered up room service, before slipping blissfully into Bach.

Back at the Konzerthaus the next day, the atmosphere, if anything, had gotten more tense, though also more thrilling for all the nervous energy in the air. I hung around backstage with Maria until she was ready to go on, and marveled at the bizarre rituals being enacted there. A plump Asian girl had gone into the bathroom to wash her hands about fifteen times in half an hour, and two Germans were doing something best described as worshipping a lump of rosin. Vlad alone seemed calm, sprawled lazily over a chair, his curls bouncing in time to the music wafting in from the stage.

I left Maria right before she was scheduled to go on, and went to find a seat. From my place in the back of the hall, I listened to every note, willing them all to be perfect. Her Bach was worlds better than her Paganini, but not good enough to counteract the damage that had already been done. Vlad was jaw-droppingly good once again, his tone intimate and welcoming.

Afterward the two of them invited me to join them for dinner, but I ran back to the hotel to practice.

The following afternoon, I played the Bach fugue, effortlessly throwing off the lightning virtuoso passages as if they'd never posed a problem for me. This time I was also pleased with the communicative power of my rendition; I'd discovered the night before that I could get a lot more out of Bach's fugue by paring down the pyrotechnics—reducing the volume at which I performed, the range of dynamics, the level of vibrato. Calling as little attention to itself as possible, the violin was better able to transmit the simple grace of the melodic line.

I rushed back to the hotel immediately after my performance, eager to lose myself in the Ebels, the one piece I had never come to like. It was still a struggle for me not to fly haphazardly through the work, and I stayed up all night laboring over the rare legato and throwing all my energy into the interminable trills. This time I didn't even try to call Jean Paul. I was sure he wouldn't be home anyway.

Again my performance went well, and again I met Vlad on my way out.

"Best Ebels, hands down," he greeted me. "Better than mine, better than Huang Long's. I've been here all day listening. You're sure to make it to the next round."

"I don't know about that," I protested, but I had been there all morning listening, too, and he was right. Some of the violinists had a rich tone I could never achieve on my best days; others had an enviable clarity to their notes; but none had managed to match the tone, the level of panache and splash, the vibrato, the attack, or any of the other infinite variables, with the underlying soul of the work—the spare, beige figure I had found staring out at me so obviously from behind Ebels's cool, restrained music. Sitting there, I had begun to think about what Masterson had once told me, that no one could have completed his concerto as I had, and the comments that Annabelle had let slide from time to time about my singular ability to interpret a work, remarks I'd always dismissed as Hungarian hyperbole. I'd always known I was good at playing the violin, of course, but I thought of this talent as similar to being good at plumbing. I knew the rules, I knew the machinery, and I did a diligent job. Now I found myself considering for the first time whether I might have a unique gift that was not a gift for composing—whether there honestly was something new I could bring to the world through the violin, even if it was not a new arrangement of notes, and whether this might not be a talent I considered worthwhile after all.

"Maria is waiting for us," Vlad continued, breaking into my thoughts. "Her husband's flown in unexpectedly, and they'd like us to join them for lunch." His face showed some distaste when he mentioned the husband.

I followed Vlad to a beer garden in the middle of the Prater, half listening while he pointed out interesting aspects of the city's eclectic architectural styles. It was his first time in Vienna as well, but you couldn't have guessed it from his mastery of the city's history and art. Maria was already sitting with her husband, who was tall and handsome, with no handlebar mustache on his boyish face. They both rose to greet us with kisses.

"Tasha, I didn't get the chance to hear you again. I was sure this time I would, but Gabriel surprised me."

"You shouldn't have missed it," Vlad stated grimly, folding himself into a chair. "It was the best."

"It wasn't the best," I protested.

"It was," Vlad corrected with finality.

We passed the rest of the afternoon anxiously staring into our beers, even Gabriel struck solemn and silent by the mood. (Or perhaps he was always like that.) We only ventured unsteadily out of our seats when it was time to return to the Konzerthaus to hear the semifinalists announced.

As we crowded into the large hall, I wondered if I looked as pitiable as the people around me, eyes wide with undisguised terror, mouth a pinch of reddish white in a sunken face. When a man's voice began booming out syllables in a thick Austrian accent, I felt my knees go limp with every name that wasn't mine.

Vladimir Stobetsky.

Huang Long.

Ryan Melducci.

Maureen Fairchild.

Seven names I couldn't put to a face. And then mine, Natasha Darsky. Dead last, but on the list. It was only when Maria embraced me that I realized her name hadn't been called.

My first instinct when we poured out of the hall was to reach Jean Paul. I waited in a long line to call from the lobby, and let the phone ring on and on before I hung up, exasperated. Didn't he know that tonight was the first cut, I fumed as I dialed my parents' number instead, and didn't he care? Though it only took me a few seconds to realize that, no, he didn't know tonight was the first cut, because I had never gotten in touch to tell him, this did not lessen my anger at all. As I rejoined my new friends, waiting for me near the doorways, I only became more irritated. Somewhere out there, Jean Paul was going about his usual life, unaware that I was experiencing a life-altering moment. I had no doubt that if he'd known he would be proud, but proud in a way that would make my triumph less solid. And this, too, fed my resentment.

Rather than head back to my hotel room to stew, I hit the Vienna party scene with three energetic Brits. Maria and her husband had gone back to the hotel to pack her things, and Vlad had left with them, perhaps to go read or perhaps to practice for the second round. That night, dancing until dawn, downing cocktails bought for me by strange and handsome men who spoke to me in a wide array of languages, I became increasingly more convinced that this was a lifestyle I could grow used to.

I woke up late the next morning, feeling woozy but determined. The next three days were free so that the twelve remaining competitors could prepare for the semifinals, and I knew I had to practice tirelessly if I wanted a shot at the prize.

The night before the semifinals began, I got in touch with Jean Paul. My stomach knotted pleasantly at the sound of his voice, and I imagined crawling into the phone and ending up in his receiver.

"I wish I could have heard!" he kept exclaiming each time I told him about the various events—the Paganini, the Bach, the announcement. "I wish I could have been there. Watch out, Tasha, I might just pull a trick like that Venezuelan husband."

I laughed, mainly because I was happy to have his familiar voice so close to my ear. The idea of his showing up, though, did not amuse me.

"Don't you dare." I kept a little of the laugh in my voice to soften the remark, but it came out forced. "You'd make me nervous. I'd never have gotten this far if you were here." It was true. His being there, I knew, wouldn't just have made it impossible for me to win; it would have made it impossible for me to want to win.

"I can't believe I make you nervous." He sounded hurt, though I'd said it many times before, explaining why his presence in Vienna was unwelcome.

"Well, you do. Now tell me about what's going on at home. Are you working like mad without me there to distract you?"

Though I thought I might be filled with unpleasant emotions when we severed our connection—my increasingly familiar cocktail of guilt, love, anger, pity—all I felt while lying in bed, trying to fall asleep, was jumpy with nerves. Another competitor had given me some prescription beta-blockers that day, claiming that she always popped them before a performance in order to steady her hands, and I decided to try them as a sort of sleeping pill instead, hoping that if my heart stopped racing I'd be able to doze off. There were three days of semifinals, with four violinists performing a night, and I wasn't scheduled to play until the third day. If I was going to be in any shape at all, I needed to find a way to sleep under pressure.

The next few days were a blur of anxiety. I practiced constantly, taking breaks only to eat and sleep and hear my competitors. I felt I was occupying a murky sliver of a dimension where only sound had any firm reality; the taste of food, the feel of my body—my awareness of these things was dreamlike, as though there were a fog separating the real me from any piece of me not engaged in making sound. Only my violin impressed itself upon me with full wakefulness, and this it seemed I heard with every part of my mind and body, as if I were just thousands of ears and fingers, hearing and bowing and fingering. When I found myself onstage, on the third night, this sense of hyperwakefulness became so strong it was almost painful to hear the A sounded from my accompanist's piano, and to tune my violin to match his instrument. But when a voice announced, "Natasha Darsky will be playing Beethoven's Sonata No. 3 and the Paganini-Kreisler *I Palpiti,*" I lost even my sense of this, and disappeared, leaving only the music behind. When I came to, I heard a rousing round of applause, and was ushered out among a half-dozen familiar voices assuring me that I would move on to the next round. When I did make it to the next round—the announcement was made the following morning—I stopped taking the beta-blockers.

We had only a single day to prepare ourselves for the finals, during which time we had one chance to run through our concertos with the musicians assigned to us from out of the many professional orchestras of Vienna. I spent the morning rehearsing with the ensemble, and was just preparing to rush back to my room (I was even considering taking the beta-blockers again, and escaping back into that murky sliver of a dimension that had seemed to be a rather productive place for me) when Vlad caught up with me.

"Don't tell me you're going to practice," he chided. I was clutching my violin case to my chest as if afraid it might run off. "Never, ever practice the day before a final round. You'll lose your mind, and then you'll lose your music. Thank God you have me here."

I let Vlad lead me to the one musical landmark of Vienna I hadn't yet visited, the room where Franz Schubert had died at the age of thirty-one, penniless and as yet uncelebrated as an artist. I had been hoping to catch this site before I left Vienna, but once we were there I hardly noticed the place; I was obsessively running through the two remaining pieces in my head, feeling them already lodged deep in my bones, every trill, every glissando. I thought I was being subtle about my mental practicing, but on the way back to the hotel Vlad said, "I see you are one of those who are already deranged, so what can I do?"

The following morning, I walked over to the Musikverein and tried to picture myself onstage. Though I'd been lagging toward the end of the playing order all along, I was now closer to the front because of the preponderance of finalists from the back end of the schedule. I was going to play my Mendelssohn concerto tonight, between Vlad and Huang Long. The following night, Maureen, Karl Steigler, and John Seabrook would play. The day after that, I would play Mozart, and then the next day—by midnight, they claimed—we would know the winners. I still wasn't sure where I saw any of this taking me, but I knew that I wanted to play well.

That evening, from backstage, I could hear Vlad playing the solo part in Prokofiev's Violin Concerto No. 2, and I changed what it was that I wanted. I wanted to play as well as he did; I wanted to play so the audience felt what I felt, so they experienced the music as I experienced it. Onstage, though, I found there was no audience. There was no stage or score, either; there was only Jean Paul rising from my violin. Jean Paul was always making his way into my music these days, taunting me and forcing me to fight for my voice, but this time he was doing neither; instead, he was wrapping me in the chords and asking me not to close him out. Through the notes I felt the terror of him slipping away from me. By the time I hit the final bar line, I was drenched in sweat and my cheeks were muddied with makeup mixed with tears. The audience was standing, a rare thing in a competition, but this made no impression on me. Nor did I feel much when backstage Huang Long, the next finalist performing that night, told me, "You know, I never understood until tonight why Joseph Joachim called that piece 'the heart's jewel.' " I left the hall numb, dazed, and even when I began to cry in my hotel room, and could not stop for nearly an hour, I was never sure what I was crying about.

The next evening, Vlad and I headed over to the Musikverein

together to hear the next three concertos performed: Maureen playing Brahms, Karl playing Mendelssohn, and John playing Beethoven.

"As far as I'm concerned," Vlad mentioned casually, as he held the door to the hall open for me, "it is only between us now. They are all good violinists, but they are not in our league."

It wasn't a compliment; Vlad didn't give compliments, and he certainly didn't flatter. He was assessing the facts, and this was how he saw them. Amazingly, they were also the facts as I saw them.

The following evening, in my hotel room, getting dressed for my final performance, I removed the necklace Jean Paul had given me on our last night together from the drawer in my bedside table, where I'd been naïvely keeping it. The jewels were too expensive, too ornate to be appropriate, and when I put them on I felt a weight on my breast incommensurate with the actual weight of the stones. I wanted to take the necklace off, but each time I reached behind my neck to undo the clasp I had an image of Jean Paul pleading, "I was hoping you'd wear it at the competition." It was painful to think of him sitting at home, thinking I was wearing the necklace when I wasn't, and so I let the cool metal remain resting against my skin as I ventured out into the frigid Vienna night.

Despite the necklace pressing uncomfortably against me, that evening I performed Mozart better than I'd ever performed it. I felt Jean Paul rising from my violin just as he had the last time, felt all the dread of losing him, and let myself collapse into the music, rather than fight it. This time the audience didn't disappear. I felt them almost as strongly as I felt Jean Paul, felt them come close, and open themselves up to me like I'd opened myself to the notes. I received another standing ovation, a longer one than Vlad's, and out in the lobby I spent ten minutes signing autographs. Back at the hotel, I reached Jean Paul for only the second time in two weeks.

"How did you do?" he asked.

"Really well," was all I said in response. I didn't feel like elaborating, going into the odd sensation I'd felt onstage, or the resounding ovation I'd received, the autographs I'd signed out in the lobby, the tentative acknowledgment that this was something I could do for the rest of my life.

"Do you think you have a chance at winning?"

"I'll come in second," I said, shocking Jean Paul into momentary silence.

I did come in second. Vlad got first prize, Huang third.

Though I'd been expecting it, I still felt woozy after the announcements were made, as if I'd had too much to drink. I called Jean Paul and then my parents, and all three of them told me independently that I was slurring my speech. My mother in particular seemed concerned by my incoherence.

"Are you all right?" she asked after I'd shouted out my news.

"She's fine," my father boomed from the other phone. "She's a brilliant violinist."

There was a warmth in his voice that hadn't been present since I'd wantonly sprouted breasts.

"I'm fine," I echoed ecstatically. "I have to go."

Jean Paul sounded even happier than my parents.

"Tasha, I canelieve it. I canelieve you!" he shouted. "Listen to me, I sound as crazy as you! I can't understand a thing I'm saying!"

I went out to celebrate at a famous disco. Vlad didn't join me, because he was eager to stay home and read as many journals as possible before his flight back to Moscow the following evening. I didn't have a drop of alcohol all night, but I was further gone than anyone there—dancing on tables and belting out songs in a language I couldn't speak, but apparently could sing. It was a visceral joy I was feeling that night—physical and fleeting.

The following morning, I awoke to something more solid and harder to define. As I dressed for the sold-out winners' concert, as I made my way over to the Konzerthaus, as I stood onstage with Vlad and Huang Lang waiting to receive my prize, and as I listened to Vlad perform, I struggled to identify this strange feeling. Was it triumph, pride, nerves? No, it was far simpler, far more basic, but I could not put my finger on it. Only when I stepped to the center of the stage, and began to play Mozart beneath the glaring lights to an audience of strangers who felt like family, did I understand that feeling. It was the feeling of being home.

I SPENT MOST OF THE RETURN FLIGHT WORRYING about my reunion with Jean Paul. I knew he would try to treat me like a returning hero, but I worried that instead he'd end up making me feel like the girl with the flashy consolation prize. That sense of being home—would it come with me?

But when I walked off the plane to see not only Jean Paul but all my friends arrayed around him, I was so disappointed at the discovery that I wouldn't be alone with him that I decided I had managed, through Bach and Mozart, to work my way back to our old love. At the townhouse, Jean Paul had gathered an even larger crowd to celebrate my victory. He'd invited Annabelle, Masterson, a few assorted others from school, and the entire music faculty. The guests stuck around for hours, eating cake and drinking champagne, and to culminate the festivities we all looked on as Annabelle hung my plaque in the most prominent spot in the living room. Through it all, I was itching to get Jean Paul upstairs and into bed, and when the last guests—Amy and Adrian—left, it was all I could do to wait until the door closed on them before pouncing on him. Afterward, lying on the couch with my head against his chest, I thought, *We're going to be OK.*

A few days later, we bought a used Volvo with my prize money. That weekend, we drove it to a bed-and-breakfast in Maine, where we spent an idyllic three days lolling around a king-sized bed. During the drive back, I announced that by my calculations we'd made love twelve times in thirty-six hours, and Jean Paul told me that, one, it was crude of me to keep track, and, two, on our next weekend excursion we would have to do better. But as it happened, that was the last time we used the Volvo together for anything other than hauling groceries.

The morning after we got back from Maine, he asked me to help him solve a problem he'd run up against in one of his compositions, and all my warmth drained out. I hated him, wanted to be far away, and then immediately felt so needy I had to grab on to him and ask him to kiss me.

"I'll ask you to help me more often," he laughed, oblivious.

That night, while he slept, I stayed up until dawn writing out a list of the things I loved about him. But then two wonderful weeks followed, and I didn't even think about the list. We had fallen back into our normal routine, cooking together, joking together, talking late into the night. The only difference was that we rarely worked on "our" music together, but even this didn't seem so strange; I was busy practicing again, this time for the modest European concert tour I'd won as part of my second-place prize. I wouldn't be leaving until July, but five months suddenly seemed a frightfully short period in which to master a masterpiece. Given the legitimate demands on my time, I was sure that Jean Paul had no idea my attitude toward "our" music had changed, but then, one night, as I sat at the table doing homework while Jean Paul prepared dinner, he admitted that my lack of interest in his music was bothering him. It was causing him to lose confidence in his ideas.

"I understood while you were preparing for Vienna that you had no time," he told me, gently, even timidly, as he ladled soup into two bowls. "But now you're done with that, and still we never work together the way we used to. Do you not think it's promising anymore?"

My instinct was to reassure him, but instead I heard a cool voice I did not recognize say, "Well, that's your work, not mine."

He let the subject drop, but the next morning I woke up to find him rereading a bunch of old scores in bed, his brows knit in consternation, his mouth scowling.

"They're amazing," I told him. "You know they're amazing,

and they're only getting better. As soon as I'm done with this tour, I'll be all yours again."

But I knew I wouldn't be, not in that way, and I racked my brain trying to think of an excuse that would get me off the hook once and for all.

At the same time, I was finding myself more tempted than ever to spy on him when he worked. I would spend at least a few minutes of every day hiding in full view in a corner of the living room. I think I was drawn to watch him, in part by a longing to be near Jean Paul in the moments he was most himself, to penetrate into the innermost aspects of his life, like just one more insecure lover obsessed with possessing. But it was also a desire to be near the act itself. By this point, the man I loved, on the one hand, and the art form I worshipped, on the other, were blurring in my mind. Musical creation was Jean Paul, and Jean Paul was musical creation. It was a dangerous situation, but I still thought it was salvageable.

After all, we loved each other. He certainly loved me. I felt it every time those eyes locked into mine, trying to see past the mercurial behavior to whatever lay behind.

But even Jean Paul could lose his temper sometimes. My flashes of hot and cold began to wear on him, and I could see irritation bubbling up periodically. The tension culminated in our first real fight, a month after I got home from the competition. The schedule for my limited tour turned out to coincide with the two weeks Jean Paul and I had been planning to spend in Cognac. Jean Paul couldn't understand why I felt funny asking to rearrange my tour so that the two crucial weeks were left open. I took this as an indication that he didn't regard my new ambitions as worthwhile, though, of course, I couldn't bring myself to accuse him of this outright. Instead, I accused him of being selfish and uncaring, and he accused me of being cowardly and shallow. In the end, I called the competition board to ask for a date change.

After this first argument, it was as if we had gotten a taste for shouting and slamming doors, and soon we fought almost daily. We'd fight about where to eat dinner, what to do on a Saturday night, philosophy, politics, the artistic merits of Philip Glass's minimalism. During every fight, I felt the almost irresistible urge to throw his original sin in his face, to let him know I had seen that letter, to make him feel so guilty that he would crumple up and expire. But to have him know I knew was too much for me—to hear him apologize, explain, to see pity on his face . . . I was fairly certain that, in the event, I would be the one to crumple up and expire on the spot. The shame would be overwhelming. It was also unclear to me whether the letter was even the worst of his sins. Was that his crime, knowing what I was and what I was not? Or was it, rather, his *being* what I could not be? Or even, perhaps, loving me, inexplicably and wholly, despite—loving me, all this time, in a form I was not yet sure I could love myself? I did not know, and so I kept silent about what was eating away at my warmth, and trumped up any number of other complaints to fill the place. I accused him of not paying attention while I spoke, of looking at other women while we were out, and once even of being a closet anti-Semite. That time, he left the house in a fury and I spent the afternoon hoping I hadn't gone too far. But when he came back, he was smiling his wicked smile, and before I even had the chance to stammer an apology he'd stripped me down and pinned me to the concave curve on our grand piano. It was only during sex that we ever seemed to be our old selves anymore.

Instead of dealing with our dissolving relationship, though, instead of thinking it through myself even if not talking it through with him, I blocked it out. I started to keep up with my class reading, and to put some effort into my papers rather than jotting down empty thoughts at the last minute. But, increasingly, the way I kept my mind off my tortured feelings for Jean Paul was to burrow deeper into my tour preparations. Though a limited concert tour did not in any way spell out instant professional acclaim, I had high hopes pinned on it, and entertained a vague premonition of artistic fulfillment. At the least, it was a remarkably cool way to lead into my senior year of college, and for the next months I reveled in Johannes Brahms the way I'd once reveled in Jean Paul. I'd been invited to perform the Mozart concerto on my tour, but I'd gotten it into my head that it had to be Brahms, with his music full of frustration and longing, that would launch my career. I wrote individually to all five conductors, requesting the change of program, and all agreed to let me go ahead with it.

One tremendous blowup between Jean Paul and me had been over the issue of where I would practice. Jean Paul had reasonably asked whether I might consider finding some space outside the apartment, and though my initial response had been to rail against this proposition, by the next day I'd arranged exclusive use of one of the Adams House practice rooms. Though I didn't live there any longer, I was still affiliated with my old dorm, and with Adrian's help I convinced them that this would be a worthy use for the neglected, drafty, yet windowless practice room. They hadn't said I could decorate, but I did anyway, turning the room into a shrine to Brahms, hanging his portrait and plastering an entire wall with the score to the concerto.

I prepared for the violin concerto in a different way from how I usually learned a piece of music. It was a method I'd wanted to try for a while, but had never felt able to justify in terms of time or effort. Now that the violin was taking center stage in my ambitions, however, I felt ready to indulge my ideas. I started by reading two tremendous biographies of Brahms. Once I'd ingested the man's life and times, I spent a solid week just reading the score over and over. I first learned every note and then moved on to my analysis—asking myself why these notes here and not those, why this crescendo, why these swells. It was only after I'd internalized the music, feeling I knew it intimately, that I put bow to violin. My purpose had been get to know the music on its own terms, unsullied by considerations of instrumentation—proper fingering and the like—so that the ideal I was trying to reach once I began playing wasn't dragged down by the reality of my skill. It was the first work, other than Masterson's, on which I placed my distinctive stamp.

Around this time, I also resumed regular contact with my friends. I'd never lost touch with them, but I hadn't made much of an effort to integrate them into my life, either. Now I went back to seeing them frequently. This was more difficult than I'd anticipated, because collective get-togethers had become out of the question. An ill-conceived one-night stand between Amy and Ari had set off a domino effect of disturbances; it had led to a confrontation between Graham and Ari, during which Graham revealed his borderline incestuous passion for Amy. This, in turn, led to Amy's feeling "violated" and announcing that she would not talk to Graham again until he rooted out any such feelings. A few weeks later, possibly because tensions were running high, there was a heated altercation between Graham and Michael over *The Brady Bunch*; Graham claimed the show was a high form of kitsch art, Michael accused him of being a secret connoisseur of the lowbrow for lowbrow's sake, and they called off the friendship. Gregory, in the meantime, had lost interest in the artsy crowd, and was dividing all his time between the math department and his debutante fiancée. And I, of course, had been living off campus in a world just big enough for two. Or maybe not quite big enough.

Now I made an effort to bring my life with Jean Paul and my life outside Jean Paul together. I began inviting Jean Paul to join me for lunches on campus, invitations he sweetly accepted even though he surely still found my friends laughable. Once, a week before the semester ended, I even invited Adrian to dinner at the apartment. It might sound strange that this should have been a singular occasion, but it was. Other than at my coming-home party, Jean Paul and I had never invited another person into our home. It wasn't any sort of explicit policy, but it had seemed obvious to both of us that no one else belonged. Only now neither of us seemed to belong, either, and it was partially my hope that by opening our home to another person we would dilute the intensity and perhaps save our relationship.

Adrian's visit was the last happy time Jean Paul and I spent together. It was the first summery day of the season, hot and sticky but still with some May breezes bringing periodic relief. I spent all afternoon cooking with the windows open, the pungent Algerian flavors mixing with the scent of fresh grass and hot dirt. I imagined it was the aroma of Mediterranean domestic bliss. For my twentieth birthday, Jean Paul's mother had sent me a handmade recipe book filled with her son's favorite dishes. I hadn't known whether I should be offended at the antifeminist implications or flattered that she was relinquishing full control to me. But other than occasionally flipping through the pages just for curiosity's sake, I'd never had much use for it; until that day, I'd never cooked without Jean Paul.

By the time Jean Paul came down for breakfast, I had every burner in the kitchen going, and every smooth surface was covered with bowls in various stages of use.

"Get out!" I'd shouted, swinging a pot holder at him as he hopped around me peeking under lids. "It's a surprise."

I'd told Adrian I was going to pick her up in the car, which I took any excuse to drive, and so at six I went to get her.

When we walked back into the house, we were met with a manic explosion of color. I heard Adrian take in a high, shallow breath beside me. Jean Paul had filled the whole place with flowers in the half-hour I'd been gone, leaving me to wonder if he'd imbued this night with as many ambiguous expectations as I had. We took a few steps farther in, and Jean Paul came leaping, uncharacteristically, down the stairs, and swung an arm over each of us.

"Welcome, Adrian!" he shouted, gaily. "Wait until you see what Tasha's done! I'm sorry, I peeped. I had to. The smells wouldn't leave me alone!"

He'd also set the table while I was gone, using the nice plates we'd bought in Maine, and heaping the center with white tulips.

"Let's eat. Tasha, please, let's eat!" He was dragging us toward our seats in childlike eagerness.

The food was a resounding success, as Jean Paul couldn't help exclaiming every few bites. I'd been worried about how he and Adrian would get along, but the three of us couldn't have had more fun together, laughing and drinking bottle after bottle of wine, late into the night.

When I walked with Adrian to the door, she was in verbal raptures.

"'From fairest creatures we desire increase, that thereby beauty's rose might never die,'" she whispered, wine thick on her breath, as I searched the closet for her backpack. It tended to annoy me when she quoted from the vast store of poetry housed in her mind, but not tonight.

"The world is good sometimes," she concluded solemnly, inspecting the floral-patterned molding around our door frame. She loved Victorian houses, with all their wooden detail, and I realized as she peered pointedly at the wall that I'd forgotten to give her the tour. "It's good tonight."

"It is," I said, misting up myself at the fantasy I'd worked us into, torn right out of Adrian's wordy imagination.

We drove in silence to Harvard Square, and before climbing out of the car, she patted me warmly on the arm rather than saying goodbye. At the door of Adams House, Adrian turned back toward me and gave a delicate, birdlike flit of the wrist that made me think of the movement Jean Paul's hair made when he threw his head back in pleasure. The association sent a shock of urgent anticipation through me.

Back at home, I raced to the kitchen, where Jean Paul was washing dishes, whistling the melody to a new composition.

"Forget the dishes," I suggested, walking up behind him.

"Just let me finish the plates. We'll get the pots tomorrow."

"I said, forget the dishes." I gave the order in my sexiest voice, and began untying the strings holding up my sundress.

"Dishes forgotten." He smiled and pulled me toward him, his warm soapy hands sliding over my skin, sliding, sliding.

Afterward, lying in bed, slick and sticky in the motionless heat of the room, he started whispering again about our shared destiny, a topic he hadn't discussed since before Vienna. I gulped in his words. I was drowning, and even then, wanting more than I had in a long time to keep on loving Jean Paul, I knew what I'd have to do to save myself.

BACK IN MY PARENTS' WEST VILLAGE BROWNSTONE after school ended, I gave myself over to last-minute tour preparations. My focus turned from Brahms to ticket finalizations, hotel accommodations, and the all-important wardrobe issue. My mother cheerily took on duties as head of costume, dragging me all over the city in search of the perfect gowns. We found two: a blue satin Yves Saint Laurent with a skintight bodice, spaghetti straps, and a flowing skirt; and a yellow silk Japanese-inspired number we unearthed in a trendy SoHo boutique. So that I would fit into these, she put me on a drastic crash diet and exercise regimen, and though I felt dizzy and lightheaded for the first few days and complained that she was quite possibly starving me to death, by the end of two weeks I was back to having only two prominent sets of curves, and my energy levels were soaring.

At school my tour had been something I kept to myself, my own private fantasy, but at home it was a collective obsession. My parents treated it like a new reason to live: "My own daughter, an international sensation," my father kept saying. "Not quite," I chided, but I loved to hear it. Though my parents specialized in the visual arts, they were confident their talent for promoting promise into celebrity would be just as effective in the world of classical music. "You're going to be a star like classical music has never seen," my mother would shriek from time to time, usually when I'd just come out of the dressing room in some thousand-dollar dress. "You're going to be bigger than the Beatles."

I didn't have much interest in being bigger than the Beatles—or in international celebrity of any sort, for that matter—but I did want to succeed in some musical art, to be worthy of my parents' hyperbole. My parents' enthusiasm made me forget, at least temporarily, that this was not my first choice of careers. To my parents, it seemed now, becoming a violinist was the greatest thing that could have happened to me. If they saw any unflattering difference between writing music and playing it, they certainly didn't let that bother them. My suspicion now is that they saw no great difference—or that presentation, for them, was, if anything, the higher good. This baffled me, since I'd always taken it for granted that they valued creation above all else. Not that I bothered thinking deeply about these issues; I was too excited.

After three weeks at home, I left for London, flanked by my exuberant managers, Mom and Dad. Whatever doubts I might have had about the sort of life I was choosing disappeared during my time in London. I was blown away by the standing ovations, the cover stories, the autographs, the constant bustle. I got to read the first real reviews of my work, and they were glowing: "compelling charm," "bewitching lyricism," "exquisite sensitivity," and my favorite: "It was as if Brahms were whispering in her ear. I felt as if I were hearing it for the first time—and I was: this was how it is supposed to be played." I got to meet my first fans.

Then on to Paris, Berlin, Budapest, Salzburg. It was the same in every city. My parents and I would take the train in the morning, and drop off our bags at the hotel, where a favorite small painting of mine by an obscure artist was always waiting on the wall, courtesy of my mother's spotty but intense thoughtfulness. She must have spent a good deal of money shipping it from place to place ahead of us. I would rest my eyes for an hour or two, then rush off to rehearse with the orchestra. At night there'd be fancy dinners, sometimes just the three of us, sometimes joined by the conductor or some other distinguished musician. I'd head to bed early, wake up for another rehearsal, and then, that evening, I'd perform.

My parents arranged incredible last-minute feats of publicity in London, Paris, and Berlin: lavish coming-out–type parties with guest lists that read like a who's who in the musical life of each city; exclusive interviews in the major papers, more appropriate for someone with three times my stature; press releases with glossy photos. I left each of these locations a minor celebrity.

In the middle of all this excitement were the two weeks I spent in Cognac while my parents jetted off to Greece to visit a potential client. I had been looking forward to this visit all summer, certain that in the romance of French vineyards everything bad between Jean Paul and me would fade away. But the minute Jean Paul picked me up at the train station, I knew the trip was going to be something else entirely. "You look exhausted," he said, taking me in with a look of concern. "Here you'll be able to rest in absolute peace and quiet and feel like yourself again." It was all I could do not to shout, "But I hate peace and quiet!" and as I forced the words down it dawned on me that, after the constant glitter and whisking of the past few weeks, there was nothing I wanted less than to be trapped in still and silent countryside, even with Jean Paul. The house itself, as we drove up, seemed to loom like a grand and ancient prison, with formal dining, near-dead grandparents, and a stiffly proper mother chosen as particularly cruel forms of torture. I could not imagine what I had found so charming about the place last summer, and wondered how I would survive the two weeks. I ended up surviving just fine, but Jean Paul and I spent a high percentage of the visit apart. He was racing to get a score ready to submit to a competition, and despite my earlier promise to resume my role as his partner when the semester was over, after the first afternoon of sitting beside him while he raved about every bar he'd written and then cursed each in turn, I was ready for a break. Luckily, Clarisse and her daughters had driven up that day for the remainder of the summer, and I spent the two weeks riding horses, swimming, and playing tennis with them while Jean Paul labored. I could tell he was hurt, but he never reproached me for abandoning him and "our" music. The car ride back to the train station was tense and silent; I was looking forward to the constant commotion of the concert circuit, and thinking how hard it was to imagine trapping myself here permanently after graduation, in just one year, which was the plan Jean Paul was now advocating. It seemed to me akin to having eyesight for one day and then poking out your eyes. I thought this through during the whole train ride to Vienna, but I could not decide what to do about it.

Of all the concerts, Vienna was the best, and this wasn't just because I was so relieved to be away from Cognac. Word of my success had preceded me, and the city welcomed me home like a returning daughter. An entourage of eminent musicians and press greeted me at the airport, and the conductor of the Vienna Philharmonic personally escorted me to my hotel. At the concert the next night, I played the first encore of my life, and also the second. Vlad was in town that weekend, Vienna being the next stop on his fifteen-city tour, and he managed to make it to my concert despite his heavy schedule. Afterward he came out to dinner with me and my parents, and charmed the socks off of them.

By the time I arrived back in New York, other offers for solo appearances were flooding in. My tour had made more of an international impression than Vlad's, not because I was more skilled, but because people seemed to find something exciting about the way I played. I had enough invitations lined up within my first week home to last me the whole of autumn and into winter, if I chose to ditch school altogether. But what was not waiting for me at home was a message from Jean Paul. I had been sure there would be something from him: a letter, flowers, an extravagant gift to let me know he was proud and had forgiven me for Cognac. Though I was disappointed to find there was no word from him, I also recognized that, in a way, this was a good thing: we were both alienated; we were in sync in that, at least.

During my first night home, pondering Jean Paul's silence, it occurred to me that if I could learn to make peace with becoming a violinist, maybe I could also learn to make peace with the way things stood between Jean Paul and me. After all, the violinist puts all her talent, her energies, the material of her whole being at the service of another mind's vision—a vision that becomes her own and yet is never hers. To be exclusively a virtuoso and enjoy it, you must be able to sacrifice yourself selflessly to music you didn't write. Though, of course, I wasn't a virtuoso in this pure way yet. In fact, though I didn't realize it, at that point I wasn't submitting to the score at all, which I think is what made me such an instant sensation. There was still that revolt against the notes I felt every time I played, which made every piece of music into a lovers' spat with Jean Paul, a tug-of-war over full ownership of the music. Because of this element, audiences found my playing raw and unclassical. "It's almost like watching an action movie," a journalist once reported in *Vogue,* and it's telling enough that I was written up there. I think if I'd been able to accept my relationship with Jean Paul for what it seemed to me to be—a partnership between two very unequal talents—I never would have made a name for myself. Not because the relationship would have prevented me from pursuing my career with full gusto, but because I just wouldn't have been the sort of person who can captivate an audience by the sheer force of will she throws up against a score.

I'm getting ahead of the story, though. I hadn't become a household name at this point, only a buzz on the classical-music scene. The word was out that something special was taking place: a young girl was playing Brahms like an R-rated flick, and everyone from Johnny Carson to the New York Philharmonic was inviting me to perform.

Egged on by my parents, Annabelle, and Mrs. Blau, I made a decision.

I had a choice: I could return to school, tough out my senior year, and then resume the touring afterward, or I could put off the schooling I'd been all but ignoring for so long anyway, and start a career. There were considerations that pulled me toward the former—the college degree it would have been nice to have under my belt (could I fool myself into thinking I'd eventually go back if I didn't finish that year?), the friends and familiar way of life to which I'd be returning, the question of who I would study with if I were so far from Annabelle. And, of course, there was the terror of giving up Jean Paul. Could I send him off to the vineyards alone, embark on a life that didn't—that, really, couldn't—include him?

It was clear to me what choice Jean Paul would have made if he were in my place: he was able to love with the same maddening ease with which he was able to create. I think, in the end, it was knowing this that made it impossible for me to choose the path that included him.

IT WOULD HAVE BEEN SINFULLY EASY TO CONVINCE MYself that it was in Jean Paul's best interest for me to break things off with him by telephone or airmail. After all, we were an ocean apart when I made the decision, and I was certain that he wouldn't want to return to the United States once he got the news. Though he was ostensibly at Harvard to study with Robert Masterson, he'd long since ceased to think of Masterson as crucial to his progress, and I knew if it weren't for me Jean Paul would have returned to the conservatoire by now; his home institution had made it clear they'd go to some lengths to reclaim him—they'd offered him extra money, a choice practice room to himself, and an assured professorship as soon as he completed his degree. What would be more merciful than to spare him the unnecessary trip abroad and the weeks of ignorance? What would be more merciful than to spare myself the sight of that face again? But I couldn't bring myself to do it. I felt that I owed it to both of us, but especially to Jean Paul, to tell him in person.

I set out in the Volvo the morning his flight was scheduled to arrive, going straight from New York to Logan airport. I cried through much of the drive, and when I wasn't crying I was marveling at the sheer lunacy of the idea—how had I ever contemplated giving up a man I loved, a man like this man?—vowing that I'd never entertain it again. I would pick him up and take him to our home, and somehow we'd manage to balance my touring schedule with our life together. This is what I was thinking when I parked the car and raced to the international-arrivals gate, gripped by the need to throw myself into his arms and bury my traitorous head against him. But the moment I caught sight of him loping toward me with an unhurried urgency, I knew it had to be done.

It's funny how a face you've seen a million times can strike you as unfamiliar after a long absence. As he came toward me, I felt I was seeing his face for the first time, and wondered how I'd ever looked at it before without thinking immediately of painful love. I was reminded of my initial impression of him: that he was a man who was waiting for despair. I recoiled from his embrace, but he didn't notice.

"I've missed you so terribly," he breathed into my ear, still gripping my ribs too tightly. "I want to devour you right here."

I tried to laugh naughtily like he would have expected, but it was hard to sound breezily lustful over the unlustful trembling.

I waited until we were in the car to bring up the topic I'd driven all this way to raise. The familiar landscape out the window reassured me that this would not be the end of the world. I just had to do it and then it would be done, something I'd been doubting more than ever since he'd wrapped his arms around me. It began to seem almost cruelly easy for me to extricate myself from Jean Paul's life; all I had to do was say, "It's over," and I would be on my own. The ease of it was almost more terrifying than the aftermath. The world was a thin and empty place if a few words had the power to destroy an axiomatic truth.

He'd been telling me about a new piece he was writing, a commission from the Paris Symphony. They were hoping, he told me, to have it from him in time for a Christmas read-through.

"You'll come, won't you? I need you there," he'd more asserted than asked, smiling his sometimes charming, sometimes aggravating grin, half sheepish and half arrogant. I would have loved to find it aggravating then, or even charming, but instead I found it pitiful.

"Probably not."

"Why not? This will be over your vacation."

"I'll be touring."

"Oh, during the entire vacation?"

"All year, pretty much, if things go well."

"All year? What about school?"

"That's my big news. I'm not enrolled this year." I tried to keep my voice as casual as possible, as if I weren't revealing a life-altering plan.

"What? You're not going to be here all year?"

"I guess not." Boston's North End rolled by our window, filled with the cozy Italian restaurants in which we'd spent so many nights. But I'd spent many nights there without him as well. I could go there again if I wanted to.

"So why am I going to be here?"

"Maybe you shouldn't be. I'm sorry I didn't tell you earlier. I thought it would be best to do it in person."

"But I'll come with you. I could have arranged it better if I'd had time."

"Don't be crazy. How will you get any work done? What about your commission?"

"I can work anywhere. The music goes where I go. I go where you go."

"But I don't want you to come."

"Not at all? How will I see you?"

"I guess you won't."

There was silence from the other side of the car. I had to keep my eyes on the road, and this saved me from having to see his expression; I tried not to imagine it. The next time his voice came out, minutes later, it was frighteningly monotone, devoid of all its lusciously deep musical qualities.

"I think I understand what you're saying, but I can't believe that I'm right."

"No, you're right," I said. "Don't you think it's time, honestly? I mean, we were miserable at Cognac. We were heading toward miserable all last spring. We don't work anymore."

"Of course we work!" The life was back in his voice, the invigorating rage I'd first heard over coffee almost two years ago, which had sent me shivering into love with its forcefulness. "I know Cognac was bad. And last spring we had our problems. But I've been thinking a lot about it, about what's gone wrong, and I think it has nothing to do with us."

"What does it have to do with, then?"

"We need a change of scenery. Boston is stifling. It's such a provincial city. This is good, your touring. I only wish you'd told me sooner. We'll travel all over. We'll both be happy. We'll go back to the way we were."

"It had nothing to do with Boston. It was us."

"No, Tasha. I think you're wrong."

"No, Jean Paul. Trust me, I wish I were wrong." I was crying now, the tears obscuring my vision. "I love you, but we don't work. I don't want you with me."

He reached into the backseat, and it crossed my mind that he was reaching for a makeshift weapon. Was he pathologically romantic enough to kill us both, with a blow to the head from an electric shaver, rather than separate? But when he straightened again, he was holding what looked like a picture album. He opened it, and I glanced over. There were some pictures of me in black and white, and some cut-out articles. My reviews and interviews.

"I collected them all summer long. It was hard to get some of them. It took me forever to track down the ones from Salzburg."

"That's sweet, but how is it supposed to make me change my mind?"

"Tasha, I need you. You need me. We belong together. You can't do this."

"I can and we don't."

"Listen to me. You don't know what you're saying. You know we belong together. You know we were made to be together."

His voice was taking on the mesmerizing tones of his polemics, and I was certain that if I could see his eyes they would have been infected with that crazed glimmer.

"Please don't make this any harder than it has to be," I pleaded.

"It doesn't have to be at all."

"It does!"

We pulled in front of the townhouse, and I looked straight at him for the first time. Because of the authority in his voice, I'd expected him to look threatening, but instead he looked vulnerable.

"Aren't you getting out of the car?" he asked. I was still gripping the wheel.

"I saw what you wrote to your mother about me." I'd been

working up the courage to say it all along; it was even more painful than I'd anticipated. So reifying. "It does have to be."

I couldn't look at him, but I could tell from the feel of his body beside mine that the mention of a letter brought no recognition. Why should it have?

"You told her I had no talent for composing."

I stole a glance and saw him pondering, looking much more calm now that he saw there was a tangible reason, something he could argue against.

"I never said that." He gave this line triumphantly. He had won; I was wrong; we belonged together.

"You meant it," I insisted, but he was shaking his head now, and I wasn't even sure if he'd heard me.

"Tasha, our music . . ."

"Your music."

"Yours, too. The pieces you wrote before me, I mean."

"Are garbage, just like you said. That's not important. I'm a violinist. That's what I am."

"No. No. That's not true. I never said that, you must be mistaken."

"I'm not."

"Come in," he said now, his voice almost back to its usual pitch, seductive and musical. I thought of following that voice inside. I thought of the scene that would follow, of the bare brunt of him pushed up against me in the foyer, rhythmically dissolving my willpower.

"I think it's better if I don't. I have a long drive back."

"You're going back tonight?"

"I think that would be best."

"You're not even going to come in?"

I didn't answer.

"What about your clothes, your books, your things?"

Again I didn't answer. I'd driven up the week before and collected everything of mine in a car-full of boxes. I'd stayed the night in the townhouse, but not alone: all my friends—except Ari, who was still at home in Israel for the summer—gathered with me, putting aside their differences and staying up all night the way we used to, shouting zealously over one another's voices, covering every topic from art to politics to the lowest sort of gossip about our classmates. In the morning, I hugged each of them, not knowing when I'd see them again, and then stopped by Masterson's office to drop off a note telling him goodbye. The next morning, he called me at my parents' house to wish me luck with what he called, in legitimately human tones, "the beginning of a brilliant career."

"It's not fair!" Jean Paul was beginning to sound desperate, panicked again. "You need to give me a chance to change your mind."

"How? With sex?"

"It's not fair!" he roared.

"Jean Paul, please . . ." I pleaded.

"No *please*!" he screamed, putting his hand on the door. I wanted him to open that door and never look back. I was dreading the moment when he would. "No *pleases* from you. I trusted you, Tasha. I gave you my soul. Not that I had a choice. My soul has always belonged to you, as you well know."

I was cowering near my own door. Of course, I'd heard him talk like this before, invoking language of necessity and unbreakable bonds, but I'd never realized until then how firmly he believed all the melodramatic absurdities he spouted.

"You've betrayed me, in the worst way someone can betray."

"I didn't mean to," I sputtered weakly, my eyes down.

"So don't." His voice was soft again, as if it belonged to a different person from the one who had just been raging at me. I felt a hand on my arm.

"No," I whispered, shaking my head.

I heard the door open, and close again. Then the back door opened and closed. I looked up and saw him walking toward our house. When he got to the porch, he turned around, and his blue-black eyes locked into mine for the last time.

I turned the ignition and sped away, feeling his eyes follow me down the street. I noticed halfway through Connecticut that he'd left the scrapbook lying on the passenger seat. I wasn't sure if it had been an oversight or a punishment.

It was nearing 3 a.m. when I found a parking spot near my parents' brownstone. I practically crawled on all fours up the narrow staircase to my bedroom. I knew I had gotten off easy. Jean Paul could have dragged our breakup on for hours, days even, and instead it was over in a matter of minutes. But as I lay in bed fully clothed, too tired even to take off my shoes, all I could picture was Jean Paul, alone in our apartment, betrayed and inconsolable. *I've betrayed him,* I kept thinking. *He gave me his soul.*

On some level I knew this was crazy. I hadn't betrayed him, I'd extricated myself from an unhappy relationship. And it wasn't as if he'd forfeited his soul in giving it to me. It was I who'd been cut to a sliver by my decision. He was still himself, in all his glory. What was I now? It was too painful to think. I was without Jean Paul.

III

p a tempo
p a tempo

I OPEN THE CAB DOOR BEFORE IT'S COME TO A FULL stop, but have to fumble with the fare. By the time I am up the steps of the brownstone, my mother is waiting in the open doorway.

"She's upstairs, in your room." She's whispering, though there's no way Alex can hear us from the fifth floor. "But I'm not sure she wants to see you."

"Did you have a fight?" I hear her hiss, as I head up the narrow staircase, now so crammed with books and magazines there's hardly room to maneuver. Her voice skirts close enough to the edge of audibility that I just keep moving. "She's not going back to Indiana so soon, is she?"

At the third-floor landing, I catch strains of an ancient and scratchy record turning on my old player. Then I see Alex's feet, heading down. I stop where I am, and I register the real displeasure that shoots through her at the sight of me, a recoil almost, throwing her backward a few steps. It is a hurtful thing to witness, but I try to smile anyway.

"What are you doing here?" she demands, still moving backward up the stairs, as I move forward.

"I came to talk to you." One step for me, one for her, one for me, one for her. We're acting out the penultimate scene in a horror movie.

"Well, if I'd wanted to talk to you, I wouldn't be here, would I?" She has stopped moving now, and looms four stairs above me, her long, lean body looking vulnerable from this angle. She crosses her arms in warning, and gives a challenging toss of her hair.

"I know you're upset."

"You know nothing about it."

"Well, I know Jean Paul," I offer, hunting. I mean to indicate that I might have some insight, after all, into what's upsetting her, since I do, at least, know the man and his maddening ways, but that is not how it ends up sounding. It sounds instead like an attempt to force the issue too soon, but the damage is done, and so be it: I *do* want the issue forced. The same ghastly look I saw on her face this afternoon has crossed her face again, and I notice now that this look is disbelief mixed with something else. Belief, perhaps. In that look I lose whatever hopeful doubt I'd been hanging on to; Jean Paul has found his way into my daughter's life.

"What does he mean to you?" I demand in as firm a tone as I've ever used with her.

She gives me nothing; even the ghastly look is gone. Her face is placid, unconcerned. She can pull this expression off at will; it's a frustrating talent.

"Do you want to know what he means to me?" I pursue, softer now.

"I think I caught the drift this afternoon. Your 'love affairs,' and all that."

Her face is still placid, but her voice wavers under the thick coating of sarcasm she's thrown up around her words. Until now I hadn't even remembered that ludicrous statement of mine, a flip, careless remark that at any more lucid time in my life I would not have made. I'd played right into that reporter's hands, though surely he'd have asked about Jean Paul regardless. It crosses my mind for a moment that those words only presented themselves to me because Jean Paul was in my thoughts, from Alex's music rife with his ideas. It strikes me that the last few days have been unfolding with notable bad luck.

"Do you want to know, or just make bad guesses?" I ask, my voice as neutral as I can make it.

"Frankly, what I'd really like is to find a spot in the world where your long arm has not yet reached. But since that's proved impossible . . ." She trails off with a dramatic shrug, but I can see tears gather in the corners of her eyes, looking incongruous on the blandly smiling face.

"What does he mean to you?" I ask again.

"Why does it matter?" She drags the last word out in a high-pitched whine, gulping in air between syllables like a small child. She is losing control, and there's nothing she hates more.

"I have no idea why it matters," I say, gently. "But obviously it matters to you a great deal."

Her placid face disappears, and she gives me what I know she thinks is a forbidding glare. To me it is anything but. Like nearly everything she does, it only makes me want to soothe her, and I can see her registering this desire in some aspect of my bearing. She takes another step backward and holds up a hand, fending off whatever emotional swaddling she thinks I am looking to envelop her in.

"Please," she says, her voice hot but back in control. "If you want to help, then just leave me alone."

I'm trying to stifle the urge to plead with her when again she says, "Please. For now?" The urge to plead with her vanishes; she is no longer ordering, she is begging, and I can tell that this conversation is too much for her, that I am causing her real pain. Still, I cannot stop myself from asking, "Are you really flying back tomorrow morning?"

"I haven't decided yet. As you might have guessed, things didn't work out there quite as I'd planned."

"I had some inkling," I say. There's a hint of her wry smile, but it could just be the light catching in one of the tears streaming down her face.

I turn back down the stairs, ready to try the only other way I know of to find out what links those two.

I HAD MY FAIR SHARE OF MEN AFTER JEAN PAUL. MY FIRST year on tour, there were a few ill-thought-out days in Paris with my fellow Vienna-launched violinist, Vladimir Stobetsky. A couple of years later, there was a month in Manhattan with the composer Albert Davies. Johann Reicher, conductor of the Berlin Philharmonic, and I lasted almost three months, though most of that time was spent on different continents. Peter Ramrock, whose punk operas were such a hit before a cocaine addiction turned all his music incomprehensible, I hardly remember knowing, though I did spend my twenty-seventh birthday among the plastic sculptures of his London apartment. There were equally short relationships with a handful of lesser musical lights, men I met on tour, in recording studios, once even on the sidewalk outside the walk-up I'd rented three blocks from my parents' brownstone. None of these relationships involved love, or even particularly strong liking. My romantic life was far more robust in rumors than in life. In fact, I spent most of my free nights watching old movies with my parents. Given my chaste existence, I found it amusing to see lines like the one in a *New York* magazine review that read, "Darsky just might be the most erotic performer in any industry outside pornography," or the *People* profile that referred to me as "a shot of sex appeal straight to the heart of classical music."

Actually, at first lines like these didn't amuse me at all. It was frightening to read such public appraisals of such a personal nature, but within a year or two it came to seem normal, just as it came to seem normal that a mystifying, one-sided conversation with strangers assaulted me by the bagful each morning—the offers for marriage, the requests for love and beauty advice, even the series of Thomas Mann quotes I received in small installments over the course of several years, as well as the more traditional fan letters, all of these answered by my father, sometimes quite floridly. But even after I acclimated to life in the public eye, every now and then all the dissection and speculation, the resilient question "Who gets all that ardor offstage?" could depress me, because the truth was, no one got that ardor offstage. Jean Paul, in some sad and strange way, was still the main man in my life. Certainly, it was still our relationship I played out day after day, in every major city in the world. For eight years I performed to a memory of him, without knowing where he was, how he was, or why he'd never burst onto the classical-music scene as he'd seemed poised to do when I last saw him.

Then, on one rainy October day, Jean Paul came back into my life.

I'd traveled to the conservatory of Oberlin College to give a master class and a performance. It was just one more stop, but it was a turbulent stop because it was the first professional appearance I'd ever made without my mother. She'd been with me since my first tour, shuttling from warm to cold to warm again, avoiding seasons, living above the laws of that awful thing, the real world. (My father, meanwhile, was stuck in the brownstone, booking concerts, arranging interviews, dealing with finances, and only becoming enraged every so often at handlers or the press. They'd sold the gallery my first year on tour.)

Not having my mother at Oberlin with me, I'd managed to get myself lost, and I'd just stopped to catch my breath and my bearings. I was disoriented and exhausted, but that was nothing new. I was always disoriented and exhausted, because touring was draining, demanding, possibly an inhuman feat. But I was also happy, because I was always happy, because I thrived on my inhuman feat, and the memory of life before seemed intolerably slow. Other than running late and getting lost, I'd been doing remarkably well without the flower-scented safety net of my mother around me, and was realizing how sincerely I meant the line I always gave to interviewers: that the reason I never felt homesick or rootless as I crisscrossed the globe was that every orchestra I ever visited, no matter how grand or dinky, felt like home to me. I was just forming this thought when my eyes wandered onto a flier bearing the name "Jean Paul Boumedienne."

It was on a bulletin board, mixed in with ads for used futons, cheap spring-break packages, and offers for professional editing help, a deep-green piece of paper that stuck out at me like a glaring inconsistency in an otherwise harmonious world. "Tonight only," it read, "new music by Jean Paul Boumedienne. *Rhapsody from Hell*. Sully Church. 11 p.m."

At first it seemed like a private message, then a cruel joke. There had been a time when I would have taken the poster for the most natural thing in the world, when I expected that any minute he would burst forth, the messiah for whom we'd all been waiting, just as his teachers and I had predicted. I expected it so vividly, in fact, that for the first few years after our breakup I truly dreaded the moment when I would walk into a party to find him there, being fêted as new Next Big Thing to emerge on the music scene. I worried that if I were locked in those blue-black eyes and they implored me to give up everything I'd built and come trap myself in the splendid quiet of the vineyards, I might just give in this second time. And if those eyes danced over me, unfeelingly, my heart might break and all my music turn bland.

But he never did show up in my circles—or any circles I heard about—and after a while I stopped expecting him to. I don't know why this should be, but once I stopped waiting to hear his name it became almost unthinkable that I would. It was as if he had ceased existing for anyone but me. For me, though, he existed acutely. I don't think it's an exaggeration to say that not a day had gone by when Jean Paul hadn't entered my thoughts, even if only in passing. Sometimes I would find myself humming an unearthly harmony, simultaneously jarring and moving, and I would realize that it had come from a piece Jean Paul had written. I'd wonder then where he was. Inevitably there would also come the wave of guilt, and I'd hear his voice saying, "You've betrayed me, in the worst way someone can betray." I couldn't help fearing that perhaps I *had* betrayed him in the worst way—that is, that I'd made it impossible for him to compose, that I'd made him disappear.

And now here he was, or at least—or perhaps not "at least" at all—here was his music. Was he here, too? I was tempted to believe he was, though he certainly wasn't a member of Oberlin's music faculty, all of whom were waiting at that moment to take me to dinner.

I looked at my watch. It was nearly eight, three hours until eleven. I assumed that "tonight" meant that night, and not some tonight in the past, because the poster was crisp and clean, and lying on top of a mess of others; it looked like it had been put up within the last few hours. And eleven? It was an odd time for a concert, but a misprint that important was unlikely on a sign that pithy. Could I make it in time to hear the concert without seeming rude to my hosts? I had to.

When I did make it to the church, after walking through the driving rain for almost half an hour—the church was about as far from campus as a building could be while still technically in Oberlin—I scanned the crowd but saw no head that looked as though it belonged to him. I settled into a pew and peeled off my soaking raincoat. There were about twenty other bodies milling around the space, holding paper cups full of juice, and munching cookies. They all looked like college students, and they were almost as aflutter with nervous energy as I was. I turned to a girl sitting in the pew behind mine, dressed in jeans so ripped that nearly her entire leg was exposed. Despite a thick ring through her nose, three through her lower lip, and stringy hair that looked as if it hadn't been washed in days, she was pretty.

"Excuse me," I said, in my least offensive voice.

She turned her head only halfway, so that she wasn't looking at me head-on.

"Yeah?"

"The composer," I asked hesitantly. "Is he here?"

She gave me a quick glance, eloquently communicating the judgment that I was an ignoramus, that I didn't belong, which I suppose I didn't.

"He never comes. He's never heard his own music performed. He says it's too painful."

"Does he teach here?" I pressed further, despite the scorn she was emanating.

She rolled her eyes. "If by 'here' you mean either the college or the conservatory, then no."

No, of course he didn't. Jean Paul certainly wouldn't need the money that would make a teaching job worthwhile; the de Rochert fortune would be more than enough.

"Does he live around here?" I continued.

"Sometimes." There was a wistfulness in the way she said it that I imagined was uncharacteristic, and I wondered whether she was in love with him. The thought made her prettiness momentarily troubling.

"Hey, aren't you Tasha Darsky?" she asked, showing a surge of interest that forced her to look directly at my face for the first time.

"No," I said, and turned my back to her.

I watched as people slowly took their seats, everyone moving with the same self-conscious sense of treading on holy ground as my unwashed tour guide affected. We were in a church, but it was clear that the son of God had nothing to do with the hushed awe in the room. It wasn't hard to figure out why a place like Oberlin would draw Jean Paul, with all these bright and eager young music students around, just waiting for a new idea to worship.

At half past eleven, a heavyset boy in glasses climbed onto the altar, in front of an ensemble of musicians larger than the entire audience, and cleared his throat.

"Everyone, please, everyone," he called out, though the room had gone deathly silent the moment he stood. "I'm sorry about the delay. Eleanor, yet again, broke a string backstage."

I was the only one who didn't laugh knowingly, confirming my assumption that this was no random assortment of music lovers. A small Asian girl cradling a violin in her lap—Eleanor, I presumed—smiled sheepishly. She was seated in front of the rest of the musicians, suggesting that the piece, though billed merely as a rhapsody, was a concerto. A violin concerto.

"But now we're ready to begin." He paused, perhaps waiting for applause, but there was only more silence, and the sound of heavy breathing. Or was that just my own heavy breathing?

"OK. Well, then, without further ado, we bring you *Rhapsody from Hell*."

There was some shuffling, tuning, a few coughs, and then one note filled the room. It was a single note, played from Eleanor's violin, but it strained the walls of the church, it was so plaintive, so absolutely hopeless. I sucked in a breath that was deeper than I'd intended, and it hurt my chest.

The note was echoed in the woodwinds, and then reverberated through the percussion, before Eleanor's violin picked it up and transformed it back into a wail. Again the notes echoed with slight changes through the woodwinds and the tympani, and then through the entire ensemble. The cycle was repeated several times, the sounds growing slowly and simply. I could understand why these children flocked to Jean Paul's music like a cult. It was redemptive in its agony. It was so affecting that I thought that perhaps this was it, this strange atonal crying, but eventually the slow progression of moans began to give way to a tender melody, longing in musical form, and as it built from the early, elegiac snatches of notes, other phrases from those notes grew around it in a dense harmony. Then, one by one, the instruments stopped playing, so that the harmony grew increasingly less elaborate, and all that was left was the violin playing the heartbreaking melody unadorned.

It was almost too much to bear, that sweet, yearning tune, without defenses, which only made it more affecting when a harsh, dissonant sound began to gain strength in the brass, overpowering the voice of the violin. The piece had begun in its full fury. The next twenty minutes were filled with a battle between the dissonant and the melodic. The melody swelled, expanded, and then was engulfed once again by cacophony, until, halfway through this second movement, the melody began to gain strength, became the aggressor, and launched an onslaught of its own. It touched random-sounding notes and showed them to be patterns, dissolving and re-forming them into melodic lines. What had sounded like pure cacophony slowly showed itself to be another theme, obscured cleverly by noise, and in the final movement, as this new theme developed around the first, and the first around it, the two became slowly indistinguishable. The result was an incredible density of texture and emotion, mesmerizing in its effects.

When the furor began to die down, instrument by instrument, I realized I was clutching the back of the pew in front of me. I released my grip but remained poised uncomfortably at the edge of my seat as the violin, left alone again, played the final plaintive note.

To say that the music was brilliant would be almost misleading. I had some insight into what it had been like for nineteenth-century audiences to hear Beethoven for the first time, or eighteenth-century audiences Bach, before the iconoclastic ideas became familiar and then establishment. This is what it was to hear something revolutionary, deliciously defying expectation. Jean Paul had managed it, the natural transformation of chaos into order, madness into melody, and it seemed clear from the looser, messier flow of this progression that what had kept his music back all those years had been his pedantic worship of the Idea, the sacrifice of passion to rules, of beauty to the Point, the manipulation of inspiration. He had given up on Sublimated Tonality as a dogma, and so managed to bring it to fruition as an art form. From that first plaintive, hopeless note, it had been obvious what had broken him free of the stubborn and stultifying notion that music ought to be pure sound, stripped of all emotion. Misery had done it. Tragedy. Heartbreak. Perhaps even I had done it, and though this realization should have horrified me, terrified me, or shamed me, instead it exhilarated me. Maybe *I* had done it. Yes, I had betrayed him. Yes, I had stolen his soul. But I might have given him his music! I might have given *the world* his music! Rather than ruining him, perhaps I had made him. I thought of my first impression of Jean Paul, back when I'd first met him, along with Robert Masterson, for lunch in a French bistro. A man waiting to be gripped by grief, that's what I'd thought of him. Had some part of him known that grief was what he needed to unleash his talent? Had some deep recess of his psyche cultivated me specifically to break his heart, then forced me to do it? It didn't seem impossible.

I wandered out of the church, amid the small crowd of equally rapturous faces, and failed to notice that I was walking around in circles until I passed the church's façade for the third time.

THE NEXT MORNING, I WOKE UP FEELING THE FULL weight of my discovery. *Rhapsody from Hell,* I was certain, was significant, not just for me, but for history. Back at Harvard, they'd predicted limitless success for Jean Paul, and probably no one had believed it more than I. But even then, I didn't expect him to produce something like I'd heard the previous night, a sound utterly unlike anything else, spiritual in its magnificence and transcendent in its pain. If he had more pieces like that, he was of a different class, even from the run-of-the-mill staggering talents: he was a great one among the Great Ones.

After breakfast, I headed back to the church, hoping to find some of Jean Paul's students still lurking around—a poor plan, but all I could think of. The building, however, was empty, though it was Sunday morning. I was about to turn around and head back to the campus when I decided to poke around in the back. I was just testing one of the doors when it swung open and a hefty frame came barreling into me.

I took a few clumsy steps backward and nearly tripped down the cement stairs, then I looked up to see a boy who looked promisingly familiar. He mumbled something incoherent and tried to brush past me, but I blocked his path.

"You emceed the concert here last night."

He didn't respond, and it occurred to me that he didn't have permission to use this abandoned church as a concert hall. That would explain the odd timing of the thing.

"I was here. I loved it." I was trying to put him at ease. "That's why I came back. I was hoping to find someone who could show me more of Mr. Boumedienne's music."

"Hey, are you Tasha Darsky?" he asked, though not with any particular excitement.

"Yes, I am." I hoped that my status as a famous musician, rather than a nut off the street, would make him more likely to help me. "So do you have any more of his music? Can you help me out?"

"I have pretty much everything he's written." He shook his head, uncertainly. "But I don't know if I should show it to you without asking him first. He's a private person. Why don't you contact him directly?"

"No, I can't. That wouldn't work. The truth is, I want to surprise him. I want to do something that would really help him, but you need to help me. Will you help me?"

He seemed amused by the choice of the word "surprise," as if the insipidly happy connotations of unexpected gifts and parties was so far from the world of the composer he knew that it was as if I'd suggested sending Castro a lollipop.

"Look, I don't know."

"Please," I begged. "I promise you. I only want to help him. Just let me see that music."

"Fine, whatever." He let out a martyred sigh. "I have copies of all the scores in my apartment. Do you want to come look at them now?"

"Yes!" I tried to stifle my excitement, but with only moderate success, and he eyed me suspiciously. I was afraid he was going to rescind the offer, but instead he let out another oppressed sigh.

"I just have to lock up."

I walked back down the steps, and watched him play around with the chains. A few moments later, he joined me at the bottom of the stairs and we walked together across the unkempt yard.

"I knew Jean Paul well in the early eighties," I said, by way of making conversation. If my reluctant accomplice had any information that bore on my connection to his hero, it didn't affect his response.

"Cool," he replied with only mild interest. "He never talks much about his past."

He led me into a ramshackle apartment building filled with

upperclassmen seeking the independence of off-campus existence. There was a distinct smell to the place, a delightful mixture of marijuana, beer, and sweat.

"Man, I hope my roommates are here. They'll freak when they see you," he exclaimed, pushing open his door. It was the first sign of real emotion he'd shown since I'd bumped into him.

I was relieved when we entered an empty apartment. I wasn't sure I could trust his roommates to keep quiet even if I could trust him, which was also doubtful.

"My room's this one." He led me inside a cluttered space littered with empty bags of chips and old beer bottles. A half-filled bong waited patiently in the corner.

I sat down on the bed, piled high with dirty T-shirts, for want of a better place, and watched as he delicately pulled a crisp manila envelope out of his desk. It was impressive, given the state of his room, how carefully he handled the scores.

"This is all of them," he said, his voice rich with feeling. "Be careful. The paper's thin."

He handed me the bunch, his fingers gripping the ends of the envelope too long.

"I'll be careful," I promised. "And thank you."

He nodded and left the room, closing the door behind him.

I looked down at the pile of music in my lap—hundreds of pages, dutifully copied by hand, probably by the young man whose room I was in. It seemed that Jean Paul had never stopped being enormously prolific. I shuffled through, and noticed that none of the pieces I knew were in there, except *Rhapsody from Hell,* which was on top. It made sense that he wouldn't want his devotees studying his early works, given how far he'd come since then, but I still felt a pang, contemplating the exclusion of the notes I had once known so well.

If I'd been tempted before to think that *Rhapsody* was a lucky miracle, an inspired aberration from an otherwise large but conceivable talent, just the briefest perusal of the scores in front of me proved that hypothesis wrong. *Rhapsody from Hell,* though certainly among his better pieces, was matched, even outstripped, by a number of other works. On the whole, his oeuvre was staggering in its breadth and the consistency of quality. The style that had been eluding him for so long, now that it had been caught, provided him with both a surety and a variability that rarely let him down.

It was already evening when my host stuck his head back in. I'd been poring over each perfect note disbelievingly for nearly eight hours.

"How's it coming in here?" he asked, without a hint of impatience. It seemed that when it came to Jean Paul's music he was all forbearance.

I stood up, feeling around the bed for my bag, and trying to hide the pages I'd managed to copy. I'd scribbled out three of the best scores, stealing some crumpled sheets of nearly empty staff paper from the considerable pile near the garbage can. It pained me to leave the rest behind, but if all went as I hoped, I would have my own versions of the scores soon enough.

I ran from the apartment building all the way back to my hotel, realizing that my plane left in only half an hour. I was already formulating a plan, and I wanted to start putting it into action as soon as possible. If I could, I would start making calls that evening.

I had known since that morning that I was going to take it upon myself to introduce Jean Paul's music to the larger community. It was ridiculous that the only people who got to enjoy his gift were these few college students. How he had managed to escape notice earlier I couldn't say, but it was one of the world's great artistic injustices that half the First World knew my name while the score of *Rhapsody from Hell* went largely unheard. I was certain that once I contacted his old teachers, the ones who had proclaimed him the next messiah of music before he'd even performed his miracles, and showed them these scores, they would do everything they could to help me preach his gospel.

The whole ride home, I plotted out how I would proceed. I decided it would be best to call Robert Masterson first and enlist his help. He'd be able to contact Jean Paul's teachers from the conservatoire, and also Jean Paul himself. I wasn't brave enough to do that yet, to speak to Jean Paul after all this time. It would be too dangerous. Dangerous because, if I had ever fully gotten over Jean Paul (and I think I had, even if I did still engage with him every time I picked up my violin), this music had pulled me in deeper than ever. It wasn't the genius of the music that had done it; it was the *him*ness of it—the pure sound of him, just as I remembered it. So, yes, it would be dangerous to hear that whispery deep Franco-Exeter blend in my ear after eight years of not hearing it, and inevitably, if all went as planned, to see him again, but it was a danger I was willing to face for the sake of this music.

By the time I arrived in New York, it was too late to make the calls, but I was beside myself with excitement and stayed up all night trying to reconstruct the scores I hadn't managed to copy. I was growing more and more ambitious, thinking now of multiple concerts, media blitzes, recordings, and so I was shocked the next morning when I got hold of Robert Masterson on the phone.

"Jean Paul's new music?" he asked brusquely, after a surprisingly warm few minutes of opening chatter. "You're kidding me."

"Have you heard it?" I asked, confused by his sudden change in tone.

"Heard it? Not exactly. But I've seen a great deal of it. He used to send me new pieces as he finished them until I told him to stop. He still sends me works now and then, but I file them away in their envelopes. It's too much when they burn out young."

"Burn out? Are you kidding? Robert, his stuff is genius."

"Genius? Seriously? Tasha, the stuff is embarrassing. It's so self-indulgent. It's all over the place."

"It's passionate."

"It's undisciplined. My first response was to cover my ears, and that was just sight-reading!"

"That's what people once said about Beethoven, you know. And Brahms."

"And a million other people, both great and lousy. Trust me, this guy is no Beethoven."

"So I take it you won't help me organize a concert."

"You're right about that. Take my advice, Tasha. Don't become Boumedienne's champion. You're asking for humiliation."

"I'll decide that for myself." But already my confidence was wavering.

It hadn't crossed my mind that Robert might fail to see the genius in Jean Paul's music. I suppose that's because I had never stopped thinking of him as the unfailing, unfeeling, purely objective ear who had run his seminar like a demigod. I'd never reconciled that impression with the less attractive one of a teacher who took his undergraduate to bed. I made the next few phone calls with ever-lowering hopes, but each time I was stung by the caustic remarks (and struck that each person I spoke with used the term "self-indulgent" to describe Jean Paul's music). I felt personally insulted by the flippant gibes of these narrow-minded fogies, but, much worse, it was easy to infer how Jean Paul would have reacted, did react, to these same unsympathetic critics. It seemed that Jean Paul's music was reviled by his former mentors almost as much as it was adored by his Oberlin cult. After five or six equally demoralizing attempts to round up partners, I decided that I would have to organize this concert on my own. I was certain I could convince any number of conductors to take on the score, and once we got the music staged, it would speak for itself to a wider and less stodgy audience. The only tangible setback was that now it was up to me to contact Jean Paul. After a few days of oscillating, I decided it might be best for both of us if I wrote instead of called. I set aside a whole afternoon to track down an Oberlin address for him, but, much to my surprise, the address was listed. I don't know why I thought it wouldn't be. It wasn't as if he were a reclusive celebrity. He was a reclusive unknown.

I wrote about fifteen drafts before I sent it off, settling on a short and businesslike note, stating only that I'd heard his music, was blown away by it, and wanted to back a performance. For days afterward I kept rewriting it in my head, and once it became plausible for me to receive a reply, my heart would plummet every time I opened my mailbox and found nothing from Ohio. It was two weeks before I received a small envelope, battered and smudged.

Like my original, his note was short, but not nearly as businesslike. He refrained from saying anything personal (other than to mention how many days it had taken him to open my letter, and how surprised he'd been by what he'd found inside), but he expressed grave concerns about my proposition. I suppose it was only natural, given the abuse he'd suffered at the hands of those whose opinions once mattered most to him, that he was somewhat loath to expose himself to wider ridicule. I could understand why it might be tempting to hide away in his cozy corner of the world, surrounded by worshipful children. But it was inconceivable to me that he'd prefer to live in safe obscurity than to risk some pain for his assured place in history. I had no doubt his music was revolutionary and, therefore, important not just to him, but to the world as a whole, and I wrote back telling him as much. This time, I also slipped in a few lines hinting at how often I'd been thinking of him lately, though I scratched them out seconds before sealing the envelope.

I had to wait through two trips abroad and one to the West Coast before I received a response.

"I disagree that I 'owe' anyone anything," it began, unpromisingly. "Least of all do I owe an unfamiliar public what is most privately mine. Still, I've given a lot of thought to what you say about art not being wholly fulfilled until it's enjoyed by an audience, and I admit that my small audience here at Oberlin is not entirely satisfying to me. Yes, as much as I hate to confess, I, too, yearn for wider acclaim. Can any artist not, and still call his work art? I'd like to think that the answer is a defiant 'yes' but I suspect that it's a whimpering 'no.' "

Though there was no explicit answer to my request, I assumed, with absolutely no doubt in my mind, that the letter constituted a consent.

I called five conductors that evening, and faxed each of them the scores. The next morning I received four tepid responses, and one enthusiastic one. The enthusiastic one was from my old friend Michael O'Shea, who had somehow managed to get himself appointed music director of the San Francisco Symphony at the age of twenty-nine—not quite his old, seemingly irrational ambition of conductor for the New York Philharmonic by thirty, but not far off, either. Not only was Michael the only one to recognize the genius of the music, he was also the only one who was willing to stage it even if I didn't play the solo part in *Rhapsody from Hell*. Michael couldn't have known what it would mean for me to play this music—to enter back into Jean Paul's talent, to throw myself into his notes—but he was smart enough to know I'd feel some sort of melodramatic nonsense, and so he suggested we sign the latest prepubescent phenomenon, Emmy Chin, instead.

The next few weeks were a flutter of activity. I was traveling around the country doing an all-concerto program with a small ensemble of other soloists, but tried to touch base with San Francisco at least once a day in order to stay on top of the preparations for Jean Paul's concert. I was running on pure adrenaline, infected with the power of the music we were going to show the world. Each night, I sent off a new, ebullient note to Jean Paul, updating him on our progress and asking him please to write back and give me a number where he could be reached. (The number, it had turned out, was unlisted.)

The only person who was less than thrilled about the upcoming concert was my mother. When I relayed the news to her, the day after I'd decided on San Francisco, she was aghast.

"You can call me vindictive or unforgiving or a worry wart," she told me as she smoothed down one of my gowns and laid it gently in its carrying case. "But I'd stay the hell away from anything connected to that guy. I say this as your mother, not your manager."

But nothing could have dampened my enthusiasm for my new project, or, for that matter, for the prospect of seeing Jean Paul again. With each new note I sent off, it was becoming more and more difficult to maintain my professional tone; the polish was beginning to sound like simple coldness, since increasingly what I wanted was to speak to him the way we used to speak, to be let into the fluid rise and fall of his thoughts, to know what this music was lit with from the inside. I was becoming convinced that when I saw him this would happen, and that perhaps this was a good thing; that perhaps it was time to undo what I'd done in my stupid youth; that perhaps I had grown into the sort of woman who could stand to be loved by him. I didn't dare to let in the thought that there could be a new woman in his life. Instead, I began to think, tentatively and furtively, of tasting the utter familiarity of him again.

Until, that is, I heard from Jean Paul.

When the musicians had already begun practicing, and the date of the concert was set, I sent a final letter with the concert details, an invitation to come watch the rehearsals, and another plea for a phone number. I ended, impetuously, on the personal note I'd been trying to resist until we met in person:

Jean Paul, I think it goes without saying that I've always regretted the way we ended, and the pain I caused. I know to you it seemed needless and wrong, and I can't say it seemed all that different to me, though from my end things were—as always—so much more convoluted than from yours. But when I hear your new music I cannot help feeling that somehow I did the right thing. I hear heartbreak here, and I think it's what unleashed you. Maybe it wasn't even our heartbreak that did it, maybe it was another heartbreak altogether, but the fact remains that if we had been what we by all rights ought to have been, then this music would not. And so I'm glad, in a way, that I made that mistake.

I thought he would take it as an apology. I hoped he might even take it as an invitation. But he took it as neither. This time, I received a reply within days.

What are these plans you're writing to me about? I never gave my consent to this concert, and I want it stopped immediately. This music belongs to me, and not to you or to the SFS. I demand you put an immediate end to anything you have unrightfully begun.

And then, in place of a signature:

I wonder, how familiar are these words to you? "Creative, genius-giving disease, disease that rides on high horse over all hindrances and springs with drunken daring from peak to peak, is a thousand times dearer to life than plodding healthiness." Meditate on them awhile.

The quote was from *Doctor Faustus*, a book I owned, and I went to my shelf and pulled it down. As I'd immediately suspected, the words Jean Paul had chosen as his sign-off were spoken by the devil himself, the one who poor Faustus believed had stolen his soul in exchange for musical genius. Clearly, my apology was not well taken.

It was late that night, after I'd stormed around my apartment throwing decorative pillows at the walls, after I'd called my mother and cried and begged her to think of something to solve this mess, after I'd lain in bed for hours, hating myself, and Jean Paul more, that I thought of the slew of anonymous notes I'd been receiving for years, all scrawled in the same manic hand, all bearing quotes from Thomas Mann. I'd received the first one soon after my initial tour: "A paternal kindness," it read, "an emotional attachment, filled and moved his heart, the attachment that someone who produces beauty at the cost of intellectual self-sacrifice feels toward someone who naturally possesses beauty."

I remember it had upset me—as an anonymous note scrawled in red ink might upset any girl—and I'd shown it to my mother with trembling hands. "A well-read fan," she said without much concern. "You'll get used to them." But whereas she read it as fan mail, I'd read it as hate mail, a conviction only strengthened when I received the next one, a year later: "His nerves greedily consumed the piping sounds, the vulgar piping melodies, for passion numbs good taste and succumbs in all seriousness to enticements that a sober spirit would receive with humor or reject scornfully." Soon they were arriving every six months, and then, out of the blue, they stopped. I hadn't thought of them since.

My skin was tingling as I reached under my bed and pulled out the box in which I stored my odder correspondence. (The Mann letters were not the strangest by a long shot; the normal stuff was filed away by my father, but the bizarre ones, I believed, belonged to me alone and not to the Tasha Darsky Enterprise.) Dumping the contents of the box out onto the mattress, I sifted through the unordered pile until I found a packet of letters rubber-banded together, all crumpled and small, with no return address. The manic scrawl of these letters was different from the careful cursive on the recent note from Jean Paul, but stamped on the front of each of them was the same postmark: Oberlin, Ohio.

I lay back on my bed, clutching the letters to my chest, and thought of a soul I didn't want locked away somewhere—in the metaphysical equivalent of an attic?—rotting, festering, threatening. I had never felt more for him.

DISCOVERING THAT JEAN PAUL HAD BEEN MY MAD Mann all along was unsettling, perhaps even devastating, but it was the least pressing of my problems in the immediate aftermath of that letter. More urgent was what to do about the upcoming concert. It was my mother's idea that we replace the national debut of Jean Paul's new music with the national debut of mine.

"I haven't written anything since college," I protested when she first suggested it. "What am I supposed to debut, some class assignments?"

But my mother was dead set on this plan, and approached Michael O'Shea without my consent. She reveled in what she saw as the irony of the situation: "The man who tried to squash your creativity is going to be the one who revives it!" "He never tried to squash my creativity," I insisted, but my mother ignored me. Soon she had turned the event from a personal triumph to a feminist cause, raving about the patriarchal hegemony enforced by the rigid institutions of classical music. She'd dug up a truckload of statistics somewhere: the rate at which women's work gets performed by orchestras, which is even lower than the dismally low rate at which men's original work is performed; that few women have been named conductor of major or even middling orchestras; and so on.

"I'd like to think my life choices have nothing to do with an extra X chromosome," I told her, but she scoffed at that. "If anyone can reverse the trend and get the public excited about music by a woman," she enthused, "it's you, darling. We've got to harness that intoxicating femininity of yours. Weaponize it."

I asked caustically whether, in that case, she considered my *Vanity Fair* cover a B-52 bombshell. The *Vanity Fair* cover and the accompanying article—"Va-Va-Va-Violin: Tasha Darsky Talks About Music, Love, and Letting Loose"—was a recent sore spot in the family, a gig arranged by my father which had caused me considerable consternation. How could I be taken seriously as an artist, I wanted to know, when anyone in a supermarket line could ogle my belly button? Not that a part of me didn't also thrill to seeing myself posed like a model, my dark hair cascading over artificially luminescent skin, my blue eyes taking on the extra sheen of the photographer's lights. It's just that the thrill wasn't worth the anxiety.

"Get over that cover," my mother suggested, "or I'll start telling people it's me."

But I couldn't get over it. Since that angry letter from Jean Paul, all my defenses had sagged, and what might have only made me wince or even giggle before, now made me feel like an artistic impostor. I was even traumatized when, in the course of a largely respectful profile, *The New Yorker* happened to call me "every thinking man's fantasy," as if I were a bespectacled Playmate instead of a classical musician. If I was every thinking man's fantasy, I wondered testily while reading it, why did I spend all my free nights watching old movies with my aging parents? Why did my few relationships never last beyond a few months? Why had I been lying in bed recently thinking about a man who wrote me hate mail?

My mother's idea to debut my music in place of Jean Paul's seemed unthinkable at first. I had nothing to debut. I had fought hard to stop thinking of myself as a composer. Most important, to replace his music with mine seemed like yet another betrayal of him. But my mother was insistent, and Michael O'Shea was desperate, and soon I was digging through hundreds of fraying scraps of paper scribbled with aborted bits of melody. I had never stopped hearing music in my head, I had only stopped trying to figure out where it led. I would write it down and stash it away, never to be thought of again. Now I reluctantly unearthed these scraps of music and strung them together into a pitiful medley I entitled *Sound Fragments.* I'd wanted to call it *Aborted Music* or *Fetal Music,* but my mother almost choked on the suggestion. The other piece we decided to debut, appropriately, was *Medea's Fantasy,* the ode to revenge I'd written for Masterson's seminar.

Sound Fragments lacked any cohesive structure, for obvious reasons, and neither it nor *Medea's Fantasy* had any interesting musical ideas, but when they were performed to a packed audience, many reviewers found something to praise in the mishmash. The critical response wasn't uniformly positive by any stretch, but that there was critical attention at all—and there was a great deal, for it seemed that, whether they liked it or not, the reviewers believed that it was worthy of serious treatment—was inexplicable to me. At first I was just baffled, but when the program was picked up by other orchestras I began to find it distressing. I could come up with any number of hypotheses for the collective self-deception being wrought by the musical community, but the reason wasn't the issue: the issue was that bad music was being taken seriously, and it was my fault. I probably should have been grateful that I'd been spared the humiliation I undoubtedly would have suffered had anyone had the guts or the sense to reveal my music for what it was, but instead I felt a strange mixture of despair and guilt. Given that I had never completely given up my equation between God and art, I suppose what I felt like was a temple-defiling heretic. That hundreds of people could hum a few bars of *Medea's Fantasy,* whereas no more than a handful had ever heard *Rhapsody from Hell,* was an aesthetic injustice of the highest order.

Yet I can't say that I didn't also enjoy my turn as professional composer. The evening when *Sound Fragments* debuted in Carnegie Hall was one of the more dreamlike events of my life. I wasn't performing, so I sat in the audience and let the music wash over me as it would over anyone else. On a purely aural level, the music was pretty. I'm tempted to say too pretty, too chirpy, which might explain why so many Americans liked it and Europeans universally panned it. It made me think of tinkling china at a tea party on a spring day in the park. But that was not what struck me about it that night, nor was I fixated on the flaws of the music—its sentimentality, its lack of interesting ideas. What I was struck with was that the music was mine. I was sitting in one of the pre-eminent concert halls in the world listening to pre-eminent musicians play notes that had come out of my own inner sensorium. I recognized the sounds as the intimate product of my mind, and yet at the same time they had taken on a foreign aspect. I was witnessing their transformation from private whimsy to public property, from thought to art.

That night, I returned home in the wee hours of the morning from a reunion dinner with my old college friends (they'd all flown in for the Carnegie debut) to find a lengthy and positively warm message from Robert Masterson on my answering machine. He, too, had been at the concert, and he'd spent a while looking for me, he repeated several times in several variations, because he had to tell me that, though he thought the Medea piece was still immature and needed a great deal of work, the sound fragments were fascinating, and clearly the product of a mind poised to produce great things. I played the message over as I prepared for bed, though I could hardly take it seriously coming from a man who'd called Jean Paul's work "a mess."

Over the course of the following day, I firmly returned to feeling dirty and dishonest. That night, when I want to dinner with my parents in the sumptuous hubbub of the Russian Tea Room, this feeling congealed into shame.

"My God," my mother said for the millionth time, as she delicately poked at a piece of chicken Kiev. She tended to find food distasteful, and only ever ordered to be polite. "I still can't get over it. I always knew you were a great composer, but every time I hear it again it sounds even more miraculous!"

I shifted in my plush red seat, wondering how she'd known I was a great composer before she'd heard a thing I'd written being performed, and whether I could eat her chicken if she didn't want it.

"Pretty remarkable," my father agreed, and while I signaled for the check, I marveled at my ability to delude. Had anyone in the world ever been better at it? Maybe *that* was my greatest talent. Not creating, not even performing, but deluding.

"Pret-ty remarkable," he repeated.

"Do you know what it made me think of this time?" my mother asked, clasping her hands together in excitement.

"Hmm, what?" My father turned toward her with rapt attention, blotting his mouth with a napkin.

"An early Barnett Newman!"

I decided not to point out that 70 percent of what my mother encountered in life reminded her of an early Barnett Newman, and instead signaled more fervently for the check. There was something about fooling my parents that made me utterly desolate. When they invited me back to the brownstone for dessert and coffee, I couldn't turn down the offer fast enough. I felt, for the first time in years, that I needed to get away from them.

A few days after the Carnegie Hall performance, I received the letter I'd been unconsciously waiting for. Or, more accurately, I received a clipping of one of my better reviews; the review was by the same *New York Times* critic who had called my latest album a "pop star's mockery of classical music" the year before, only now he was saying that *Medea's Fantasy* was "hypnotic," "fascinating," and, ironically, "promising." Scrawled across the newsprint in red ink was a quote from Thomas Mann's *Death in Venice:* "There is inborn in every artistic disposition an indulgent and treacherous tendency to accept injustice when it produces beauty and respond with complicity and even admiration when the aristocrats of this world get preferential treatment."

Like the original letter in what I'd come to think of as the "Mad Mann Series," this one was ambiguous enough that I could have read it as bizarre fan mail if I chose. Instead, I felt myself chastised, and cleaner for it. The quote, as I read it, was painfully dead-on: my success, at least with regard to composing, was an injustice, born of my fame and the tendency of fame to breed on itself, though the only people willing to admit it were me and the love of my life, who scrawled anonymous, red-inked notes. Now that the injustice had been aired, it was as if I had been forgiven my sins and had only to repent by keeping my bad music to myself.

But *Medea's Fantasy* was being played by classical radio stations all over the country, and Sony wanted an album, and there were requests pouring in for more Darsky music. My mother began hounding me to sit down and write something. After dinner one night in my apartment, I showed her the letter, declaring, "This says it all."

She stared at it, and I saw her struggling not to erupt. "Tell me something and tell me honestly," she finally demanded, giving me a look that was intense even for her. "Why did you end things with Jean Paul? It clearly wasn't that you'd fallen out of love. That was obvious."

I'd been brewing coffee while she pondered the letter, and I bought myself some time by retreating into the kitchen to pour the drink into two mugs. When I came back to the table, I knew what to say. "I suppose it was because I was just me and he was him, and that was unbearable. I couldn't stand him loving the lesser of us; I couldn't understand why he did."

She looked down at the letter again, and I believed the conversation was at an end. When she looked back up at me, the expression in her eyes had changed dramatically: there was no glint or glitter, no determination; only sadness.

"The lesser of you two?" she asked. "Only you could have believed anything so far from the truth as that. I doubt even the bastard himself believed it; he was selfish, not deaf."

THAT NIGHT, LONG AFTER MY MOTHER HAD GONE home, I was awoken just before dawn by a loud clap of thunder, and found that there were a few notes running loose in my head. Usually I would have huddled deeper beneath the covers, but, thinking back to that look of utter defeat on my mother's face as she'd declared me Jean Paul's equal, I made my way to the piano I'd recently bought so I could practice at home with accompaniment. I sat there for hours, but I couldn't unearth the rest of the music those few notes had suggested; for days I tried, but nothing came. Whatever talent I'd once had—big, small, or infinitesimal—there was nothing left of it. I'd rooted it out.

Perhaps this wouldn't have been so bad—after all, I hadn't composed in years, and those years of noncomposing had been among the happiest of my life—except that I cared again, and caring drained the joy from my playing. Months passed, blandly. I was still crisscrossing the globe, swept up by the glamorous whirl of celebrity, but orbiting wasn't nearly as much fun as it had been. Whereas before every performance had been an exhilarating struggle of eros and identity in which I'd fought for my own voice from out of the notes, now I'd lost the will to fight. Feeling failure swirling thickly around me, I didn't want to claw my way out of the music anymore. I wanted to crawl inside it and never come out. I wanted to be nothing *but* that music, and I wanted Jean Paul gone, ultimately and irrevocably, from my mind, my notes, my life. Instead of confronting the score—which to me still meant tussling with Jean Paul—my performances became a timid tiptoe around it. The critics called the transformation of my playing a "maturing," but I knew it was a regression. I suspected I was going through an early midlife crisis, but I kept plugging along, because I was afraid of what would happen if I stopped.

My mother noticed the change in my mood, if not in my music, and decided I was overworked. "What are we doing to you?" she lamented. "We're making you an old woman at twenty-nine." She imposed a new rule: we would never stay in a city fewer than three days, and on at least one of those days we needed to be frivolous. My father was unhappy with this new rule, arguing that it was bad business, and I—afraid of slowing down—couldn't have agreed more; but my mother was firm, and when she was firm there was no getting around her.

That was how I ended up one night at a dinner party outside Paris, hosted by August and Edmund Rozmarin, friends of my parents whom I'd known since childhood. Edmund had financed a few of my parents' more ambitious projects—in my father's words, "handing over obscene sums of money without so much as a flinch." He was one of that wonderful breed of creature that my parents were always seeking out in far reaches of the globe, bulwark of the artistic vanguard: a financial mogul with sincere aesthetic aspirations. Now at the height of his wealth (the 1980s had treated him well, as they had most investment bankers), he had abandoned the meaner pursuits and retired to the French countryside to begin his magnum opus, a novel set in the lost city of Atlantis.

His greatest talent, though, was as neither novelist nor artists' pocketbook muse, but as dinner host. He and August threw weekly parties, and my mother decided this would be the perfect place to start living it up. Their parties drew an interesting mix of people—artists, writers, businessmen, politicians, and intellectuals—who, under the infectious influence of Edmund's jovial Texan joie de vivre, soon shed their disparate exteriors and became a homogeneous blend of raucous good-timers in varying states of intoxication.

August and Edmund were the sort of people who were so happily in love that they couldn't understand why anyone wasn't, which is probably why, when I arrived an hour late, missing the sherry and the introductions, I found myself seated next to a handsome Kuwaiti oil-tycoon who happened to be a huge fan of mine. But as he slathered on the charm—"The only thing in the world that rivals the beauty of your Brahms Violin Concerto," he actually told me, "is your face"—my attention wandered to another face seated all the way at the other end of the table, about twenty bodies away: tragic, harried, obsessed. I happened to know whom that face belonged to: Aleksander Pasek, the legendary Polish filmmaker, whose movies were credited with rallying a nation behind Solidarity, and whom many now wanted to see as Poland's new president. But when I looked at him I didn't see an old man who'd brought down a regime with art; or, rather, I did, but within the wrinkles and crags I also saw another face staring out at me: darkly beautiful and single-minded. I couldn't have said why exactly, but it was as if they were one and the same. All through dinner, I watched him out of the corner of my eye, wishing someone would introduce us. No one ever did, and so, while we both waited for our coats in the foyer, I saw my chance and seized it. He was standing alone. I went up and tapped him gently on the arm.

"Hello, Mr. Pasek," I said. He gave me a startled, not particularly friendly look, but it was what I'd expected. He was known for his gruffness. "I'm such a fan, it's a pleasure."

"A pleasure," he grunted, shaking my hand.

"My name is Tasha Darsky," I offered. He nodded, and I thought he was about to say something else, but just then August handed him his coat. He turned away, and my Kuwaiti fan sidled up, inviting me for a sail on his yacht. By the time I looked around for Pasek again, he was gone.

Back in the hotel room, I mentioned to my mother how intriguing I'd found Aleksander Pasek, and hinted that I might look him up when we were in Poland, which happened to be the next stop on my tour; I was performing at a last-minute star-studded concert in Warsaw, an artistic celebration of Solidarity's recent victory in that June's partially free elections.

She looked concerned and remarked that he seemed old for me. Laughing, I explained that my interest wasn't romantic, that there was just something magnetic about him, and she said if that wasn't a description of romantic interest she didn't know what was.

"*Bloody Earth is* one of my favorite movies," she mused, as though trying to acclimate to the idea of him in our lives.

The next night, she brought home a few of his films. "You got me thinking about them all over again," she explained.

We traded in a few hours' sleep to watch *Treny.* The film is based on the long poem by Jan Kochanowski, and, like the poem, it chronicles the travails of a father who's lost his young daughter. There are subtle hints throughout the film that the loved one isn't a human child but the independent nation of Poland, which had also died in its infancy, taking its few short, gasping breaths between world wars: Orszula, the dead daughter, is always dressed in shades of red and white, the national colors of Poland, and she is referred to as a soaring eagle, symbol of Polish sovereignty. The film is powerful, and by the time it was over, both my mother and I—each of us sobbing—would have taken up arms for the cause of sovereignty if anyone had stopped by to sign us up.

The next day, we left Paris for Warsaw. There was a storm blowing in from the north, and the train listed perceptibly from side to side. I stared out at the deserted French countryside, brooding, and only halfway through the trip realized that I was imagining myself as one of Pasek's fate-defiant characters, taunting the storm and whatever auguries of history it represented. When we pulled onto Polish soil, the weather lifted, and we were greeted with a dull but pleasant sunshine. I could almost feel the credits rolling across the scene.

Though I was hoping he might, Pasek didn't show up at the independence concert, as far as I could tell. I asked around, but though many people edged into mania at the prospect of his being present, no one had seen him. That didn't necessarily mean he wasn't there. The concert had drawn performances by famous musicians from around the world, and thousands of Poles filled the audience. Warsaw's Lazienki Park looked for three days like

Times Square on New Year's Eve, with the eighteenth-century Theatre on the Isle, where the concerts were staged, as the hub of the mob. One man, however famous, could get lost in the crowd. I continued to search.

On the last day of the celebration, my mother said to me, "Just go to Kraków and find the guy."

"But what about you?" I asked. In keeping with her "de-stress Tasha" plan, we were supposed to spend a month lounging in a resort town in Switzerland.

"I'll wait for you in Bruen," she said. "Just go."

So I went.

THE FIRST SIGHT I CAUGHT OF PASEK IN KRAKÓW WAS of his gray hair flying around his head like a halo gone haywire, his face tight with rage. He'd suggested that we meet by the Adam Mickiewicz Monument, in the middle of the city's large, medieval Main Market Square. I'd thought initially that the choice might be meaningful, since Adam Mickiewicz, I had read in my guidebook, was considered Poland's greatest Romantic poet—I flattered myself into believing that this might be a nod from one artist to another; we would meet under the eyes of a third. But the monument was such a popular rendezvous spot that I found the sentence "Let's meet at the monument" in my *Quick Polish Phrases* book.

When I arrived midafternoon, the square was thick with people, but only three were paused near the base of the statue: one was a woman reading from a small bright-green book that contrasted startlingly with her coppery hair, and the other two, Pasek and a smaller man, were engaged in an intense argument. Or, rather, Pasek was shouting heatedly at the smaller man, who cowered, his face half hidden in the stiff gray collar of his jacket. I approached cautiously, awed by the study in gray, and Pasek stopped his invective long enough to look up and ask with relative calm, "You are Ms. Darsky?" I nodded. "One moment. Please, your patience." And then, holding one hand up in my direction, which I took as an attempt to indicate that he hadn't forgotten me, he continued to voice his displeasure.

It was probably no more than a minute before the small man skulked away, leaving me alone with the legendary filmmaker, the man whom many Poles wanted as their highest political leader, a man with an incredible set of lungs, but it felt to me like ages, watching the fearsome contortions of Pasek's face. I focused on that face because it still drew me strongly, but also because I couldn't comfortably look at the other one; in the single glimpse I'd caught before turning away from the smaller man, I'd been disturbed by something in his expression, an indication of some perverse enjoyment that I felt hit too close to home. He never cast his eyes my way, either, not in the least curious to see the third party who was now observing them. When he turned and ran in the other direction, it was without so much as a glance at me. In fact, neither man cast his sights my way. Until I took it upon myself to remind Aleksander Pasek of my presence, lingering just beyond his still-outstretched hand, I think he was considering chasing after his friend and continuing his harangue.

"Mr. Pasek," I said quietly, peeking out from around his looming limb.

"Ah, yes. Miss Darsky." He dropped his arm and turned his tremendous face in my direction, a tremendous face that was nonetheless overcrowded with features. There was nothing soft or delicate or fine in that face. Nothing at all artistic. If I'd seen him on the street and had to guess at his life, I'd have pegged him as a factory worker, someone who labored in a clanging, metal-filled place, and thrived on the noise and chaos of it. But despite the obvious contrast between this harsh, clanging face and the darkly romantic one, up close the similarity between the two was even stronger than it had been from across a long table: the intoxicated intoxicating look of the eyes, the defiant set of the jaw. And now there was the shared talent for raving. Whatever Pasek had been shouting about, it had surely concerned themes high and impersonal.

I realized I'd been staring for an inappropriately long time when he raised his eyebrows at me.

"Shall we find someplace to talk?" I asked.

I followed him to a small outdoor café, emerging as if by natural outgrowth from the Renaissance arches of the red-and-yellow-bricked Cloth Hall. I'd spent the morning on the ground floor of the imposing building, browsing through the stalls of folk arts and crafts, and was reassured to return to its shadow. The monument was still in view, not more than twenty feet away, and I slipped myself into a seat facing in the opposite direction. I would now forever associate the statue with the sight of that small man's face, an association I did not want looming over me as I tried to become acquainted with Aleksander Pasek.

A girl with puffy cheeks that marred the charm of her clear green eyes approached our table. Aleksander ordered a glass of vodka for himself and a coffee for me. I hadn't asked for a coffee, had no desire for it, but I thanked him anyway.

The strain of a polonaise, played by a mandolin, a guitar, a harmonica, and an out-of-tune violin, was hovering in the air, and, looking around for the source, I saw a group of young musicians who must have just set themselves up on the far side of the monument. A small circle had gathered around them, and one couple danced in jittery, lighthearted movements around the onlooking pigeons.

"Poland is so different from what I imagined," I mused, turning back toward Aleksander. "I expected it to be drab, but Kraków is one of the most colorful cities I've ever visited."

He nodded as he lifted the drinks off our waitress's proffered tray.

"May I call you Natasha?" he asked, fondling his glass as I adjusted myself in the cheap plastic chair. "Natasha, I must tell you something right off the start, because I would not feel honest if I failed to mention it. Would that be suitable to you?"

"By all means." I liked his direct manner, not only for itself, but because it fit with the folksy atmosphere of the teeming square with the music, the dancing, the pigeons, and the smell of the café's pastry on the hot air.

"I have no idea who you are."

I flashed a meager smile, and then stared into my coffee. I was irritated with myself for being flustered.

"I understand you are a fiddler of no small talent, very famous," he continued. "This, anyway, is what people told me when I asked.

But I had never once heard your name before you called me. I don't disbelieve when you tell me we shared a dinner not long ago, and now that I see you I do recall that we exchanged some words—I never forget a pretty face—but when we first spoke I thought you might well be a lunatic; I get many calls from lunatics." He shrugged, an incredibly expressive gesture as played out by his two rocklike shoulders. "Maybe you are a lunatic."

"I'm not," I interjected needlessly.

"Anyway, I asked around, you know, to see if I should keep our date—because if you were a lunatic, well, I have no interest in meeting with crazy people. But those I asked said, 'Hey, she's famous. She's great.' So I came. You don't like coffee?"

I'd been glaring into the cup, and I smiled meekly, lifting the drink to my lips. The steam was sticky and unpleasant in my face.

"So now here we are. A great musician, and a great misanthrope. A real meeting of the minds."

I moved my dumb stare from the cup to his clanging features. I realized, with some mild surprise, that when he let his face relax he was still a good-looking man, with the strong jaw and intense blue eyes as roughly striking as they had been in the much younger pictures of him I'd seen in scattered newspaper articles over the years.

"I haven't offended you, I hope." His tone suggested exactly the opposite.

I was about to tell him that he hadn't, that I was tougher than I looked, but he had started speaking again.

"My father was a great Polish historian," he said abruptly, as though I'd asked. "Piotr Pasek. He was a professor at Jagiellonian University here in Kraków."

"The Oxbridge of Poland," I offered, quoting from my guidebook. My guidebook had been my sole companion for the past few days.

He gave me a puzzled, impatient look, then continued.

"My father was an important man. The Second Republic of Poland even appointed him the official state historian—this was between the two world wars, you understand, so Poland was an independent nation."

I nodded, which seemed to irritate him. It had not yet become clear to me that the "you understand"s which peppered his speech were meant to be taken more as orders (you understand!) than questions (you understand?). He cleared his throat purposefully before picking up his narrative.

"What I mean to say is that when the Nazis came to power we hardly considered ourselves Jews. My grandfather, you understand, had been the chief rabbi of Kraków, and his father before him, but we . . ." He waved away the rest of the sentence, his knotty hand taking on an air of graceful insouciance in the gesture.

"I was angry when my father told me that we were running away to England, just when things were looking bad for our country, with the invasions just begun. I told him, 'We're going to beat the Germans. They won't get so far as twenty kilometers into Poland.' This was the talk I was hearing around me then. That this invasion was nothing to worry about."

He paused for a moment, and motioned toward my cup. "Polish coffee too strong for you, eh?"

The coffee was disgustingly weak, but I didn't bother to say so, merely shrugging in response. He seemed satisfied—gratified even—and continued on.

"In England I had one pleasure only, and that was the Polish film office. Their filmmakers were recording the war, the gathering soldiers, the battles, everything. I would sometimes spend whole days watching them over and over, hiding in the back of the theater between showings. When the war ended, I returned to Poland alone. My family refused to come. 'What are you going back to?' my sister Rosa asked. 'There is no country to return to.' My father agreed. 'It is the last Partition,' he told me. 'Soviets now. There is no Poland.' But of course I came back, of course Poland was still Poland, and for over a year I did almost nothing but aimlessly wander the streets of Kraków, watching my father's predictions come true. These walks were my own private documentary film, entitled *Everything Is Going to Hell.* I'm not sure when I first got the idea to enroll in the film school at Łódź. I had the notion that I could do something much like the wartime documentarians had done, only now I would need the subtlety afforded by fiction to do what they had accomplished so honestly. In 1981, after martial law was declared, it was only my film unit and one other that were disbanded.

I took this as a sign that I had done what I had set out to do. I was inspiring the people, keeping their nationalist spirit alive, and the government was afraid of me. You know, Lenin himself once said of film that it is the most important of the art forms. That is probably our one point of agreement."

"Fascinating," I said, because it was, but also because I was unsure why he was telling me all this, and how he wanted me to respond.

"This is what you must understand," he continued, as if he'd read my mind, which did not seem at all impossible given the penetrating way he held my eyes. He stabbed a thick finger down on the table for emphasis. "You are an artist. You think that here, before you, is one of the same. You think, Let us talk, let us compare, let us theorize together about truth and beauty"—here he raised an eyebrow with some amusement—"and I am saying, 'Beautiful Natasha, this is not who I am. I am simply a man who loves Poland.' "

"Oh, but that's not why I . . ." I began, but then trailed off. What was I going to say next? That I'd tracked him down because his rabid gaze and ideology-soaked art reminded me of a man I was trying to forget?

"I'm just moved by your films," I ended up offering.

"And I am saying that was not my intent."

"But surely it was."

"No."

"Not to move people?"

"No. To keep them from giving in."

"I'm not sure I see the difference."

He gave me one of the more evocative scowls I'd ever seen, and I was more than a little curious to know what would come out of his mouth next. Unfortunately, just then Pasek's small, harried friend come scurrying up to our table. Again without even glancing in my direction, he whispered something in Pasek's ear and then stood at attention, as though awaiting orders.

"Ah." Pasek rose more fluidly than I'd have thought his large body able. "You must excuse me for my rude behavior. Two days of filming are perhaps in jeopardy, and this I cannot allow."

He threw a few crumpled bills on the table, and barked some

words to his friend, who went running off in the direction from which he'd come.

"A rain check?" he asked, but before I could respond he was striding determinedly across the stone slabs of Main Market Square. I watched his thick back, covered in a woolly gray workman's shirt thinly lined in red, retreat. There was an elegant brusqueness to his movement, and I let my eyes follow him until the broad swath of gray disappeared into a crowd.

I was sure then that I'd never hear from Aleksander Pasek again, and that this impetuous trip, with its short and weird culmination in Main Market Square, would be the sort of memory I'd shrug at, uncomprehendingly, in future years. More than that, I suspected I should be grateful for the abortive nature of our acquaintance. That Pasek intrigued me seemed more dangerous than promising; all I needed was another monomaniac with whom to get tangled up.

But the next afternoon, when I returned to my hotel following a morning of sightseeing—I'd secured myself a tour guide, a young woman studying Polish literature at the university who offered "tours for the erudite," which I was not, but wished I was—I was reluctantly excited to find an invitation to dinner waiting from him. It was the sort of invitation I could imagine no one but Pasek leaving—a voice message containing simply the name of a restaurant and a time. The unabashed idiosyncrasy of it was what convinced me to go, because a large, sane portion of my mind was telling me that to do so was idiocy.

The restaurant wasn't listed in my guidebook, and when the concierge tracked it down for me it turned out to be an hour's drive from the city, in the village of Wislica. Again I hesitated, but again the strangeness convinced me to proceed. I hired a car, and dressed carefully, choosing a businesslike linen skirt suit.

The drive took even longer than the concierge had estimated, but the view was picturesque as we rolled past darkened farmland, forests, and sleeping villages. In one of these villages we pulled up along the side of the road, in front of a drafty-looking thatched-roof structure that I hoped was not our destination. The driver told me to wait in the car and climbed out to consult a group of men singing by the side of the road.

"Is close," he said as he climbed back in. "But roads is narrow and muddy. Better we leave car."

I didn't like the idea of wading through muck in my strappy heels, but I deferred to my driver's better knowledge of the byways of Poland. I followed him out and onto a small road, so small that our car almost certainly could not have fit between the wooden houses lining each side. He pointed to a well-lit building, larger than the wooden houses we were walking past, several yards ahead: "There, yes?" It wasn't far, just as he'd claimed, but the ground was spongy from an afternoon rain shower, and I felt that I was in distinct danger of losing my shoes. I was afraid to slow down, not wanting to fall out of shouting range of my driver, who was rushing along at his own loose-legged pace. I was about to call out to ask him please to wait for me, when I felt my feet lose contact with the earth. I thought, at first, that I'd fallen, that I was heading downward toward the slosh of a road, but I had been lifted up off the ground into strong male arms. There was a stench of vodka.

"Welcome to Wislica, Tasha Darsky," Aleksander Pasek barked. "Sorry about the mud."

He carried me the rest of the way to the inn, which might have been disarming if it hadn't been so disconcerting. I was relieved to feel the clink of my heels on solid stone steps.

The dining room was simple and rustic, filled with a soft yellow light. A small old woman approached us, her face radiant with a toothless grin.

"Witaj!" she exclaimed, as Pasek took her in his arms. They exchanged a few more words in Polish before she led us to a table, tucked into a far corner of the room. The remoteness of the table seemed unnecessary given that there were no other guests.

My driver had disappeared into some other part of the inn, and the old woman vanished as well. I stared across the table at Aleksander Pasek; I couldn't keep myself from staring at that face. There was a lot to learn from it.

"You are surprised," he said. I thought he meant surprised at the shift in his behavior, which, naturally, I was.

"Confused," I admitted.

"No restaurant in Kraków is as good as the Golden Egg." My

surprise, I gathered, was not supposed to be directed at his sudden familiarity, but at his dining preferences. "I discovered this place while I was filming *Treny.* I don't know what I'll do when Framka passes on. No one else can cook to my liking."

I was glad for the return of the man I'd expected: crass, blunt, transcendentally egocentric.

Again, as if he could read my thoughts, he changed his tone. "I'm sorry. You think that I am tactless. You think I am an uncaring, crotchety old man. But I love Framka. She is like my second mother." He leaned in close to me, and whispered, "I send her a check every month. She thinks it's from the government. From the government, can you imagine!" He let out a low throttle of laughter.

There seemed to be no end to variations on the theme of Aleksander Pasek.

"So now, Tasha Darsky, let me hear the other relevant facts."

"About me, you mean?"

"Yes, what else?"

"Well, I should warn you first that I am an artist, and my aim is to move people." He looked hurt at this, as if it were unfair of me to hold him accountable for statements he'd made just the day before.

"I'm afraid that, aside from that, there isn't much to tell," I demurred. "I haven't lived a life like yours."

"Everyone has a narrative to their life. You just have to find the relevant plot." And now here was Aleksander the sage, to round out the full cast of personalities.

"I think my plot might simply be my career," I offered, apologetically.

"Ah, the story, much loved always, of success."

"It's far from inspiring, I know. No wars or heroism, no lifelong causes. An embarrassingly self-focused existence."

"Your life, as far as I can see, has not been very long," he cut me off. "I would guess you're no older than twenty-five."

"Twenty-nine," I corrected, wondering why he hadn't let me continue. Had I been making a fool of myself?

It had started raining again, and the drops were creating a resonant patter on the wooden roof above us. The windows across the room rattled. We both stared intently at the glass. Framka reappeared with two bowls and a large pot. She set the pot down between us, and ladled a thick, beefy stew into the bowls. She had set my driver to work: he came out behind her with a bottle of vodka and a bottle of wine, and filled four glasses.

"You're not one of the American vegetable-eaters, I hope?" Aleksander asked.

"I eat meat, if that's what you mean."

"Good, because this is all that Framka cooks. The one item on the menu."

He winked at her, and she burst out into a deep belly laugh. It sounded like the laugh of a much younger woman.

"Does she understand English?"

Aleksander began laughing, too, the laugh of a much older man. Framka slapped him on the arm, and he returned the gesture. They looked like a couple of children stabbing at flirtation. Then Framka and my driver hurried out as unobtrusively as they'd hurried in. I tasted the stew. It was pungent and earthy, tasting strongly of potatoes and some other flavor I could not identify.

"You like it?" he asked, and though it was more like "You like it!" I treated it as a question.

"It's delicious. Really delicious."

"Framka"—he lowered his voice again—"has a very engaging story to her life."

"Oh?"

"She was once famous, too, like us."

"For her food?" I asked.

"Her sex."

"Excuse me?"

"She was a famous whore. In Kraków, between the wars."

"Are you sure?" I found it difficult to imagine, though I suppose it's hard to imagine any battered old woman as she might have been in the lusty blush of youth. The laugh, though, deep and greedy for life, lent the idea some plausibility.

He shrugged. "I believe what she tells me."

He paused, one finger to his thick lower lip, and considered my question again.

"Well, if she were inventing the tale, it might be even more interesting, no? But this is not so. She can describe everything about the high society of interwar Kraków with perfection. She could not have been correct on so many details by chance."

"What kind of details?"

Aleksander put his finger to his lips again, this time to silence me. Framka had returned with a dark loaf of bread. It still wasn't clear to me whether she understood English. Aleksander tore off a piece from the loaf and handed it to me. It was hot, and I dropped it into my bowl by mistake. He pretended not to notice. Perhaps he really didn't; he was watching Framka's retreat.

"Facts about important government officials, and other eminent people in the city. About their private lives and private spats. I knew enough from growing up in these circles to authenticate her version of events. She was heavily involved with these men. That is for certain. She knows some intimate secrets. Secrets even a household servant would not know."

"How do you know she wasn't one of their wives?"

"If she were a respectable woman, why would she tell me she was a prostitute?" he asked. "And, besides, how would she know about so many men's secrets?" It seemed like a reasonable inference, and yet I couldn't quite get myself to believe that this brittle remnant of a woman had once led a life of dissipation.

"She sounds like more of a courtesan than a prostitute," I ventured. "I mean, if she was so well integrated into these high circles."

"Yes, a courtesan. That's a good word for it. She was a courtesan. Like Dumas's Camille."

"How did she end up here?" I asked.

"That, Natasha, is the good part of the story. Of all her admirers, her most ardent was Jan Krzesło. You know of Jan Krzesło?"

I admitted that I did not, though I suspected this would lower me in his estimation.

"He was an important man in Kraków back then. Very important. He owned many factories. One of the richest men in Kraków. He poured much money into the city, was involved in local government. A good friend of my father's. I knew him as 'Uncle Januk.' "

"And she was this man's lover?"

"Not just his lover, his love. Jan was married with a big family, you understand, but he had an awful wife. Aunt Ewa. Mean, and dissatisfied, and fat. Mean and fat children, too. My sisters and I were afraid of them. We felt bad for Uncle Januk. We didn't know, though, that he had a bewitching mistress. We would have been happy to hear it."

"Was she very lovely?"

"She must have been. I imagine her to look like you."

He smiled dashingly as he said this.

"When the war came, Jan was afraid for Framka. Did I mention that she's Jewish? Well, she is. That's important. Naturally, Jan was afraid for his Jewish courtesan." He drew out the last word, and winked. "Everyone had some inkling that things would not be good for the Jews under Nazi occupation, even if they could not have imagined how bad. So this is what he did: he secured for her the best fake papers, saying that her name was Framka Swetsław. You know, she never told me her real name? Perhaps you think here is a hole in her story. Then he bought her this inn in Wislica, from a couple who were happy to retire in luxury. What genius, eh? He sets her up, not far from Kraków, in an inn. It was a wonderful hiding place, plus a convenient spot for him to visit! Unfortunately, he did not get to take advantage of this clever arrangement for long. He was killed by the Gestapo in 1940, for propagating anti-German sentiment."

"And she just stayed here?"

"You mean in this small village, far from the glamour of city life? Yes. Who knows why? Maybe this life suited her better. Maybe she was afraid of the city once it was under communist rule."

"Maybe she was heartbroken over the loss of Jan," I suggested.

"Doubtful. She was a prostitute."

"Still," I insisted. "It's possible."

His shrug was an eloquent rebuttal.

"Certainly it is not a choice either of us would make, eh?"

I sensed he was posing it as a bond between us, and so I didn't object. I wouldn't have had the chance to anyway, since right then Framka bustled back in, said something to Aleksander in Polish, and left again.

"Your driver is staying the night," he told me after she'd gone.

"You're kidding."

"The roads are too bad for driving. Dirt roads, you know. Not safe."

"Well, how am I supposed to get back?" I asked.

"He'll drive you tomorrow." Again the shrug. "I'm staying as well."

"Where am I supposed to sleep?"

"This is an inn," he laughed. "I think we can find you a bed."

I felt heat rising to my cheeks. It was not unpleasant.

"I have things I need to do," I stammered, because I was sure this was an invitation, but wasn't as sure that I wanted to accept it. "I'm meeting someone tomorrow morning."

"Someone important?" he asked.

"My tour guide."

He laughed again. "I'll give you a tour tomorrow. I'll introduce you to real Poland."

I hesitated, afraid that whatever I said next would commit me.

"Framka decided to stay here her whole life, so you can manage one evening," he ventured, portentously, when the silence began to grow uncomfortable.

I smiled and nodded, though the statement made little sense to me, then took a sip of vodka. I hadn't touched it all night, sticking with the watery wine instead.

"Are you finished eating?" Aleksander eyed my empty bowl.

"I guess I am." I took another swig from the vodka. It went down easier than any vodka I'd had before. There was a hint of potato in it, which made it taste less like poison. I liked it much more than the wine.

I noticed then that Aleksander had his hands spread on the table as if he was about to push himself up. I tried to imagine kissing him, but realized I was picturing my face pressed up against a far younger version of his, an image stolen from the pictures I'd seen over the years. He stood, and I ran through the reasons I should not do this. I wondered whether I would. But the question turned out to be moot.

As I joined him on my feet he said, "I hope you don't mind if I excuse myself. I'm very tired."

Seconds later, he'd gathered our empty dishes, and disappeared the same way as Framka and my driver. Framka turned up at the bottom of the stairs, as if they'd arranged a relay system. She beckoned for me to follow her, and we climbed together up the creaky staircase. I tried to conjure the image of a young Framka leading her lover up these steps for the last time. It was just like Pasek to bring me to a place once brewing with improbable romance and then abandon me at the crucial juncture.

Upstairs, there was a long hallway, longer than I would have anticipated, lined with identical doors. Framka opened one of them and revealed a room so small there wasn't even space for the two of us to stand inside together. I walked in and sat on the bed. Though it was tiny, the room was clean, as were the bedclothes, which was more than I could say for my suite back in the supposedly posh hotel in Kraków.

"It's perfect," I told her. "Thank you."

She smiled, leaving the question of her English still unanswered.

"Good night," I said.

She smiled again and left, closing the door behind me.

In a moment of paranoia, I formed the idea that she had locked me into this confined space, but a push at the door sent it flying open. I found then that I couldn't get it to close properly again, and so I left it stubbornly ajar. I turned my face to the wall, away from the dim light traveling up the stairs from the dining room, and listened to the ping-ping-ping of the raindrops falling on the roof, just feet from my head.

I'd been lulled into a pre-sleep trance, my breath falling into the rhythm of the relentless pinging, when I realized that I'd forgotten to ask Framka about the washroom. I opened the door and tiptoed down the hall, unsure whether there were other guests to disturb, though I strongly doubted it. None of the doors opened, and I shuffled back toward the stairs and down into the dining room.

Framka was sitting very still at one of the tables, and I was about to approach her for direction when I realized that across from her, talking in low tones, was Aleksander.

Back upstairs, I found the bathroom behind an exceedingly narrow door I'd assumed opened to a closet. While I splashed water on my face, I tried to shake my juvenile horror at the possibility of being left out or rejected. I pictured the two of them downstairs talking, and wondered why I'd been removed from the picture. It took me hours to fall asleep, the ping of the rain only aggravating.

I woke up the next morning to sun streaming through my tiny grate of a window, and the delicious smell of freshly baking bread saturating the dense air of my room. Aleksander and my driver were already seated at a table when I came down, sipping from cups of a strong-smelling coffee.

At another table there was a young man in an old suit, reading a newspaper.

"Good morning," I called cheerily from the base of the stairs.

Aleksander turned around, a piece of bread poised halfway to his lips. "You slept well?" he asked.

"I did," I lied. "And you?"

"Always."

I sat between Aleksander and my driver and piled some slices of cheese and tomato onto a thick hunk of warm black bread.

"So when are we leaving for Kraków?" I directed the question at my driver.

"Not until later," Aleksander answered. "First we are going to do my tour."

"Not of Kraków?"

"Of course, no. Of Poland. The tour guides can show you the city. I will show you the important things."

His boyish enthusiasm as he said this prevented me from protesting.

Within the hour, we'd left behind Wislica, heading wordlessly northward into the primeval forests. Eventually, when we were nowhere in particular as far as I could tell, Aleksander asked the driver to pull over. (He called him "Stanisław," making me realize I had never bothered to learn his name.)

Hefting a basket out of the trunk—packed, I supposed, with a picnic courtesy of Framka—Aleksander barked to Stanisław that we'd return well before dark.

"How are we going to find our way back to the car?" I pressed. It had not escaped my attention that the forest was vast and thick.

He shrugged. "This is my concern."

I didn't see how the problem, should it arise, would affect him any more than it would me, but I decided not to point this out. I had the sense that today he was poised halfway between the boor and the gentleman.

We walked in silence, he a few paces ahead, moving as if he had a definite goal in mind. I found it difficult to maneuver the uneven terrain in my mud-soaked heels, and struggled to keep up with him. If he noticed me lagging, he didn't give any indication; he seemed to speed up whenever my feet felt on the verge of giving out. He finally paused in a spot not significantly different from many others we'd passed. I wondered what minute considerations were guiding his choices; perhaps they were invisible to any but the discerning eye of a director; or perhaps he was just enjoying toying with me.

"Here?" I asked, desperate to sit.

He looked uncertain, but nodded.

I opened the basket and removed a blanket, which he then spread on the ground for me. I leapt at it, sliding my burning feet out of their straps. He lay down next to me.

"This," he motioned around him, "is Poland. Untouched by the hands of communism. This is what I love. This is my tour."

"You do love it, don't you?" I remarked. "You must be so happy now."

"I am," he said, grabbing my hand and then letting go. Other than his gallant effort to protect me from the mud the evening before, he'd given no indication that my body exerted a pull on him. I wanted to grab his hand in turn, and keep it, but the gesture seemed false.

"No, I mean, now that Poland is becoming Poland again," I corrected, thinking that he was saying that he was happy here, right now, with me.

"Yes, I understand." His tone wasn't impatient, but I bristled. To hide my embarrassment, I continued, "What does it feel like? I mean, to want something so much, to want it even when it seems impossible, and then to get it. It must be wonderful."

The subject seemed not to interest him, because in response he pointed to a particularly large beech and asked, "You know about trees?"

"Not much."

"This tree was probably around when King Władysław Łokiełek hid here from King Wenceslas of Bohemia. This tree. You can tell from the thickness of the trunk."

I thought he was going to continue musing about Polish history, but instead he lapsed into a tutorial on Polish flora. It wasn't until hours later, until after he'd finished his long tutorial, and we'd eaten Framka's immense lunch, and had lain staring up at the trees, lightly grazing each other's side, that he returned to the question I'd posed.

"It isn't wonderful," he said, not loud, but loud enough to startle me after the silence of the past few minutes, disturbed by nothing but the rustling leaves.

"What isn't?" I asked, continuing to stare upward. He hadn't sat up or even rolled onto his side, and I followed his lead.

"Getting what you have wanted all along. It isn't wonderful."

"I could see that," I sympathized. "I mean, that it would be anticlimactic. You can't help thinking beforehand that once it happens everything will be perfect. You don't realize how many new, serious problems even the most hoped-for wish will bring with it."

We were silent again for a while after that, and I felt close to him, or at least I felt that he felt close to me, that I'd understood him, and that he was grateful to me for it. But eventually he muttered, "That's not what I mean at all."

"Oh." I was amazed I could have read the lull so wrong. "Well, what do you mean?"

"I mean it's not wonderful for me. Just for me."

"I don't understand. Why is it different for you?"

I was still on my back, as was he. I sensed he wanted us to remain this way, turned toward the heavens instead of toward each other. He laid his hand on my stomach. It felt reassuring. For minutes, that's how we lay, on our backs, his heavy hand on my belly. Then his hand glided downward, slowly but not tentatively. Seconds later, it was him I was staring up into, his severe face less severe as it lowered down onto mine. I opened my mouth, tasted the meat and cheese on his breath, the vodka I hadn't noticed him drinking. He tasted like food, but he also tasted like earth, like forest. I mused that he tasted like the country he loved, but perhaps it was just the dirt flying around us in the breeze.

I felt him reach for the buttons on my blouse, thought I should stop him, and found I had no desire to do so. His hand sliding onto my breast felt as good as his hand sliding onto my belly, and his body, pressed now on top of mine, was invigorating. His bulk was more muscle than fat, a powerful body, a purposeful body. I let it carry out its present purpose.

Afterward, lying half clothed among trees that had once shaded Polish kings, my sights returned toward the thick canopies, I wondered what I had just done. Was it Pasek I'd just allowed to make love to me, or was it an association I'd stamped onto him? That I was now feeling so settled and righted beside a man with whom I'd forged no real connection, made the latter seem disturbingly plausible.

"It isn't wonderful for me because I have become the lowest form of being," he murmured in a voice so low I could hardly make out the words.

"A communist?" I guessed. Had he sold out and joined the party after all? Would he soon suffer for that?

"An artist," he corrected.

"An artist?"

"Yes. I started out as a patriot, with selfless goals. I took a wrong turn and became an artist. I ended up with only selfish goals."

"Why do you always speak as if there's such a contrast between patriotism and artistry?"

"Because Poland was my art. Now if Poland becomes Poland it's no longer my art."

"You mean, you'll lose your inspiration once Poland is free from Soviet control? Is that what you mean?"

"Something like that."

"I don't see why that needs to be. You have so much new material now."

"*Needs to be, has to be,* doesn't matter. The important thing is *is.* My art is dead. Maybe the essence of my art, as you say, was nothing so broad as Poland. Maybe it was just something so narrow as freeing Poland from Soviet control. Maybe I was just an artist of

Polish independence. For some people the medium is paint, some film, some music, some bodily motion. Why not for me independence?"

"I doubt that's possible."

"Well, *I* have no desire left. No ideas." He sounded exasperated, almost angry. I wanted to lay my hand on his stomach like he'd done to me; it had felt so reassuring. But I wasn't sure it would have the same effect on him.

"So, since you ask, it is not wonderful for me, no. There you have it. Aleksander Pasek, the great patriotic filmmaker, the man some people say should run for highest office, wishes the communists would come back to power. Alone at night, that's what he prays for. Not the safety of his country, but its vulnerability."

"I doubt it's so dramatic as all that," I reasoned, though the rawness of his sentiments fascinated me. "It's only natural to feel some ambiguity in a situation this loaded with expectation. If someone gave you the choice to personally undo the elections or not to, we both know what you'd decide."

He reached over and kissed me one last time, and I thought it was because my words had soothed him. It occurred to me only later that something in his manner indicated that he hadn't heard me. He sat up, and began to gather our clothes and scattered dishes.

"We should find the car," he suggested, pulling a shirt over the smooth expanse of his chest. "It will be dark soon."

I helped him stuff the blanket into the basket, and then resumed my place stumbling behind him, trying not to trip over roots and rocks. As on the way there, we exchanged no words.

Stanisław was waiting where we'd left him, reading the same thin newspaper we'd left him with that morning.

"Good time?" he asked. His thick eyebrows rose just short of insinuation, as though he was trying to offend me without upsetting Aleksander.

"Yes, very," I said.

Aleksander said nothing.

He was silent for the rest of the trip home, but so was I. We were both tired. And when he reached for my hand across the backseat, I didn't pull away. We sat hand in hand during the entire ride back to Kraków.

When we reached the city limits, he leaned over and directed Stanisław in Polish. I thought it was rude that he would ask to be let off first, but it didn't bother me. I smiled at him as he climbed out, and was surprised when he poked his head back in to give me a kiss on the forehead. The gesture seemed more tender than our afternoon warranted.

"Shall we get together again soon?" I called out after him, emboldened by the trace feel of his lips still lingering below my hairline.

He nodded without turning around, already retreating into the old brick house he had lived in since childhood.

"Yes, very soon. Call my home."

That night, one of his movies happened to be playing on the rickety television set in my room. It was one of those he'd claimed was his best, *Mothers and Ministers,* about an affair between a nineteenth-century French minister and a Polish noblewoman. I didn't like it all that much, and I told myself, the next afternoon, that part of the reason I was calling to invite him to dinner at my hotel was to ask him why he considered it a favorite. There was no answer, and so I left a message, then headed out to meet my well-paid traveling companion. When I returned to the hotel early in the evening, I was in a foul mood because my day of sightseeing had turned into a fraught reunion. My guide had been sullen until we reached the spooky underground cathedral of the Wieliczka Salt Mines, at which point she proceeded to bawl me out in front of a large group of Italian tourists for the previous day's absence. The experience made me keen on a quiet dinner with a friendly face, and I figured Aleksander was the closest candidate, and so I was annoyed to find, when I returned to the hotel, that he hadn't returned my call. I dialed the number again, but again he didn't pick up, and I wasn't going to leave a second message. He didn't return my call at all that night. I decided I wouldn't try reaching him again—let him call me if he wanted—but late the next morning, uninspired by the prospect of another journey alone with my guidebook, I dialed his number anyway.

This time he answered on the first ring.

"Today, you mean?" he asked, when I invited him to take me around to his favorite spots in the city. "Oh, that would have been so nice. Only, unfortunately, I must leave this afternoon for Łódź. It's the Polish film festival, you understand. Otherwise I would have loved to show you the charm of Kraków. I will be away from Kraków precisely one week. Will you still be here when I return?"

I couldn't help hearing in that last question a bit of dread, as if I was a pest: Will you *still* be here?

"I hadn't been planning to stay that long," I answered truthfully.

"Oh no? So it is a shame. Perhaps we can meet up again next time!"

I was about to reply, something about having no idea when, if ever, my next trip to Kraków would be, when I heard the line go dead.

Within the hour, I'd packed my bags and headed off to Bruen.

My mother took me at my word when I said that Pasek had been scary and strange and that we'd only met twice; she was more concerned with the house we'd rented sight-unseen, distraught that it was closer to a bungalow than a villa and that the second bedroom was a partially enclosed terrace. But the bungalow was pretty and well cared for, with a small garden out back skirting the edges of the lake, and the weather was so pleasant, with cool winds rising off the water, that I preferred my veranda to a normal bedroom. For a couple of weeks I swam and rested and ate a tremendous amount of cheese, and the memory of Pasek faded.

That is, until I discovered Pasek's legacy to me, at the beginning of the third week. Instead of a new us to throw myself into, he'd given me a missed period. I waited seven days before reacting. Then I went to the pediatrician whose bungalow was next door to ours. She confirmed what I already knew.

The pediatrician tactfully suggested the name of a doctor nearby who she happened to know was good at taking care of such problems. It might be best to do it here, she said. If I returned to America, or even traveled to Geneva or Berlin, there was sure to be press. I agreed, and thanked her for the advice. Then, leaving only a cryptic note for my mother while she was sunning herself by the lake, I boarded a train bound for Kraków. It seemed only fair to let him know.

I called Aleksander as soon as I got to my hotel, told him I was back in town and had an important matter that I wanted to discuss. He invited me to come to his house that evening, but I told him that I was too tired from the trip, that I'd come the following morning.

The next day he greeted me at the grand mahogany door of his grand house, with a worried look on his face. He took my arm authoritatively, guided me to a seat in the formal turn-of-the-century living room. There was a tremendous grandfather clock chiming the hour in the corner. I thought that, in an odd way, the clock looked like Aleksander: appealing in its outsized charmlessness. He asked if I felt all right. I said I did. He asked if I wanted coffee. I said I did not, I just wanted to tell him my news and be done with it. He nodded, then saved me the trouble of giving the report.

"You're going to get rid of it, I assume."

"I'm not," I told him firmly, my voice much stronger than my convictions warranted. I had only just made this decision on the way over.

"You're not," he repeated calmly, perhaps patronizingly.

"No."

"I hope you're not making any plans that involve me, then."

"Of course not." I actually had been making such plans. I'd even hoped he'd feel transformed inside, just as I did. "Flesh and Blood" sounded like the title of a Pasek film.

"Good." He patted my leg, an incongruous gesture given the sentiment it accompanied.

He asked again if I wanted any coffee. I shook my head, and told him I'd said all I wanted to say and would go now.

He put his hand on my arm; it felt reassuring, as it had the last time.

"Natasha." He said my name in a voice that was not gentle. "I hope that you have thought out this choice of yours."

"I'm not a child," I whispered in a treacherously childlike voice.

"No, you are not a child, but are you a mother?"

"I'm about to be." The word sounded alien. Was I going to be one of those? "Do you doubt my competence?"

"I suppose I don't know you well enough."

"That's certainly true."

"I hope you don't think I'm a bad person." He looked at me searchingly, and I was inclined to believe he did care. But the remark sounded too naïve, the simplicity of the phrase "bad person" almost comical, and I wondered whether imminent parenthood wasn't regressing both of us.

"I don't," I told him, though I did.

"You think I'm cruel, but I'm not."

"I understand. This is my choice, not yours."

"What's cruel is to have a child you don't want."

"Maybe that's cruel. I don't know."

"It is very cruel to have a child you can't love."

"You think I can't love my child?" Just saying those last two words—the first time I had ever put the possessive pronoun to that noun—brought me close to tears.

He shrugged his uniquely eloquent shrug.

"What an awful thing to say!"

"I never said you couldn't love your child."

"I think you did."

"Did you think you could learn to love me as well?" he asked. It seemed like a particularly mean question; I was beginning to dislike even his unshrinking honesty.

"Maybe. I hadn't given it much thought. I don't know what I'd hoped could happen." Why, I wondered, was I even answering him?

"You could never love me."

"Why, because you're so unlovable, or because I'm incapable of loving?"

"I don't presume to know you that well."

"So you claim."

He stood up and began pacing, stopping in front of a bank of photographs. I strained to see, from across the spacious room, what faces were staring out at him. Then he began to laugh, his ancient-sounding rumbles shaking his whole body.

"Remember," he said, turning back to me, "I told you I saw only one movie before World War II?"

I nodded, though I didn't remember his telling me this.

"Did I tell you what it was called?"

"I don't think you did. Not that I remember."

"I didn't tell you. I'm sure I didn't. It was called *Everyone Can Fall in Love.* A silly title, eh?"

"I've heard worse." I had the puerile urge to throw out some of the titles of his own films. *Spoons and Scarves* came to mind.

"It's silly," he continued, "because it isn't true. Not everybody can fall in love."

"I'm not sure I believe that."

"You of anyone should."

"Why's that?" My eyes burned with indignation. I didn't know much about prenatal health, and I worried whether this high level of emotion would be harmful to my baby.

"Only because I suspect you might be one of those who can't."

"I have been in love, deeply in love. And what happened to not presuming?"

The shrug was slower this time, and even more suffused with expression. "Perhaps I know more about you than you think."

"What does that mean?"

"Consider this." He ignored my question. "You might have only thought you were in love. Is that possible? I think you only love one thing. Same as me."

"What? Myself?" Is this why he'd chosen me as the receptacle for his dark secret? Decided to bury his shame in my body? Because he'd gotten the impression that I was a soulless mate? How flattering.

"No. God, no! We don't love ourselves at all. If we did we would surely let ourselves fall in love. No, we love something higher."

"Not art?" What a cliché. I almost laughed, but I was too furious to smile. How dare he equate his own misplaced ideals with my emotional capacity. How dare he assume that because he had lost his selfless patriotic fervor I was as cold and dead inside as he. Even in my furor, though, I might have dismissed the whole conversation in a single liberating burst of jollity if it weren't for my pity—how could I not feel for this man who believed that art had emotionally castrated him, and that he had found in me a similarly dismembered spirit?

"Yes!" he shouted. "Yes, art! That devil's altar!"

"That's ridiculous."

"Is it? Tell me something, would you ever sacrifice personal happiness for your art?"

"I think most people sacrifice personal happiness for their work, artistic or otherwise."

"Yes, but what would you sacrifice? Or, rather, what wouldn't you sacrifice?"

I didn't answer at first. I thought of the paralyzing fear of artistic failure I'd often felt in my youth, thrashing in the sheets at night. I thought of Jean Paul, a man I'd confused with an art form, who still believed that I'd sacrificed his soul to my own ambitions. (And was he entirely wrong?) I thought of my life, empty of everything but music and fame, empty of any real companions but my parents, empty of any prospects for love. What would I not sacrifice? What had I not sacrificed? And then I knew.

"This child," I told him. "I wouldn't sacrifice this child."

He was still standing near the bank of photographs, handling one absentmindedly. I'd had the urge a moment before to hurl the tasseled pillow at him, or something heavier, but now I felt all the frustration, anger, and fear dissipate. The thick swirls of sadness and bitterness wafted away. For the first time in my life I felt strong—not just defiant or determined, which I had felt often enough, but strong in the sense of capable and, more important, certain.

"You don't have to worry about either of us bothering you," I assured him again, calmly gathering myself. "Please don't walk me out."

I gave him a long, memorizing look then—his face angry and stricken, his eyes clanging their displeasure—and then I stepped calmly out the door.

IV

p a tempo
p a tempo

BY THE TIME I GET HOME FROM MY PARENTS' BROWN-stone, it's past midnight. My body wants nothing more than to crawl into bed, but I cannot imagine letting go of this day before I know something more definite about what connects my daughter to Jean Paul. Musical snooping is one thing, I realize, and physical snooping another, but I go into her room anyway.

The space is nothing like it was three weeks ago, when it served as a neat and tidy shrine to an absent child. Now it is filled with the actual presence of that child, which in Alex's case always means a mess. Discarded clothes are flung everywhere, mixed in with used dishes, half a bagel lying at the foot of the bed. But the primary material of this chaos is staff paper, reams of it, covered in notes and covering every surface: stacked in piles on the desk, spread across the bed, littering the floor in clumps.

I go to the piles on the desk first, and am surprised to find lying on top of one of these stacks a bunch of old reviews and programs from performances Alex and I gave together, as well as three photographs, all taken by my mother. One shows Alex, aged five years, pulling me impatiently by the hand down a street in Amsterdam; the two others are snapped in indeterminate European hotel rooms, and in both Alex and I smile at each other rather than at the camera: my mother has caught us off guard, and the easy tightness of our bond is made palpable through her sharp eye. Alex must have removed these from the closet in my bedroom within the last few weeks, and this, paired with her surprising decision to play her new music for me last night, makes me queasy with the thought that she'd been on the brink of finding her way back toward me. Again, I am struck with the bad luck of it, and as I curse the reporter under my breath I begin to tear through the piles more recklessly, no longer taking care to leave everything just as it was.

It takes only a few seconds of this reckless tearing to find something promising: the piece of music I'd been trying to reconstruct from a thin memory until last night. I look it over and let out a hiccupped cry of triumph, because staring up at me from the top of the second page of this score is a phone number. I stare at this number a long while, knowing there's nothing I can sanely do with it—it might not even be his—but moving toward the phone anyway, wondering what I'll say, dialing the numbers, hating, hating, hating the man who will answer at the other end.

It seems to ring forever, and I am about to hang up when his voice comes on, that whispery-deep Franco-Exeter blend.

"Hello? Hello? Who is this? Alexandra, is this you?"

"No, Jean Paul, it's me."

"Ah, Tasha," he breathes my name heavily, and it sends shivers up my spine. "I've been hoping you'd call."

AFTER THAT SCENE IN PASEK'S HOUSE, IT WAS MONTHS before I told anyone else I was pregnant. Instead, I continued to go about life as if nothing had changed. Not even my mother suspected, though she was still traveling with me more often than not. In private, though, I tore through libraries' worth of baby books, then stuffed them underneath mattresses or deep in drawers. I whispered conspiratorially to my belly. And I plotted ways to break the news to my parents. It never seemed like a good time.

As the weeks wore on, of course, my secret became harder to keep. My stomach was growing, not dramatically but perceptibly, and I was forced to buy an emergency wardrobe of suspiciously looser clothes during a three-day stay in London. I was also making brief, furtive trips to ob-gyns in every other city I visited. Still, I put off telling my parents. I might well have tried to put it off until I had a child to show them, if I hadn't gotten sick in Milan when I was just five months pregnant. The cautious doctor I ducked in to see didn't like the sound of my deep coughs, and ordered me to cancel all engagements for the foreseeable future.

If telling Pasek had been trying, it was nothing compared with what I encountered in the brownstone upon my unexpected return. Had my mother been with me in Milan, I'd have told her first and had her help me tell my father, but since she'd skipped this trip, I decided to tell them both at once, which was probably a mistake.

"This is bad business!" my father shouted, glass tinkling in its frames in response. "There are dozens of concerts that have already been scheduled!"

"Maybe I can keep touring for a while after all," I told him, knowing I couldn't.

"We have performances scheduled for up to a year from next month, for God's sake. Can you keep all of those?"

My mother sat on the couch across from mine, looking down at her hands.

"Tasha, you will get rid of this problem," my father finally ordered, looming above where I sat huddled in a corner of hard leather upholstery.

"I won't," I said, and though it was true that nothing could make me yield on this point—not when I felt I had already come to know this child—my voice wavered.

My mother stood.

"Stop," she ordered, and my father shrank back; he had never been silenced in the middle of his rage. "Just, please, stop."

My father threw up his hands as if to say, "You're all insane," and stormed from the room. I looked at my mother in triumph, but now she was crying, and she followed my father out. I was left by myself, coughing frantically into my sweaty palm, wondering whether I'd just made the most selfish or the most selfless decision of my life.

Yet, tense as this afternoon and those that followed were, it was over the course of the next few days that I first began to feel real, unadulterated joy about my impending motherhood. In Kraków, I had felt conviction; while traveling, I had felt a giddy nervousness, mixed in with heavy doses of guilt for keeping such a vital matter to myself; but now that it was we two, mother and child, who were battling together against the rest of the Tasha Darsky Enterprise, I felt touched by a maternal light like the one that glowed from the painted faces of that most famous mother-child pair. Firmly ensconced now in my parents' brownstone—my mother insisted that I move in, so that she could take care of me—tending to my cough and my belly, fending off my father's glares and my mother's anxious ministrations, I spent the happiest month of my life. I played the violin, I continued to read baby books, I went for long walks, alone or with my mother. I passed most afternoons in the small enclosed playground in Washington Square Park, watching mothers play with their children, overcome with dramatic sighs and teary smiles that shot a warm, weepy feeling through my limbs, like an injection of estrogen straight to the heart. It was a true maternal high. Everything was right; everything made sense.

Until, one day, it didn't anymore. I'd spent the morning as usual, practicing the violin, sharing a tense and silent lunch with my parents, complaining to my mother afterward that my father seemed poised to hold a grudge forever. In the afternoon, I walked over to the playground and waited for my maternal high to kick in. This time the reaction was slow to take hold. Instead of weepy warmth, I felt chilly in the mid-December wind, tired out by the walk over from the brownstone, tight around the lower stomach, where my coat had ceased to fit right. My thoughts wandered, I tried to push them back to children and mothers and weepiness; they wandered again, and I pushed harder. A panic began gathering in the back of my mind: Was this it? Was it over? Had I lost the maternal instinct I'd been cultivating? Used it up? Somehow misplaced it? *Look, look,* I reprimanded. *Look at the children and mothers and feel something. This will be you soon: sigh, smile, tear.*

Nothing, nothing, and then something I could not have anticipated: horror. This would be me soon, and there was nothing I could do to stop it.

In place of my loopy, light-infused, estrogen-altered mood, a creeping desperation began to take hold: I was overcome, in stages lasting over the next twenty-four hours, by the realization that every minute brought me closer to a fate I could not avert. The sight of my swollen stomach, once a source of proud wonder, terrified me by the following morning. I was disgusted by its heaviness, wary of brushing my arm against its roundness. Within a week, my thoughts had begun to flirt with Victorian scenes of a fall, belly-first, down the long, narrow staircase of the brownstone. I recoiled from these thoughts, but more and more this meant I simply recoiled from me.

Behind the growing dread that kept me up at night, I sensed the prophecy of Aleksander Pasek. There was a disgusting similarity between these new shudders and those I'd felt while lending myself to other people's music. Was it possible I could be so perverse as to consider myself used by my own child?

For the next three months, I entertained these heinous, hateful thoughts late at night, and then played the part of the eager expectant mother for the benefit of everyone else during the daytime. I began to see myself as monstrous, unnatural, surrounded by dark, telltale colors which swirled thickly in angry strokes, repulsing other figures from my frame. The shame was nearly as debilitating as the fear, and I could hardly stand the company of other people any better than I could stand being alone. I'd emerge from sweat-stained dreams to find my mother demanding that we spend the day buying a small collection of gender-neutral baby clothes, or my father, who had abruptly and rather dramatically come around to the idea of a grandchild just as I was rebelling against it, telling me to choose the artists who would paint the walls of the nursery, his gift to me. And then there was the surprise baby shower which my mother and my old college friend Adrian Brown organized, importing acquaintances from around the globe into the Palm Court at the Plaza Hotel so they could reproach me with their smiles and well-wishes and concerned questions about my health and hopes. I spent most of the party in the bathroom, sobbing into a thick, muffling towel that a sympathetic bathroom attendant sneaked in for me.

It was in the taxi, hospital-bound at last, that I lost all grip on propriety and let myself be seen for what I was. It was a relief to hurl myself against the sides of the car as my mother tried to calm me, and my father looked on in bafflement. I gained an odd pleasure from seeing their faces contort with anxiety when I begged them not to make me go through with this.

For a brief, grateful moment, right after I'd given birth, I thought that my perversity had ended with my pregnancy: seeing my daughter for the first time, I was overwhelmed by awe and protectiveness. After eighteen hours of labor, I had done my penance and regained the right to love my child. But then the moment fled, and with it the ability to tolerate the sight and smell of her. I asked my mother to take her away, and refused to see her for the rest of my stay in the hospital. I also refused to name her, until they insisted, at which point I chose "Alexandra," perhaps to solidify the alienation between us.

Back in my parents' house, I lay in bed with the shades drawn, and the stereo constantly playing a recording of a score from one of Pasek's movies, which I had purchased right before leaving Paris for Poland. In my head I followed the music, my right hand instinctively fingering whenever there was a part for violin, and I tried to imagine that there was nothing else in the world but these notes: somber, luminous, taking their faith from the sheer depth of their own despair.

For days, my mother, father, or Adrian, who seemed never to go home, would pierce through my aural delusion, forcing Alexandra into my awareness. She was never quite visible underneath layers of pink blanket, or audible in her contented sleep, but she overtook the room with her presence. I had tried in the hospital to breastfeed her, but she'd gagged on my milk (the nurses blamed "hyperlactation"), and I took this now as an excuse not to touch her at all. Each time my parents tried to force her into my arms, I'd turn my head to the wall, pleading sick: my story, which no one believed, was that I was afraid to infect her with my imaginary germs. What was I afraid of, really? Before, my acute sense of doom had rested on the birth itself: all my fears had focused on that event, and its unswerving approach. Now that it had taken place, my terror took on a new target: I was frightened by my daughter, by Alexandra herself, that tiny bundle emitting the periodic gurgle and the smell of talcum powder mingled with insufferable sweetness. I could not have said why, precisely, except that she was so much me, and yet so much not: she scared me with her sameness and her strangeness. Even my own body had a sickening sameness and strangeness for which I held her accountable. My breasts disgusted me in particular, painfully filled with milk, and leaking, as if I were a barnyard animal.

My mother and father, out of either misunderstanding or pigheadedness, brought Alex with them every time they came to my room, but Adrian came in alone a few times, and this is probably what kept me tethered to sanity. Not that it was a particularly strong connection. After a week and a half in bed, I realized I wasn't fooling anyone, and so I began to get up in the morning. For several days, I busied myself making phone calls and reorganizing my life, but this didn't make me feel any better. Instead of a barnyard animal I felt like a ghost haunting the living, sneaking from room to room so I could avoid human contact.

After three days like this, I announced that I was going back to my apartment for a while. I had gotten the idea that once I was alone I'd feel liberated, but instead, finding the place exactly as I'd left it four months earlier, when I had lived there speaking cheerily to my stomach, I hit a new low. I headed straight to the bedroom closet, seeking out a steadying force, some distraction to lose myself in. I'd been thinking of favorite old recordings, but instead I stumbled on scrapbooks of early review clippings, and spent the rest of the afternoon pawing through these. When I woke up the next morning, I was beaten and resigned. I seemed to have made a decision while unconscious: If I was to feel this way forever, if there was no escape, then Alexandra, at least, should have a mother. I may have been unnatural and hollowed out, a sorry shell with no inner component other than artistic ambition, but there was no reason that my daughter had to suffer for that. One of us was going to be miserable, and it ought to be me.

It was my father who asked if he might put Alexandra on the phone when I called there minutes later. I doubt he was expecting me to agree. I hardly expected it myself, despite my recent resolve. She made no sound as far as I could hear, and I couldn't bring myself to try to induce any from her. Then my mother came on the line. Without indulging in any unsettling reflection, I launched right in, my tone casual and light.

"I think I should take Alexandra off your hands."

There was only quiet on the other end; I was disappointed. I was expecting a different reaction.

"Mom?"

"Are you sure?"

"Yes, of course. She's my daughter. I miss her."

"Alex misses you, too."

We both knew that Alexandra had no notion of my existence,

much less longed for me, and forming this thought made me sad, which struck me as a promising change from hopeless.

"So should I come get her?"

Again there was silence. I knew what my mother wanted to say to me and why she couldn't say it. The optimism I'd been generating over the course of the conversation threatened to fizzle with this reminder of how things stood.

"I'm taking Alex for a walk now. Why don't you come with us?"

"OK. Right, no, that's perfect. We'll do it slowly. We don't want her to be frightened."

"Right."

"Well, where do you take her?"

"All over. We mix it up. She likes to see new things."

I laughed, thinking about her having likes and dislikes, about her wanting to see new things.

"Do you ever take her to the playground in Washington Square Park?"

I was waiting in the familiar spot when my mother rolled up with Alex in her stroller, a tiny face peeking out of purple rolls of flannel. At first I was only conscious of this bland, broad impression, signaling *baby* loudly in my mind. And then a barrage of facts hit me: how she was closer to making real eye contact now, and how her body propped up against the pillow was holding its position more securely. I was surprised I could chart her progress in such detail, as if I'd been observing her carefully every day, instead of turning from her, frightened, as I had been for the past three weeks.

I'd planned to tell her in greeting how we used to come and sit here together, but when I saw her, this real person aging by leaps and bounds, it didn't feel natural to speak, and so I only smiled. My mother, with her spotty acuity, noticed the last-minute indecision, and the disappointment it must have produced on my face.

"You can speak to her. Babies like to listen. It's how they learn to speak themselves."

"Well, I know that."

"Tell her something."

I felt the tiniest spurt of that old warmth, of the glow, and then, before I could savor it, I burst out crying.

"I can't."

"You can," she said firmly. She was clutching my arm to the point of pain, but I knew it was meant as loving support. I buried my face in the soft cashmere of her coat.

"I don't know what's wrong with me. What's wrong with me?"

"Nothing's wrong with you, sweetie. Keep talking to her. She likes the sound of your voice. See how she perked right up when you started speaking?"

"Do you think she recognizes my voice?"

"Definitely."

"Alexandra, do you remember me?" I bent my face down close to hers, and was overpowered by the fresh smell she gave off. I breathed it in, realizing that the scent wasn't turning my stomach. Her light-blue eyes reflected recognition, or at least they seemed to.

"Hey, Alex, look who's here," my mother broke in, and I could hear that she was crying, too, though she was trying to hide it.

"I feel so strange," I confessed, still looking into Alex's eyes. "But not in a bad way, I don't think."

"It's normal to feel strange," she said.

Crouching in a thin layer of freak April snow, I took in this tiny source of terror. I wasn't nearly as afraid of her, I realized, as of this strange sensation she brought out in me. It was just as Pasek had said: In my life I'd been unable to deliver on a single passion other than the violin. Beyond my instrument, my inner world lost its substance in translation to the outer. The musical rumblings that swelled in my mind were flat and dull outside of me; my emotional attachments, which seemed so thick and weighty, were too fragile to stand up to my ambition. So how could I be sure I would make good on this one?

The uncertainty was awful, and threatened to pull me into panic once again. But instead I took a tiny, elegantly shaped hand, and kissed it, while I made a promise that I had no notion how to keep: that this time I would get it right.

ALEX MOVED IN WITH ME A FEW DAYS LATER. SHE ARrived with my parents, and simply stayed on when they left. After they'd gone, I knelt beside where she lay on the couch, so contented in her new blue onesie bought specially for the occasion, and laughed. Alex joined in, making a sound not unlike a deep rumble of a chuckle; I knew it was probably gastrointestinal, but it thrilled me anyway. *She's happy,* I thought. *She's happy with me.*

It wouldn't be right to say that I eased seamlessly into uncomplicated maternal feelings that afternoon. In the coming days, even weeks, there were still moments of frightened disbelief, those "God, what have I done to my life?" minutes while contemplating what I might be doing if I weren't cleaning spit-up off yet another sweater. But, slowly, steadily, these bad moments began to give way more and more to moments when the world seemed ideal, seemed to close in around me and my daughter, protective and nourishing. It wasn't so much that I came to any conscious reconciliation to my fate, as that my life was becoming so transformed by Alex that it didn't seem worth contemplating what it might be like without her. She'd saturated everything: there was her smell, her sound, the innumerable toys and books which my mother had been compulsively purchasing, strewn already all over the floor and furniture. But, more than that, there was a texture to the air, a feel to time; a weightiness had descended around us, calming and exciting. Over the next few months, watching her grow, watching her change, watching her watch the world, I actually began to pity anyone who spent his or her days in any other way.

My parents indulged me for two years of this happy blur. They even allowed themselves to indulge, trading in talk of press releases and concert bookings for squeaky-voiced chatter about such pressing topics as Peter Cottontail and *Goodnight Moon*. But eventually they lost patience with a life that was nothing but story time and playtime and began to pester me to pinpoint a date when I could begin touring again. I recognized that they were right to raise the issue, but I brushed the topic away each time they raised it. Alex changed daily, hourly, by the minute; I couldn't imagine missing any of it. I couldn't imagine flying off without her, willingly exiting our cozy shared space. So, when my parents spoke about my "comeback," I smiled and blocked it out.

"You'll wake up one morning and realize you want to go back and it will be too late," my father urged me, ominously, one day over the phone, while I watched Alex do a wobbly dance to the Mozart CD booming through our tiny apartment (any minute now, I knew, there'd be a broom knocking against our floor, but Alex loved for me to play the music as loud as it would go). "You'll regret it then."

But, crawling across a rug strewn with toys, books, and Cheerios in order to brush a strand of hair out of Alex's face, I could not imagine that such a day would come. Alex completed me, calmed me, filled me like nothing else ever had, more than music, certainly more than the adoration of an audience. She neatly gathered together the dangling ends of my longing so that they reached toward nowhere but her. I would not have believed this if you'd told me two years before, but there it was: Alex made me not miss the stage. And so I spent another few months only intermittently wondering what to do about my career. Though I still played the violin daily, these sessions were often undisciplined and short—more playful fun than professional practice. I increasingly suspected that perhaps it would be best to give up the performing life for a teaching life; it wouldn't be as exciting, but surely it would be rewarding in its own way.

I might have gone ahead with this plan if it hadn't been for the day when my mother found me staring at the painting that had always languished in a partially hidden alcove of the brownstone's stairway. In place of bold colors and strident strokes, there was the muted dockyard at night, men working, a girl looking on from her corner of the frame while the world went on without her. I was on my way to the study to put in a few phone calls regarding teaching jobs I was pursuing at Juilliard and Curtis, but, as I so often did, I had to stop and stare. Alex was downstairs, trying to tell my parents about the clown we'd seen the day before, and the bits of chatter that drifted up to me from this conversation were for some reason making the picture appear that much more poignant. It's possible that I stood there looking for a long time.

"Failed abstraction with girl in corner," my mother said, and I jumped, startled to hear a voice right behind me. I hadn't heard her come up the stairs. "It's the last thing I ever painted."

"Is it?" I asked, regaining my composure. "I wondered. It's so different from your other works."

"Not all of them," she replied, weightily.

"No? Which ones?" I would have been surprised if she'd been honest and said something like "The ones I painted before your father and his rigid notions found me," but not nearly as surprised as I was when, instead, she pulled me farther into the alcove and, lowering her voice to a whisper, said, "You're a wonderful mother. But remember, sweetheart, you're not *only* a mother."

"Is this about teaching?" I asked. Her voice was a husky hiss, and if I didn't know any better I'd say she sounded angry.

"Yes." She kept my eyes locked intently in hers. "A million times, yes."

"I thought it was only Dad who couldn't . . ." I began, but she held up one elegant finger to silence me, and her eyes drifted toward the painting.

"Do it," she said, "for me."

She sashayed up the stairs then, and I could hear her feet striding up three flights, all the way up to my old fifth-floor bedroom, now also the defunct office of the Tasha Darsky Enterprise, from which I knew my father had been "secretly" calling various conductors, trying to get them to pester me into engagements.

I glanced one more time at the painting, thinking what a strange exchange that had been, and that it was unlike her to speak so elliptically, when I heard Alex struggling up the stairs.

"Who's that?" I called out, forgetting my mother as the top of Alex's golden head appeared over the last step, then her face, ice-cream–stained and beatific. I was kneeling down to wipe the chocolate off her chin when the grin melted into an expression of grief. (Her face was every bit as expressive as her father's, though fortunately lacking any other of its features.) When I turned to figure out what had caught her eye, I saw it was my mother's painting.

"What about that painting makes you sad, Alex?" I asked, scooping her into my arms.

"The little girl. She's sad," she told me as we stood beneath it together, taking it in.

"Yes, she is," I admitted.

"Why?" Alex asked.

I buried my face in her silky hair, savoring the delicious smell of her.

"Because she's forgotten how to paint," I told her.

It was the most powerful persuasion my mother could have hoped for: I did not want Alex living under the weight of my disappointments, terrified of failure, vowing to avoid it at all costs. I did not want there to be some equivalent of this painting in her life. I understood now what my mother had been telling me in that strange, elliptical way. Five months later, I was on a plane to San Francisco.

"NO CHIRPY CRAP," my father had called out to me as I boarded the plane ("What's crap?" I heard Alex ask my mother as I was walking away), and no chirpy crap I gave them. Several months earlier, when I'd first put a score in front of me with serious intentions, I'd been terrified of what would come out of my instrument: what would I do if the music was pastel-colored joy? But by the time my father called out his charming farewell, I knew that this was not a possibility. In the months I had been practicing for my comeback performance, I had found that the sounds I made now were, if anything, even more gritty and raw, more *sexual,* than ever before. *How strange,* I thought, *because I am still all pastel-colored joy inside.* But there must have been some untapped core of defiance lurking in there still, and perhaps it had only grown stronger for being so drastically deserted by the rest of me.

The performances I gave in San Francisco were the most intense I'd ever delivered. Playing Brahms to three sold-out audiences, I threw myself so violently into the music that I bled into it, losing my sense of where I stopped and the notes began. I could feel old pain and struggles lay against me like a favorite worn sweater, and the adulation of the audience was a magnetic pull. I realized for the first time that I was carrying on a love affair with them, the audience, as well—that, even while I struggled against Brahms, I was submitting to them, laying myself prone and vulnerable. Hitting the final bar line was a searing tear of flesh from flesh. Backstage afterward, I wondered, *Who was that up there, and what is her relation to me?,* but the following night I transformed again. I wondered why I had never noticed before that there was someone else I became while I played. It explained the mystery of how I could be called "the femme fatale of violin," "every thinking man's fantasy," and even among "the sexiest women alive" by *People,* while never feeling particularly attractive. Recognizing this schism frightened me, as if the stage Tasha might blot out the other if I let her out too often. As long as the notes poured out of me, I was intoxicated by the music, by the *performance,* and Alex was a ghost from a former life. Could that be healthy?

When I stepped off the plane in New York the next day to find Alex waiting with a bouquet of roses almost as big as she was, I found myself crying and laughing so loudly that everyone around us turned to stare.

"Did you think we were going to kill her, for God's sake?" my father asked.

The next day, I made a bid on a four-bedroom penthouse duplex on West End Avenue. I needed a weighty, costly permanence to convince me that my life with Alex was more real than my life onstage. The walk-up was getting too cramped for us, anyway. I was enchanted by the flood of light streaming in on all sides through the abundant bay windows. To me, the place just screamed happy childhood, and for the next two years I all but barricaded us in there. Though I made several recordings, and gave performances all around the country, each time my parents brought up another international tour I batted away their entreaties with the reply "We'll see when Alex starts school."

By the time she was four, though, I knew the gig was up. I reluctantly enrolled her in the same private school I'd attended as a child, and tried to figure out what to do now that I had my days to myself. I had a lot of time to fill, especially since unfilled time was time I knew I should spend thinking about returning to the international circuit.

Some of this new time I filled by practicing my violin for an extra two hours each day, and some I filled by firing my housekeeper and doing all the cleaning myself. I also reclaimed the responsibility from my father of opening and responding to the invitations, gifts, and fan letters that still came by the bagful in the mail each morning. That was how it came to be that I was the one, and not my father, who opened the invitation for a panel discussion at NYU's Tisch School of the Arts entitled "Does Beauty Have Any Place in the Arts: An Afternoon of Exploration," and saw the name "Jean Paul Boumedienne" under the heading "panelists."

As I held the unexpected thing in my hands, my first thought was only: *Good for Jean Paul.* He was getting some recognition outside of Oberlin. But I couldn't bring myself to put the invitation down and move on to the next envelope, and so I thought: *Maybe I'll go.*

Then, for three weeks, I put the looming date out of my mind.

I woke up in a sweat on the day of the panel. I'd been dreaming about making love to Jean Paul in the vineyards of Cognac, and Alex was due at school in ten minutes. As I threw clothes onto her, and raced her out the door, images from the dream kept floating back at me, unbidden. These images, and the effects they were having on my body, made me feel filthy, fluttery, lonely, and seriously ambivalent about going to see Jean Paul. When I strolled into the large auditorium later that morning, dressed with what I considered chic modesty, I had already had three changes of heart. I took a seat toward the back of the medium-sized crowd, and scanned the dais up front. By the time my eyes found him—looking gaunt, older, but still so inordinately attractive I felt a choke catch in my throat—he had somehow found me, too, and his eyes were boring into mine with their old intensity. It took some effort to smile—a dreamed image I hadn't recalled before, this one of him beneath me, his mouth reaching for my nipple, had floated aggressively back to me, making my cheeks burn and my heart race and my own mouth strain toward a surprised "oh"—but the effort was wasted. He looked away as soon as our eyes met.

The gesture was hostile, angry, and it convinced me that my coming had been a terrible idea. He hadn't been the one to invite me. He still hated me. He always had. I was about to change my mind one last time and sneak out the door when the moderator, a young ham of an art-history professor listed on the program simply as "Joe," leapt to the podium.

I settled down unhappily into my seat, trying to pay attention while Joe read a comic poem about the flight from beauty in the arts. I felt too aware of my own lost chance for flight to take in his words, but I perked up some when he began to introduce the panelists. There was a painter, a sculptor, an installment artist, the brutal music critic Arnie Glasswasser—one of my most ardent admirers and no doubt, I realized with a thud of recognition, the source of my invitation—and, staring at the ceiling, looking lost, Jean Paul.

"By way of introduction," Joe said, after waiting for the polite applause to die down, "why don't all the panelists say a few words about themselves and also, perhaps, one place they definitely *do* see beauty belonging."

A short titter from the audience and panelists followed—Jean Paul's face alone remained uncreased by a smile—and then all eyes turned to my old love. He had been staring at the ceiling throughout Joe's address, and now he moved his head in a quick jerk to face the audience, fixing the whole lot of us in that blue-black stare, and said, "My name is Jean Paul Boumedienne. I am an unknown composer. And I believe beauty is the only thing that has a right to be anywhere it cares to be."

I let out an appreciative laugh along with the rest of the audience, but I couldn't help noticing that Jean Paul didn't laugh along; he looked downright wounded at the audience's appreciative explosion, and turned his gaze back to the ceiling as Arnie Glasswasser made the obvious crack about a ten-ton gorilla in a movie theater. (Where does he sit? Anywhere he wants.) I stared at Jean Paul, bemused, but he didn't look my way, and even if he had I'm not sure what his glance could have told me. Perhaps he was just nervous. Perhaps he didn't know how to act in front of an audience.

But when Joe asked whether the concept of beauty was anything more than a social construction, and, rather than make the typical noises about context and authorship, Jean Paul responded by lecturing the room on the moral stake of beauty—claiming, specifically, that all of morality boiled down to aesthetics, so that what was good was just what was beautiful, and vice versa—I knew bad showmanship wasn't the explanation. Arnie Glasswasser broke in to challenge Jean Paul on his definition of "morality"—surely he must mean something weaker than what we usually mean by the word—and in return Jean Paul explained that what he meant by "to be good" was to have a beautiful soul. I doubted that anyone realized how substantial the word "soul" was for this impassioned speaker; the thoroughly postmodern audience surely assumed he meant the word metaphorically. I actually found his speech rather moving, but the earnest, raging way in which he gave it—and its minimal connection to the question posed—was alarming.

I found it increasingly difficult to stay in my seat as the hour progressed. I wanted to jump onto the stage and huddle Jean Paul away. While the other panelists discussed such questions as "Is beauty a sexist notion?" and "Is beauty a prerogative solely of the ruling class?," Jean Paul gave what seemed to be a single speech, broken up, to his annoyance, by the panel format: from beauty's underpinning of morality, he moved on to claim that beauty stood at the heart of all knowledge, and then, in response to three successive questions about the place of sex in aesthetics, explained how he believed our conception of God to have grown out of beautiful sounds. At one point, when asked by Arnie whether he believed in anything so naïve as an objective ideal of beauty, he rose partway out of his seat and, as if rallying the troops for a great last-pitch battle, called out, "If beauty falls, the world falls!" After that he stopped looking away between questions, keeping his gaze locked onto the audience. He seemed to be warming to the topic and to the spotlight, and also to be oblivious to Arnie's increasingly derisive baiting of him. The first time Arnie referred to him as "our friend from the agora," Jean Paul flashed a delighted smile, as if overwhelmed by the compliment.

Can't you see he's not made for such things? I wanted to scream into Arnie's fat, satisfied face. The man was making a mockery of Jean Paul, and poor Jean Paul had no idea. But the tenor of the audience was turning decidedly in Jean Paul's favor; they broke into applause after each one of his rants. He was the only one getting ovations, though it was difficult to tell whether these were ironic or just appreciative of the unexpected spectacle of his monomania—or, I suppose it was possible, responding to his ideas. Most of the other panelists, for their part, smiled indulgently as Jean Paul spoke, and a few glanced at one another with smug expressions of amusement during the bouts of applause. When it was time to take questions from the audience, nearly a third of these were directed to Jean Paul, and though he rarely responded directly—why treat the audience any differently from the moderator?—the applause continued after each of his tirades. The discomfited gestures of the other panel members also continued.

By the time Joe began thanking the panelists and inviting all of us to a reception downstairs, I had managed to shred my program to bits in my anxiety. I crept from my row while Joe was still thanking sponsors, and moved for the door.

Out in the hallway, I tried to gather my thoughts. What a strange display that had been. Had he always been so . . . ? And had I just not . . . ? I was making my way carefully down the staircase, unused to wearing high heels anymore (*Can you believe you dressed up for . . . ?*) when Jean Paul called my name.

I turned to see him bent over on the landing, his hands on his knees, gulping in air. Joe's voice was still booming from behind the closed doors of the auditorium. I pictured the empty seat at the dais and the puzzled, delighted looks of the audience and felt weak.

"Jean Paul." The name felt strange in my mouth. "It's great to see you again."

"Why are you here?" he demanded, straightening, his eyes narrowed suspiciously. "Did you organize this event?"

"No," I told him, confused for an instant before I understood his concern: This invitation had been a big deal to him, a sign that his career was taken seriously by someone who mattered. He didn't want to find out that that someone was me, that I was pulling the strings behind this, too, as I had been pulling the strings behind what should have been the national debut of his new music. "No. An invitation came in the mail a few weeks ago. That was the first I'd heard of it."

"They're all idiots," he said. "I wish you hadn't wasted your time."

"Well, you weren't an idiot." I realized I was speaking to him in much the way I spoke to my four-year-old daughter.

"True," he said. He smiled his dazzling smile—oh God, that smile!—which had once made me melt with desire, but now only deepened my sadness, because I saw that the smile itself was a little mad. Though part of me wanted to turn and run and never look back, another part of me wanted to reach out to that smile, comfort it.

"So—do you want to grab a cup of coffee, maybe, or . . ." I suggested, wondering even while I said it whether this was a good idea.

"You have a daughter now," he broke in, revealing this information as if he thought it would be news to me.

"Yes, but she's in school." I thought he was questioning whether I had the time to spare.

"But now it can never be the same between us. There's someone else."

He watched for my reaction for a moment and then burst out with his lusciously musical laugh, his face transformed to what it had been when I'd known him. Then he turned and disappeared into the hallway he'd come from. I could hear the crowd filing out of the auditorium, and hurried down the stairs.

Outside, I was about to turn toward home when I thought better of it and headed to the brownstone instead. I burst in on my mother reading a magazine.

"He's very off," I said to her about twenty minutes later, concluding my story as we sipped coffee at the dining-room table, the reds, blues, and golds raining down on our hands and faces.

"Wasn't he always?"

"I don't know, was he?" This was precisely the urgent question I wanted answered.

She smiled, shook her head, gave me a pat on the cheek, and seemed about to change the subject.

"Mom, seriously, tell me, was he always this, well . . . loony?"

"How can I say? I didn't know him all that well."

"But if he was . . ."

"There's something appealing," she said then, cutting me off, "about the delusion that the artist is a being apart, that his talent is sacred, and that it makes him immune to the rules the rest of us need to follow. The grandeur, the heroism of the artist." She shrugged. "It's very appealing to be with someone who sees himself in that heroic mold, but no one who sees himself that way can be entirely sane."

She stood and gathered together our coffee cups. I felt that she was being overly dismissive. Could artistic arrogance alone account for what I'd witnessed that afternoon? I couldn't say why I felt the question deserved so much serious consideration except that Jean Paul had been the love of my life and . . .

I didn't hit on the "and" until I went to pick up Alex from school. Watching her run toward me, arms swinging at her sides, grin plastered across her face, I thought, *. . . and her father was the same way.* I had fallen for Aleksander Pasek for a brief moment because I saw Jean Paul looking out from his obsessive, single-minded face, Jean Paul shouting through his rants, even Jean Paul telling me he'd sell his country for the price of a single film.

If Jean Paul was crazy, did that mean that Aleksander Pasek

was, too? And if Pasek was like Jean Paul, well, it was too easy to slide to the worst worry, that Alex might have the seeds of this mania, this misery-inducing, rabidly single-minded obsession, germinating in her. She was singing in her trumpet of a voice, running ahead toward our apartment, eager to show me something she had made in school, and all I could picture, watching this sweet, boisterous child bounce along the sidewalk, was a vision of her screaming non sequiturs at a crowded room one day, a raving madwoman tethered to an Idea, a laughingstock, affording an ironic downtown audience a few moments of amusement. I ran up behind her, swooping her into my arms despite her shrieks of protest.

IT WAS SOON AFTER THIS THAT ALEX STARTED TO COMplain about having to go to school in the mornings.

"Do I have to go?" she'd ask every day, appearing half dressed in my bedroom, waiting cross-legged on my bathmat when I stepped out of the shower, tugging on my skirt as we left the building. "Just for today, could I stay home?"

The other kids were mean to her, she said, they colored on her drawings, they didn't want to be her partner for dance time, one boy had threatened to bite her. When I look back on it, it's clear these could be the complaints of any four-year-old, and that her desire to play hooky had nothing sinister motivating it. But because it came so soon on the heels of my run-in with Jean Paul, I panicked. *She's an outcast,* I thought. *They're being cruel to her. This is just how madmen are born.* But I had no idea what I could do about it.

One day I came down from my study to find that she had turned on the television. I didn't allow her to watch television, and so I went to shut it off. But as I approached I saw that, instead of the cartoons she usually sneaked on, she was watching a music performance on PBS, and I thought, *Well, that's not so bad.* Then I noticed that the performance she was watching was one of mine: a rebroadcast of a concert I had done at Carnegie Hall the year before. I sat down next to her on the couch, and she turned her heart-shaped face toward me with a serious expression.

"Why don't you play the violin anymore?" she asked, her tone every bit as serious as her face.

"But I do, sweetie. I play it every day. You know that." She often sat and watched me practice, always drawn to wherever the music was.

"No," she said, her face grim and stern. "Why don't you ever play like *that*?"

"You mean on a stage?"

"No, just *big*. Like a mountain. Like an ocean," she corrected me, sounding impatient. She dragged out the last word, her mouth in awe of the size she was describing.

"Big," I repeated, mulling her words over, wondering how a child so young could see what it had taken me years to notice: that I altered in front of an audience.

"Maybe I will," I said, wrapping my arm around her and settling in to watch the rest of my performance. "Maybe I'll be big again. And maybe you'll come along."

Saying that, I felt a cacophony in my head go quiet: my mother's husky whisper—"Do it for me"—beneath the picture of a girl who had forgotten how to paint; the whining minor chords of failure, defeat, bitterness that those words had stirred up again after so many years; and Jean Paul's lunatic rants sounding out in the voice of my daughter. I could not believe I hadn't thought of this solution sooner.

ALEX AT FIVE took to life on the road almost as quickly as I had at twenty. When she wasn't organizing elaborate make-believe games with the staff of lavish hotels, or taking the grand tour of innumerable zoos, or dressing in my old gowns and parading around foreign streets, or hamming it up for the press (she'd break into song whenever a group larger than five was lingering, and she called these people, whoever they were, the "press"), she was studying under the gentle care of her British nanny, Mrs. Bottom. I knew many people disapproved of forcing an itinerant life on a child—many people told me as much to my face—but I didn't see what the fuss was about: academically she was excelling; under Mrs. Bottom's care she was soon reading at nearly twice her age level, tearing through math workbooks as though they were a treat, and even picking up French and Italian. More important, she could not have been happier. As with me, there was nothing that pleased her more than being near music.

Even before she was born, Alex had loved music, kicking to anything with a melody. She loved music played loudly, she loved it played often, and she loved it in all its varieties. In India she became enchanted by the pop songs of Bollywood; in Japan she fell in love with Gagaku. In every country we visited, she seemed to find some native sounds to thrill her, in part because my mother and I made it a top priority, second only to finding the zoo, to suss out the local favorites for her. What she loved most of all, though, like her mother, was a full orchestra pounding away at a score. By the time she was six, she could hum nearly my entire repertoire bar by bar, and the most persuasive reward we could use to bribe her to do something unpleasant was the chance to stay up late and watch one of my performances from the wings with my mother. Backstage, her blond curls bobbing, she would tell anyone who passed by, "That's my mother." (She announced this bit of news to anyone who caught her eye, regardless of where we were or what we were doing, but she announced it most proudly when I was performing.) Sometimes she would even pretend to be performing herself, first announcing "I'm the Big One" (she took to calling me "the Big One" that first year on the road; my parents and I were never sure whether the capitals belonged or not) before taking a deep bow and then drawing an imaginary bow across imaginary strings.

But, for all her love of music, it never occurred to her until one afternoon in Bilboa that she could make music herself. It was my mother who encouraged her to climb up on the piano bench in the lobby, while they waited for me to finish lunch with a reporter, and my mother who greeted me in paroxysms of excitement when I emerged from the dining room, while Alex grinned up at me from her bench, taken by the power she'd found within herself.

What had happened was this: Alex had announced "I'm the Big One," bowed deeply, and then started to bang around on the keys. She had banged around for a while, as she had many times before, and then she'd stopped. Purely by accident, she'd struck a series of notes that formed part of the first theme from the first movement of *Eine Kleine Nachtmusik.* She'd stared at the keys in amazement, and then started to pick at them. She managed to pick out the entire melody. She had just turned seven.

"Another Tasha Darsky," my mother whispered in my ear as Alex picked through the keys again—her third time in a row. But I could never have done such a thing at her age.

The day after we returned to New York, I started interviewing piano teachers who might be willing to tour with us. I found Madeleine Chan, a recent Yale grad who had played Carnegie Hall at thirteen and was now looking for an excuse to put off law school and keep herself immersed in music. Under her care, Alex was soon playing so well it was hard to believe she *did* play that well.

To be honest, I wasn't sure I *wanted* her to play that well. Not that I wasn't thrilled, mostly, at the discovery of Alex's gift. I knew the joy my daughter was experiencing: the rush of hearing beautiful sounds fly easily from beneath her hands. But there was something else mixed in with the joy and pride: fear. Creeping into the perfect cocoon I'd created for Alex—creeping in along with that sly smile, and those agile hands—was the realization that, try as I might, I couldn't shield her absolutely, that certain things are bound to happen unexpectedly.

It was soon after Alex started studying piano under Madeleine that the most unexpected thing of all happened: we found ourselves in Poland. I hadn't been back to the country since that strained afternoon in Pasek's Kraków home, and I hadn't planned on going back. I had an irrational hatred of the place, thought of it as the land of Pasek and, therefore, as a place that laid unwanted claims on my daughter, whom I liked to think of as mine alone. But my father had called mid-tour, begging me to squeeze in a stop in Warsaw for a live television special, and I felt too foolish saying "no."

For years I'd been trying to form a passable fairy tale out of the legendary Polish filmmaker who'd sold his country for art, and confessed his sins into my womb. I presented Alex's father as a character in a story—not someone you expected to come off of the page and into real life. Not someone to *meet.* Unless, as it turned out, you found yourself in his fictional world.

"Poland?" Alex had repeated, wide-eyed, when I told her where we were headed next. I might as well have said "Hundred Acre Woods." And just as she would have hoped to meet Winnie-the-Pooh or Christopher Robin if that had been our destination, now she hoped to meet her father. I got through to him on our last day there, after leaving innumerable, increasingly desperate messages on his machine.

In a vodka-soaked voiced, he basically told me to get lost.

"It was your choice to have this child," he told me. "Remember this, Natasha. Remember this, that I said to you, 'Do not.' "

"Yes, I do remember," I said, my voice tight with the effort not to sound hate-filled. "I made that choice, and now there's a darling girl in Warsaw who would like to meet her father."

"Well, I am in Kraków and cannot make the trip. And over and above this particular reason, in general I say to you 'no.' " He hung up before I had the chance to reply.

I made my way into the next room, where Alex was just starting to open her eyes. The night before, she hadn't let me turn out the light until I'd sworn up and down that he would not come while she was sleeping. What should I say now? That I hadn't been able to reach him? That he was tied up?

"About your father," I told her, sitting down on the bed and idly rearranging the covers around her. "I have some sad news."

Her face went rigid in anticipation, and I found I couldn't force the words out.

But then some new words came to me, and they seemed so much easier to utter: "He died."

"He died?" she repeated, and then went limp, her eyes several degrees duller. It occurred to me that I had just done something unforgivable, not least because death might not be a concept a seven-year-old could deal with. But it turned out that she could, at least if it was the death of a semi-fictional character she only half believed in anyway. Looking down at her daintily clasped hands, she recovered quickly from the blow, and when she looked back up at me, she was only as sad as she had been when Charlotte had died in *Charlotte's Web.* Certainly less traumatized than she would have been had she learned that her father was a drunken lout who hadn't even asked her name.

"How long?" she wanted to know.

"Years and years ago." I knew it would seem less tragic the more remote I made it. "But I only just found out today."

"How?" I wasn't even aware that she knew there was a "how" necessarily associated with every death.

I shrugged. "By being very old."

I reached for her hand and saw that my fingers, interlocked with hers, were trembling. *She's better off being spared,* I reassured myself as I hustled her out of bed and into the bathroom. I could hear her singing sadly to herself as she dilly-dallied with a wash-cloth, and wondered whether I hadn't been too eager to kill him off. Maybe I had wanted all along to set things straight this way, to establish finally and firmly that she was mine and mine alone.

But what right did he have to be alive to her?

This was something I would ask myself a lot over the coming years.

FOR MONTHS AFTER OUR VISIT TO WARSAW, I TORtured myself with the various ways I could be found out in my lie: there could be a newspaper profile of Pasek, she could catch sight of him being interviewed on television, he could even have a change of heart and try to contact her himself. But eventually, as we moved about in a seemingly Pasek-less world, these worries came to seem unfounded. Yes, it was possible that she'd catch wind of him, alive somewhere, but it was much more likely that she wouldn't. Eventually, when she was old enough, I would tell her the truth. For the time being, there was no use worrying about it. What was done was done. And there were so many new worries to consider.

For one, there was the question of Alex's career.

My parents had begun to make an issue of this. To me it seemed criminally premature. She may have been coming to sound like a professional pianist at seven, but she was behaving no less like a child.

Part of her irrepressibly boisterous behavior involved commandeering any untended piano for her own use. She could sit and play for hours in hotel lobbies, shopping centers, or restaurants. These impromptu concerts drew satisfied crowds, but they were also public disruptions, and I tried to keep them to a minimum. I certainly would not have indulged her on the stage of Brussels's Palais des Beaux-Arts, messing with a piano that had just been tuned for my performance, which would open the annual Fête de la Musique that evening. For that level of indulgence, Alex turned to her grandmother, while I was talking backstage with the music director. By the time I arrived on the scene, she was halfway through the *Moonlight* Sonata, my mother was beaming, and by my mother's side was a young man whom I recognized as the Belgian composer Van Rheede. He'd been getting a lot of international attention for his *Cantatas on War.*

"She's magical," he told me. "A fairy child. I'm going to write something for her."

I figured he was just being kind, or at most swept up in the moment, but two months later a score arrived by airmail. What he'd ended up writing was a piece for both of us: a duet for piano and violin. Along with the score, he sent the request that Alex and I debut it. My parents, of course, loved the notion, and while we were still weighing the pros and cons together, my father was calling around for interested venues behind my back. Brussels, unsurprisingly, was the most eager.

I hemmed and hawed for weeks, until my mother sat me down one afternoon and convinced me. We were in my living room, and I could hear Alex prancing around upstairs in the elaborate Cinderella costume my mother had brought over with her. "Just this once," my mother told me. "Can't she do it just this once? You know she'll love it."

I gave in, but it was not just that once, and I'd known it wouldn't be. Alex was a sensation on the stage. She transformed up there. One second she was in our hotel room making herself sick on pillow mints, the next second she was a formidable maestro. Ageless and overwhelming.

We had five more offers by the time the run in Belgium was over. "Just like with you," my mother said, but I had been twenty-one when my offers started flooding in, and Alex was only seven. The idea of making Alex into a child performer frightened me, but I had to admit that she'd loved being onstage in Belgium, and I could well understand why.

Pestered half to death by my parents and a handful of conductors, I decided that, as long as we always performed together, it would be fine. And it was. It was more than fine. As a musician, I experienced the strange and maturing sensation of *not* wanting to draw all the attention to myself. Instead, I played protectively, always far more aware of the sound of the piano than of anything else. Alex and I became more entwined than ever, through music, which was the deepest part of either of us. I could play a single note, and she'd know where I wanted it to lead.

Exhilarating as our new closeness was, I kept a suspicious watch on her, looking for unhealthy signs. But I never saw any. She loved every aspect of her new life. She was never fazed by attention. She adored being recognized on the street; as time went on, she craved, absolutely craved, reviews, even if they were bad.

I still worried about making my child into a professional so young, but nothing *felt* particularly professional about our lives. Our traveling sextet was chaotic and fun-loving. In addition to Madeleine Chan, Alex's jet-setting piano teacher, we had now traded in Mrs. Bottom for the far more educated and far more rowdy Amanda McGrath, a bespectacled wild-woman with a Ph.D. in math, who served as Alex's academic tutor and our resident gossipmonger. My father also began to leave his post at home to accompany us on our travels. He claimed it was because he'd figured out how to run a business from the road, but we all knew that it was because he loved to be near Alex. She brought out a side of him we hadn't known was there: soft and calm.

Of course, she also brought out the old man's ravenous ambition again. In the immediate aftermath of our first few overseas performances together, my father began to agitate for Alex to strike out on her own. I didn't like this idea at all: yes, she was clearly a child who loved performing, but why not make sure that all her onstage appearances took place within the cozy confines of our duo? Why put her out there all alone, when she was content to be up there with me? When Alex was nine, my father announced, in a beer garden in Bavaria—the event came to be known in family lore as "Grandpa's beer-hall putsch"—that he'd arranged for Alex to have a stage all to herself the following month. Alex looked at him in puzzlement and asked, "Why would I want to do that?" She didn't begin to perform on her own until she was twelve, when she demanded it because it would mean significantly widening her repertoire.

When Alex was fourteen, she gave the most widely acclaimed concert series of the year, performing the *Pathétique, Waldstein,* and *Appassionata* sonatas over the course of a week in Bonn. It was a program my father had titled "Darsky Does Beethoven," and it drew tremendous crowds. Two days after it ended, my mother announced that she was feeling her age, and could no longer live out of a suitcase. Shortly thereafter, Madeleine Chan decided that it was time to stop putting off law school, and within the week Amanda McGrath was engaged to a minor Italian aristocrat who'd sponsored a music festival I'd helped to organize.

On the heels of her greatest professional achievement, Alex was abandoned. Not knowing what else to do, we took some time off to regroup. I was relieved by the break, but Alex was restive. I could only imagine what it was like for her to find herself alone and stationary after almost an entire lifetime of constant excitement. For the first time in her memory, the penthouse on West End Avenue was more than just a place to recoup between gigs. She was supposed to feel at home in the beige-and-cream rooms we hardly recognized—my mother had had them redone by some much-touted decorator the year before, while we were away on tour, and the woman had done them so tastefully they looked unlivable, even when there were clothes and books scattered around.

And, what was more, Alex was now expected to go to school like any other child her age. I enrolled her in the same tiny and stodgy but excellent private school I'd attended until the third grade. Instead of hotels, restaurants, concerts, parties, she woke up and caught the subway every morning, coming home to nothing in the afternoon but dinner and perhaps, if she was lucky, a movie rental.

At first, spending her days around hundreds of other kids was not without some compensatory thrill—particularly since Alex's fame and golden-curled good looks catapulted her straight to the center of the junior-high "it" crowd—but after a few weeks the newness wore off, and she announced to me wearily one night over dinner, sounding like someone twice her age, that she found herself bored by the small intrigues and large crises that seemed to make up her fellow students' world. To take the place of everything she'd lost, she threw herself wholly into the one thing left to her from her old life: music. Whenever she was home, she was at the piano.

I filled my time with far less noble activities: talks, honorary awards, charity galas. These events were nothing but glitz, and they often left me empty inside, as if I were just glitz, too—eye-catching, empty, ultimately worthless—but I kept going because they gave me something to do while we were docked, and because Alex seemed to gain so much vicarious pleasure from hearing about them.

It was at one of these events, a thousand-dollar-a-plate dinner to benefit leukemia research, that I was reunited with Robert Masterson. He served on the board for this particular charity, and it had been his suggestion that I be the celebrity guest this year. Yet somehow I was taken by surprise when he was the one waiting for me in the lobby of the Helmsley Palace.

"You know," he chided, walking over to me, "it's established custom for people to become *less* attractive as they age. But you always did do things your own way. *Grazioso* without fail."

I said something to the effect of "You're too much," and let myself be pulled stiffly into his embrace, though I was put off by the peculiar spicy, clean scent of him. His presence was embarrassingly familiar and frighteningly aged. Grasped in his stolid embrace, I found myself viewing him with suspicion, through a mother's eyes, and I pulled away coolly. I saw him take notice.

But by the time I lost Robert, several minutes later, to a small man who apologetically informed me that they needed to talk "shop," I was reluctant to remove myself from his side. I kept track of his massive silver-haired head bobbing above the impeccably dressed fray, casting my eyes about every few minutes to see where he had moved. I enjoyed keeping my eye on that head, feeling that it anchored me to something stable I could not identify. The past, maybe.

I was disappointed when we were instructed to find our seats to discover that Robert was not eating at my table. That honor went to those nine people willing to pay not one thousand but five thousand dollars a plate, which put on the pressure to be scintillating. With everyone sitting down, Robert's head was brought level with dozens of other heads, and I could no longer spot him simply by scanning the room. I stopped looking, and concentrated instead on trying to be simultaneously divine and approachable for the benefit of my tablemates. This is one of the trifling skills I have perfected over the course of my career. It was not until the crowd was thinning considerably, and I was plotting making my own timely escape from my tablemates—who were still sitting over their plates of half-eaten Black Forest cake and their third cups of decaf coffee, and showing no signs of wanting to go home—that Robert appeared, hovering above me to say that my car had arrived.

"I didn't order a car, by the way," I mentioned as we walked out into the lobby, stopping to shake various hands as we went.

"Well, then, it was a poorly chosen lie. I just wanted you to myself for a while. You looked like you were fading anyway."

"Oh, I was." I laughed, feeling oddly girlish in his presence.

"Are you too tired for a nightcap?" The way he looked at me gave me a surge of excitement, not sexual, but, again, the old, girlish desire to be the teacher's favorite.

"No, I'm not too tired," I said. "But let's walk instead. I've been spewing hot air all night. I could use some cooling off."

As we strolled up Madison Avenue, enjoying the crisp December air, he filled me in on old names from the music department I hadn't thought of in twenty years—who got tenure and who was denied, who divorced, who had affairs, whose book was a tremendous flop. He told me that he had seen Jean Paul a few months earlier. He had shown up uninvited to a conference and raved on for days that revenge has driven all great art.

"That guy has officially cracked up." He shook his head. "He shows up everywhere without warning, raves like a lunatic, and yet students somehow flock to him. They're calling him the Pied Piper of the Ivies. But, you know, it seems you and his enchanted students aren't alone in thinking his work is worthwhile. I have quite a few colleagues who agree with you. Perhaps I've become an old fuddy-duddy in my musical tastes, because I still don't see it."

I couldn't help feeling a flutter of joy to hear that Jean Paul was getting his well-deserved recognition, but the satisfaction was dampened by the news of his showing up unannounced to rave at academic conferences. I confessed my own run-in with Jean Paul years earlier, at the panel discussion on beauty in art.

"Sounds like Jean Paul all right," he said, laughing, and I didn't feel like telling him why I didn't find Jean Paul's eccentricity particularly funny, why hearing about it caused a shudder to run down my spine.

We were both silent for a while after that, and I began to calm again in the brisk wind and the relative quiet of midtown at midnight. "It's so nice to see you again," I said, thinking how true that was. "I mean, really, really nice."

"I've always thought about you a lot," he replied.

"Oh?" I felt myself tense, as though I were still nineteen and fighting off Jean Paul's insistence that Masterson's sole interest in me was erotic.

"Yes, I really have. You know what I've always wondered?"

"What?"

"Well, I don't want to imply that I think you made mistakes in your life, especially since we're having such a nice time, and since it's none of my business. But I've always wondered why was it that you . . ." He stopped then, arresting both his legs and his mouth, and it was clear that he was wondering whether to finish what he'd started.

"Here's what I don't get," he continued after a few moments, choosing his words carefully. "I always considered you to be one of my most promising students. Probably second only to Boumedienne. And you seemed so passionate about writing music. You seemed to really want it, that sort of success. I'd say you were second to none in that regard. And yet . . . nothing. You've let your talent go to waste. Why? I feel I have a right as your teacher to ask."

"You really thought I was good?" I asked.

"Sure. Didn't you know that?"

"I guess I didn't."

"You had, have, an exceptional talent. I mean, beyond your talent on the violin."

There was a burning feeling in my chest, but it was so physical that I attributed it to the heavy cream sauce the caterer had slathered on that evening's salmon.

"Well, you did write those fragments, though."

"I did write those." I gave a fake laugh, wishing, without much passion, that we could change the topic.

"It depressed me to hear them, to tell you the truth. It sounded like each of them was part of a much larger piece of work that you never let out."

"I don't know about that."

"I'm just saying how it sounded to me. I think you've denied the world something, and I can't figure out why."

"God, you're making me feel terrible," I said, though I wasn't feeling terrible at that moment. I felt happy, praised, even proud. It was only in the cab, headed home, that I started to feel terrible. I was overcome then with a lesser version of the same enervating revulsion that had settled over me fifteen years earlier when, egged on by my mother's concern, I tried to a follow a string of notes and learned I no longer could. If it was true I'd once had a talent for composing and had let it wither away, why did people have to keep bringing it up?

I was looking forward to slipping quietly into bed, downing a couple of sleeping pills, and drifting out of these thoughts. I hoped that Alex wasn't waiting up, as she so often was, eager to pump me for every last bit of information stored in my memory: What had I eaten? Who had I met? What had they said? How had they gushed? Was I the most attractive woman there, and had every man instantly fallen in love with me? (She took it on faith that the answer to the last two questions was always "yes," and that my consistent responses in the negative were simply the result of modesty or stupidity.)

At home, though, I found all the lights on, and Alex hopping maniacally from foot to foot on the second-floor landing. Instead of starting in on her deluge of questions, she was chatting circuitously and incoherently around some piece of information she wanted desperately to divulge, behaving so frustratingly unlike herself that I likewise behaved uncharacteristically and spluttered,

"What on earth are you talking about?" She responded by drawing me into her bedroom and shutting the door purposefully behind her, as though there were anyone else in the apartment to keep out. Once I was planted on the bed, Alex weightily drew a folder from a notebook inside an envelope inside a drawer, and handed it to me. I ran my fingers along the sheets covered in tiny notes, meticulously scribbled out.

"You wrote this?" The timing of the revelation made it harder to believe.

It was Alex's first creative effort, completed just that morning, she told me. I was amazed at first just to see that she had any interest in composing—she had never expressed any desire to learn. But I was even more amazed when I read through the short piece and saw that, in raw power, it was extraordinarily promising.

"Thank you," I told her, knowing I was being corny, but not caring. "You've given me an extraordinary gift tonight."

She didn't care about my corniness, either; she flitted around the room, leaping over stray socks and twirling between half-eaten bowls of ice cream, and told me how the music had come spilling out of some special place in her mind she'd always suspected was there.

AS WITH PIANO, once Alex began her composition lessons she progressed at lightning speed; the "year of rest" became all about finding a suitable composition teacher to take on the road with us when we resumed our touring life again in mid-July. For the time being, I just signed her up for lessons at Juilliard and continued to marvel at her progress.

To me, her talent seemed almost too prodigious to be believed, and I began to wonder whether a mother's ear was reliable. But when, one month into her lessons, I met with Ed Lambert, her teacher at Juilliard and a recent recipient of a MacArthur Fellowship for his own compositions, I got the sense that maybe instead my maternal ear hadn't given her enough credit.

Tucked into the corner of a small restaurant across from Lincoln Center that smelled of egg salad, I tried to shake off the chill of the cool February rain that had insinuated itself under my skin.

Shivering and dripping, I listened to the overly thin, thirty-something Ed tell me that there was "no telling what Alex might be." No telling? What did this mean? That her music gave no indication whether she had talent or none, whether she was a hack or a natural?

"No, no, exactly the opposite," he'd enthused. "Judging from her music, there's no telling how far her talent might extend. It's staggering."

Staggering. I liked the word, and let it trip off my mind's tongue several times in a row. I had stopped shivering, even my nerve endings held rapt.

He pulled out the latest work she'd given him.

"See how it develops inward?" he asked, pointing to several instances where melodies and harmonies interlocked and spiraled in on one another. "It's so precise, obsessive almost, don't you think? In a good way, though. It looks on the surface like such small music, but it's humongous. It implodes, rather than explodes."

I peered at the music, trying to see what he was saying. Yes, he was right, it was there, the implosion. I had missed it. "Small" was exactly how I'd described her music to my mother, failing to notice how it grew in intricate insinuations, burrowing ever more deeply into itself. How strange that I of all people would fail to see that. And this man, who actually used the word "humongous," had noticed.

"It's truly original, isn't it?" I said in a tone of voice that implied that I, too, had noticed this aspect of my daughter's music immediately.

"Definitely. She's something else."

Without realizing what I was doing, I reached my hand out and traced the length of the paper. When I caught his eyes lingering over my renegade fingers, I laughed.

"Have you noticed," he asked, growing increasingly more excited, "how untentative she becomes when music is involved? I mean, it's like one second she's just this, like, you know, this normal girl. And then, the next second, she's a force to be reckoned with. It's like her intuitions are so strong she doesn't have a choice whether to believe them or not. You know?"

I nodded, well aware of how true this was, and how true it had been for years. I wondered, not for the first time, whether she recognized this division in herself, remembering how she had identified a similar schism in me.

Ed chuckled and said, "Sounds like our girl," when I mentioned that old exchange to him. ("Big as an ocean," she'd told me, and was soon swept up in the current.) He dabbed at his mouth with a napkin, and then leaned forward, planting his elbows on the table conspiratorially.

"This is a good story, you'll like this. Last week, we were discussing a piece written by a former student of mine, and out of nowhere she goes, 'He made a mistake here. It shouldn't flat this last time.' Oh my God, you should have seen her face when she heard herself say that! You could tell she just didn't even know where a comment like that came from. A criticism, jeez, you'd think she'd insulted the guy to his face. The sweetest kid on earth. Those intuitions, though. It's like they have a life of their own. She's something else."

Trying to catch a cab outside in the downpour, I thought to myself, *Well, she's got it,* and I felt such a rush of emotions in response to this casual thought that I let out a strangled, feline cry that turned several passing heads. I was overjoyed. I was proud. I was frightened. I pushed away an awful image of her spewing non sequiturs at a crowded room, only to be assaulted by an image of her realizing, on a rainy night, that she had forgotten how to write music.

That night, while I lay in bed marking up a score sent to me by a young composer, Alex came in and crawled under the covers with me. I couldn't remember the last time she'd done that, but her body lying against mine felt different from whenever that last time had been—lanky where once she'd been round, bony where before there'd only been soft flesh, the last of her baby fat gone. I gazed down at her face, and realized for the hundredth time what an interesting face it was—her small, perfect features so full of expression: her pale lips eager to please with an ever-present smile, her narrow nose turning upward, stoically, all forbearance, but her eyes, those long almond-shaped eyes, sapphire blue and hot with determination, telling a different story. I found myself wondering what secrets other than music lurked beneath that face.

IT WAS SOON AFTER THIS—while I was still basking in the glow of Alex's newfound talent, spending almost every night on the couch with her, listening as she spun out new ideas, watching her run manically back and forth between the piano and me, trying to play out her inner mind for my listening pleasure, and constantly asking, "Do you see? Do you see?" as if she would expire on the spot if I didn't—that Alex first started to show signs of finding me unbearable.

It began one night when I suggested that a movement end differently from how she'd written it.

"No!" she shouted, her eyes flashing ferociously, her face contorted, as she jumped up from the piano. "Don't you understand at all?"

"I guess I don't," I apologized, and all the rage fled from her face as suddenly as it had appeared.

Another night, she asked whether I might get her work performed. I was taken aback that she was already thinking in such ambitious terms, and explained that even professionals had a terrible time finding orchestras to perform their music. She grew sullen then and said I hadn't understood her question. The following day, she wouldn't speak to me at all, except to say once, under her breath, something that sounded like "If you played it, they would do it," but which, when questioned, she insisted had really been, "I want some tuna fish," though when I offered to fix her some she said she'd changed her mind.

"I'll tell you what this is," my mother told me when I broached it with her, after the worst display of anger yet. (I'd made the mistake again of offering a musical suggestion that revealed my utter lack of understanding.) "It's her launching point."

"Her what?"

"Her launching point. For separating from you. Every child needs to do it, especially when you've been as close as you two have been."

"So what do you suggest I do?" I asked.

"Wait it out. It'll pass."

"But I'm afraid."

"Of what?" I pictured her wrinkling her nose dismissively on the other end of the line.

"I don't know. She just seems so . . . so vulnerable to me sometimes." I thought of that ethereal face in rage. Maybe *she* was obsessively imploding inward, just like her music.

"That kid is tough as nails," she scoffed. "The only one I'm afraid for is you."

I was about to object when my father's voice appeared in the background, peevishly reminding my mother of a fast-approaching dinner reservation.

"I've got to go," my mother apologized. "But trust me: Alex is not a child one should worry about."

IT WAS ABOUT A MONTH AFTER THIS THAT I CAME home from another charity event, eager for Alex to come bounding down the stairs with a hundred questions—though she bounded less frequently these days—and found instead that she was holed up in her room, with the lights on and the stereo blasting Tchaikovsky's Symphony *Pathétique.* Alex often listened to Tchaikovsky to, as she put it, "neutralize my brain," and so I figured that she'd worked herself too hard. The school year had ended the week before, and she'd been spending her days composing nonstop. I considered peeking in on her, but decided not to disturb her in case she'd dozed off.

I was already changed, washed, slathered in creams, and just slipping under the covers when I noticed that there was a sheet of paper lying on the pillow next to me. It was one of those pink "while you were away" memos, filled out in Alex's barely legible scrawl: Under *from* she had written "beyond the grave," and under *message,* "My dead dad is dying. Care to explain?"

Seconds later, I burst into Alex's room to find her posed amid the towering pile of denim, linen, and paper that covered the pink-and-white flounces of her bed, her head held very straight. She was staring determinedly at the opposite wall. The Symphony *Pathétique* had recently started up again and was just then edging out of its reflective opening and into its first desperate frenzy.

"Thanks for knocking," she said without looking at me.

"Who called?" I asked.

"The undead's lawyer."

"Oh." So he was reaching out from his deathbed, was he? It was a twist worthy of the most sentimental of prewar Polish films; I would have thought Pasek incapable of it on purely aesthetic grounds.

Taking in the stiffly held head and the crisp tone of her voice, I decided to launch straight into my apology. "I'm sorry I lied," I told her, my voice straining above the swelling, frantic music. "I thought I was doing the right thing, but it was wrong of me. I just thought it was too hard for you the other way. You know, knowing that . . ." I trailed off. Even now I couldn't bring myself to say what she would have known had I not lied to her.

She still hadn't turned her face to me, and inside I was pleading, *Come on, look at me, get the anger out, and then I can comfort you*. But when, after what seemed like minutes, she did turn to glare at me, it was not with a face that looked like it wanted to be comforted. It was not with any face of my daughter's I recognized. It was a face distended with rage, flushed a deep crimson by what I immediately thought of as her Pasek blood. I'd seen her angry before—especially in the previous few months—but I had never seen her look like this. I had only seen a fury this expressive once before, beneath the Adam Mickiewicz Monument in Kraków.

"Alex," I said, venturing toward her, wishing that she would turn the music off; it was paining me to hear it. There now were the trombones quoting from the Russian Orthodox Mass for the Dead; I could almost sense her fuming the words at me (I knew she knew them): "With your saints, O Christ, may the soul of the departed rest in peace." Well, he was no saint.

"I'm sorry," I repeated, coming closer.

She tensed at my approach, her lips pursed tighter, her eyes more piercing. "Sweetie," I said, taking another tentative step toward her, walking as if I were trying to keep an untamed animal from fleeing.

"You lied," she said, her voice a flat monotone, expressing none of the ferocity in her stormy eyes. "I don't understand why, and I don't want to talk to you now."

"I appreciate that," I said. "But if you could only let me explain. You see . . ."

"Go away," she ordered, cutting me off. "I need to think."

"We'll talk when you're ready, then." I backed away.

"Oh, and, Mom?" she called out, just as I was closing the door behind me. "I booked us two tickets to Kraków. We're leaving tomorrow."

IN THE STARK FLUORESCENT LIGHT OF DAMIANA HOSpital, Alex saw her father for the first time. His face was yellow, vague, and bloated, and he was sleeping, but other than that he was much as I remembered him. Even at this advanced stage of hepatitis, even unconscious, he had the blaring clang of metal on metal emanating from him.

"That's him?" she whispered, incredulous, walking without hesitation to his bed, while I hung back uncertainly in the doorway. I think she had been imagining him all these years to look like the Polish actor Bruno Swelitski, who played the hero in so many of Aleksander's early movies, but she didn't sound disappointed, only surprised.

"That's him," I confirmed.

"I don't look like him." She moved her delicately featured face close to that monstrous one to inspect, and then, before I could stop her, kissed him on the nose.

"Alex!" I reprimanded, but he had already woken and was looking, startled, into her unfamiliar face. He turned his milky eyes my way.

"Ah." He turned back to Alex. "The girl."

She nodded, but looked less sure of herself than she had when her father was just an endearingly helpless lump peeking out from a blanket.

"Alex," she said. "I mean, Alexandra. Like you. That's my name."

"How old? Ten years now?"

"Fifteen," Alex corrected.

"You look younger," he told her. "Much younger. Like a baby."

I stepped closer to the bed.

"Hello, Aleksander," I said. "How are you feeling?"

"I'm dying!" he said, not taking his eyes off Alex. "What a question. Your mother tells me you write music," he continued, still looking only at Alex. We had spoken on the phone a couple of times since we'd arrived in Kraków, and I had passed along this information, thinking he might find it of interest. He hadn't given any indication until now that he'd processed it.

Alex nodded solemnly.

"Show me," he ordered, and she looked at me in distress.

"We didn't bring it with us," I told him. "We have some in the hotel. Maybe tomorrow."

"Yes. Tomorrow. Fine." He waved my words away with his beefy hands. I remembered the gesture well. "Nice to meet you, Aleksander the Second." He pulled the thin blanket farther up on his chest. "Now, if you excuse me, I do the only thing I can do anymore with any finesse. Sleep."

We walked from the room, and out into a hallway smelling of bleach. We were both silent as we made our way back to the hotel, and I was sure she'd been traumatized. But out in the weak sunshine and bustling crowds she said, "I like him."

We stayed in Kraków for a month, and what a strange month it was. Every day we visited Pasek, and he and Alex would whisper and giggle like schoolgirls. Someone had managed to uncover a keyboard in the bowels of the hospital (or maybe a nurse had brought it from home, I don't know), and the two of them would bend their heads together over this keyboard for hours. It turned out Pasek had a penchant for the piano as well, though he primarily played Chopin. What was more, though he himself didn't compose, he had a great interest in composition, and soon he and Alex were talking about rescoring his entire oeuvre with works she'd write with his input. I think if he didn't tire so easily they might even have done it. A lot of what they did, bent over that keyboard, somehow pertained to that project, anyway. I know she wrote a ballad to accompany the opening credits to *Treny,* which, like me, she considered his most moving film.

It was one of these afternoons, while the two of them were bent over the keyboard working on the *Treny* ballad, that I noticed that their skulls were precisely the same shape. For some reason, noticing this—more than discovering his love for piano, more than the joint project they'd hatched—gave me an irrational pang, which reminded me of the pang I'd felt watching Pasek whisper to the old whore in Wislica. I knew I was supposed to be happy that Alex finally had a father in her life, but the timing of the whole thing seemed a little too perfect. Just as I was starting to wear on her, he had to appear. Strike one parent, bring in the other.

It did not help my mood at all to see how obviously superfluous my presence in the hospital room was as far as both Alex and Pasek were concerned. Pasek only ever addressed me to say that Alex was a gift, a treasure, a mouse of gold, a darling music chest. Yes, I wanted to say, but she is *my* gift, my treasure, my mouse of gold. *My* darling music chest. After a while, I started sending Alex in on her own, as I waited in the cafeteria or in shops, or back in Pasek's house, where he'd insisted we start staying. I hated being in that house, though he did have a great collection of films, some in English.

Sometimes, sharing muffled translatlantic calls with my mother, I found myself saying awful things, along the lines of "God, this guy takes a long time to die," but the truth was that I'd expected him to putter out of existence as soon as he saw Alex. On the plane ride over, I'd even worried he wouldn't hold out that long. Instead, he was fading slowly, dying in bits and pieces: his liver, his spleen, and, most recently, his hold on reality, so that he wove in and out of the past and present, in and out of his own life and films. Alex would come home from the hospital with the most bizarre questions:

She'd say, "Who's Framka? Aleksander said she visited him this morning and she was sad she didn't get to meet me."

And I'd say, "I have no idea," because I didn't have the heart to say, "Framka's an old prostitute who surely died years ago."

Another time she came home to report that poor Pasek was in a state because his niece, Orszula, had just passed away. "You don't think he meant the Orszula from his movie, do you?" she asked, her voice grave with concern.

"It's possible he did have a niece named Orszula, who happened to die," I said, unconvincingly.

A few weeks into our visit, Alex came home clutching a frayed and crumpled piece of paper, which turned out, upon close inspection (the type was badly faded), to be a newspaper article dated June 19, 1920. It was a profile of Aleksander's father, Piotr, upon his appointment as state historian of the Second Republic of Poland. On the back was a note that read:

My dear daughter (if I may call you that).

Your mother and I loved each other for an instant, and for an instant I saw you in your mother's belly. Would you believe me if I said I loved you, too? I wonder, what has your mother told you about your family? Perhaps someday I will tell you about your Polish history. I could be accused many times over for many crimes, if I were only worthy of accusation. Forgive me.

The note was dated June 19, 1991, just a year after Alex was born. Handing it to her, Pasek had said, "I wrote this for my daughter. You remind me of her. Give it when you see her, you understand?"

Alex was upset in the hours following that visit, but most of the time she was upbeat—shockingly upbeat for a kid spending most of her time with a dying, deranged old man in a decrepit East European hospital. Of course, she'd also managed to befriend a group of neighborhood kids, language having long ago ceased to be a barrier for her, and I think she might have even found a boyfriend among these, though she became enraged whenever I asked about her connection to this tow-headed Sasha.

She seemed content to stay in Kraków forever.

But we both had concerts coming up, and I was starting to panic, wondering when Pasek was going to die already. What if it took years? We couldn't stay here that long, could we? I supposed we could travel from Kraków as our base, but . . . But, then again, Alex had been denied her father for fifteen years, and shouldn't she be allowed as much time as possible with him now?

One night, over dinner, I broached the topic.

"I hate to bring this up," I said, sitting across from her in the formal old dining room that Alex insisted we use for all our meals because many of Pasek's semi-coherent stories took place around it. "But I have to give some concerts in London in two weeks. What do you propose we do?"

Alex's response was unexpected. "Of course you'd do this," she hissed, "I knew it," and for a moment the Pasek blood flooded her face. But then it washed away, and her pale skin seemed almost an icy blue in contrast; it was a beautiful color, but not for a face.

I was too taken aback by the heated response to reply, and so she continued, "It's just like you. I knew you'd never let me stay with my dad. You never let me do anything. I'm like a kid in a bubble."

"That's absolutely untrue," I protested. "You've seen more of the world than almost any other child your age."

"Yeah, with you and a bunch of hand-picked adults by my side. I mean, you never let me do anything *normal*."

"Normal's not all it's cracked up to be, you know."

"No, I don't know," she shouted now, her eyes fierce. "How could I know, when you never let me learn anything on my own?" She paused, gathered her breath, and then continued much more calmly. "It's what you do," she said. "You hoard me. You even tried to hoard me away from my father. You lied to me when you should have just let me feel whatever I would have felt. You can't protect me from the world; it's going to find me sooner or later. It's my right to be found. Aleksander said that if I want to be an artist I have to experience pain and that you do me a great disservice by treating me like a china doll. He said I need to sacrifice at the devil's altar."

I'd been preparing a response in my head as she spoke, but I was struck silent by this last remark; I wouldn't have thought even Pasek could want his own child to go through the emotional castration he still believed was required for art. And wasn't the artist supposed to be the lowest sort of person, according to his scheme of things? Or was that only as compared with the patriot?

"That didn't strike you as at all disturbing," I asked, "that your father told you to sacrifice at the 'devil's altar'?"

"He meant it metaphorically, obviously," Alex said, rolling her eyes. "He told me you wouldn't understand."

"I see," I said.

"I doubt that," she returned flatly, before getting up and walking from the room.

Two days later, Pasek died. It happened overnight, and no one thought to let us know. Alex simply came back from the hospital, only half an hour after she'd left the house, and without giving any explanation said, "So when do we leave for London?"

That night, she locked herself in her bedroom, and didn't emerge. I watched *Treny,* sifted listlessly through Pasek's old photo albums, and looked forward to going back to New York the next day.

I might have felt relieved, but I had a hunch that Pasek would be coming with us.

THE DAY BEFORE WE LEFT NEW YORK FOR LONDON, WE received a package in the mail from Pasek's estate. It was Alex's portion of the will, and contained all of her father's original screenplays and a few of the original reels of film. For some reason I cried as we sifted through them, but Alex didn't, instead telling me blandly, "As long as I have his work I'm not at all sad."

It was the first time I'd ever had the sense that Alex was lying to me, and it felt like the tonic note of some long-lingering progression from transparency to translucency to opacity. I looked at her over Pasek's scripts. Somewhere in that body was my daughter still, but all I was being shown by her—all I had been shown by her since Pasek's death—was someone else, the sort of person who said, "As long as I have his work I'm not at all sad," about her own father; who laughed derisively when I asked if she was in pain; who smiled knowingly when eyes trailed after her. (Alex had shot up seven inches seemingly overnight, without gaining any breadth or depth, and though to me she looked like a flower whose stem was about to break, that was apparently not the way she looked to the rest of the world.)

"It's OK to be sad," I told her, reaching for her hand across the coffee table strewn with her paltry paternal legacy. "He was your father."

"Thanks." She pulled her hand away. "I was just waiting for your permission; you know I don't emote without it."

I decided to let the comment go. We were leaving for London the next day, and I was hopeful that once we resumed our old life of nonstop movement our interaction might go back to normal.

But London was a disaster. I blame this at least in part on that leering gaze always following Alex. I was noticing it all over Heathrow Airport, grown men eyeing my child's body, taking her in as if she were spread out in a magazine for their viewing pleasure. My odd response was to think, disjointedly, of Asian paintings on thin sheets of rice paper and then wonder how such a frail, new creature could possibly give rise to intricate notes that coruscated on sheets of music paper as if they were painted in gold, and then feel that the world was horribly cold and cruel. By the time we arrived at the hotel, I'd forgotten all about this, but I think the experience of realizing Alex was becoming a woman, and a dangerously attractive one at that, is possibly what lay behind my instinct to say "no" when Alex announced she was going to hang out in the lobby for a while.

"No?" she parroted back, disbelievingly, as I continued to unpack my suitcase.

"No, I'd rather you didn't. Go unpack, get some rest."

"Are you kidding?" Her hands were clenched in tight fists in her lap, but she didn't move from the bed, where she'd been rather unhelpfully unballing all my pantyhose.

"Do I sound like I'm kidding?" I didn't have a great deal of experience saying "no" to Alex, so I actually wasn't sure. I wasn't even sure why I wanted her to stay in her room, except that it made me feel calm to think of her there.

"What you sound like is insane," she said, and before I could respond she'd gone.

I put aside the dress I was about to hang in the closet and went after her. I found her sitting on her bed, staring out the window.

"Yes, I'm still here. I was obedient," she said, without turning to look at me.

"I wasn't checking," I told her, honestly, but the idea that perhaps I should have been was so upsetting that I paused too long, and didn't launch straight into my apology. The lag gave her time to decide I truly had been checking in on her, and when she looked at me it was with utter disgust.

"Well, if I'm stuck here," she spat, "could I at least have my privacy?"

"Yes, that's fair," I said, and slunk away.

That night, I didn't sleep at all, thinking about this exchange. The next afternoon, I gave the first terrible concert of my career. I knew it would be terrible before I even started to play. Usually in the moments before a performance I feel the notes in my fingers, itching to get out. This time I felt nothing: not only no itching in my fingers, but no music playing in my mind, no urge to transmit anything to the audience, and, perhaps worst of all, no heart to tussle with the score. I was not surprised, when I put bow to strings, that all that came off my violin was technical razzle-dazzle. But I only became fully aware of what I'd done when I walked backstage to find Alex sitting in the corner of my dressing room, fuming.

"What was that?" she demanded.

"Off day, I guess," I told her as I sat down to take off my makeup.

"Well, don't play like that in Brussels." We were slated to perform together again in three weeks—Beethoven's Triple Concerto, accompanied by our friend the cellist Norman Rashman—and it had been something we'd spoken about a lot over the past few months: the only subject that could bring out her old self lately. Just hearing her mention Brussels made me relax, and I smiled and told her I doubted I'd ever play that badly again.

But I played just as badly the following night, and then in the three concerts I gave in Paris, and then in a series of concerts across Italy. It was an unbroken string of terrible concerts, of pure technical skill and nothing more, and the reviewers were not letting this go unremarked. Worried about what I was doing to his enterprise, my father announced that he was flying out to meet us in Milan. Unfortunately, Milan turned out to be my worst concert yet. Even my technique was less than dazzling, the result of a fight Alex and I had had that afternoon, over whether or not she'd be allowed to go to a nightclub with a couple of unsavory-looking adolescents she'd met in the hotel dining room. I'd allowed it, and all I could think of onstage was what unspeakable dangers she might be facing at that moment: alcohol, drugs, lurking rapists looking to slip something into her soda. By the time I hit the final bar line, I'd forgotten I was even onstage, and the round of weak applause that greeted me took me by surprise. Backstage, all I wanted was to check my cell phone and make sure Alex hadn't tried to reach me, but I instead found my father waving my clean shirt over his head like a rally-flag.

"Better to cancel any number of engagements than ruin your reputation," he was shouting. "Better to disappear rather than this! What a mess you've made of things. Do you even know how to play the violin anymore?"

"I'm not canceling anything," I told him. "At least not until after Brussels."

I was living toward Brussels, and I think Alex was, too. Not that I could have known for certain. Alex had managed, over the course of a few weeks, to make privacy into a high art, and since I was terrified of being the pathologically controlling mother she accused me of being, I served as far-too-willing an accomplice. Yes, I always put up a fight (those friends she kept meeting, for instance, and the nightclubs they took her to seemed worth fighting over), but I always lost. All she had to do was remind me that I had stolen her chance at a normal childhood, and I was demurring that, yes, of course I believed she only smelled of beer because someone had spilled it on her.

There was also another reason I fought against the protective instincts that were telling me to start learning how to forbid: when she wasn't partying with the young jet set, she was threatening to disappear into a world of pure sound. She'd developed a new goal: to create a piece of music that was as self-contained as possible. I didn't know what she meant by this, but I didn't like the way the idea or the resulting music sounded. It took only two weeks for her brand-new composition tutor (who doubled as her piano tutor) to quit in a fury because Alex had stopped showing up for lessons, explaining to him that there was nothing he could teach her because she was on to something altogether new. Two days later, her academic tutor quit as well, and was cruel enough to say in front of Alex that he "quite frankly found the girl unnerving," before leaving us with no buffer. With his departure, I began to feel so utterly isolated that I begged my mother, to no avail, to travel with us for a while. I finally understood why other soloists were always trying to commiserate with me about our lonely lifestyle.

But through all this unpleasant hubbub, whenever it came to the Brussels concert, everything seemed to resolve magically into the way it used to be. When we practiced together she was her old exuberant, easy self, enjoying the music, assessing our progress, cracking jokes. Even if an hour before she'd called me a "cynical bitch" and hurled a shoe at me (because I had the temerity to press her on the question of whether I smelled marijuana in her room), while we were playing together it was hard to believe anything had changed. Outside the music, I often had the dizzying, nauseating sense that I had no idea who my daughter was anymore—was she still the child I'd raised, hidden beneath layers of anger and sullen sophistication, or was she just those layers without the familiar core? and, either way, what sort mother was I not to know?—but when we played together I felt certain I could hear her old self rising from the piano, and I was calmed. I think the soothing effect that all things connected to Brussels brought out in me accounts for my doing the unthinkable that night in Milan by walking in on Alex unannounced. I'd just finished convincing my father not to cancel our performances in Brussels, and I suppose I was high on this triumph and on the anticipation of the one event that could still bring out the old Alex, and I wanted to tell her how excited I was to share the stage with her again. I suppose I also wanted to reassure myself that she'd come home by midnight, as promised. I walked in to find her crouched on the ground, feeding her scores to a blaze.

"What are you doing?" I gasped, taking in the scene: the roaring fire casting shadows on the sumptuous reds and creams of the suite; Shostakovich's eerie *Lady Macbeth von Mzensk* saturating the air; and Alex looking every inch the fairy creature reviewers had compared her to as a child—that sad, chic body—performing a solemn magical rite.

She straightened on wobbly legs.

"You're drunk," I ventured recklessly, knowing my observation might be perceived as an accusation.

But she only giggled. It wasn't the lusty, indulgent, mocking laugh she'd developed in the past few months, but a scared, girlish titter. And in place of the knowing smile I'd grown to hate was an uncertain twist of the lip, which took on a ghastly cast in the orange glow of the room. I looked from her face to her burning scores—those melodies and harmonies that nearly smothered one another in the name of self-containment—and became aware that I was watching the musical implosion escape from the page and into her life. I'd been right to mistrust that music.

"Why are you doing this?" I was hovering in the doorway, afraid to push farther into the room, strewn with empty beer bottles and overflowing ashtrays, though the smell of alcohol and tobacco had been all but erased by the smell of burning paper.

"They're all wrong." She staggered toward me. "They're all wrong, and I don't know what to do about it."

I told her not to do anything about it right then, just to lie down and rest. Then I noticed that the sheets of her bed were in a tumult. Had there been someone else in that bed with her? I wondered with much less urgency than usual. I sometimes suspected it, but she was far too good at keeping secrets for me to be able to confirm my suspicions. Anyway, it somehow seemed utterly unimportant at that moment, in part because, seeing her like this—so childlike—I also found it utterly impossible.

"Yeah, I'll lie down and rest. That'll solve everything," she said unkindly.

"Well, maybe I don't always know what's best for you." I was struggling to keep my voice steady. "But I know I want it."

"I'll tell you one thing." She was laughing—the lusty, knowing laugh now. Her long, narrow arm swept an arc around the grand room, taking in the rumpled bed, the staff paper burning in the fireplace. The action and her voice were like her presence onstage: ageless and overwhelming. It was amazing how abruptly she could dart between the vulnerable child and the distanced sophisticate. "This isn't it."

"We'll figure it out," I promised her and myself, looking steadily into her rapidly blinking eyes. We were only inches apart now, since she had been lurching toward me all along, and I grabbed one of her long, elegant hands in mine. "We'll figure out what's best for you."

"Will we, Mommy?" she asked, the stage presence giving way, her child's voice wafting toward me on alcoholic breath. I felt the old pounding desire of a composition deep within me that I needed to yank out, and knew that there was a solution hovering near.

"We will," I told her. "Don't you worry, I will."

But I didn't.

ON THE TENSE, SILENT PLANE RIDE HOME THE NEXT morning, I tried to avoid thinking about the concerts we were skipping out on, the loose ends we were leaving untied, the anger this would almost certainly engender in people upon whom our careers depended. I wondered whether I had been too rash in making the flurry of phone calls that morning and huddling us onto the first flight home; whether I hadn't just panicked and done the first thing that had come to mind, and not necessarily the best. Why would the situation be any better in New York? Perhaps it would be worse. The privacy she was craving would be harder to come by in our apartment. As though she were reading my mind, she turned toward me just then and announced, "I think I ought to start at a conservatory."

"You're fifteen," I reminded her, bracing myself for a fight.

But instead of lashing out at my complete lack of comprehension, my nefarious cocooning of her, my desire to control her life like a demiurge, she returned to staring pensively out the window. I wondered whether her sincere entreaty the night before had marked an important turning point in our relationship, whether she was prepared to trust me again. But this happy delusion lasted only until our ride home from the airport, when Alex began bawling me out for calling a limousine service instead of hopping in a cab.

"Why do you think you're so special?" she demanded, though for all her life we'd been using this same limousine service and she'd never complained before. "This is total bullshit."

When I failed to rise to the bait, she started to complain about the concert she would be missing in Brussels. "You realize I've been practicing the triple concerto for months, right? You realize this is the first time I would have played anything as major as Beethoven's Opus 56 in an important city. You realize this concert would have been important to my career even if it was nothing to yours. God, I would have been sharing the stage with Rashman!" This last remark was meant as a jab (one that missed its mark), because the cellist Norman Rashman was a relative unknown compared with me, or, for that matter, her. Really, this concert was not terribly important for her career. The piano part of Opus 56 was the least challenging project she'd taken on in years; she no longer had a teacher to help her work through performances like the remarkable Beethoven's Sonatas series she'd given under Madeleine Chan's tutelage at age fourteen. But I also knew the concert had been important to her, just as it had been to me, and it was with real apology in my voice that I said, "But you have to realize that just over twelve hours ago I found you burning all your music, and begging me to help you."

"I was drunk," she mumbled under her breath, but she returned to staring pensively out the window.

It was clear to me then, and became increasingly clearer over the next couple of days, that I had been a fool to think that one unabashed show of need would save our relationship. If anything, knowing that she'd revealed some lurking dependence seemed to stoke her resentment, and as we spent the next week and a half hustling to get her re-enrolled in the same private school she'd attended the year before, her mantra became "I don't need your help." She didn't need my help picking out a new wardrobe for school (only my credit card), she didn't need my help deciding on a class schedule (she went to Adrian for that), she didn't need my help finding nourishment (she ate all her meals at my parents', or in fast-food joints), and she certainly did not need the suggestions I was stupid enough to make while she played the piano. This last she told me while storming out the front door, vowing never to play in front of me again.

Once she started classes, the situation improved somewhat, but only because we fell into a routine of largely ignoring each other. Though I could demand that she start eating the dinners I cooked, I couldn't force her to speak to me while we ate, couldn't force her to stay in on weekends, and couldn't ask her to stop spending so many nights at my parents' house and on Adrian Brown's couch. From what I could tell, she was glad to be back in New York, glad to be back in school, and I was content to remind myself periodically that I had made the right decision by taking us off the concert circuit.

In place of the social butterflies from the previous year, who still longed to claim her, Alex gravitated this time to a group of artsy, edgy kids who dressed like bums but spent money like shahs. They didn't bore her the way her initial group of school friends had. I think she was in awe of them, using the term "my friends" as though referring to a team of Nobel laureates. "My friends think you're nuts to ask me be home by two a.m.," she would tell me, as if their opinions would make me rethink my curfew. Or she'd tell me, "None of my friends see the point of this constant checking in." At least once a day, I would hear how her friends thought it was a crime possibly on a par with child abuse that I was holding her back from applying to conservatories. That she was fifteen, that she hadn't completed a high-school education, that she was not responsible enough to call and let me know what time she'd be home, let alone to fend for herself on a college campus, none of this mattered to the panel of experts who judged me guilty of high crimes on a daily basis.

One of the nights that she threw this particular accusation in my face—it was about a month after she'd started school, and I was short-tempered because I hadn't slept much that weekend thanks to Alex's liberal interpretation of the 2 a.m. curfew—I looked at her over the dinner table and, in the most disdainful voice I'd ever used in her company, said, "Conservatory for what? You don't even play the piano anymore. I don't know *what* you do anymore."

Her face went rigid and flushed, and she could barely speak through her anger.

"Is that what you think? Do you know me at all?" she managed to stammer with difficulty, before rushing from the room.

When I called my mother minutes later, I was upset to find that she, too, was surprised by my outburst. It turned out that Alex was over there playing the piano all the time. (Later I found out about several unannounced late-night visits Alex had made to Adrian's apartment, when it was too late to bother my parents. Adrian had apparently once offered Alex twenty-four-hour use of the keyboard we'd given as an ill-chosen birthday gift and Alex took this offer literally, sometimes letting herself in with her spare key at 1 or 2 a.m. to bang around lightly on the keys, imagining that Adrian was sleeping through her soft concerts.)

"Doesn't she practice at home at all?" my mother wanted to know.

"No, as a matter of fact, she doesn't." I was angry at my mother for knowing more about Alex's life than I did, and I didn't try to hide this in my voice. It was only a few moments later that I remembered Alex's vow never to play in front of me again because of the small but strongly unwanted suggestions I'd made. With that realization, all my anger turned from my mother toward myself. Any idiot could have predicted those suggestions would have been unwelcome.

"She hates me," I said flatly.

"Far from it."

"Everything's been wrong since Kraków. I'm sure Pasek said all sorts of nice things about me."

"Maybe," she said. "But I doubt that's where this is coming from. I think maybe it wasn't so much what he said as what he was."

"What? A man? A drunk? A Pole?" I was being snide, but my mother's knowing tone was infuriating.

"No, her father. A whole other source of her DNA," she said in a soothing tone that was even more infuriating than the knowing one.

"You're sounding very pseudo-philosophical. I know what a father is."

"Yes, I know you do, but did she? I mean, you two were awfully close, you seemed practically fused sometimes, what with the music and your itinerant universe. I think it's possible that meeting her father helped her accept that she wasn't just a knockoff of you. That she was someone different, and that she could be independent."

"Huh," I said. This was sounding frighteningly plausible.

"It was bound to happen," she continued, emboldened by my nonconfrontational "huh." "It was already happening before Kraków, wasn't it? Don't you remember how angry she was when you made those suggestions she didn't agree with about her compositions?"

"So you're saying we were unhealthily close and this is the inevitable result?"

"No, no, it was inspiring to watch you two." The past tense was not at all lost on me, but now I was hanging on to every word. "But maybe she *does* need some time to grow an identity apart from you. You're rather a forceful presence, you know."

"Am I?"

She guffawed into the phone, and then declared, "I've got to go. Your father is calling. But if you don't know you're a forceful presence, I have to question whether you've ever met yourself. My God, even I sometimes need to stop and remember who I am when I've spent too much time with you."

"That's not funny," I said, but she'd already hung up.

The next morning, when Alex came into the kitchen to grab some breakfast, I was waiting for her, sipping coffee.

"I'm sorry about what I said last night," I told her.

"It's no big deal," she said, tossing her hair as she scanned the refrigerator. "Just know you were wrong."

"It is a big deal, and I'm sorry. Grandma told me you've been practicing over there. That's not necessary. I promise I can behave myself. Not a word from me when you're at the piano."

"Don't make a production out of it. Like I said, it's no big deal."

"Alex?" She'd found the juice and was taking small sips from the container. She looked at me over the lifted carton.

"Do you feel overwhelmed by me?"

She put the juice down on the counter and stared at me for several moments. I'd clearly taken her by surprise, but she was able to rearrange her features back into their new near-permanent state of placid blankness, and scoffed, "Don't flatter yourself," while shoving the juice back in the fridge.

That night, though, as I was lying in bed reading, she crawled in beside me like she used to.

"Busy?" she asked.

"Not at all."

"You look tired," she said. "Are you OK?"

As a matter of fact, I was far from OK. I'd just gotten off the phone with my father, who was urging me in increasingly imperative terms to retire. I might have considered retiring, but managing my career was the one pleasant distraction I still had, and throwing myself coldly into the technical challenges as I practiced brought a welcome numbness. And then there was the question of who I would be if I wasn't the busiest violinist working the circuit. But the bad notices were still pouring in, though I hadn't performed in over a month, and negative press was not something my father could abide. I had the feeling that if I did continue performing, my mother would find herself sole manager.

"I'm fine," I told her. "Bad conversation with Grandpa. You?"

"I'm good, but this guy I've been hanging out with? Jerry?"

I had no idea she'd been hanging out with one particular boy, but I nodded anyway, as she told me about the various things she did and did not like about him. She didn't ask my advice, just ticked them off, pros and cons. It was clear she was only telling me any of this for the sake of sharing something with me, and though I wasn't at all sure why she suddenly wanted to share, I went to sleep that night in something of a maternal bliss. In the morning, she flew into a rage about a pair of pants that had gone missing (she accused me of leaving them at the dry cleaner's, but they turned up at my parents' house), and it was as if the previous night had never happened. But a week later, she crawled into bed with me again, and I learned how she'd forgotten all about Jerry and was now into a guy named Mike. Two weeks later, I learned that she and Mike had decided it might be a hoot to perform something in the school talent show, and then how a bunch of her friends were going to volunteer to paint a mural at a local homeless shelter. I never tried to anticipate these moments of sharing. It was impossible to predict when they'd come, but when they did, they could sustain me for days through her tantrums and silent treatments, and, what was perhaps the most painful for me, her rebukes about my foundering career. Alex, it turned out, hated the bad reviews as much as my father, and was just as annoyed with me over them. But whereas my father saw the string of terrible concerts across Western Europe as a signal that we'd reached the end of a good run, Alex simply saw them as yet another infuriating and indecipherable piece of my generally infuriating and indecipherable behavior. I liked to think she cared so much because beneath it all she still loved me as much as she ever had, though I also considered the possibility that her stance on the matter was somewhat different—that, as she saw it, if her life was going to be unjustly controlled by someone, that someone ought at least to be objectively formidable.

One Sunday about two months after we settled into New York, I came home to find her on the couch pawing through a folder she must have stolen from my bedside table. My father had sent it to me, filled with an assortment of my nastiest reviews.

"What are you doing with that?" I didn't sound nearly as alarmed as I was. If there was one reason these reviews bothered me, it was how much I knew they would upset Alex, and yet here she was reading through every last one.

Without looking up, she began to flip through, reading out the highlights as she went: " 'Tasha Darsky seems to have lost all the ardor that once made her as thrilling to watch as to hear. Darsky's Brahms has become as flat as it once was textured. The aging femme fatale has gone from sensuously dangerous to dangerously boring.' "

She looked up at me then and said, "You're still *my* favorite femme fatale, you know."

"Thank you," I replied, trying hard to smile as I continued to hover uncomfortably near the doorway. "Maybe you can write in to the *Times* and tell them I've still got it."

"Why are you doing this?" she asked, ignoring my attempt to lighten the mood. "You're so good."

"Nothing's changed," I lied. "It's just a few bad reviews."

But I knew she didn't believe me.

It was two weeks after this that we went to dinner at my parents' brownstone to celebrate my father's seventy-fifth birthday. Beforehand, Alex and I had one of our worst blowups yet. I wanted her to change into something nice, and she wanted to wear the pair of ripped jeans she'd found on the street and hadn't taken off in weeks. I gave in, of course, but we arrived in complete alienation, and Alex didn't even jump in to do battle with my father when he greeted us with his continuing monologue on why I needed to retire. (Usually Alex was my greatest ally—far better than my mother, who was surprisingly weak on the matter.)

When my father wore himself out, we settled down into a wordless dinner beneath the reds and blues and golds of the dining room's stained-glass windows. Halfway through, my mother disappeared into the kitchen and turned on the radio. It was tuned, as it always was, to WQXR, and they must have been doing an evening of contemporary music, because it was one modern piece after another that wafted in to fill the tense space around us. We sat nibbling our salt-crusted sea bass through two terrible electronic pieces and a decent atonal piece, before something breathtaking came on the air. Truly breathtaking, because, though for a few seconds what I was taken with was its thoroughly modern classicism, before long I was taken instead with the certainty that it was by Jean Paul.

That a piece by Jean Paul would be included in this roundup wasn't nearly as surprising as it would have been a few years earlier. He wasn't a household name yet, nor would he ever be, but I was convinced that within half a century the name Boumedienne would overshadow that of Schoenberg in the educated consciousness. His devotees were gaining clout, ascending to positions of power, and he was ascending with them. As well he should have: the music piping into our dining room was just as assured and mesmerizing as any of the pieces I remembered from my visit to Oberlin; this music was unlike anything else, and yet, listening, I could hardly believe the sound hadn't existed somewhere, waiting to be discovered, all along. At least that's how it struck me initially. After a minute or two, all I was aware of was the anger and pain roiling through the notes, raw as ever. Perhaps it was just that I was sitting with a daughter and a father whose love I was doubting, but what I heard in that music was hatred. I thought of the Mad Mann letters, our run-in at NYU, the univited appearances he'd been making to alert the public that revenge has spurred all great art, and I felt that we were sitting there listening to an indictment of me put to music. It didn't help that Alex was clearly lost in the sound, her face gone slack in religious ecstasy.

As my mother cleared the dishes, I followed her into the kitchen and switched off the radio, calling out as I did, "This is Grandpa's birthday, and we all need to pretend we love each other tonight." When I returned, the mood was much improved. My father and Alex were mumbling that I was being melodramatic and that of course we all loved each other, my mother was slicing birthday cake, and the specter of that angry music was gone. I tried to relax as my mother made an effort to be chatty about the store where she'd bought the cake—it specialized in pastries for both humans and dogs, which led my father to declare he wasn't tasting his slice until someone confirmed it was species-specific—but I found that it was harder to banish the music from my head than it had been to banish it from the room. I was still hearing it, and it was forcing me to acknowledge that I was the sort of person who could engender enough fury to fuel an entire oeuvre—no wonder, then, that my daughter had come to hate me.

That night, I dreamed of all sorts of unpleasant confrontations with Alex, my father, Jean Paul, sometimes all three at once. I awoke in a fog, and spent most of the day muddling around the apartment before I remembered that this was the day of Alex's school talent show. I'd received an invitation in the mail weeks earlier, and though Alex acted indifferent when I asked if she wanted me to come, I had no intention of missing it. By the time I arrived in the auditorium, most of the seats were filled, so I had to make my way into the front row, where I prayed Alex didn't think I'd intentionally planted myself. I sat there for two hours, pleasantly bored by the nearly identical, unsubtly sexual dance routines, the pop songs sung poorly, the solid but uninspired violin, flute, and piano sets by kids with glasses. The only impressive performances were given by a boy named Mike Leoni, whom I placed as Alex's Mike halfway through his strangely intriguing mix of stand-up comedy and action-painting, and, of course, by Alex, whom they'd placed last on the program, no doubt as an incentive to keep these well-cultured parents in their seats. She played Schoenberg's Three Piano Pieces, Opus 11, and she played it majestically; it was hard to believe she'd worked through the piece on her own, and in just a month or two, but I knew she must have, because I'd never heard her tackle it before. Better than the music itself, though, was how happy she looked up there; it was soul-soothing to watch her relishing every note, and I began to doubt whether I had done the right thing by taking us off the concert circuit after all. Maybe the stage was her natural habitat, the way it once had been for me; maybe taking her away from it was cruel.

When she finished, I had to hold myself back from rising in ovation; I waited until there was a critical mass already on their feet before I joined in. Alex soaked in the roar of approval, kept soaking it in even as the headmaster came onstage to tie things up. As long as the applause kept coming, she wasn't going to leave. She bowed again and again as the headmaster stood anxiously by; she was hamming it up, beaming, looking happier than I'd seen her since before she got a phone call from her undead father's lawyer, and I was gazing up at her, almost as happy as she was. Suddenly she caught my eye and reached for my hand. I reached up for her as she reached down for me, and then there we were in the middle of the auditorium, hand in hand, reconciled. By this time the headmaster had stopped looking nervous, and started to bask in the applause himself, and, seeing this display of filial affection, I guess he decided he ought to milk it, and so he began to wave me onstage. I shook my head "no," he waved me on again, I shook my head "no," he waved me on again, and then I thought, *Well, why not?* and I let go of Alex's hand and made my way to the stage steps. The moment I was up there, I knew I'd made a mistake. Ever the professional, Alex was still smiling, still bowing, but there was a strain to that smile now, and she refused to look my way. The headmaster was unsure what he'd wanted me up there for in the first place—he'd probably assumed Alex and I would embrace, which is what I'd assumed as well—and now he was just standing by, watching me stand there awkwardly, as Alex disappeared from the stage, still smiling and bowing. I gave a quick bow myself, shook the headmaster's hand, and then went after her. She was gone by the time I arrived backstage.

It took me nearly half an hour to find her, sitting at a desk in an empty classroom, and by that time I'd already thought through dozens of ways to apologize. Seeing her, though—not tear-stained, not red-faced with fury, just slumped against a desk like a rag doll, her face a resigned blank—I forgot my well-worded speech.

"Let me go," she said, while I stood wordlessly and helplessly in the doorway.

"To a conservatory?"

"Yes."

I thought of all the reasons to say "no"—she was fifteen, she hadn't graduated from high school, she'd hardly proved herself levelheaded in the past year—but I couldn't bring myself to list them again.

"Or don't let me go," she said now, wearily. "But in that case don't ever say you want what's best for me. Don't pretend to be trying to figure out how to make me happy. There's only one thing that I want, and I mean this in the nicest way possible. Just let me get away from you."

"OK," I said, and that was that.

SHE WAS A DIFFERENT PERSON FROM THE MOMENT I UTtered those two syllables—something close to her old self—and it was with an ease bordering on closeness that we sifted through the campus brochures over the next few weeks. I might have taken this as a sign that I'd made the right choice—my parents certainly did, and even Adrian called me up after a lunch date with Alex to tell me how wise I was being—but I was far from confident that I had. What I felt, instead, was that I had no choice: Alex had convinced herself that this was what she needed, and since *I* was now convinced that my instincts were abominable as far as she was concerned, I simply had to trust hers.

Still, it was hard for me to reconcile myself to letting her go, and when she was accepted everyplace, I pushed for her to enroll in one of the schools closer to home, thinking that at least I could keep an eye on her that way.

"They say Juilliard still has the best faculty," I'd tell her, or, "You can't beat Curtis's department in terms of variety." When she leaned toward any place too far away, she received only a skeptical "hmmm" from me. But I knew all along that she'd choose the conservatory at Indiana University; it was impossible to ignore the way she'd taken to the flat greenness of Bloomington, and, more important, the way the faculty had fallen all over themselves trying to convince her to come, before they'd even formally admitted her. Like so many, they had followed her career closely and were shocked to find her applying, but only they were smart enough to gush over her compositions instead of her performances. (Indiana was also one of three schools that didn't ask Alex to pass a GED exam before enrolling; they were satisfied with Amanda McGrath's assessment that Alex was already better read in most subjects, and mathematically more sophisticated, than most American college graduates.)

In the months leading up to her departure, my anxiety mounted steadily. I would wake up in the middle of the night asking myself, "Why am I letting this child go out there?" I flirted with drastic ideas of enforced captivity. I counted down the weeks unhappily: five weeks, four, three, two. Then, out of the blue, she announced that her flight was leaving a week from Sunday, cutting my time in half.

"There's a week of freshman orientation before classes start," she said as if she'd told me this before, which she certainly hadn't.

I'd been planning to help move her in. I wanted to see where she'd be living. I wanted to make sure everything went smoothly. I wanted to hold on to her for an extra week. I'd thought that when I put her in touch with my travel agent she was booking tickets for both of us; now I suspected that my missing ticket was the only impetus for her taking on the task herself.

When her flight started boarding, she had to order me to detach myself. She gave a laugh then, as she walked through the gate, shaking her head with those familiar motions so that her hair fell in gentle waves, and I felt a stab to the gut because I knew the joy in her laugh was relief at escaping from me.

And yet, once she was gone, life alone didn't seem so bad. She called the day after she arrived to tell me in breathless tones about her three music-crazed roommates, the orientation events they'd attended together, and the professors she'd already gone to meet, and I hung up feeling that I'd spoken with a girl who was exactly where she wanted to be. Though her calls after that weren't exactly frequent, they did continue steadily, and her ebullience never ebbed as she chattered on about the classes that were even better than she'd hoped, the rolling green campus she found to be a charming contrast to the cement of her dozens of home towns, the roommates she'd now decided to hate because of their ability to peg a person by the sort of clothes she wore. She admitted that she was having trouble making friends because people out in Indiana seemed unnerved by her, but told me not to worry, that she was there for the music, and that, anyway, she knew there must be people she would like lurking in some dark corner of the practice rooms. She just had to find them.

As for me, I was trying on a new role. I'd agreed to give an advanced class at Juilliard, and though it only met twice a week I was surprised to find it taking up nearly all my time. Being at the front of a small classroom was a far cry from the rush I got onstage, but it was nice to feel close to music again, and particularly satisfying to acknowledge that I was helping other talented musicians hone their craft. I wasn't letting myself think too thoroughly yet about whether this was the new form of my career, though both my father and Alex were doing all they could to make me face the issue—my father, of course, urging me to secure a permanent faculty spot, and Alex taking every opportunity to tell me what a monumental waste of my talent even this one year of teaching constituted. My mother was finally chiming in on Alex's side, though hesitantly; I think she was fighting the conviction that I'd fallen prey, despite all her efforts, to her curse, and lost my gift. The sticky family drama aside, I enjoyed my time as a teacher, and enjoyed even more my considerable free time. Real free time—time when I shouldn't have been practicing, recording, marking up a score, giving an interview, making an appearance somewhere, or tending to Alex—was something I hadn't experienced in decades, and at first I didn't know how to fill it. But soon I was reading novels, seeing movies, catching up with old acquaintances as though I'd been doing this all my life. I went to a reading of my old college friend Graham Rockwell's at the 92nd Street Y; I heard my fellow Vienna-launched violinist Vladimir Stobetsky perform at Carnegie Hall; I read a mortifying tell-all memoir by my college roommate Amy Wyatt's daughter, who claimed that her mother's famously militant books on feminist musicology were responsible for turning her into a music-hating, low-achieving nymphomaniac; I went to many long, lingering dinner parties. And though I missed Alex even more than I'd anticipated, there was something pleasant in being able to simply miss her; simply missing her suggested I wasn't worried about her.

Alex came home for a week over Thanksgiving. At first I didn't even recognize the tall, self-possessed woman who walked off the plane. She had the air of someone ten years older, but as soon as she spotted me the air fled, and she was running into my arms, her face grinning with childish delight. Seconds later, she was composed and adult again, but the childlike warmth remained as she eagerly told me about the few promising friends she'd found, the professors she worshipped, and the new piece of music she was writing for a student recital that was taking place in a few weeks. Would I come? she wanted to know. Parents were invited. My instinct at this last piece of news was to fall at her feet in gratitude, but instead I calmly said I'd love to come. This ability to rein in my messy maternal instincts lasted through our entire visit, and was no doubt part of the reason we got along so splendidly. All it took was for her to bristle once when I suggested a course she might want to check out the following semester, and I was instantly reminded to leave inviolate the independent realm Alex was building for herself. My behavior for the rest of her stay was so impeccably laissez-faire I think even she could have stood a more uneven performance. On our last night together, as I listened to a meandering story involving a drinking game some boys from her dorm had formed around the movie *Amadeus* (the rules were that they had to take a gulp of beer each time Mozart brayed with amusement or a D-minor chord was sounded), without uttering a word of reproach, she looked at me with a sly smile and said, "So what does a girl have to do to raise an eyebrow around here, anyway?"

For the first few days after she went back to school, I was feeling lonely and achy and wishing I didn't have to wait two weeks to fly out and see her again. But, luckily, much of those two weeks was taken up by a trip to California that Adrian and I had planned in order to see Michael O'Shea's debut as conductor of the Los Angeles Philharmonic. After the performance we flew to Sonoma, where we found Amy Wyatt uncomplicatedly basking in pride over the literary splash her daughter had created by making Amy out to be the devil of academe. Back in New York, I returned to the pleasures of teaching and relaxing for several days, gave one short and terrible recital in Avery Fisher Hall, and then, before I knew it, I was flying out to Bloomington to hear Alex's new piece performed.

If our time together over Thanksgiving had reassured me that Alex was better off in Indiana, this visit erased any doubt. Showing me around campus and introducing me to new friends, Alex seemed more comfortable in her skin than she had in years. Even when her despised roommates clamored for my autograph, she simply rolled her eyes and gave an understated snort of contempt.

The night of the concert, I took her out to dinner with a few friends she'd found in a composition class. She regaled the table with stories from her childhood on tour with "the Big One," a term she dredged up with no disdain or irony. She told them about the nights spent watching me from the wings and telling anyone who passed, "That's my mommy," about the impromptu shows she'd put on in hotel lobbies before she became a tiny professional herself, about the bumbling romantic adventures of her teachers Madeleine Chan and Amanda McGrath, about the beer-hall putsch her grandfather staged in a failed effort to speed up the start of her solo career. And when one of the three girls broke in at this point to exclaim how much fun it sounded to be a Darsky, she replied, with only the thinnest coating of irony on her voice, "Oh yeah, it was fun all right."

But, as happy as it made me to hear her speak nostalgically about her childhood, this was nothing compared with what I felt a couple of hours later, when I heard her new music. It wasn't so much that it was staggeringly good—though it was; it was leaps and bounds beyond the other work performed that night, and also leaps and bounds beyond anything she'd done before—but, rather, that it was unfettered. The sound was young and light, despite the mature weight of the actual skill involved in bringing it about. I think perhaps what I was hearing was simply that she'd released herself from the goal of a self-contained piece of music; the notes soared away on the freedom she'd given them.

Back at home, I was as buoyed by the memory of those happy, life-embracing notes as I was by Alex's fast-approaching winter break. I would have her with me for nearly a month, and I would spend that time continuing to prove that I posed no threat to her independence. I found my mind wandering, whenever I wasn't careful, to the meals I'd cook and the places we'd go and the conversations we'd have when Alex and I were together again. It was hard to prepare for classes, much less to listen as my students played; I was kinetic with anticipation.

Then, two days before Alex was supposed to fly home, she called to tell me she wasn't coming after all. She was working on a piece that was her "best by far," she gushed in a voice I didn't recognize, and she couldn't bear the thought of taking time away from it. "But can't you work here?" I pleaded, wishing I didn't sound so needy. "I don't think so, not as well. With the dorms cleared out here, there'll be no distractions." I'd never known Alex to be distractable where music was concerned, but I didn't say this. Instead, I pointed out that, with the whole school gone, they'd probably turn off the heat in the dorms. "I'll layer," she told me.

Still staring at the phone minutes later, I felt loneliness creep so thickly over me that, before I knew what I was doing, I found myself outside, heading toward the brownstone. My father was there alone and wasn't overjoyed to see me.

"Are you behind this?" he asked, holding up a copy of *Strings* magazine with the words "Where's Darsky?" in small print on the cover. The article, which I wasn't behind but had already seen, was nothing but a quarter-page speculation about my return to the stage.

"Alex isn't coming home," I told him, rather than honoring his accusation with a reply. "She just called. She's staying out there."

Unlike me, he put his finger on the cause of her absence immediately. "We've been passed over for a young man," he said, waving me inside. "Mark my words: Alex has a beau."

But I didn't buy it and instead spent the holiday season nursing images of her huddled under a mass of sweaters, hats, and gloves, lost in a swell of melody in an empty dorm.

The next time I saw her it was March, and I was in Bloomington for another recital that included her work. I'm fairly certain that there was nothing different about the way she acted then, no giggliness, no sheepishly ecstatic smiles off into space, nothing outward in her person. But there had been that music exploding its gorgeous passion out into the world, the notes striking me as exposed and sickening, like eggs on the underbelly of a sea creature. I'd hated that music, with its confusing familiarity, and wanted to reach out and pluck it from the air. Not that I told Alex this. I told her it was fascinating, because it was, and a new direction for her, because it was that, too. And, anyway, outside of the concert hall the notes no longer seemed threatening, simply different, and I wondered how I could have worked myself into such an irrational state.

That was the last time I saw Alex until she turned up in my doorway nearly a year later.

She'd call me frequently enough, but I wasn't able to call her, since she'd moved off campus and claimed not to have a phone. "No phone?" I screamed when she told me this. "Are you crazy?" A pause. "I don't want any distractions." She said she was working day and night on something "wonderfully new." But whenever I asked when I'd get to hear this wonderfully new something, she'd change the subject. In May, my parents went out to visit her, and reported that she was flourishing: she looked wonderful, she was upbeat and energetic, and she was in raptures over some musical revolution in which she was taking part. She was, they told me, looking forward to spending the summer in New York. It was something she told me a lot as well, and it kept me from giving in to missing her too much.

But then, in June, just three days before I expected her home, she called again, almost as an afterthought, to tell me she wasn't coming after all. I'd just finished my last class, and was sharing a bottle of champagne with my students, but I didn't let their presence in my office keep me from a pitiful display.

"Please come," I begged her, knowing I was wreaking all sorts of damage to my new image as a laissez-faire mother. "Please, just for a while."

"Mom," she said sternly, "don't make me feel guilty. I can't come home. I have important things to do here."

"But just for a week or two," I wheedled.

"We'll see," she relented.

But she never came.

I spent most of the summer hoping Alex would at least invite me out to Bloomington, and batting away my father's demands that I formally announce my retirement. He wanted to begin publicizing a final concert, a farewell that he thought he could make into the musical event of the decade. When I asked why he'd even want me to play one last time rather than put me in mothballs immediately, he looked at me in wonderment and said, "Because not to milk an end like this would be bad business." I told him I'd think about it, and then avoided him assiduously for weeks. I did sign on to teach another year at Juilliard, though, and I was beginning to grow comfortable with the thought of making that a permanent gig. After all, for all his brusque business-talk, my father was right: I could not put on a good show anymore. If London, Paris, and Milan had suggested it, that short recital at Avery Fisher Hall back in December had clinched it. The violin and I had grown apart. We still had warm regard for each other—even real affection—but not the fusion and fury of love. I no longer had the energy for that affair, or perhaps what I lacked was the interest. Regardless, what was the use of dragging out a moribund relationship? Perhaps if Alex had been there to fight me on it I would have resisted, but in the end, with Alex lost in her musical revolution, calling less and less frequently, and always sounding like she was in a rush to be off someplace else, I gave in. We scheduled the farewell concert for the following April, which gave me a nice buffer in which to continue putting off playing in any serious way. Practicing for this event, I knew, would be torturous.

It was my mother who suggested I pick up biographies as a distraction when Alex's semester started up again, and the chance of a visit from her faded into oblivion.

"She's drowning in music, I'm sure of it," I'd just confessed to her. "How do I even know if she remembers to eat, to sleep?"

"She's not an idiot," my mother replied, and then suggested the biographies. "They worked for me," she intoned dryly, "When I was wondering whether you'd ever make your way home from Massachusetts."

That fall, in addition to teaching my class, and participating in the sort of normal social activities that still struck me as excitingly new, I tore through the lives of Purcell, Telemann, and Leonard Bernstein. I was a third of the way through *Shostakovich and His World* when Alex called from the lobby downstairs, announcing in a choked and defeated voice that she was coming home.

What happened after that I've already put down: how I said, "I'll come get you," feeling I could fly through the wires with the sheer force of my desire to be near her; and how she'd replied, "No. I'm here, I'm on my way up." How minutes later, she glided in the door, looking thinner, pale, tired, and shot me a tragic look as magnificent and overwhelming as anything she'd ever displayed on stage. I could see every age of her in that look, every day of her, and I wanted to take all those Alexes and stuff them somewhere secret, where I could try to raise them all over again.

Instead, I regained my composure, and asked in as unalarmed a voice as I could muster, "Do you want to tell me what's wrong?"

"Not really," she replied, already escaping up the stairs with her small suitcase.

Seconds later, the bedroom door slammed heavily behind her, and it stayed closed for most of the next two weeks. Whatever had happened to bring my daughter back to me in this state had left her not only wounded and tight-lipped, but also furious, and not just at me: at her grandparents, at her beloved Indiana, at the world in general, it seemed. Each time one of us tried to penetrate that bedroom and ask what had happened, or even simply mentioned the words "conservatory," "Indiana," "classes"—if we did anything but talk about impersonal, unmusical topics—she would either fly off the handle, attacking us for our complete lack of understanding, or else she would get up and leave. My parents had never been on the receiving end of her fury before, and they were afraid, but I wasn't. I wasn't happy, certainly, but I wasn't scared.

As she holed up in her room playing music at ear-breaking levels—perhaps she thought it drowned out the sounds of her sobbing, but it didn't—and avoiding human contact whenever possible, I tried not to think too hard about what exactly had gone wrong out in that flat fantasy land of hers. A concert gone awry? A professor's bad opinion? A painful breakup? A falling out with friends? There was no way to know, because there was no way she'd tell me, and, really, what did it matter? Eventually—I hoped before her winter break ended—she'd get over it, realize it hadn't destroyed her universe, go back out there, and continue her life.

I just had to keep reminding myself of this, using all my energy to hold myself back from gathering her in my arms and trying to comfort her, from shaking her hard and saying, "What are you so upset about?"—because, of course, whether it mattered or not, I wanted to know. I just had to mind my own business. I turned my focus toward reconstructing the music that had sickened me the previous March with its echo of something strangely familiar, made me want to reach out and pluck it from the air and carry it home in my handbag. I had the notion that there might be a clue in that score, but it was the distraction that was a godsend. I was making slow progress unearthing the music from my memory, though that still earlier piece—the light, young, unfettered one—I could recall with almost perfect precision. Knee-deep in dim memories, I was able to keep myself from prying face to face. Only a stubborn kernel of my mind believed the project had any urgency until two nights ago.

We'd just finished dinner. I was lying on the couch, marking up a score, while Alex sat at the piano. When the sounds came I wasn't prepared for them. Not that I would have been prepared for them even if she'd stood in front of me and announced what she was about to do. These sounds were meant to startle: an unmoored, chaotic jumble that held on to music by the tips of its teeth (I imagined them bared and bestial). It was hard to believe this carefully measured cacophony came from Alex's lyrical imagination, but there was an expansiveness and generosity even to these raw notes that marked them as hers. There was no doubt that I was hearing her "something wonderfully new," and though I wasn't at all sure I liked it (or saw what was particularly new about it), I was glad to be hearing it. I came close and stood behind her, and as I watched her long fingers move fluidly across the keys, I strained hopefully to hear some hints of melody that I thought I caught amid the noise. I strained harder, felt certain I heard something, strained harder yet, and then I didn't need to strain anymore, it was rising to the surface, diamonds forged in hellish heat and grime, but she was pulling it off so subtly, so organically, that she was halfway through before I realized that what I was hearing was Sublimated Tonality. There they were: the two lush melodies that had been growing from the chaos all along. There they were, incandescent and triumphant, circling around each other, melding and molding, but ultimately keeping their hard-won forms. She had pulled it off nearly as well as he ever had, chaos spiraling naturally into beauty, but any pride I might have felt was swallowed by the sense that the room was filling with Jean Paul. I felt him as strongly as if he were right beside her, whispering instructions in her ear, and it took all my strength not to shout out, "You can't know him!" When she laid her hands lightly across the keys, I was scared of what might come out of my mouth, so for several seconds I didn't speak. My mind was jumping between the many means he could have used to take revenge on her for my wrongs—didactic, professional, *romantic*—and it was only with great difficulty that I forced out the sort of praise she was expecting. I might have been able to force out more, but she had had her fill of human contact for the evening, and with only a few quick words of thanks exchanged, she hurried back behind her shut door.

I might have run after her, decided to pry (though probably not), but, with her gone, Jean Paul vanished from the room, and my spasm of shuddering displeasure seemed overwrought to me. What on earth made me think she knew the man? I wondered, collapsing onto the couch. Clearly, she'd had a teacher who was a student of Jean Paul's, or else she'd been learning from Jean Paul's music on her own, from recordings or scores she'd picked up. Maybe she'd even independently arrived at the notion of atonality dissolving into tonality—it wasn't such a strange idea, after all, just a hard one to pull off, though, granted, she pulled it off using a lot of his tricks. More likely, then, that she'd learned from his music or from one of his students, but not from *him*. Why on earth would I think from him? What operatic melodrama I'd conjured! I recalled the night of my father's seventy-fifth birthday, nearly two years earlier, when we'd heard a piece of Jean Paul's on WQXR, and Alex's face had gone slack in a religious sort of ecstasy. Of course she would have tried to track down those sounds, and of course she'd have found them. Jean Paul was no unknown these days, particularly not in a musical hotbed like Bloomington.

By the time I crawled into bed an hour later, all thoughts of Jean Paul had vanished from my mind, and instead I was wondering what it meant that Alex had played her new music for me.

I woke up in a buoyant mood, and when I came downstairs to

find Alex waiting for me at the breakfast table, which she had set for two, I had to bite my lip not to show the exultation fighting its way onto my face.

"So you liked it, right?" she asked, as I sat down and poured some cereal into my bowl.

"Liked it? My God, Alex, I loved it!" Without my teeth grinding into my lip, it was impossible to keep the exultation down, and so I let it pour out. She seemed pleased. This sort of messy maternal behavior she had never minded.

"I finished it the day before yesterday," she told me, while stuffing a spoonful of cereal in her mouth so that milk dribbled down her chin as she continued. "While you were at Grandma and Grandpa's."

"It's the best thing you've ever done," I told her honestly.

"I know." She'd swallowed her mouthful of food, and was smiling beatifically now, looking like she'd forgotten she was supposed to be broken and battered. I was wondering whether I ought to mention that I knew of another composer who'd accomplished what she'd accomplished—whether she would want to know of him if she didn't yet, and whether, if she did know of him, she'd want to know that I knew him, too—when her hand fluttered down on mine for an instant.

I looked across the table at her then, preparing to tell her how proud I was of her, how in awe I was of her talent, her strength, her resilience, but instead I found myself noticing the color of her eyes. When she was young her eyes were a pale blue, and as she aged they darkened. For much of her life her eyes were the same unremarkable sapphire color as mine. But now, as I looked across at her, they were a deep and raging blue, a blue so dark it was almost black, and for an instant their similarity to another pair of eyes flustered and confused me. By the time I'd recovered enough to acknowledge that this coincidence could not possibly have any significance—what would the significance even be?—there was a knock coming from the front door. It was the reporter, of course, there on his mission of sending our lives back into disarray.

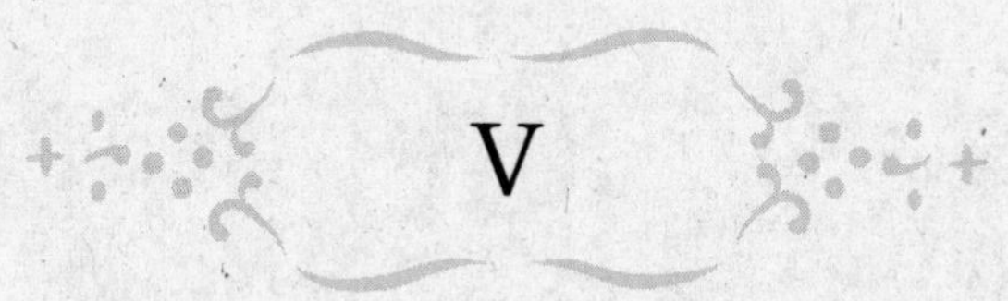

V

p a tempo
p a tempo

"I LEFT OBERLIN ABOUT TEN YEARS AGO," JEAN PAUL tells me. We're sitting in a coffeehouse far downtown just twelve hours after I phoned—twelve anxious hours in which sleep was unthinkable. Instead, not knowing what else to do, I began to put my memories to paper, while keeping my eye on the phone all the while, willing Alex to call.

Though I chose to meet downtown to ensure our privacy, I'm wishing I'd picked a more familiar neighborhood. I need something to anchor me. That his face is unchanged is no help at all, of course. I almost feel it's in poor taste for him to look so good. Gazing at the man who wrote the Mad Mann letters, who raved unbidden at dozens of conferences, who refused to let his work be debuted by the San Francisco Symphony out of cowardice or spite, I still see the boy who sent me shivering into love with his raving ambitions, and my heart is deviously, traitorously aflutter.

"Some members of the music faculty asked me to leave. They thought I was whipping the students into a frenzy. Obviously they had no power to force me to move, but . . ."

"So you went to Indiana?"

"Yes. I'd heard the students there were similar to those in Oberlin. Iconoclastic, you might say, or at least hoping to be. And, you know, I'd found that the Midwest rather suits me."

"And you met Alex?" I'm trying to speed up this narrative; I certainly don't want to sit here looking at his unchanged face any longer than necessary, not to mention that I'm growing almost crazed with the need to know. But he's twirling the spoon in his cappuccino, his disheveled hair falling into his eyes as he stares at the swirling liquid. The pierced girl behind the counter is taking no pains to hide that she's staring at him. We're the only customers, but even so we clearly don't belong. The six small tables are made of chrome, and the walls are lined with grainy photographs of motorcycles. A whiny boy is singing about masturbation on the stereo. We are too old to be here, and I am irritated with Jean Paul for suggesting we duck in. Actually, given the reason we're meeting at all, I'm far more than irritated.

"She came to one of my sessions."

"Your . . . ?"

"Sessions. They were just these . . . Some of the students would come by on Sunday nights. We'd order pizza and talk about music. I'd play them my new work, and sometimes they'd play me theirs. It was a rotating group, people came and went, but there were usually about ten or twenty on any given Sunday. Alex came with one of her classmates."

He pauses and sighs, staring down at his cup again as if his memories are stored inside. It occurs to me that his language itself is a kind of sigh: nothing florid, nothing grand. I've never heard him speak so simply, and I wonder whether this is a permanent change in him, or just a tailoring to the circumstances.

"I still remember seeing her as she came through the door. For a second I thought it was you."

"But we don't really . . ."

"The way she held herself, and something about the expression on her face. It was you. I can't . . ."

Perhaps he realizes this is a bad line of thought to keep pushing, because he gives up and says, "Of course it was no surprise to find she was brilliant. How could it be otherwise? She was alive with ideas that night. She was incandescent. I don't know, I felt . . . proud."

I'm taken aback by the choice of words and let it show on my face, but the only one who notices is the girl behind the counter.

Jean Paul is still staring downward. The one thing I'm glad to find unchanged in him is his whispery voice; strain as she might, it's clear our audience can't hear a word he's saying.

"She became a regular. She came every week. And then she started coming more often."

I know my face has blanched, and I'm not at all sure I can handle what's coming next. I wish—not for the first time—that Jean Paul had told me this story over the phone. I suppose it was good of him—right, even—to fly out to New York, but I wish he hadn't.

"Go on," I urge, because he's stopped and is staring now at one of the photographs on the wall: it shows an electric-blue motorcycle with tail fins.

"Do you know what it's like to find a student that good, Tasha?" His voice has dropped several decibels, and now even I'm having trouble hearing him. I have to lean closer, and I can smell the old smell of him, the expensive lavender soap his sister would send from Orléans that I used to tease him for using. "I'd had talented students before, but her gift is something altogether different. Exquisite. What I'd had before were acolytes, you see, people who could mimic, but Alex could do so much more. To mold talent like that, to transform it—it's gratifying, to say the least."

I'm reluctant to ask the obvious question, but I force myself. "Did you ever tell her about our connection?"

"No." He pauses, thinking about this, then continues in a firmer tone. "I should have. I know. But it seemed so strange to mention it. It's hard to explain, but, Tasha, it didn't *feel* so clear-cut, so easy to pin down who knew whom when. When we were sitting at the piano together, when I was playing her my new music, or speaking to her about my work, I could almost believe you were in the room with me. Yes, there you were, and you were just as you had been, and I was so aged. Like some horrible fairy tale, a reverse Rip Van Winkle, only I was glad for it."

He gives a broken smile that seems a cruel parody of his younger smile, and I find I'm almost pitying him. I realize then that I'm picturing this story unfolding in our Cambridge townhouse, and I want another background to play the scene against.

But I can't very well ask him to describe his home for me. I settle for leaving the space around Jean Paul and my daughter indeterminate.

"It's possible I let it infect my behavior. Maybe I looked at her in a certain way sometimes, when the borders between the mother and the daughter became momentarily confused in my mind. I might have. I don't know."

He lets his head fall into his hands then, and tugs at his disarranged hair with what looks like painful force. When he looks up at me abruptly, seconds later, there's horror on his face, probably reflecting the horror on mine.

"Go on," I urge, not kindly.

"I think perhaps that was why she turned to me, that confusion on my part," he continues, his voice wavering under the cold of my tone. "It held out a promise to her, and I . . . I failed her, Tasha, I hurt her, perhaps even worse than Benjamin."

"Benjamin?" The name is a distraction, a decoy thrown in my path, and I want to bat it away and get at the truth I have been preparing to stare down since I first heard Jean Paul rise out of Alex's music: Alex falling in love with Jean Paul, Alex having her heart broken by Jean Paul. I am as furious with him in this moment for trying to derail me as for anything else, though I'm even more furious with myself: the naturalness of Jean Paul's move from Oberlin to Indiana, the predictable music-session—I see now that I'd been recklessly naïve not to expect this melodramatic improbability all along. That eventually they would meet would have been obvious if only I'd let myself consider it. How many people were there in the academy working seriously on avant-garde composition? Thirty? Fifty? Perhaps not even so many as that, and all of them centered on six or seven tight hubs, all of them keeping their ears on the others. And among this rarefied group, how many were actually producing music worthy of commotion? Of course they would meet eventually. If not now, then years from now, and it would have been no better then. Because, of course, once they met, she'd be as lost as every girl playing in Jean Paul's ensemble at Harvard, as the girl with the torn jeans and the filthy hair pining in a pew toward the back of a deserted Oberlin church. As lost, even, as I was.

He looks at me with surprise, which turns, terribly, to pity before he says:

"You don't know."

I can barely bring myself to say the next words.

"Clearly not."

"Maybe I shouldn't, then."

"She's my daughter, Jean Paul." My voice is so steely it frightens even me.

"Benjamin broke her heart, I believe."

"Before you?"

"No!" The word is abrupt, an arm thrown up to block a punch. He looks at me with some alarm, then says more softly, "Oh no, Tasha. Is that what you thought?"

I stare across the table at him, at the embarrassment on his face, which is embarrassment *for me.* I expect a flood of relief, but it doesn't come immediately, and I find this puzzling.

"Benjamin?" I roll the name over in my mouth, tasting the three unfamiliar arcs of it. "I don't remember hearing the name."

"Ben Guerrero." He pauses, waits for recognition, and when I give none, he continues.

"She met him at one of my sessions, actually. He was a regular before she was. A graduate student at the conservatory. Quite talented. He was one of my more promising students before Alex came along. I can't say for certain how long it was going on between them. I'm hardly plugged into the students' love lives. I suppose it's fair to guess, from the way they interacted at my sessions, that there'd been something there since at least last winter. As I said, I don't know much about it. I couldn't even have said for certain that they were a couple until she showed up at my house in the middle of the night. That was a shock, I can tell you. Perhaps it's why I behaved so badly."

"I'm really not following," I admit. My head is spinning, and I'm still not experiencing the relief that is my rightful due. It occurs to me that for days I have been gripping the notion of Jean Paul and Alex like a wound I'm too afraid to assess. I've been gripping so tightly that even now I'm afraid to loosen my hold. This is making it nearly impossible for me to take in the new information Jean Paul is handing me.

"This was about three weeks ago," he says. "Right before she left Bloomington. She simply showed up at my house, out of the blue, at two in the morning. I'd been asleep for hours, and woke up to hear this pounding on my door. I think she must have been knocking for a long time before I heard her. She was frantic. Her face looked wild. She seemed utterly unlike herself. I told her to sit down, but she couldn't; she started pacing. She asked me whether I had always thought her strange, too caught up in her music. I told her I knew her as a music student, and as a music student she seemed admirably devoted to her art.

"You have to understand that Alex and I never spoke like this. With other students, sometimes there was a personal element, they would talk to me about their lives, about current events, about art and culture. With Alex, it was not like that. Probably I have never worked more closely with a student than I have with Alex, but with us it was *always* music. I could not have told you the classes she was taking, the names of her friends, her political stances. Her musical mind I had come to know intimately, but I knew very little else about her. I sensed this was how she wanted it. She always behaved with a charming formality; she had a way of being friendly and engaging while maintaining her distance. I rather admired this about her, to be honest. She seemed so self-contained, so mature."

"What happened then?" I ask impatiently. I don't like hearing his assessment of my daughter's demeanor; I know this self-contained quality of hers far better than he ever could, and I stifle the urge to tell him that it's not a blessing, for her especially.

"She kept asking me questions. Whether the other students thought her strange, cold. I told her I really didn't know. She asked me whether Ben ever spoke to me about her. I began to understand then that this was about her romantic life, that something traumatic had happened to her in that sphere. I told her that he never had, but that she should feel free to talk to me about him if she wanted. That was when she began to cry, and threw herself into my arms."

I reflexively shudder, the image of my willfully self-possessed daughter in such visible distress painful to entertain.

"To say that I was taken aback would be an understatement. It was two in the morning, I'd just been woken from a deep sleep, and here was this child curled up against my chest. Here was this child, who was *your daughter.* When she began to speak again, with her mouth so close to my head, I could smell alcohol on her breath, and I admit that frightened me. A lot of what she said then was lost on me—her voice was muffled and hard to make out—but I gathered that Benjamin had ended things with her earlier that evening, and that his reasons had been deeply wounding, had had something to do with what she was now feeling out, this sense that she was inaccessible, locked off. And he was right, she said, he was right, and she was so sick of it, so sick of keeping passion locked up. Her whole life she'd been cocooned. It had always been . . ."

He looks guiltily at me then, as if he hadn't meant to let this last part slip, and when he resumes speaking his voice is barely audible. I refuse to lean any closer, and instead just strain harder to hear him.

"I'm afraid I misunderstood. This all came so quickly, and in such an impassioned jumble, and then, suddenly, she was looking up at me, pleadingly, telling me that she had always sensed that, with me, it was different, that we had a deeper bond, a special bond, the sort of connection she lacked with others. It must have been a difficult thing for her to say, a desperate thing, and it kills me now to think of how I reacted, but, Tasha, I really did think for a moment that what you implied earlier . . . that her feelings for me were . . . romantic. This child. Your child. And the worst of it would have been that she would not have been delusional, but perceptive. She *had* roused a deep passion in me. Only it wasn't new, and it wasn't for her."

He makes a move as though he's going to reach for my hand, and though I hardly believe it's possible I don't want to take any chances. I pull back abruptly and knock over my mug, so that dark liquid pools over the scratched metal surface of the table as he says:

"I could have been softer, but I was just . . . I was ashamed, and I reacted with some horror. She ran out of the house before I had a chance to explain myself better. The moment she'd gone, I realized my mistake. She wasn't declaring her love for me. She was seeking confirmation that *someone* had felt close to her, cared for her. That was what she had seen in the way I looked at her when I thought of you. A friend. Someone who loved her and was proud of her. I *was* that. I could have told her that. All that night and the next day I kept calling her apartment. There was never an answer."

"She had a phone?" The instant the words are out, I want them back.

He looks at me with puzzlement, then continues.

"Finally, I found out her address and went to her building, but the woman who rented her a room told me she'd taken off with a suitcase early that morning. You know the rest better than I, I suppose."

The girl from the counter chooses this moment to saunter over with napkins, and as she drops them next to the puddle of coffee, I shoot her a look of disbelief that seems to have no effect whatsoever. She loiters a few seconds, then walks slowly back to her spot behind the counter.

"I'm so sorry, Tasha."

I do believe that he's sorry, but I can't bring myself to say this to Jean Paul. I cannot tell him it's OK. Instead, I ask why he never made an effort to contact her here.

"I wanted to call her, Tasha, believe me. I've been so worried. But I thought . . . perhaps she wouldn't want to hear from me. I sent her a letter explaining how sorry I was for my confusion, expressing my deep regard for her, my concern. I told her to call me. I never heard back. It occurs to me that the letter made little sense without that extra piece of information. The conclusion I jumped to, the horror I felt . . . I should have just told her, but I sensed that perhaps this would not be wise, that this was not the time."

There are dozens of responses I could give to this, but I'm exhausted and can't make the effort to say any of them, so I just nod.

"Why did you do it?" His voice is loud and firm as he says this—for him it is almost shouting—and it's clear that he's practiced it. His eyes have stopped roaming, too, and he's locked me in that blue-black gaze. It's only because my heart is pounding that I say, "End things?" as if I weren't sure.

"I've never understood."

"Because, Jean Paul." I am amazed at how easy it is to say what I once could hardly allow myself to think. "You were you, and beside you I was nothing."

"But, Tasha," he starts, but I cut him off.

"Please, it was so long ago. That's the answer."

He's quiet for a while, and I can tell that he accepts what I've said. I wish I'd told him sooner, and wonder how things might have been different if I'd only had the courage. But back then it was unthinkable.

"You have so many reasons to hate me now." This, too, he says in loud, rehearsed tones. It makes me wonder whether he knew I'd give an honest answer. He pauses for a while, and out of the corner of my eye I watch our audience come out from behind the counter again, this time to arrange a stack of newspapers a foot away from where we're sitting. I want to tell Jean Paul she's eavesdropping—I know he'd stop speaking so loudly if he knew—but before I have a chance to say anything he starts in again, now in unrehearsed fits and starts that come at a much softer pitch. "The way I behaved, so angry. The letters. The music. Mine, I mean. You have no idea. God, I was angry. I think 'angry' isn't even the right word. You don't live in anger, do you, like you live in sadness or hopelessness? Does normal anger have that sort of stability? Sarah asked me that once. She came soon after you. Not that it improved with time; it was like that with all of them. I hardly remember their faces. Now I realize. I see."

"What do you see?" I ask this urgently, much more urgently than I would have liked.

"Tasha, you weren't much older than Alex back then." Now he does take my hand, and I let my fingers lie limply sandwiched between the table and his palm. To have his skin pressed up against mine is uncannily nice, and I let myself stare directly at him as he says, "The woman who broke my heart was a child. I've been so angry at a child all these years."

For a few seconds it's hard for me to speak. I am feeling something strongly, but I have no idea what it is: anger, fear, love, desire, satisfaction? It is none of these, or perhaps it is all of them, but then it turns disappointingly to pity, and I say, "Well, you were a child, too."

"I think I still am." He gives a sad half-smile, with none of his dazzle in it, and I have the urge—easily stifled—to reach out and stroke his cheek.

Instead, I tell him, "No, I think you're not." It seems true to me. It seems that this is an adult sitting before me, that something—maybe this experience with Alex—has snapped him out of his youthful romanticism. I wonder whether this is the end of the Pied Piper of the Ivies. But, despite the pity that's overtaken me, despite the renewed urge to reach out and stroke his cheek, I am not ready to forgive him for hurting Alex, and so I say, "But Alex certainly is."

"How is she?" he asks then, and it sounds as though he does care.

"She's doing better."

"Is she working on the piece in A minor? She was struggling with that one. I thought perhaps she'd put it aside for a while."

The piece in A minor must be the one she played for me two nights ago, and of course it is finished and, as Jean Paul might say, miraculous. But because I'm still angry at him for not telling her immediately of our connection, for not understanding what she needed from him in her moment of distress, for shaming and mortifying her far beyond her fairly meager endurance (I can only imagine, and I am trying hard not to), I don't want to give him the gratification of knowing this, and I say, "I don't think she's working on anything right now."

He looks alarmed. There is something fatherly in this look, and for an instant I feel warm toward him. I feel, bizarrely, that this is what it would have been like to raise Alex with someone I loved, and then I am disgusted by this thought, and by him, and by the girl beside us who has given up on the newspapers and is just staring open-mouthed. But most of all I am disgusted by myself, and so I say, "She finished the piece in A minor. Just a few days ago."

"Ah!" He smiles, and it is the old smile, in all its glory. "Ah!"

he says again, and it is driving me crazy that he is so pleased, so unchanged, so affecting, and all I want is to be away from him.

"It was good to see you again," I say, and I pat his hand, though the gesture comes off as false.

"It was wonderful and painful," he amends, honest as ever.

As I walk out the door, I catch a glimpse of him still sitting there, motionless, locking the spot where I'd just been in his blue-black gaze.

I LEFT JEAN PAUL AT A CHROME TABLE FAR DOWNTOWN nearly eight hours ago. I've been sitting in my living room since then, watching the windows go dark, willing the phone to ring. I've finished putting my memories to paper, and now I can't figure out why I did it. Though the project did help distract me from the unringing phone. Now I can't stop staring at the slick black receiver, which rests in its cradle staring back at me. We've been staring at each other for at least an hour, and I am just deciding that I ought to give up and go to bed when, suddenly, the front door opens and Alex is standing there, looking haggard and hard.

"So what is he to you?" she asks, and though her face is tear-streaked and her lips are trembling, her voice is steady and strong.

"Nothing anymore," I assure her, and before the words are even out I'm angry at myself for this cowardly response, disappointed that this is all I can dredge up for her.

"What *was* he?" she demands, angry, too. There's a bit of a groan in her voice, which makes it almost impossible to reply.

I force myself to say, "Everything, I guess."

She hasn't stepped through the doorframe yet, and she looks for an instant like she's going to turn and leave again, but instead she walks inside, and sits herself stiffly at the far end of the couch from where I'm seated.

"So you two were, like, involved."

I nod. "When I was hardly older than you are now."

"Did you love him?"

"Yes."

"And he loved you?"

"Yes, he did."

"How long were you together?"

"Two years."

She nods, seems to be assimilating the information calmly, then suddenly her face becomes liquid, she is dissolving onto the couch, but through the tears her voice still comes out calm and controlled as she asks, "Did he break your heart?"

I think of saying "yes," of sharing this bond with her, saying we both had our hearts battered in, but we're already so far into unpleasant truths that I know it would be a mistake to taint it now with a lie.

"I broke his, actually," I say.

"Oh God," she says. "So you're her?"

"Who?"

"The woman. The woman who broke his heart, the woman he writes all his music for."

"He told you that?"

"Every Boumediennite knows that."

"Boumediennite?" I want to say, but instead I say, "Yes, that's me."

Her hand goes flying up to her mouth again, and I think she's going to start a new bout of crying, but instead she laughs, then grasps my gaze in a steady, challenging stare and says, "You have to admit it's funny. I mean, I go halfway across the country to get away from you, and I end up working with a guy obsessed with you. Funny, right?"

"Darkly, maybe," I admit, cautiously.

"No, it's fucking slapstick!" She's laughing wildly now, shaking her head, hitting her palm against her rail-thin, denim-clad thighs. "I mean, seriously, it's slapstick, right? I carefully circumvent the banana peel and slip in the pile of *horse shit*." These last words she screams. The scream propels her off the couch, and now she's pacing all over the room, her head bent down purposefully, as if she's trying to find the rest of her lines in the carpeting.

She's moving so fast I have to dart my head from side to side to keep sight of her as I say, "He thinks the world of you."

At this she stops pacing, and all the energy from her swinging legs races into her face in the form of her red Pasek rage. "How do you know that? You don't know anything about it! Anything he thought of me, anything he did for me, it was all tangled up, once again, with the fact that I'm your daughter! He seemed to care so damn much. I always thought it was weird, you know. I thought it was, like . . . that we had some sort of special bond, like, I don't know, like something deep, some teacher-student communion. I thought . . . It's so dumb. It's so incredibly dumb, because now I see why he cared so damn much. It was because of you."

"That's not true," I say calmly, refusing to be cowed by her fury this time. "He cared because you're the best student he ever had. He told me that today. Far and away the best, he said."

She opens her mouth but doesn't respond, maybe because she's too angry, or maybe because she recalls that just yesterday she all but forgot her shame and her anger in the thrill of having finished the piece in A minor, a piece she never could have written without his mentoring, without his deep and real involvement in nurturing her talent. She stands there looking at me with an open mouth for what feels like minutes, and then she shakes her head, and returns to her spot on the far side of the couch, but this time she lets her body fall so formlessly into the cushions she looks inanimate for a moment.

"It's not really funny." Her head has fallen against the back of the couch, and her eyes are closed. "It sucks, actually. You have no idea how much it sucks to be the daughter of Tasha Darsky." She sits upright now, and looks at me somewhat regretfully, as she continues. "And I know that's a mean thing to say. I know you love me, and you try hard, I know you try hard, but it's true. It's not your fault. You're not human; you're, you're *omnipresent*. I don't think there's anyplace I can go to take a break."

"I love you so much," I say, because it's all I can think.

I wish I could tell her that I know about Ben Guerrero, that I understand the way in which her heart was broken by the boy she loved, and then broken again by the teacher she worshipped, and how unloved and unlovable she feels; I wish I could tell her that I know she believes I did this to her—made her this way, inaccessible, self-contained—with my cocooning, my hoarding, and my omnipresence, but that this reading of cause and effect is far too simplistic, too unfair, and concedes far too much to Ben Guerrero. I want to tell her that there is a part of her capable of *great* passion and love, of great openness—that I know this part well, and some man will know it, too, someday, that, in fact, it is this part of her that has brought her back here to have this painful conversation with me. But it is too soon to let her know how aware I am of the events that sent her racing out of Indiana—that I spoke to Jean Paul about them, no less—and I feel certain that eventually I will have the chance to say all of this, because she will tell me herself, on her own terms, what passed between her and this Ben.

"I love you, too," she admits, letting her head fall languidly back again, before bolting it upright with what looks like a painful snap. "But sometimes I wonder."

"What do you wonder?"

"I don't know." Something has broken the strangely easy fluidity of this exchange, and she's back up off the couch, and heading toward the stairs.

"What do you wonder?" I ask again, because I don't want her to disappear into her room now.

She looks at me for a while, and it feels for all the world as though she's sizing me up, wondering whether I'm worth enduring this conversation. I suppose she decides I am, because, with one leg on the first step and one arm already draped across the banister so that she seems to hang into the room rather than stand there, she says, "I wonder what the point is of being the secondary Darsky."

She might have expected a big response from this, or she might not have, but I am so nonplussed I cannot say a thing, and so, rolling her eyes, and hanging from the banister more exaggeratedly, she explains, "You know, when the Big One's already done everything I could ever have hoped to do, and probably done it as well as it could be done, well, I mean, what's the point? You break hearts easily and I get easily broken. You inspire oeuvres and I inspire freak-outs. I mean, our genes have clearly reached their height in you, so maybe we should just give it a rest, you know?"

She's climbing the stairs now, but I am not going to let her leave it at that. This girl overshadowed by me? That she can believe it almost makes me laugh, and there is a bit of a laugh in my voice as I say, "You've got to be kidding."

Maybe it's this laugh—this unexpected, perhaps wounding hint of a laugh in my voice—that makes her stand still, and then, slowly, turn around.

"Do I seem like I'm kidding?" she asks, and I am surprised by how hurt she sounds.

"But, Alex," I plead softly, feeling guilty for that hint of a laugh now, realizing how hard it must be for Alex to say these things, unfounded as they are. It occurs to me that it took me over two decades to say as much to Jean Paul. "You're so incredibly gifted. It's just so hard to believe."

"You just don't see . . ." She trails off, and I can see her face tensing angrily again, before she breathes deeply and her muscles relax. "You don't see, because you're you."

"And you're you."

She rolls her eyes dramatically at this, and I cannot imagine how we've gotten to this point, to this conversation that seems like a farce, but somehow we have, and so I say what I would have thought had been obvious. "Alex, do you realize all I ever wanted was to have the talent you have?"

She gives me a look of utter disdain in response to this, a "try again" glare that would dry the words in my throat if they weren't so true.

"Do you know, I left the only man I ever loved because I couldn't do what you do: write music like that?"

Now she throws up her hands in despair, but I can see that she's trying on my words to see if they hang comfortably between us.

"I know you know this," I press, because at any point up until five minutes ago I would have sworn by it. "I know you know how proud I am that you can do what I never could."

She cocks her brow now, and, rather than challenging me or agreeing, she simply asks, "*Sound Fragments*?"

I nod. "Pretty embarrassing."

"They might've been good, if you'd gone ahead and finished them."

"But you have to admit," I prod, "there's no comparison."

I can see a subtle smile creep onto her face, and though she suppresses it, it's still there in her voice when she says, "Well, we're not in competition."

"I'm glad to hear it," I tell her. "Because I'm afraid the first Darsky would be trounced if it came to that. And not just in the composition round, either. You're a far braver woman than I think you know. Braver and more generous in art and love than your old mom could ever hope to be."

"Don't push it," she sighs, flopping down onto the step she's been occupying these last few minutes, and dropping her head into her hands. "We're still not OK."

"I know," I tell her. "But we will be."

"Yeah," she sighs, back on her feet and heading to her room. "Probably."

EPILOGUE

There's a familiar and thoroughly terrifying frenzy coming off the audience; it's the anxiety of people who have paid a ridiculous sum for a ticket and are not sure the show will be worth it. I used to call this frenzy "energy" and viewed it as a challenge. That was back when I knew I could deliver.

Tonight, of course, the frenzy is worse than ever. This is, after all, the biggest event in classical music in the past fifty years, at least according to my father's press releases. This is the farewell performance of the great Tasha Darsky, advertised for months, hyped half to death. My father outdid himself this time. He created a rush on tickets for "Swan Song" ("Why so morbid?" my mother asked, but I liked the title) by limiting it to one performance, and taking out ads in the *Times* from fictional people desperate to find a ticket, when there were still plenty left at the box office. Tactics like this were so effective, tickets sold out months ago.

Even from backstage I can feel the crowd thrumming in the aisles, wondering why they paid so much to see an artist who is leaving the stage because her concerts have become dull and plodding. Who is leaving, in other words, because she is no good anymore.

"Oh, Tasha, you're being a bore," my mother chides when I mention this to the crowd in my dressing room. "Lighten up, *enjoy* this night."

She's in a surprisingly good mood, given that this is the moment she's been dreading: the moment when I give up, and forget how to play. She's been in this happy, dippy state for weeks, ever since she got into a car accident on an interstate and walked away with nothing but a broken arm. She believes she has averted fate, slunk out of a long-lingering curse. She cradles her cast lovingly, while my father tells me that by all means I should *not* lighten up and *not* enjoy this night if either of these means giving the sort of careless, unimpassioned performance he had the pleasure of catching in Milan. "Heavy up, heavy up," he splutters, pouring himself a drink from a cart someone wheeled into the corner for him.

Alex is in another corner, flipping through a magazine. It's the first time I've seen her since she went back to school, and she almost didn't come in for this event. "Why should I watch you throw in the towel?" she'd complained every time I asked her to be there. "I'd rather watch you *not* throw in the towel." But she came in the end, and though she can hardly look me in the eye, she hasn't left my side all day.

When I swoop onstage in my long, white, feathered gown (too cheesy? my father won that argument), the frenzied thrum is gone. There's only silence as I take my place before the orchestra, and the silence is even worse than the thrum. The audience is frightened for me, and I feel a gratitude that might once have inspired me to a particularly tender performance. For a moment I think that perhaps I won't disappoint them after all, that, inspired by their care for me, my playing will be rejuvenated. But as soon as the music starts, I know this won't happen. My heartbeat slows, I become calm, almost bored, and I'm hardly aware that I'm playing the Brahms Violin Concerto, that music full of frustration and longing that was once, tensely, mine, and is now not. I play it as if it's something I've borrowed from a friend, something I've been asked to keep warm until the real owner comes back. The audience keeps its distance, realizing that the music's not mine to offer them. I feel them disengage until I can't sense them at all, and it's just me alone in the room, going through the motions without making any music. I have lost my desire to tussle with a score, to fight for my own voice and take part in a lover's spat with the composer. And this, after all, is why I'm leaving. So what did they expect? I ask myself as I reach the final bar line with relief.

But I still can't help feeling guilty for the roaring ovation, the shouts of "encore," which are just desperate attempts to affirm that they did not waste their money. I know I've let them down. I hear my father's voice yelling "encore" above the rest, from front and center. I am standing at the edge of the stage, probably ten feet from him, but I can't see out, of course, and I suddenly feel depressed by this fact. *So this is how it's going to end?* I think. *Just like this? Opacity between me and my audience, no connection? And music nowhere in the room.*

I picture my father out there, yelling "encore" simply to save appearances. I picture my mother, cradling her cast and realizing that only one piece of destiny is going to be averted this month. I picture Masterson, who sent a tremendous bouquet of flowers to my home last night with the note "I'll be listening and hoping to hear a change of heart." Somewhere out there he is shaking his head and writing me off. Then I picture my daughter, seated next to that booming voice out in the audience yelling "encore" louder than the rest. And before I can be overtaken by yet more maudlin thoughts, I am overtaken by something else: I am taken over by music.

I drop the bouquets that have been coming at me from every angle, and I move back to my place in front of the orchestra. As I pick up my violin from the case, a hush falls over the room. I can almost sense the collective thought, *We didn't mean it. Please, no more.*

I unleash a tremendous note; it is expansive and exuberant, and it meets with a strangled, euphoric yelp from front and center that I'm not sure anyone else can hear. The note is followed by a series of intricately chaotic bars that only an imagination as luxuriously prodigal as my daughter's could have conjured.

I'm improvising a great deal, playing on the violin the melody of a piece meant for full orchestra, but the essence is all there, I remember it note for note—how could I not? It's nothing less than the sound of Alex, her something "wonderfully new"—and I am inside a piece of music like I haven't been in years. Like I haven't been inside a piece since I learned how much Jean Paul hated me and I first, temporarily, lost my will to fight. Not that I am fighting now—no, I've exhausted that mode of relating to music, literally played it out. But why fight with this music? This is my daughter's sound, and I lay myself before it undefended and unresistant. I feel it slip over every part of me and into me, and when it slips back out it is transformed by my love for it. I have an aching need to bring out the full power lying latent in this score.

I know I'm succeeding, too, because I feel the orchestra breathing heavily behind me and I feel the audience come close. I feel them exploring the contours of this new musical place I have brought them to, and I feel them loving this music, too, loving my daughter. I feel them loving all the people I love, because all the people I have ever loved have found their way into these notes now: my whole life has found its way into these lush and large melodies, because what is my life, after all, but who and what I've loved, rightly and wrongly?

The rich and mysterious smell of Robert Masterson, sherry and cigars, comes wafting out of the mathematical precision of the intricate melodies slowly taking shape out of the unbridled notes; the oddly reassuring feel of Pasek's hand on my stomach reaches out from the defiant reveries that break into the score at the oddest times; there, in that one chord progression, is my Great Artist giving me my first heartbreak; and even my father booms out his devotion to art from inside some flourishes I add on a whim.

And Jean Paul. Jean Paul is coursing through everything. Coursing through this music, making it unlike anything ever created before. Coursing through our very selves, dripped into our genes, so that his blue-black eyes look out from Alex's face. He is everywhere in this music and he is nowhere, because she has taken his ideas and made them her own. And I love him. I love him for giving her this music, and for giving me *my* music, that glorious fight with the notes that I only recently lost. And I love him simply because I do and I always have and always will.

My mother is in there, too, of course, whispering small scenes in muted colors—delicate, tentative notes that resonate a few layers below the surface. She's in there, and so is the girl in the painting, though in this music the girl's not sad at all. She's unleashed.

But it's Alex, of course, who's really been unleashed, vibrating ecstatically through every inch of Carnegie Hall, coruscating on the air. I hear every age of her, every stage of her soaring over the audience, and I want to stay here remembering with each of them indefinitely. I want this music never to end. But then it does. Hitting the final bar line is a searing rip, a tearing of flesh from flesh, and at first I mistake the terrifying roar that greets me for a sound coming from myself, my own animalistic wail. It is only a moment later that I notice that the deafening sound is coming from the audience and that it's joyful. They are on their feet, on the seats, yelling and shouting and carrying on in a way totally unbefitting an audience in Carnegie Hall.

I try to take it in, this ovation unlike any I've ever had before, and while I'm doing that a single stage of Alex echoes down from the chandeliers: She is four years old and wearing a loopy grin. She tells me I'm as big as an ocean. I grin back just as loopily and tell her that she is, too. And just like that, I'm a musician again.

1. Tasha Darsky seems blessed with every advantage—beauty, brains, talent, money, fame. Did this make it harder for you to sympathize with her story? Do you think it would have been easier or harder to care about her story if it were told through the eyes of another character?

2. In what ways do you think Tasha's parents shaped the woman—and the mother—she ultimately became? Do you think she's fair to them when she recounts her childhood? What do you make of the scene beneath her mother's partially hidden masterpiece? Do you think that moment of recognition was instrumental in guiding her later life choices?

3. Why do you think Tasha allows herself to become involved in a romantic relationship with Masterson? Did her behavior with her teacher make you think less of her? Or did the insecurity involved in that choice make you feel more sympathetic to her? Why do you think Masterson became involved in the relationship?

4. When Tasha breaks off her relationship with Jean Paul she is still very much in love with him. Why, then, does she do it? Did this decision ring true to you? Do you think the relationship would have ended if she had never seen the letter he wrote to his mother? Do you think Tasha would have continued to compose her own music if she had never read the letter?

5. To what extent does Tasha's relationship with her parents resemble Alex's relationship with her? Do you think Tasha is a good mother? Do you think it was responsible of her to bring Alex on tour with her and to let Alex become a professional musician at such a young age? How do you think Tasha's choices as a mother would have been different if her parents had not functioned as the only other authority figures in her daughter's life?

6. *The Passion of Tasha Darsky* is an exploration of the interactions between three different forms of love—romantic, parent-child, and artistic. How does Tasha's artistic passion play into her human relationships? How do her human relationships play into her relationship with the violin? Do you think she would be a better mother, daughter, and lover if she were a less committed artist? Do you think she would be a better musician if she could separate more effectively from the people she loves? Do you think there is anything her artistic passion *adds* to her ability to love and care for people?

7. What does Tasha mean at the end of the book when she says, "And just like that, I'm a musician again"? In what way did she ever stop being a musician? What has changed?

8. *The Passion of Tasha Darsky* can be read as a meditation on the possibility of devoting oneself wholeheartedly to both career and motherhood. What, if anything, do you think the final scene in the book is meant to suggest about this fraught and timely issue? Do you agree?

© Steven Pinker

Yael Goldstein Love graduated from Harvard College in 2000. She lives in Cambridge, Massachusetts. This is her first novel.